Dividing
by Ø

ONYXIS STONE PRESS, First Print Edition, March 2016

www.bryanperkinsauthor.com

Dividing by Ø

Bryan Perkins

ONYXIS STONE PRESS

For you.

Table of Contents

XLIII. Nikola

Nikola took a deep breath of the cool air and held it in her lungs for as long as she could, her hand set gingerly on the doorknob in front of her. Letting the air out as slowly as possible, molecule by molecule almost, she adjusted her glasses. She knew that Tillie would be happy to get out of the Hellish prison the protectors had put her in, but she wasn't as sure about how Tillie would feel concerning where they had taken her. She huffed and fixed her glasses again. There was only one way to find out.

The door creaked open to reveal an official looking reception area, something requiring a high level of security to get past. The walls and carpet were two slightly different shades of gray, and the short chairs lining the room were a third. Behind the reception desk a gray-haired old man peered like a fish through the bulletproof glass that separated his side of the room from hers.

Nikola crept up to the desk, trying to make as little noise as possible—all these drab gray offices made her feel like she was in a library—but the door creaked closed behind her and slammed shut. She jumped at the sound of it, pretty sure she saw the old man behind the desk groan and roll his eyes, and when she got close enough to speak, he cut her off before she could even get started.

"Bonjour," he said in a slow, drawling voice. "Comment puis-je vous aider?"

"Oh—*uh*…" Nikola blushed. She knew enough French to understand the old man's question, but she wasn't confident she could speak her response. "*Eh*—Je m'appelle Nikola. Je suis ici pour...*uh*...I was sent to see the American." She shrugged at the English bit.

The old man behind the desk rolled his fishy eyes for sure this time. "*Ah*." He nodded. "L'American. Oui. Let me see here..." Somehow he spoke even slower in English. "Here it is. Yes. Nikola Montpierre, Special Agent First Class in the Revolutionary Workers

Defense League. Here to put one Tillie Manager through orientation. Is that correct, mademoiselle?"

Nikola nodded. "Yes, sir. That's me. What do you—"

"Please place your thumb on the scanner in front of you."

"Oh—*uh*…" Nikola pressed her thumb to the tiny window on the desk in front of her and the camera behind it scanned her print. Satisfied, the glass door next to her beeped and opened.

"Agent Pierre of intake will give you further directions," the old man said, not even looking at her anymore as he spoke, back instead to staring at his computer screen. "Just through the door there."

"Oh—*uh*… Thanks." Nikola nodded and went in the clear glass door, through a short hall, and into a smaller, darker reception area. There were no chairs in this room, and the colors bordered closer to black than gray, but there was still bullet proof glass between her and who she assumed was Agent Pierre behind the desk in front of her.

"Bonjour," he said with a smile and a twinkle in his eye. He seemed much nicer than the old man already. "How can I help you?"

"Oh, *uh*—I'm here to see Tillie."

"Oh, oui, oui, mon couer." He chuckled, his eyes twinkling. "Of course. But I already knew that. I intended to ask if there was any further assistance I could offer."

Nikola blushed. She didn't know what to say. She didn't know what she was doing, or what to expect. She just wanted to talk to Tillie. "*Uh*…"

"I see." Agent Pierre winked. "It's your first time, then, huh?"

Nikola nodded.

"Well, she'll be right inside waiting for you. And remember, you can do whatever it is you have to do in there. The walls are thick, see. You might as well be in an entirely different world." He laughed a big hearty laugh, still somehow managing to maintain his French accent as he did.

"Um…okay," Nikola said. She wasn't sure why she would need soundproofing but Pierre seemed to be trying to help. "So I just—I just go in then?" She looked around for a door but there was only the one she had come in through.

"Oh, no, sweetie. You don't go anywhere. We take you there.

Adieu."

Before she could respond, the floor fell out from underneath her. She hadn't realized she was in an elevator until just then, gasping at the jolt of inertia. The walls were all bullet proof glass and she could see the rest of the building as it fell up up and away around her. When the elevator stopped, it was in front of some frightened soul who was hunching in a metal chair with a bag over their head. Through the glass, whoever it was seemed as far away as the old man in the reception area—and even more fishy. The doors slid open and Nikola rushed to the person's side, hurrying to remove the bag from their head.

Tillie flinched away at first, jumping up and struggling against the unknown assailant. "Stop! Let go! Stop!" she yelled as Nikola wrenched the bag from her head. Tillie still must not have recognized Nikola, though, because it took her some time to stop struggling, even with the bag removed. When she finally did recognize Nikola, she started weeping and repeating Nikola's name over and over.

"Nikola. I never thought I'd— Nikola, help me— Nikola, Nikola."

What had they done to her?

Nikola tried to hug Tillie to calm her down but Tillie's arms were cuffed to the chair. "They tied you down! Why would they tie you down?"

"Nikola. Ni*k*ola. *Nikola*," Tillie muttered. Her head looked heavy and her eyes wouldn't stop blinking at a rapid pace. It seemed like she could lose consciousness at any time.

"Yes, Tillie. It's Nikola. I'll get you out of this. Just let me— let me…"

Tillie went on repeating her name while Nikola scanned the room. It was tiny and dark. There was nothing in it but the chair Tillie was tied to and a button on one wall which Nikola ran over to press.

"Bonjour. C'est Pierre. Puis-je vous aider?" came a voice over the intercom.

"Why'd you cuff her?" Nikola demanded of the red button.

"Qui?"

"Tillie Manager. This is Nikola Montpierre. Why did you—"

"*Ah*," the voice cut her off. "L'American. You did not say

you wanted her uncuffed, ma'am. I did ask if there was any way I could help you. Remember?"

"Why'd you cuff her in the first place?"

"Standard procedure, mademoiselle. Much like asking for the keys *before* you go down the hole. Perhaps you'll remember that in—"

"Just bring me the keys!"

"*Nikola*! Nikola, Nik—cola," Tillie mumbled louder at the sound of Nikola's yelling.

"Oui, mademoiselle. Right away, mademoiselle. Be down in two shakes of a lamb's tail, mademoiselle," Pierre said in an overly subservient tone, dripping with pomposity.

"I'll have you out as soon as I can," Nikola said, crossing to Tillie to stroke her hair as the elevator fell from behind the fishbowl door and soon reappeared, coming from the top down and carrying Agent Pierre. The doors slid open and Agent Pierre bowed low, presenting a keychain and key to Nikola who rushed to grab it and ran back to unlock Tillie.

"Je t'en prie, ma chérie. Is there anything else I can help you with?"

"No!" Nikola stomped a foot at him then went back to comforting Tillie.

"Then, *adieu*." Agent Pierre bowed low, the fishbowl elevator doors slid closed, and he fell out of the picture.

Nikola unlocked Tillie's hands and feet, but still Tillie wouldn't stand. She kept rocking in the chair, repeating Nikola's name over and over.

Nikola sighed, pushed her glasses up on her nose, then took Tillie's face between her hands to look her friend in the eyes. "Look at me," she said. "Tillie. It's me. It's Nikola. *I'm* Nikola. I'm here to help."

"Nikola," Tillie said, smiling despite her red puffy eyes. "Nik-ola, Nikol-a, Nikola."

"Yes, dear. It's—I'm—" Nikola's own eyes went red. She let go of Tillie's face to wipe away the moisture. "Nikola's here, honey. What did they do to you?"

"Nikola?" Tillie started crying again.

Nikola did, too. She didn't know what else to do. They weren't supposed to treat Tillie like this. They were supposed to be saving her from that horrible place, not putting her somewhere worse.

"Alright," Nikola said, grabbing Tillie's hand and helping her stand. Tillie protested at first but eventually gave in, standing with some effort and a lot of assistance.

"Nikola?" she said, looking like a sad, lost child.

"Yes," Nikola said. "It's me. And I'm getting you out of here. You need some fresh air and a doctor. Now come on. Up you go." She lifted Tillie's arm over her shoulder and walked her to the elevator.

"Nikola," Tillie said, smiling as the elevator's fishbowl doors closed and the floor fell out from underneath them.

Agent Pierre didn't look happy to see Tillie when they arrived. "Mademoiselle," he said with a sneer. "I don't think you have clearance to take *L'American* with you. I'm afraid—"

"I have clearance!" Nikola said, banging on the glass between her and Agent Pierre, Tillie still holding onto her shoulders for support. "Let us out of here!"

"I—*uh...*" Agent Pierre was flustered. He looked this way then that, trapped in his fish bowl, then typed and clicked on his computer, gaping wide-eyed at whatever it was he saw there.

"Oh, mademoiselle," he said. "*Je suis désolé.* Go ahead. Go ahead," he added, waving them through the now open doors.

Nikola practically carried Tillie through the reception area into the cool air outside. They came out of the tall, official looking cement building into the center of everything. To Tillie it probably looked like a war zone from some movie produced in Outland Three. They were surrounded by crumbling buildings—all but the gray behemoth they had just come from were crumbling into piles of rubble at their feet—interspersed with huge canvas tents, all in various shades of browngreen. To add to the effect, most of the people walking around the rubbled streets wore big black combat boots and camouflaged uniforms, whether they were working one of the many food stands—one on each corner practically—or actually parading from one assignment to the next in preparation for a military maneuver. To Nikola it looked entirely different though. To Nikola it looked like home.

Tillie's eyes brightened as she squinted against the sunlight. She looked this way and that, taking everything in, then smiled at

Nikola and said, "Nikola." with a nod.

Nikola tried to smile back. "Yep," she said. "Though I was hoping some fresh air might help with that. I can't imagine what they did to to you to make you—*hmmm...*"

"Nikola?"

Nikola sighed. "*Exactly.*" She took Tillie by the arm and led her through streets lined with rubble, toward nowhere in particular. She didn't know where to go. What would cause a person to lose the ability to speak anything but a single word? Why did that word have to be Nikola's name? And what could she do to change it?

She looked up from her thoughts and they were in front of her parents' half building, half tent office. Where all the other tents they had passed were more like canopies, this one had dark green walls held down with big slabs of rubble and armed guards at either side of the entrance flap. Nikola stopped in her tracks but Tillie kept going, pulling Nikola's arm a bit before coming to a halt, too.

"Oh, I'm sorry," Nikola said. "I—it's just—"

"Nikola Nikola." Tillie shook her head, not wanting to go in.

"Right, well. It's just that exactly," Nikola said, adjusting her glasses. "You keep saying that over and over, and I'm not entirely sure what to do about it."

"N—N—Nik—ol—a," Tillie said with some effort, like she was trying to say something else but couldn't.

"No, no no." Nikola waved her arms and stepped closer to Tillie, patting her on the back. "I mean, I'm sure you're fine, you know. But I—but— *Okay.* Well, let me start from the beginning. You see that tent building?" Nikola pointed and Tillie looked at the two armed guards.

"Nikola?" she said with raised eyebrows.

"Yep," Nikola said, nodding. "The one guarded by those two big guns. Well, behind those guns are my parents—my whole family probably. And—well—since they were the reason I was in your country in the first place, I guess they're the best people to ask about what happened to you because of it. Besides, they're gonna want to know how you're doing anyway. They've been pretty worried about us ever since I left."

"Nikola?"

"Well—no—of course it would be better if you could actually talk when you met them, but you'll have to meet them sooner or later anyway and they can probably help get your words back. Two birds with one stone, you know."

Tillie shrugged with a sigh, shaking her head.

"I'm glad you agree." Nikola grinned. "And whatever you do, don't mention our smoking on the balcony, okay?" She chuckled a little, but Tillie wasn't ready to find the situation funny. Nikola couldn't really blame her. "Alright. Well, let's do it then," she said, taking Tillie's arm.

Nikola pulled Tillie between the guards, and she could feel Tillie's fear rise up through the goosebumps in her skin as they passed inside the tentbuilding. If Nikola hadn't grown up with the guards always there, twenty four seven, she might feel the same way. She might also have gasped—like Tillie—at how official the inside of a canvas tent and crumbling building could be made to look, almost exactly like the inside of the holding cell Tillie had only moments ago been released from. Tillie must have noticed the similarity, too. After her gasp she struggled trying to get away from Nikola and out of the building, but Nikola held her tight.

"Nikola. *Nikola*. Nikola!" Tillie begged as she tried to escape.

"No—it's okay—I—" Nikola argued, but she couldn't formulate words and hold Tillie at the same time.

Luckily, her little brother—she loved to call him that even though he was so much bigger than her (or anyone for that matter)— Curie ran around from behind the reception desk to help her. "Woah . there, lil' Nikkie," he said, holding Tillie still but somehow managing to be gentle about it at the same time. "Who's this frightened little bird you brought us today?"

"Tillie," Nikola said, more to Tillie than her brother. "It's okay. This is my little brother, Curie. He can—he'll help us, okay. You're safe now. You're safe with us."

Tillie was still darting her wide eyes back and forth between their faces, but she was struggling less and less, and as Nikola's brother continued to talk, his voice seemed to have a soothing effect on her.

"Ah. *Tillie*," he said with a smile. "The beautiful American you've told me so much about. And one of a very few in her country to really see the truth of the worlds, from what I understand. I embarrass myself by calling her a mere bird. No, she's too intelligent for that, *too fierce*. I must be blind to miss a majestic eagle as it stares me in the eyes."

Tillie stopped struggling, staring Curie in the eyes. Nikola had let go of her a long time ago, but Curie still held her one hand in both of his, looking deep into her eyes just the same. Nikola fidgeted and coughed. "*Ahem*," she cleared her throat. "So, Curie, this is Tillie. Tillie, Curie. You two seem to be pretty well acquainted by now."

"Not well enough," Curie said, not taking his hands off Tillie's.

"Curie?" Tillie said.

"Tillie!" Nikola cheered, clapping her hands together. "You said something else. You—"

"Nikola, Nikola!" Tillie exclaimed, deflating again when the words only came out Nikola.

"It's okay, my eagle," Curie said, rubbing Nikola's hand in his palm now. "We'll take care of your injuries and have you flying again in no time. Singing, too. I promise. Just, please, come with me. I'll make you right again."

Tillie gave in to him, lost in Curie's eyes and words. Nikola kept her feelings of awkwardness quiet this time, instead following them in silence and letting Curie continue to do what seemed to be working for Tillie.

There was no elevator in this building, nor any bullet proof glass. Curie led Tillie hand in hand through grayed halls into a brightly lit, clean white room. Tillie jumped up onto the hospital bed just as Curie asked her to, and Nikola began to hope that she might get better sooner than later.

"Now," Curie said, looking Tillie in the eyes again. "Look at me, okay. I'm going to get you some paper." He rummaged through a drawer and handed her a pad of paper and a pen. "Okay. Are you ready?"

"Nikola," Tillie said, nodding.

"Good," Curie said. "Very good. You anticipate me already. So, first, I want you to write my sister's name for me," he said, pointing at Nikola. "Right there on the pad." He pointed at the paper.

Tillie wrote the name with ease and held it up for them to see. Nikola smiled and nodded, trying to be encouraging.

"Very good, my eagle," Curie said. "Now, this time I would

like you to write my name on the pad, please."

Tillie struggled hard to write something down then scribbled it out with a sigh. She wrote something else then scribbled it out again in a huff.

"It's okay, Tillie. You can—" Nikola tried to say but Curie shot her a look, cutting her sentence off with his ice blue eyes.

"You can do it," he said to Tillie. "You remember what it is. I know you do. You just said it. And it's not hard to spell, just five letters exactly how it sounds."

Tillie was sweating by the time she finished, and the letters looked like chicken scratch when she held the notepad up for them to see, but Curie and Nikola smiled, nodded, and cheered her on as if it were a much more difficult task.

"*Perfect*," Curie said, bringing Tillie in for a hug. "Now, what's your name?"

"Tillie!" Tillie blurted out, holding her hands to her mouth when she did. "My name is Tillie Manager!"

"Yes, my eagle," Curie said, smiling wide and hugging. "Your name's Tillie Manager."

"Tillie!" Nikola screamed too loudly. "I knew you'd be okay." She grabbed Tillie and squeezed her tight. "I'm so glad you—"

"What is all this racquet down here?" asked a voice from behind them, Nikola's mother's voice. "How many times do I have to tell you kids that this is an official building and not a playground?"

"I'm sorry, Mom. We were just..." Nikola trailed off, not sure how to finish the sentence.

"Sorry, ma'am," Tillie said, bowing her head.

"Mother," Curie said, standing taller and stepping toward their mom. "This is the American. She was in need of medical attention. We took care of that and we were just about to send her to you."

Nikola's mother looked between the three of them suspiciously. "Is that so?"

"Yes, Mother," Curie said, nodding earnestly.

"Of course, Mom," Nikola said. "Why would we lie?."

Her mother looked around at them one more time. "Of course," she said. "Well, then, Curie, you get back to the desk now.

You've already left someone waiting for you, which is why I'm down here in the first place. And Nikola, you bring the American up to my office. Your father will want to speak with her."

"I was about to do exactly that," Nikola said, "but I—"

"Then go," her mom said, clapping her hands at Nikola like she was still a child. "Allons-y. Rapide. I have business to attend to." She kept clapping until Nikola grabbed Tillie by the hand and ran up two flights of stairs, the first of which her mother followed them up, clapping all the way.

Nikola stopped to catch her breath between flights, hunched over and trying not to curse. She looked up and Tillie was hunched over, breathing heavily, too, but she was smiling at least. Nikola couldn't help but chuckle at the sight of her, and soon they were laughing together, their laughs echoing through the empty stairway.

"So," Nikola said when they had gotten their laughter under control. "That was my mom." She shrugged.

"And your *brother*." Tillie smiled.

"Yes. And my *brother*," Nikola repeated, giving Tillie a look she probably couldn't decipher. Something along the lines of *Watch it sister*. Nikola wasn't quite sure how she felt about Tillie and Curie's rapidly developing relationship, and she had bigger issues on her mind for the moment so she didn't want to think about it at all. "And you're about to meet my father," she went on, trying to change the subject. "Him and my mother being the reasons you're here now."

"*Right*," Tillie said. "You said that already. What I still don't know is where *here* is, though."

"Oh. Of course." Nikola chuckled nervously and fixed her glasses. She forgot about the basics in her need to get Tillie talking again. "Well, you're in my home now," she explained. "This is my country, or—*er*—our world, or whatever you Americans call it."

"So you *are* a Russian, then," Tillie said, taking a step back from her. "And we're in—you took me to...Russia?" She held her hand to her mouth, as if terrified.

"What?" Nikola chuckled. "No. Of course not. I told you I wasn't—"

"Then where are we?" Tillie demanded. "If we're not in Russia and we're not in America, then where could we be?"

"Lots of other places," Nikola said, trying not to laugh now that she remembered how dismal Tillie's American education must truly have been. "There are many more than two countries, you know. Too many more. This one included. Come on. I'm sure my dad can explain it better than I ever could, and I know for a fact that he'll end up explaining it to you again, anyway. So let's just go and get it over with."

Tillie hesitated.

"Honestly, Tillie," Nikola said, "It's the only way forward, whether you're actually in Russia or not—which I guarantee you're not." She extended her hand.

Tillie looked at it for a second then took it. "You're right," she said. "Y'all got me out of that prison. I should be thanking you, not complaining. Let's go."

The office was up a few flights of stairs still. The walls were all gray and slightly crumbling—patched in parts with green canvas—and there were two big desks facing each other on either side of the room. Nikola's dad was at his desk, on the right hand side of the office, furiously typing at something, and the other, her mother's desk on the left hand side, was empty. Nikola's dad didn't even look up when they entered the room.

"*Ahem*," Nikola cleared her throat, adjusting her glasses. "*Uh*—Dad—or—*er*, sir. It's me. Nikola."

"Just a moment, dear," her dad said, lifting a hand just long enough to wave it once and get back to typing. "Almost done."

"Oh, well..." Nikola looked at Tillie and shrugged, mouthing, "I'm sorry."

It wasn't more than a minute before Nikola's dad stopped typing and looked up from his work, satisfied. "Ah, there we are," he said with a smile. "Now, dear—*oh*—you should have told me there was company." He stood up fast and ticked off a salute. "General Andre Montpierre at your service, mademoiselle."

"Oh—*uh*—" Tillie blushed.

"It's just Tillie, Dad," Nikola said. "No need to salute. She's here—"

"Nonsense, Nikola." Her dad scoffed. "And *just* Tillie? That's all the more reason to show our respect. She's an ambassador from another country, dear. Practically another world!"

"Yeah, well," Nikola said. "I thought maybe you could hold off on the theatrics a bit. At least until she feels more comfortable in her transition, you know. She's been through a lot."

"Oh, no. I mean, of course. I'm sorry, dears." He crossed from behind the desk and led Tillie to a soft chair by a window. "Here, take a seat. Can I get you anything? We don't have much, but there's some ice in the freezer and a mighty nice tap for water, if I do say so myself."

"No, dad," Nikola said. "We're fine."

"Actually some water would be nice," Tillie said, getting comfortable in her seat.

"There you have it," Nikola's dad said, crossing to a sink on the far wall. "One ice cold water, coming right up."

"Thanks," Tillie said, taking a sip of the water as Nikola's father sat in one of the chairs himself—not his desk chair.

"So," her dad said. "America, huh? It must have been a long trip getting here."

"*Ugh.* You wouldn't believe," Tillie said with a sigh. "It was a nightmare."

"Yes, yes. I'm sorry about that, dear. *So sorry.*" He shook his head, staring off into the distance. "But," he said, brightening up, "that's all behind us now. Now is the time to look to the future. Are you ready for that, Tillie?"

"I—*uh…*" Tillie looked like a landlord caught in a rent strike. She couldn't even move or speak. Nikola was worried Tillie might revert to repeating Nikola's name again so she tried to come to Tillie's rescue.

"You know, Dad," Nikola said, "maybe you can kind of explain what's going on—or—I don't know, why Tillie's here or whatever. I only just got her out of holding, you know, and they still had her locked up with a bag over her head when I got there."

"Locked up and bagged? No!" Her dad looked seriously concerned but Nikola knew better. Nothing on base went down without his knowing it. He might be a good enough actor to fool Tillie, but Nikola had lived with him for long enough to see through it.

"Yes, Father," Nikola said. "Now why would they do that?"

"Oh, you know," he said, shaking his head and waving her concerns away. "They're soldiers, dear. All they do is follow orders, live by regulations. It's procedure so they follow it. That's all."

"Procedure set by—" Nikola started to say, but her dad cut

her off.

"Now, Tillie," he said, "I know this must be pretty overwhelming for you, but do you have any questions for me? Let's start there."

Nikola wanted to drive the point further, but she knew her dad wouldn't react well so she just sighed and let Tillie speak.

"Well, sir." Tillie shook her head. "I have a lot, actually."

"Of course. Of course you do, dear. *Ha ha ha*! Who am I kidding?" He rocked back and forth in his chair, clapping his hands and laughing. "Well, then. Go ahead. What first?"

"Well, sir. *Uh*... I guess, where am I?"

"You're in my office. Where else? *Ho ho ho*."

Nikola groaned.

"But really," her dad said, putting on a straight face, "you're at Bitburg Revolutionary Base in The People's France. Right now you're in one of the most closely protected and highly classified buildings—nay rooms—in the entire country. Welcome, little American. Welcome to our workers' paradise."

"Oh, *uh*..." Tillie hesitated.

"Don't make it seem so great," Nikola said. "The People's France isn't a very protected place in general. And besides that, it's tiny."

"No, well, for now it is," her dad said. "But we're working on that. We're growing, aren't we? Step by step, every day, the incessant march of modernization drives on. You know."

Nikola shrugged. "I guess."

"So what am I doing here?" Tillie asked. "When do I go home?"

"You are being protected here, child," Nikola's dad said. "You're being protected from the ones you Americans call protectors. You were there. You experienced it: A bag over your head, shoved into a drawer to rot. And let me tell you, the things they had in store for you are so much worse than that. It's unimaginable. If we hadn't secured your escape... Well, let me just say that you have no idea what would have happened to you and you should be happy for that fact."

"Dad!" Nikola said, slapping his arm.

"It's true, Nikola," he said, rubbing where she had hit him. "And Tillie should know it. That's why you're here, Tillie. We saved you from things unthinkable inside those prison walls."

Tillie shook her head. "Like what?"

"*Torture*," Nikola's dad said. "A fate worse than death. They'd kill you a thousand times and keep you alive to do it again. Human or android, it makes no difference to them. They'll make you suffer until you give up and then make you suffer a little more. That's just the way they like it."

"I…" Tillie looked to Nikola who nodded. Nikola knew that much wasn't an exaggeration. At least that's what they had told her when she agreed to go undercover, that she, too, would be risking a fate worse than death. "I can't believe that," Tillie said.

"I know, child," Nikola's dad said. "It's unbelievable. But it also happens to be the truth. I think you'll find that all truths are a little hard to bear, especially when you first learn of them. We live in unbelievable times, girls, so what else can we expect but unbelievable things?"

"No, but…" Tillie started.

"Dad, maybe that's a little—" Nikola tried to say but Tillie cut her off.

"I want to go home!" she demanded.

"I know, child." Nikola's dad frowned. He shook his head. "I know. But you can't. Not yet. It's not safe for you. We'd be sending you back into exactly what we rescued you from in the first place. I can't have that on my conscious. I'm sorry."

"Then when?"

"*Hmmm.*" Nikola's dad thought on that for a moment. "When the time's right is all I can say. Sooner than later, I hope. But I don't know. It's out of my control. In the meantime, there are a few things you could help us with around here. The more help we have the sooner we can make our world and yours safer for everyone, and only when it's safe will I send you home."

"*Ah.*" Tillie nodded. "I see."

Nikola frowned. She didn't like the tone of Tillie's voice or the look on her face, something. Her father didn't seem to notice anything suspicious, though, because he just smiled and nodded and went on talking.

"Good," he said. "Great! Then let Nikola here show you around, and once you're settled in, we'll see what exactly it is that you can do to help us help you. How does that sound?"

"Sure." Tillie nodded. "Whatever you say, sir."

&   ✖   ∅

XLIV. Laura

Two girls played dominoes on a dirty carpet. One was supposed to be the other's daughter, but Laura thought they looked more like sisters. No one cared what Laura thought, though.

The girls laughed and bantered. Nothing scripted, just simple improv, most of which wouldn't make it into the final product anyway. If Laura had her way, none of it would. Laura wouldn't have her way, though. Laura never got her way.

They were shooting b-roll. It's called b-roll because it's not A grade work. It's not scripted. It may not even be used. Those crucial shots of roadside flowing by in all the most famous movies, that's pretty much the epitome of b-roll. Laura hated shooting b-roll for the projects she enjoyed working on. For this particular project, it was Hell.

She had been standing there, watching them for hours now, statuesque and silent. She hardly even breathed. Her only movements were to lift a finger, press a button, and drop the finger. Lift a finger, press a button, and drop the finger. Watching the two play dominos, do each other's hair, or some other nonsense until her phone rang and one of the girls screamed, causing Laura to jump and almost knock over the camera.

"Fortuna, Jen!" Laura yelled. "It's a fucking phone and you're a fucking adult. *Act like one.*"

"Oh, *uh—sorry*," Jen said, standing from the floor and brushing herself off. "I was so deep into character I couldn't help it."

Laura scoffed. "Whatever." She answered the phone. "We're working on it, Cohen."

"Shut it down," Cohen said on the other end of the line. "Shut it down now. We need you and Jen here ASAP."

"We're not done yet," Laura said, both because she wanted to piss Cohen off and because she didn't want to do what she knew came next. "We're only at dominoes. We still have to go through—"

"I don't care," Cohen said, cutting her off. "You can do that any time. We've got a conveyor belt and not for long. So grab your shit and get your asses over here."

"*Ugh.* Fine. Whatever." Laura hated when he tried to boss her around. Stupid fucking directors. If only it was him they needed out of the picture instead of Emir, that she wouldn't have any qualms about. "Where is here?" she added for cover's sake even though she knew the answer already.

"Loch Ness Studios. Lot 37. *And hurry.*"

Cohen hung up before Laura could respond. "Well fuck you, too," she said anyway.

"Hey!" the other girl—not Jen, but Laura couldn't remember the poor extra's name—gasped, holding her hand to her mouth.

"Shut up, kid," Laura snapped. "You're off the clock. Get out of here. I'll call you when we need you again."

"*But—*" she squealed.

"Go!" Laura stomped her foot at the girl who scurried away.

Jen chuckled. "Dude," she said. "You don't have to be so mean. The poor girl's just trying to do her job. We don't pay her enough for all that."

"Yeah, well." Laura scoffed. "We don't pay me enough for all this, either. Shit. We don't pay me anything."

"Alright, alright." Jen waved her hands defensively. "I get it. *Me neither.* So what does the slave driver want now?"

"*We're to go to Loch Ness Studios,*" Laura said, mocking Cohen's stupid voice. "We've got a small window of time in a studio with a conveyor belt."

"Just fucking great," Jen said, pulling out her phone then sliding and tapping on the screen. "The only lines I haven't practiced yet. Of course we get a shot at it today."

"Well, I have some gear to pack up," Laura said, getting to it. "You can go over your lines while I do it."

"Sure," Jen said, getting exasperated. "I could memorize them on the elevator ride over there, too, but that wouldn't give me the time I need to perfect my part. I mean, I understand the script is a piece of shit, like Guy—*wherever he is*, Fortuna protect him—tried to warn us, but I don't want my performance to play down to it. Okay."

Laura scoffed, hefting a bag of gear onto the anti-grav carts. "You're telling me," she said. "You think I enjoy rigging and shooting this crap? We're all on the same crew."

"Oh, yeah, yeah." Jen waved Laura's concerns away. "It's not the same, though. They'll see *my* face up on that screen. Everyone will know for sure that it was me. *You* can put a pseudonym in the credits, but I can't wear a mask through my performance. My face is my tool."

"It is all the same," Laura said, packing the last little bit as she talked. "And it doesn't matter anymore anyway. We're off to the Loch. Let's go."

She pushed the cart out through the hall and into an elevator. Jen followed close behind, not paying attention to where she was walking because she was reading the script on her phone. She bumped right into the back of Laura when they entered the elevator, then complained about it as if Laura were responsible.

"It's not my fault you don't watch where you're going," Laura said. Then, "Loch Ness Studios. Lot 37."

The elevator doors slid shut and the floor fell out from underneath them. When they slid open again and Laura pushed the cart out, it took Jen some time to follow, still reading her script. They walked through a long hall, with a cement floor and steel walls, into what appeared to be an assembly line. Cohen was deep into a lecture while Emir sat at the conveyor belt, listening to the director drone on and trying to snap little bits of whatever was on the line together at the same time. He wasn't very good at either task, though, so he kept messing up at both.

"There you are," Cohen said, finally breaking away from his lecture some time after Laura had already gotten to setting up the lights and cameras. "What took you two so long?"

Laura scoffed.

"We came right here, dude," Jen said. "We're not your fucking on call slaves, ready to bow to your every whim and whimsy."

"You are my crew though, aren't you?" Cohen asked with wide eyes, feigning offence as he always did. "Emir was here on time. He didn't have any trouble. I don't see why it took y'all so long."

"We were shooting your fucking b-roll!" Laura snapped. She stopped what she was doing for a second, took a few deep breaths, then went back to rigging the lights like she hadn't said a thing.

Jen gasped at Laura's attitude, putting one hand to her mouth but still holding her phone so she could read the script with the other.

"Well we're here now so let's get to it," Cohen said, flustered. He clapped his hands together. "Emir are you ready?"

"*Muahahaha!*" Emir laughed, standing from the conveyor belt and pushing his chest out. "I am a robot. I am always ready."

"If only you were," Cohen said with a grin, turning to Jen. "What about you? I see you're still going over the script. And is that the right costume for this scene? Where's Steve?"

Jen scoffed. "You tell me, *director*. And I wouldn't be reading the script right now if you had given me a little warning that we were going to do this scene today."

Cohen took out his own phone and pulled up the script. Emir laughed at them and did the robot. "Silly humans," he said in a monotone voice. "I am a robot. I already memorized—"

"Yeah, yeah. *We get it*," Cohen said, waving him away. "You're in character. Way to do your job. Now, Jen. No. This isn't the right costume. I need you to find Steve and get changed."

"Find him?" Jen said, dropping her phone from her face for the first time since they had left the other set. "Where the fuck is he?"

"I don't know," Cohen said. "Probably in the green room. Just go." He waved her away.

"*Ugh*. But—" Jen tried to complain.

"I said go!"

Laura stopped her work and Emir stopped doing the robot so they could both turn around and gawk at Cohen's attitude.

"*Whatever*, dude" Jen said, flailing her arms and storming out of the room.

Laura went back to work, wishing again it was Cohen instead of Emir that was the star of the show.

"Fuck," Cohen said, pacing the room and brushing back his already slicked-back hair. "I can't deal with divas right now. Do y'all hear me? We don't have time for this shit, okay. We only have this lot for—" He looked at his phone. "—a few more hours and we have plenty of shots to get to while we're here. So if y'all could just fall the fuck in line for once in your pathetic lives, that would be fan—*fucking*—tastic. I'm under a lot of pressure here. So let's all do our part to relieve a little bit of it today."

Emir nodded. "I am a robot," he said. "Your wish is my

command."

Cohen took a deep breath then chuckled. "Good," he said. "What about you, Laura? You gonna give me shit when I tell you to set the lights and cameras—"

"Exactly where I have them," Laura stopped him, crossing her arms and giving him the evil eye.

"I—well..." Cohen looked back and forth between his phone's script and the rigging a few times. "*Uh...* Yes, actually. Exactly that."

"Good," Laura said. "Now maybe you can stop giving me shit for no reason."

"*Oooooohhhh.* Damn, buoy," Emir said, finally breaking character to snap his fingers together three times in a zigzag pattern. "She *told* you."

"Shut the fuck up, Emir," Cohen said. "No one asked you."

"There," Jen said, coming back on set and striking a pose. "Is this better?" Laura thought she looked almost exactly the same as before, though—maybe a little dirtier.

"Is that what Steve gave you?" Cohen asked, stepping toward her to get a closer look.

Jen nodded, holding her pose.

"Then, yes. It's better," Cohen said, clapping his hands together too loudly for Jen's taste. "Places everyone. I think one take should be good for this. The scene's not difficult. We're starting from Alice's entrance and going through Adam's attack. We'll cut right before he puts her on the conveyor belt. Y'all got that?"

Everyone nodded, taking their places. Emir sat at his seat, stretching his fingers in preparation for snapping pieces together. They'd be able to speed it up in post production but he would have to give them something they could work with if they wanted to make it look at all natural. Well, not really, in the end, but he didn't know that yet. Watching him, Laura almost felt sorry for what she had done, for what she had to do, but he would be okay in the long run and she had no other choice.

"Laura, what about you?" Cohen asked, breaking her away from her reservations.

She shook herself out of them. "I—*uh.* Yeah," she said. "*Sure.* This is just a long shot anyway. Set it and forget it." She chuckled to hide her apprehension. Emir'd be alright, she assured herself over and over again. Emir'd be alright. Emir'd be alright. Emir'd be alright.

"Okay. Good," Cohen said, looking around at everyone again to be sure they were in their places and ready. "On my count then." Laura's heart skipped a beat and her palms slickened up. There was no stopping what had been set into motion now.

"Lights!" Cohen called.

Laura flipped a switch, turning off all but the camera lights.

"Belt!"

She pressed a button and the conveyor belt hummed into motion.

"*Aaaaannd* action!"

Emir set to piecing together bits of nothing. Jen gave him a few seconds to do it before slowly walking on camera, surveying the empty seats around Emir.

"No," Jen said, her voice only slightly trembling, not her best acting.

Emir ignored her. He kept piecing together bits of nothing.

"It can't be you," Jen said, voice cracking a little bit.

Emir turned his head to look at her but kept on with his work. He was going slower now, but again, post-production would remedy that.

"Yes," Emir said in his monotone robot voice.

"But..." Jen held her hand to her mouth. "But you're—"

"A robot," Emir said. "*Muahahaha.*" He threw his head back in laughter, still piecing together nothing.

"But my family," Jen said. "My coworkers. They'll—"

Emir stopped working. He stood slowly and turned to face Jen, smiling wide. "I am a robot," he said. "I don't—"

But he couldn't finish the sentence. A heavy, hard light fell from above, landing on his head and knocking him to the ground. Jen screamed, Cohen rushed to Emir's side to see if he was okay, and Laura simply flipped the camera off, calm and collected. She had expected everything. She had rigged the light to fall in the first place. So, naturally, it came as no surprise to her when what had been planned ended up happening.

"Shit! What the fuck was that, Laura?" Cohen demanded, holding a limp and bleeding Emir in his arms.

"I—I don't know," Laura said, mustering all of her acting

abilities for this one scene. Sure she was a grip now, but she had gone through the same school system as everyone else, and she couldn't help but pick a few things up along the way. "That wasn't one of my lights," she said, which was true even though she *had* rigged the light to fall. She knew better than to commit a crime with one of her own babies. "You'll have to ask the studio owner about it."

Cohen looked around wide eyed at Laura, then at Jen, then back to Emir who still lay lifeless—the trickle of blood from his forehead slowly and alarmingly turning into a stream. "Yeah, well," Cohen said. "I—I guess I'll take care of that."

"What about Emir?" Jen's voice cracked as she said it. "Is— Is he...*dead*?"

"What? *No*," Cohen said, looking back at Emir and trying to shake him awake. "Of course not. He can't be. Right, buddy? You're not dead, are you?"

Laura was starting to worry that he might be. That wasn't part of the plan. She had just wanted to put him out of commission for a while, not forever. This couldn't be happening when she was so close to being free of her chains. She was not about become a murderer, even for that freedom. "I think we should—" she started to say, but Emir blinked his eyes open.

"*Emir*. Emir, baby," Cohen said, still on the ground and holding him, brushing his hair like a child. "You're alright, aren't you?"

Emir shook his head, still groggy.

"We need to get him to a doctor," Jen said.

"No!" Cohen snapped. "We can't. They'll ask too many questions. We weren't— Just trust me."

"Well what the fuck are we supposed to do then?" Jen started to cry.

Emir blinked a few times and shook his head. "I am a robot," he said in a weak voice. "I don't care."

"*There*," Cohen said. "There, you see. He's fine. He doesn't care."

"I don't think—" Jen said.

"*No*," Cohen cut her off, standing now that Emir could hold his own weight—though only barely. "It has to be this way. Laura, take him to the green room and get him some water. I need to—"

"I don't think—" Laura said.

"I don't care what you think! Do it!"

"*Ugh.* Fine. Whatever." Laura went to help Emir up while Cohen brought Jen to a far away corner of the set, whispering angrily at her. Laura hefted Emir's arm up over her shoulder and had to carry most of his weight all the way through the halls to the green room.

Steve gasped when she pushed the door open. "Fortuna!" he said, holding a hand to his mouth. "What happened?"

"I—*uh*—" Laura heaved Emir onto the couch next to Steve who went to comfort the injured actor. "I don't know," she said, breathing heavily. "A light fell on him."

"A light?" Steve shot her a look and went back to comforting Emir.

"*Not one of mine,*" she said. "A studio light."

"A studio light?" Steve crossed the room to get some water for Emir. "No way."

"Yes way. Why? Do you think it was my fault?"

Steve put his hands up in defense. "Now I didn't say that."

"It sounded like that's what you were implying."

"Well it's not. I was just saying—"

"Alright, alright," Cohen said, coming into the room with hands clapping. Emir flinched at the sound of it. "How's our star doing?"

Jen scoffed as she came in behind him. "*I'm fine,*" she said under her breath.

"I am a robot," Emir said, louder this time at least.

"He doesn't look good," Steve said. "I think he needs a doctor."

"No!" Cohen and Jen said together.

"That is," Cohen added, chuckling and rubbing his hands together. "He looks alright to me. What do you say, Jen?"

"Oh, yeah," Jen nodded, giving a thumbs up. "Sure thing, boss. Right as rain."

"You see." Cohen smiled.

Steve dabbed a wet rag on Emir's bloody forehead. "Right as rain, huh?"

"I am a care," Emir said. "I don't robot."

"That sounds right as rain to you?" Steve scoffed.

"Well he's a little dizzy," Cohen said, chuckling and trying to avoid eye contact with both Steve and Laura. "But nothing too serious. Right, Jen? *Tell them.*"

Laura scoffed. "He doesn't look like he'll be able to act any time soon," she said, hoping they'd see that at least. "It seems pretty serious to me."

"Fuck, fuck, shit, fuck," Cohen repeated, pacing the small room. "You're right about that."

"Well, why don't we complain to the studio manager, then?" Steve asked. "It is their responsibility, isn't it? Maybe they can send a doctor for us."

Cohen shot him a look then turned to Jen. "No, I don't know," he said, urging Jen to say something. He obviously didn't want the studio managers alerted to the fact that they were using the lot.

"You know what," Jen said, putting on a fake smile. She never really was that great of an actor. She had a pretty face, though, so she got work. "I think I'll go and alert them myself. I'm pretty sure—no—*I'm certain* that I saw someone with a Loch Ness monster on their shirt on my way in here. I'll—I'll go alert them to the problem, and we'll get to the bottom of this in no time."

"*Yes,*" Cohen said, clapping his hands together as she started to leave. "That exactly."

"You know," Laura said, holding her phone over her head. Jen stopped in her tracks, and Cohen stared at Laura, annoyed, while Steve went on dabbing Emir's forehead with a wet rag and Emir kept mumbling about being a robot. "I happen to have the studio manager's direct line. I could save you the trouble." Laura smirked.

"Oh, no, no," Cohen said, looking to Jen for help. "Nonsense."

"It's no trouble at all," Jen said. "*Really.* I'll just go out and—"

"Por que no los dos?" Steve said, shrugging.

Cohen shot him a look. "Yes," he said. "Of course." He chuckled nervously, rubbing his no doubt sweaty hands together. "Both. *Great* idea, Steve. Top notch." He shot a big fake smile at Jen, nodding. "Go ahead, then."

"Oh, well…" Jen said. "Okay, I guess. I mean. *Yeah.* I'll just be on my way then." She walked out as slowly as she could, but even with all that time Cohen couldn't come up with a way to keep her from leaving.

"And I'll just make that call, then," Laura said with a chuckle, trying to stall a bit herself. She did have a direct line to someone in the ownership line of Loch Ness studios, but she wasn't really supposed to call him until *after* all this dirty deed was done, not right in the middle of it. "I'll let them know they're dealing with Cohen Martin," she said, "the soon to be biggest director on any TV set in the entire world."

"No—well—" Cohen stammered.

"Do it," Steve said. "Can't you see this man's injured?" Emir nodded off again as if to illustrate the point. "And tell them to send a doctor." Steve went back to dabbing Emir's still bleeding head with an already bloody rag.

"Alright, then," Laura said, hitting send and putting her phone to her ear. "I'll tell them what's up."

"*Good,*" Steve said with a single curt nod.

"No," Cohen said, stepping closer to Laura and trying to tear the phone out of her hand. "No, you can't— You don't understand."

Laura held tight, though, and took a step back. The phone had rung three times and there still wasn't an answer. She was starting to worry that no one would answer when he finally did.

"It's about time, sweetheart," came the sickening voice from the other end of the line, the voice of the man who had kept her in the chains she was trying to free herself from for so long now. Cohen tried one more time to grab the phone away, but Laura took a quick step back and dodged his advance.

"It's done," she said as she did.

"You can't!" Cohen complained.

"Good," the voice on the other end of the line said. "Very good."

"Yes," Laura said. "I'm calling about Loch Ness Studios, lot thirty seven. This is Laura Concierge."

Cohen gave up, slouching on the couch next to Steve and rousing Emir who groaned, failing to sit up despite trying. "Wha— Where am I?" he said.

"See, he's fine!" Cohen said.

"Yes," the voice on the other end of the line said. "Very good, child. Keep up the charade. Tell me what happened."

"Yes, sir," Laura said, turning her back to her crew as she spoke. "Lot thirty seven, sir. We were filming a shoot when one of the studio lights fell on top of our star. He was knocked unconscious, sir. We're not sure he'll ever act again, and we only had the lot for a limited time at that. This is your responsibility, and we demand a refund and credit for more time in the studios as reparation."

Cohen held his face in his hands, shaking his head, probably crying. Emir seemed a little better already—which Laura was happy to see—he was sitting up now, at least, and Steve was crossing the room to get him some more water.

"Very good, child," the voice on the other end of the line said. "I assume you mean Emir when you say *star*, of course."

"Yes, sir," Laura said, nodding even though the voice couldn't see it. "He... He doesn't look good. We need a doctor. Someone to tell him just how bad it is, sir."

Emir still looked dazed on the couch—though he was drinking water by himself now—when Jen returned to be furiously updated by Cohen who really did start to cry.

"I've sent someone already," the voice on the other end of the line said. "My personal doctor. She'll give you the diagnosis you seek. And I expect to see you shortly, dear. In my office as soon as you're done there. You know the way."

"Yes, sir," Laura said, nodding. "And we expect a full refund on our rent for the day. Nothing less." But the second part she said to a dead line.

"So?" Cohen and Jen asked at the same time, both with red puffy eyes.

"They said they'd—"

The green room doors burst open and a young woman in a long white coat rushed in with a black bag over her shoulder. "Where's the patient?" she demanded, setting her bag on the coffee table in front of the couch.

"Oh—*uh*..." Everyone kind of pointed at Emir whose head still seemed to be too heavy for his neck to hold up.

"Alright, then," the doctor said, grabbing some tool from the bag to examine him with. "Let me just see here."

Emir blinked his eyes against the light that the woman's tool emitted, shaking his head. "I am a robot," he said. "I don't care."

The doctor kind of chuckled then shook her head, like she

realized that laughing was poor bedside manner only too late. "What was that?" she asked when she had gathered herself. "He's a robot?"

"It's one of his lines," Cohen said, talking too close to the doctor. He looked like he wanted her out of there before she could cause any trouble for him. "He has a hard time getting out of character. That's nothing out of the ordinary for him."

"It's true," Jen said, nodding.

"Still, I don't like it," the doctor said, shaking her head. She put her tool back in the black bag and got a bottle of pills out. "A glass of water, please."

Emir held the glass he was still drinking from up to her and said, "I am a robot. Your wish is my command."

"Oh, well..." The doctor shook her head, pushing the glass back to him and handing him two pills. "It was for you anyway, dear. Drink up and take those. They'll have you feeling better in no time."

"I am a robot," Emir said, swallowing the pills and the rest of the water. "I don't care."

"Well," the doctor said, grabbing her bag and crossing back to the door. "I'm afraid that's all I can do. He should be better soon, but not today. Probably not tomorrow, either. Just don't let him go to sleep for the next twenty four hours. Wake him up every fifteen minutes, at least. Otherwise he may not wake up ever. And then give him some rest after that. A few weeks of it, in bed, with no work. That's the only thing that'll make him well again. Okay, then. *Ta ta*." She slammed the door closed behind her as she left, apparently in a hurry to do something somewhere else.

"You shouldn't have done that," Cohen said, standing in Laura's face.

"What?" Laura asked, stepping up to him. "Get Emir medical attention?"

"Calm down you two," Steve said, standing between them to push them apart.

"I was just trying to help," Laura said, shrugging. "I would hope that one of you would do the same if it was me about to die like that."

"*You* were being defiant," Cohen said. "*I* had everything under control."

"I don't know," Jen said. "Nothing bad happened, right?

Emir should be fine, I mean. That's what the doctor said, isn't it?"

"That is what she said." Steve nodded.

"Still," Cohen said, pacing the room. "What the fuck? What are we supposed to do now? We don't have a star."

"Wait until he's better," Steve said. "What else?"

"We don't have time to wait," Cohen said. "Our time's almost up here. Not to mention the investors…"

"What about them?" Jen asked.

"Yeah," Laura said. She still didn't even know who these mystery investors were. "What about them?"

"They want their product," Cohen said. "What else? They're investors. What the fuck do you think?"

"I think you need to calm the fuck down," Laura said.

"Yeah," Jen nodded. "Settle down, dude."

"Well we need a fucking star or we don't have a movie," Cohen said.

"And Emir should be fine again soon," Steve reminded him.

"I am a robot," Emir said, groaning.

"We need him sooner than soon," Cohen said, flailing his hands in the air. "We need him right now. Fuck it. Fuck this. I'm out of here." He stomped out of the room, slamming the door closed behind him.

"Fortuna!" Jen said when he was gone. "What an ass."

"Right?" Steve nodded. "You need some more water, honey?"

Emir nodded. "I don't care."

"What an ass," Laura repeated, packing up her lights and cameras. "Y'all can take care of Emir, though, right? I have some pretty important business to see to right now."

"Uh…" Jen looked to Steve, obviously not wanting the responsibility herself.

"Yeah, sure." Steve nodded and shrugged, rinsing his glass— of everclear, probably. "I have some sewing to do anyway. What the fuck? I'll make it an all nighter."

"Great," Laura said. "Awesome. I hope he'll be alright." And she knew he would be but not soon enough. The wheels had been set in motion.

෨   ✄   ♨

XLV. Anna

In her tiny little kitchen, it was a pleasure to cook breakfast—a pleasure not many people knew how to enjoy, sure, but a much needed diversion in these tumultuous times nonetheless.

Rosa was off in her study, no doubt. She always woke so much earlier than Anna and set to work straight away. Anna couldn't do that, though. She had to ease into her day, get prepared for it, test the water with her toe before diving in. And what better way to prepare for the day than to cook and eat a hearty breakfast? This particular breakfast was one of the heartiest in her repertoire. She had already grated the sweet potatoes—specifically chosen to provide as much energy as possible for the day's inevitable drainage—and pan fried them along with the sausage and bacon before that. She had it all in the wok now, with some diced bell peppers, onions, and tomatoes—already sauteed—when she added a dozen eggs and set the resultant slop to cooking over the gas stove's heat.

The energy was going to be needed, that was for sure. No. Maybe that wasn't quite right. The energy was there already, no doubt about that. An outlet was what they needed. The residents of Five and Six were all hot kinetic molecules, bouncing against one another and the walls that were put there to contain them—walls which did contain them, for the most part, but not for much longer. With so many molecules absorbing so much energy in such a small space, it was only a matter of time before some of them found a seam to escape through—or created one themselves. That was the natural order of things.

When all the eggs in the wok had solidified—changing phase from liquid to solid thanks to the kinetic energy they had absorbed from the stove top—Anna turned the burner off and left the frittatas to congeal. When it came to cooking, like many things in life, Anna knew that you had to let things cool down a bit before you could really enjoy the work you had done.

With breakfast cooked, she made her way to Rosa's office—

their office, really, since there was only one in the entire Family Home, but Rosa claimed it as her own because she used it most often. Rosa was there, of course, behind her desk, scribbling furiously on some notepad, just as Anna had expected.

"*Ahem.*" Anna cleared her throat. "Breakfast's ready, dear."

Rosa scribbled a few more lines then looked up at Anna absently. "Oh—*uh*—I'm sorry. What was that?"

"Breakfast," Anna said, crossing around the desk to massage Rosa's shoulders. "You need your energy for the long day."

"*Ahhh,*" Rosa groaned, reacting to Anna's fingers. "That feels so good."

"So will some food in your stomach," Anna said, really digging into Rosa's muscles. Rosa let out a little yelp that was tinged with pain and pleasure at the same time, a result of the satisfying, painful release of lactic acid build up in her muscles. "I made frittatas," Anna went on, "the perfect start to an important day."

"They don't get much more important than this one, do they?" Rosa stood from the chair to embrace Anna and kiss her.

"No," Anna said, giggling as she caught her breath. "They don't. So come on." She took Rosa's hand and led her out to the kitchen to sit her in one of the bar stools. "So," Anna said as she loaded a plate and set it in front of Rosa, "how do you feel?"

"*Aaaaahhhh.*" Rosa yawned, stretching her arms as wide as they would go. "Tired."

Anna scoffed. "That's it?"

"I don't know," Rosa said between bites, using her fork more like a shovel than an eating utensil. "What did you want me to say?"

Anna shrugged. "I don't want you to say anything. I want you to say how you feel. It's a big day today. I thought you would think so, too."

"Of course I do." Rosa chuckled, spitting some chewed up slop onto her plate. "But every day is big with our Family. Every day I put everything on the line for our prosperity. Today's no different. You know that about me."

Anna cracked a smile. She did know that about Rosa. It was one of the main reasons she loved her: the woman's indomitable will and incessant optimism. Today really was just another day to her. The inevitable success of the Human Family was just as inevitable as it had always been. Whether they were simply pulling new members one by one, or taking the biggest risk that either of them had ever taken, it made no difference to Rosa, the Human Family would overcome all odds.

"I'm glad to see you're so confident," Anna said, kissing Rosa again.

"And why wouldn't I be?" Rosa asked with a wry grin. "It remains impossible for the Human Family to fail as long as we stand united."

"But this?" Anna asked, breaking the embrace and taking a step back. "Are you sure it's the only way? Aren't the protectors humans, too?"

Rosa scoffed. "You saw what they did to us, honey. When they reacted like that, they showed us that they aren't human. They aren't a part of my Family at least. No one who crosses us like that could ever be."

"I don't know," Anna shook her head.

"What then? You'd have us do nothing? Should we just let them murder us en masse again the next time they come around?"

"No," Anna said. "We have to protect ourselves."

"Exactly." Rosa smiled. "*We* have to protect ourselves. We can't expect the protectors to do it for us. Our only other option would be to give up on the Family altogether, to get back under their radar by doing nothing to fight back against them. You don't want that, do you?"

"No way," Anna said. "Of course not. Not an option."

"*Good.*" Rosa kissed her on the forehead. "Then why don't you go on downstairs and get the consoles running. I have a few more things to tend to here, but I'll be along to help as soon as I can."

Anna chuckled as she left the room. "Sure thing, dear," she said, waving and closing the office door behind her. Rosa wouldn't be down until it was time to go through the rings and Anna knew it. There was no point for her to be. There was nothing Rosa could do in that basement to help prepare for what was to come. She would only get in the way. Anna was one of only a handful of people in all the worlds who knew how to operate that particular model of transport ring, using the control consoles she herself had designed and built, and that handful didn't include Rosa. Rosa's strengths lied in other areas—areas where Anna was weak—so it made no difference to Anna whether Rosa tried to help or not. In fact, it was better if she didn't.

The transport rings were stored in the basement of the Family Home. Where there used to be piles and piles of boxes containing various supplies—mostly paper and drawing utensils, but a little bit of food here and there, interspersed with the occasional clipboard, there could never be enough clipboards—there were now six giant rings lining the walls and the two consoles in the middle of the otherwise empty room.

Anna's fingers moved over the consoles' controls with the deft speed of a practiced musician. The buttons and levers were her piano keys. The music she made was only audible in the clicking and swiping as she worked, but her composition was performed in a medium far different from that of sound. The sounds were only the tip of the iceberg, and the rest of Anna's symphony spread deep, submerged in the darkness of nameless dimensions, shaping and reshaping her very plane of existence.

This was when Anna felt her best. She could almost see those deeper dimensions of existence as she molded them with her very hands. Here and there were once thought to be separated by a great chasm of nothingness, but that nothingness was not nothing after all. On the contrary, it was something. As she poked and prodded at that nothing that was really something, the very foundations of existence began to untangle in Anna's hands. These distances weren't separated by a single path from A to B, they were separated by many paths, infinite paths perhaps, and all of varying lengths. The more she played with this ball of yarn at the heart of her universe the more it unfolded, the more it opened up to her requests, and the more she could control the world around her.

The tricky part—Anna had determined after a not insignificant amount of trial and error—was in finding the path you wanted, the shortest path you could catch with the technology at your disposal, and making sure you ended up with that particular one rather than any of the seemingly infinite other possibilities. Getting the paths to shuffle themselves was the easy part. Getting them to shuffle a royal flush to the top of the deck was where it got hard. But then again, you didn't always need the flush to win. Sometimes you could get by with two pair—especially when you had six hands, one per transporter ring, to work with—and Anna was getting better at shuffling aces to the top, at least, if not the full flush.

She set the timing patterns and outlet depots for the mission—they weren't going to any costume closets this time—and by the time she was done, she could already hear Rosa upstairs, riling the crew who had volunteered to go through. She climbed the stairs into the neatly packed conference room, filled with thirty-five of the bravest Family members Anna had ever known and listened to what was left of Rosa's speech.

"They have brought us to this," Rosa spoke—almost sang, really, in that commanding tone of hers. "It is their fault!" She slammed her fist on the podium and the group hooted and hollered in response. "We try to feed our Family and what do they do to us? Murder us in the streets. Step over the dead and dying bodies of *our* brothers and sisters in order to come into *our* homes and disrespect *our* rights. I say no more!"

The crowd raged again. Anna was nervous to hear shouts of "Kill them all!" and "Eye for an eye!" but she couldn't blame them. She couldn't stop them, either. Hell, she couldn't even stop herself from helping them if she wanted to. She could only hope that their heads would cool once they finally carried their fate in their own hands. That might be the only way to prevent the apocalypse she thought was probably inevitable no matter what she did.

"Tonight we endure no more," Rosa went on. "Tonight we take responsibility for our own protection. Tonight we take the fight to their home and we earn their respect. Are you with me?"

Anna joined in with the cheering this time. She couldn't help it. Rosa had the same effect on everyone.

"You know your assignments. You know your objectives. You've studied up on the blueprints and know exactly when and where to go. Don't let me down. Don't let yourselves down. But most importantly, don't let your Family down. Because it's not only our lives on the line out there, it's the life and livelihood of each and every one of our human brothers and sisters. We will not fail them!"

Everyone cheered to that, standing from their seats and stomping their feet. Anna's heart raced at the sound of it.

"Let's do this. Troops, forward!" Rosa waved her hand and Anna was pushed down into the basement, riding the crest of a wave of soldiers dedicated to protecting the Human Family. Anna took her place behind the consoles, and when Rosa came down—last out of all the Family—she called them to attention. Their excited chaos suddenly dissipated into a steel sense of resolved solidarity. At three words from Rosa, the fluid mass that had seemed too large to be contained by the small basement coagulated into six tight columns, one directed toward each of the transport rings.

"Now is the time for discipline," Rosa said over the silent and still platoon. "Now is the time for resolve. Together with our Family we cannot fail. Now let us succeed!"

Rosa shot Anna a hand signal and everything around her disappeared. There was no platoon of soldiers, stuffing her basement too full. There was no basement at all and no Rosa inside of it, waiting to guide her platoon through the transport rings. There was only Anna and the music she loved.

Soon the rings were humming into action. Six of them all together in such a tight space must have been deafening to the troop, but Anna couldn't hear a thing, she was too busy listening to the subtle notes of her song. The strings of creation jumped and jittered as Anna wove them together into the most elegant universal tapestry that any of them there had ever been a part of. Never before had Anna controlled six rings at once. Three she had done, and there was some thrill to it, but nothing like six. Each hand was working a different console, and it became as if half her brain controlled three of the rings and the other half the rest. There was no time for anything else but the music.

Then the humming stopped. Anna shook her head and looked up. The basement was empty. The thirty six brothers and sisters—including Rosa—who had only just filled the room to bursting were now in another world entirely. It took them only three steps to get from the Family Home to Outland One, across six worlds—three steps and Anna's symphony.

Anna sighed in relief and frustration. This was the worst part about being the Queen of the Consoles: waiting for the action to finish without being able to see it. She wasn't sure she would go across with them even if they didn't need her to run the rings, but she had a hard time picturing how it could be any worse over there than it was waiting helpless at Home to see which of them returned alive.

Then she did the worst thing she could do. She started imagining all the terrible possibilities of what could be happening to her Family members in One, to her Rosa and the others who Anna's own hands had sent into whatever terrible fate that awaited them. She imagined the protectors being there just as her Family stepped through the portals, waiting to gun Anna's brothers and sisters down before they even had a chance to move. She imagined her Family making it all the way to the guns they were seeking, only to be shot in the back as they lay their hands on salvation. She imagined the look on Rosa's face as the life left her body, never to be caressed or kissed or loved by Anna again. And she began to weep.

She shook herself out of the crying after only a moment, though, wiping the moisture from her eyes. Those scenarios were all in her head. They weren't reality. The only way Anna could find out what was actually happening over there was to wait until her now three and a half minutes—still three and a half!—were up and she could let them all back to fill her in on every little detail.

She paced the room as she waited, trying to get her mind back on the path settings she would need to set for her Family's triumphant return rather than imagining the horrible things that could be happening to them. She kept slipping back into the daymares, though, until she set her hands to work on the consoles, preparing another symphony. There was still more than a minute before an escape was called for, sure, but this way she could distract herself with the music.

Before she knew it, the rings were humming into motion. She didn't even have to check her watch. She had come to be so in tune with the rhythms of the universe that she probably kept better time than the old ratty thing ever could. The doors opened, her masterpiece finally coming to fruition, but something had gone wrong. One door wasn't in the right place. The entryway had opened exactly where it was supposed to open, but it didn't lead home. It led... Where? Where the fuck was it going?

The pace of Anna's fingers on the console quickened. Who was messing with her strings? Who was trying to play over her? Why were they doing it? And most importantly, how could they?

Voices tried to break through her shell of concentration, but Anna pushed them away. Or rather she let them go and pushed her mind away from the noise, deeper into the fourth dimension. Some of her Family had made it back safely, at least. She could work harder and smarter with that small comfort, but she wasn't going to stop until all her brothers and sisters were safe again at Home.

At first sight of it, she thought the breach had come from the protectors themselves. Maybe it was some kind of defensive system she hadn't noticed when she was first planning the pathways. But that wasn't true. It couldn't be. There was no activity from One at all, and why would the protectors ever send her people to… Where were they being sent?

It was an eternity in her mind—or three seconds in reality—before she caught the other end of the rope. She had a grasp on both sides now and set all six of the rings alternating between various portals near the location of the missing Family members. She kept shuffling the deck and dealing hands, shuffling the deck and dealing hands, confident that eventually she would hit big.

She didn't know how long she had been at it when the humming stopped. Did she stop it? Had she done anything to help anyone this entire time, or was she just a waste of effort and life?

Hands patted her back until there was no more rustling in the basement. Everyone had scurried upstairs to run away or been left on the other side, in One with the protectors. Anna didn't care anymore. The symphony had taken every ounce of her brain power to compose and conduct. She had no energy left with which to worry. She sat straight down on the ground behind her consoles, ready to give in to the world, and cried silently to herself.

Then came the voice, her voice, the only voice which could possibly bring Anna back to reality after all that. "Nanna," it said. "No more worries in your eyes, now, Nanna. Your Rosie-Posie's here."

Anna cried and jumped up and hugged Rosa—all at the same time. "I thought I had lost you," she said through her tears.

"And I you." Rosa grinned, kissing Anna. "But you came back to me, and you brought our brothers and sisters with you."

"I—I could never—" Anna said. She gathered herself and wiped her eyes, remembering how little she actually knew about what transpired in One. "But what happened? How are you— How did it go? Is everything alright?"

Rosa chuckled. "It's more than alright," she said. "But there's plenty of time for that later. Come on."

Rosa led Anna out of the basement—almost carrying her up the stairs into a frenzy of motion all through the halls, each Family member doing their work with a big black gun strapped over their shoulder—into the kitchen to get a glass of water. Anna's heart skipped a beat, though, when she saw one body bleeding on the dining room table and another doing the same on the kitchen counter, and she was torn violently back into reality.

Again her muscles seemed to work by reflex. Rosa handed her a glass, and instead of drinking the water, Anna fed it to the injured party on the counter who sipped it up with a groan. "There you are, child," Anna said. "Let me see what they did to you."

One of the other soldiers was already snipping off the injured party's shirt so Anna helped with the last little bit and peeled the shirt off as gingerly as she could. It stuck to the poor woman's skin, right under her breast, giving Anna a good idea of where the wound was. The injured woman groaned in pain as Anna tried to get a better look. Anna wanted to groan herself at what she saw, but she held it back. This was a pretty bad wound. She lifted one side of the woman's back and felt around as softly as she could. No exit wound. It was getting worse.

"I'm gonna need some tweezers and bandages," Anna said. She turned to Rosa. "And some pills, dear. Injections preferably, but I'm not sure we have any at the moment. You'll have to take a look-see."

"I—but— Are you sure, dear?" Rosa said, caressing Anna's lower back with one hand. "You just fainted down there in the basement. I don't want your health getting any worse than it already is. There are people here who can do this for you."

"*I'm sure*," Anna said, kissing Rosa's cheek at the same time that she took the rags and bucket from some assistant's hand. "I was worried that I had lost you, but now that you're back, I'm over it. Just go get those injections."

"Injections, huh?" Rosa raised her eyebrows. "Are you sure pills won't do?"

"It doesn't matter," Anna snapped, working on getting the shrapnel out of the woman's abdomen at the same time as carrying on the conversation. If they asked her to cook a meal and write some slogans, too, she might need as much brain power as she had needed earlier to reshape the universe with six rings at once, but reshaping one human body would have to suffice for now. "Either would've done," she said. "Like I said already. But now that you've taken so long, pills should be more than enough because...*ah*." She held up the bullet which was, luckily, still in one piece. "I've got the bullet."

"Right, right," Rosa said, kissing Anna on the cheek one more time before heading down to the basement. "I knew my Nanna could take care of everything."

"You, take care of this," Anna, stitching the wound closed, said to the soldier that had been assisting her. "Bandage her up and keep her watered. And there are beds in the basement. When you're done here, go ahead and put two or three of them in the conference room. I don't think we'll be having any more public meetings here after all of this so it shouldn't matter in the long run."

"But the basement's clear," the assistant said. "There weren't any beds down there a minute ago."

"Rosa will show you," Anna said, crossing to the next patient. "*Go.*" That was the one thing Rosa did now how to use the consoles for, a pre-programmed room change.

"Okay, what do we have here?" Anna asked, looking down on a too young boy who was holding a bloody rag to his own forehead.

"I'm fine," the boy said.

"I don't know," the nurse who had been tending to him said—if she could even be called a nurse she was so young. "You bled a lot."

"Let me see," Anna said, taking the rag from his head.

The boy winced in pain.

"*See,*" the nurse said, crossing her arms.

"It doesn't look too bad," Anna said, dabbing some more blood away as the boy winced.

"*See,*" he said with a groan.

"Looks like it could use some stitches, though," Anna said, dabbing the wound one last time.

The boy jerked away from her. "Stitches?" His eyes widened and his face lost that rebellious resolve he was trying so hard to maintain. "I don't know about that, ma'am. Are you sure?"

"It won't hurt," Anna said. "*Much.* Besides, I thought you were fine." She grinned.

"I am," he said, crossing his arms.

"Then lay right down like a good boy so I can stitch you up."

He hesitated then gave in, probably trying to impress the

nurse who, for her part, looked genuinely worried about the boy's health. "*Ugh*. Fine."

"Great," Anna said when he was on his back. "You," she said to the nurse, "get a light over here please."

"Oh—*uh*." She ran to the other room and came back holding a floor lamp. "Will this do, ma'am?"

"Yes, yes," Anna waved her closer "Just put it close so I can see. There you are. Okay. Now this is going to hurt. Are you ready?"

Anna didn't wait for an answer. The boy winced and groaned and ground his teeth, but he didn't jerk his head at all, and soon Anna was tying off five stitches.

"There you are," she said with a smile as he sat up, trying to scratch the stitches. Anna slapped his hand away. "Don't touch them. That'll make things worse. Nurse…" She looked to the girl who was still holding the lamp."

"Oh—*uh*—Ellen, ma'am," the girl said, almost hitting herself with the lamp trying to shake Anna's hand.

"Nurse Ellen will fit you with some gauze. You keep it covered and dry, then come back to me in the morning—after you've gotten some rest. You understand me?"

The boy nodded, going to scratch his head again, but Anna slapped his hand away. "*And no scratching*. I mean it." Anna looked at Nurse Ellen and gave her a big smile, patting the girl on the back. "You did well, Nurse," she said. "Just wrap his head up with some gauze and be sure he doesn't scratch it. If you can handle that, maybe I'll teach you how to sew the stitches next time."

Nurse Ellen's white-knuckled grip on the floor lamp finally loosened. She set it down, her hands trembling, and the lamp rattled. "Yes, ma'am," she said. "Right away, ma'am." She took a few steps then turned around, blushing, to go the other way toward where the gauze was stored.

Anna surveyed the room. Two bodies wasn't bad. She had expected her kitchen to be a morgue after what Rosa had planned. And the mission was definitely a success, the guns on everyone's shoulders was evidence enough of that. As long as that bullet wound didn't become infected, they might not—

"I'm here!" Rosa said, storming in with a bottle of pills and a handful of syringes held up over her head. "I got what you asked for, Nannie dear." She smiled, holding her bounty out to Anna, proud of herself.

Anna chuckled. "Too late again, Rosie," she said with a grin, shaking her head. She still couldn't decide if Rosa did these things because she was cheap and didn't want to waste the supplies, or if Rosa was simply too queasy to witness the blood. Most likely it was the former, but probably a little of both. "But give the kid a pill anyway. And the woman a few." Anna handed the bottle to Nurse Ellen then turned to Rosa. "Come on." She held out her hand. "You have to tell me all about what happened now."

Rosa smiled and took Anna's hand, kissing the back of it before letting Anna lead the way into their office.

"So," Anna said, sitting Rosa in the desk chair and taking the seat across from her. "Those injuries weren't too bad. Everyone else is back safe then? No other injuries for me to tend to?" She smiled wide, hopefully.

Rosa's smile slowly faded to a frown. She broke eye contact with Anna, fumbling through the desk for nothing in particular. "Well, yes and no," she finally said. "Yes those are the only injuries for you to treat..." She smiled a fake smile, not going on.

Anna sighed. "But not everyone else is home safe?"

Rosa shook her head, breaking eye contact again.

"Well what then? Who? *Go on*. It's not like not telling me is going to change what happened."

"No...well... A few of us didn't make it back. And some of those who did make it back aren't alive to be treated. And that's just from my squad. I haven't had reports from the others yet."

"*No*." Anna fought tears. "Who?"

"Yujin and Melody were murdered just as we got our hands on the guns. They were so close, but the *protectors* who did it paid the price. We got Yujin's body back, but reinforcements came and the protectors took Isha when she tried to retrieve Melody's. They— they still have her. We're not sure if she's alive or dead."

"No. But they'll—"

"That's not all," Rosa said, stopping her. When she was giving the bad news, Rosa sure liked to pile it on. Why could it never be the same with the good? "One of those doors you sent us to get home didn't bring us back here like it was supposed to."

"I know, I tried—"

"I'm not entirely sure where it took us, actually. But

wherever that is, Kara's still there. The rest of us made it to your second door and back home, but she... *She didn't.*"

"I know where she is," Anna said. "That door wasn't sent by me. There was some kind of interference or something. I don't know. I had never seen anything like it before."

"But you know where she is?" Rosa asked, sitting up in her chair and leaning forward on her desk with a big smile. "You can get us back there?"

"Yes," Anna said, though she wasn't as sure of herself as she sounded. "Of course I can."

"Good." Rosa smiled. "Not now but soon. No Family members left behind."

"No," Anna said. "Of course not. That's why I wouldn't give up—I didn't give up—until I got you back from wherever they took you."

"Whoever *they* are."

"I'll find out."

Rosa chuckled, standing and crossing around the desk to massage Anna's shoulders. Anna loved the feeling of those fingers on her skin. "I know, dear," Rosa said. "Just like I knew you'd get me back from wherever they sent us to. And just like I knew that we couldn't fail in this mission as long as we worked as a Family."

Anna rolled her shoulders under Rosa's massaging fingers, groaning with pleasure. "You think it was a success, then?"

Rosa laughed. "Of course, dear." She kissed Anna on the cheek. "And now our Family's invincible."

⅋   ✳   ⅌

XLVI. Roo

No one in the worlds understood the fourth dimension as well as Roo did. She was pretty certain of that. And, no, she didn't mean time. She was talking about dimensions in timespace. Humans could sense three dimensions of space, and time could be thought of as a dimension, but technically that wasn't quite true, and technically was all that mattered to Roo.

Technically, time was an emergent property. It was a result of changes in space. Without changes in space there would be no way to measure the passing of time. Roo often wondered what it would be like to live in a universe with no changes in space, no time, but it seemed impossible. Nothing existing in such a universe could really be said to be alive. Always she came to the conclusion that, no, without change there is no life.

Maybe that's why she liked jumping so much. It was never really the act of getting from here to there that appealed to her, it was the act of changing the universe, being alive. That's why she preferred to call it bending rather than jumping. But no one else understood the fourth dimension like she did, all they cared about was getting from here to way over there in one hop, so jumping it was if she wanted to be mutually intelligible with the rest of the worlds. When Roo was bending, though, she wasn't doing it to run away, she was taking it upon herself to consciously change the space she occupied, and it was the only time she ever felt truly alive.

"Did you have something to add Miss Sommelier?" came her teacher's voice, breaking Roo from her daydream.

"*Um*, no, ma'am," Roo said, shaking her head. She had no idea what the old lady had been going on about all day and she didn't really care to find out.

"Well then I'll ask you not to interru—"

A metallic clanging bell went off, interrupting the teacher's sentence. Roo jumped out of her desk as quickly as anyone else, and the entire class filed out despite the teacher's demands that they re-seat themselves and subsequent defeated pleas that they all do their homework when it was clear that none of them were going to. Roo chuckled at the poor old slob as she pushed her way through the mass of nerdlings and outside. She was almost out scott free when she heard her name.

"Roo!" Mike called, running to catch up with her. "Wait up!"

"Hurry up!" Roo called, slowing her pace but not stopping to wait. "I've got shit to do."

"That's exactly what I'm here about," he said, catching up with her and pulling her to stop. "What you gettin' into?"

"Whaddya think?" Roo asked, crossing her arms. She only did one thing with her free time so it wasn't that hard to figure out what she was getting into.

"*Jumpin'*," Mike said. "I wanna come along."

"*Psssh*." Roo scoffed. "First of all, it's bending, not jumping. I'm not one of those neckbeards who're in this for the sole purpose of jumping into girl's locker rooms when they least expect it. I'm in it for something else, something deeper."

"Yeah, sure." Mike scoffed back. "What then?"

"For—for..." She thought about the complex enigma that was the fourth dimension and almost fell back into her daydream from class. "For the serene feeling I get when I'm actually capable of shaping the universe I live in. For the awe and wonder I experience when staring into the fourth dimension. For reasons beyond anything your puny little brain could ever understand. That's why." She picked up her walking pace, almost to a jog.

"No one understands that crap," Mike said, actually jogging to keep up with her. "You're the only one who ever talks about it."

"*I know*. That's why I need to be alone. So git."

"No, wait." He stopped her again. "Look. This is for real, okay. I'm—I might be in trouble."

"Then definitely go away. Trouble's the last thing I need in my life."

"No, look. I think you can help me." The look in his eyes was so desperate it made Roo pity him for a moment. Honestly, he had to be in some seriously deep shit to be coming to her for help. "*Ugh, God. Okay*," she said, giving in. "What do you want?"

"Well..." Mike looked away, embarrassed now to even be speaking to her, it seemed like. "So, it's not really for me, okay," he said. "Or it is for me, I guess, but it's not me who's in trouble. And mostly it's for my brothers, you know, because I couldn't give a fuck about that inconsiderate asshole who tries to call herself my mom. You know what I mean?" He nodded expectantly.

Roo did not know what he meant, though. She had no clue. So she said it. "No. I don't. What inconsiderate asshole? What kind of trouble? WTF am I supposed to do about it?"

"Oh—well— Okay, well... Let me start again."

"Spit it out fast, kid. My patience is running thin and I have an urge to bend."

"Okay, well... It's my mom, right. Well, I don't know how to put this, but she got in with the wrong people, you know. And well—she's been—she's been... *jumping*." He leaned in close and whispered the last word, not looking as excited about the prospect of "jumping" as he did before. At least he didn't seem to be in it for the thrill of going through the portals like all those other jumpies.

"Okay," Roo said. "So what? What am I supposed to do about it? Or are you just here looking for the same thrill your mom's always after?" She never knew the urge could be genetic.

"*God, no*. Fuck that. Thrill? Talk to me about thrill when you're stuck at home, changing your baby brother's diapers, your other brother crying for food, or mom, you're not sure because, even though he's old enough that he should be able to, he doesn't talk yet, and the whole time your mom is out who the fuck knows where doing who the fuck knows what with some stupid jumpies. *No offence, okay*. But I'm not personally interested in becoming a jumpie like y'all. Trust me. That's the last thing I intend to do."

"*Well*." That was a little much, sure, but at least it seemed like the kid meant what he said so Roo would let him get away with the attitude this one time. "What the fuck do you expect me to do about it then?" she snapped, showing a little attitude of her own.

"Well..." Mike looked at his feet, losing confidence already after his rousing speech. "Honestly, I didn't really think this all the way through yet. I don't even know what this jumping shit is. That's why I came to you. You're the only person I could think of who even knew anything about it."

"You're right on that point," Roo said with a grin. The poor kid didn't know how right he was. She was probably the only person in all the worlds who actually knew what *this jumping shit* was all about. Plus, a little flattery went a long way. The only problem was that Roo still had no idea what she was supposed to do about his family problems. "But I still don't know how you expect me to help."

"Well, me neither. But you can, right? I mean, you can at least teach me about jumping, or show me how you do it. I don't know. Maybe that way I'll figure it out for myself and won't need your help to find her."

"*Pffft*. You know, I'm not sure that's gonna help you, kid. I mean, what if your mother's addiction is hereditary? What might happen to you if I teach you how to jump then?"

"Hereditary?"

"Yeah, you know, inherited. Genetic. As in: if your mom has it, so will you."

Mike scoffed. "That's fucking stupid."

"Not really. Actually it's supported by a lot of evide—"

"I don't give a shit." Mike stomped his foot. "I'm not gonna get addicted. I'm gonna help my mom. You got any better ideas?"

"I could just walk away and leave you to figure out all this shit for yourself." Roo scoffed. "In fact, that's sounding like a pretty good idea. See ya." She made to leave but Mike grabbed her by the arm to stop her.

"No. Please," he begged. "Just—I won't get addicted, okay. I don't even want to take part in it at all after seeing what it did to my mom, but it's the only way I can think to help her. And you're the only person I can think of to teach me. So… What do you say? Partners?" He held out a hand for her to shake.

Roo slapped it away. "No," she said, walking on toward the way she had been going before she was interrupted. "We're not partners. You owe me big for this, and don't you forget it."

"Of course, of course," Mike said, jogging to keep up with her quick pace. "Whatever you say." He somehow managed to maintain a smile through his heavy breathing.

Roo didn't say another word until they were there. She led him on roundabouts, doubling back and criss-crossing paths so he would have a harder time remembering where they were. When she was at the right alley, she crossed it then came back through on the other side.

"Shit," Mike said, hunched over, huffing and puffing. "I never knew jumping was such exercise."

"*Bending* is illegal," Roo said, crossing back to check the other side of the alley again. "That's your first lesson. What we're about to do is against the law. We can't let anyone see us. If the protectors catch us doing this, we're fucked."

"Right, I—"

"*Shhh*." She held a finger to his mouth. "Now this is my secret lair, okay. So—"

Mike chuckled.

"I'll fucking leave your ass out here," Roo said, raising a hand as if she was going to hit him—she never really would have but he didn't know what she was capable of.

"No, no, no." Mike put his hands up in defense. "Please. I'm sorry. It's just, secret lair sounds totally superhero. I like it."

"Well it's secret for a reason, okay."

"Yeah, yeah. I got it," Mike said, stepping back and looking around at the alley. "So, this is nice. *Uh*...I guess. But I don't see how you can jump from here. It's just an alley."

This time Roo laughed. "Not *here*, dumbass. C'mon." She grabbed his hand, and it was a little sweaty, but she didn't let go anyway. It was far too late for that. "I'll show you." She walked him up to the brick wall, behind one of the dumpsters, and spun him around so she could step closer, putting her face so close to his that she could feel his breath. "Are you ready?" she whispered, looking at his lips instead of his eyes.

"I... *Uh*..." He fidgeted, staring at her lips, obviously nervous.

"You'll have to be." She pushed him, and he fell back, but instead of hitting his head on the wall behind him, he fell through the wall as if it weren't there at all, landing on his ass with a yelp.

Roo stepped gracefully through the wall, and over Mike, into her secret lair. "*Ta da!*" she said, taking a bow, then she hunched over laughing.

"*Shit*," Mike said, standing and rubbing his ass. "You didn't have to push me so hard."

"Sorry," Roo said, still chuckling. "I couldn't help myself. I always wanted to do that to somebody."

"I thought you were gonna..."

"Kiss you? *Ha*! Yeah right, you sicko. I had you fooled. Kiss *you*? That's grody."

"Yeah…" Mike looked at his feet. "Sure. *Gross*."

The secret lair wasn't much. It was more of a closet. The ground was made out of metal grating, which was loud when you walked and painful to sit on. The cement walls were lined with shelves carrying various supplies—technical bits which came in handy when Roo had rigged the wall unit for the first time but only got in the way now that she was trying to get back to her baby.

"So *this* is your lair, huh?" Mike said. "It looks like a janitor's closet to me."

"It's not a janitor's closet," Roo complained. "It's a Sommelier's secret lair. But really it's a supply closet." She patted a box of circuits on the shelf that was closest to her.

"So how are you supposed to jump from a supply closet?" Mike asked, still confused.

"We just jumped to get here," Roo said, crossing her arms. "And we'll jump again when we go back out to the alley."

"You mean, that was…" Mike looked at the wall he had just fallen through. "We jumped?"

"Not so great, is it? That's why I told you I prefer bending to jumping."

"And I told you I know nothing about either. What's bending?"

"Bending is when you mold the universe to your liking," Roo said, imagining the feeling as she described the process. "Bending is reshaping three dimensional space, through four dimensions, in order to transform the world around you. Bending is pretty much the greatest experience in existence, and if you've never done it, I'll never be able to explain to you how great it feels."

"Sure." Mike shrugged. "I guess my mom thinks the same way. But I still don't see what's so great about it or how you're supposed to do anything like that from this closet."

"The key," Roo said, removing some boxes from one of the shelves so she could get to the metal door behind it, "lies in where this closet is located. It's not any old supply closet, you see. We're somewhere between E and F right now. FG, technically, but that's another story. What matters is that this is a supply closet in the subterranean maze of tunnels where the walls are maintained."

"Walls?" Mike was looking even more confused than ever. "What are you talking about?"

"The walls. The walls… *Hmmm*. Okay. So we come from World F, alright. Everything you've ever known, every place you've ever been, all of that exists, and or takes place, inside of World F, now FG. You follow me?"

"*Uh…* sure." Mike shrugged, not looking like he followed.

"Well there are other worlds, too. A through E, of course, and G, which only recently became a part of our world, hence the FG."

"Okay." Mike nodded, still obviously not following.

"*Anyway*. The walls—though they're not really walls, more like fields or portals or something. Well, they're kind of like the hole we passed through to get into the lair here."

"Through the wall…" Mike said.

"*Yes*. Exactly. But not physical walls. Metaphysical walls. Giant portal walls separating the worlds."

"And these walls help with jumping how?"

"*Bending*. Not jumping. The walls are where space has been bent already. The people who live in E are the ones who first discovered how to do it, and they bent and curved space everywhere in order to separate the worlds into how they exist now. Hell, the same people bend space to move our elevators, fill the 3D printers, and perform countless other little actions we never notice every single day. Bending is part and parcel to every aspect of human life and…and… *And I'm sorry*. I get a little carried away. I could go on talking about it forever. Is any of this getting through to you at all, though?"

"So these *walls* or whatever," Mike said. "Whatever it is that separates these different worlds. You're saying that this room here is where they come from?"

"This room is in the world where the hardware that bends space exists. If you went out that door right there, you'd find a maze of tunnels that went further than you could explore in one lifetime. There are so many miles of portal walls it's ridiculous. And I can jack into them all from right here." She swung the metal door open as she said it, revealing her masterpiece.

The box she had opened was really a circuit breaker, but Roo knew that more than electricity ran through the breakers in this world. From here she could use the touchscreen tablet she had implanted—thanks to the supply closet—and a one handed keyboard—from the same place—to access every part of the wall system and bend the worlds to her heart's desire—not without some annoyance from security bots, of course, but they were nothing she was incapable of finding, tracking, and hiding from with ease.

"That's it?" Mike said, scoffing. "That's all you use. It looks like a half a computer. It doesn't even have a full keyboard. I bet the graphics are shit."

"Graphics aren't the point." Roo scoffed. She flipped on the touch screen with a swipe then tapped out a few shortcuts to bring up the blueprint for all of F. "You see that?"

"Yeah," Mike said, yawning. "It looks like a map. *Bo-oring.*"

"That map is the blueprint for every single wall in F. That's the map of your entire world, bucko. Everything you'll ever experience, all on one shitty computer screen."

"Yeah, sure. Like your life's better."

Roo tapped some more shortcuts. "It is," she said as more blueprints came up, dwarfing F. "This is my world. This and beyond because I know even these can't be the end of it. That's what bending gives me that you don't have, kid. *I'm* free to traverse all the worlds."

"Sure you are. Free just like my mom is to ditch me with her kids. The same kids who prolly need me to do some menial shit for them right now. Thanks for your help, Roo. *I guess.* I mean, you at least helped me understand how much of an arrogant ass my mom might turn into if she keeps on doing this jumping—or, oh, sorry, *bending* thing—much longer. So I guess that helps. See ya." He made for the closet door then turned around, remembering that it wasn't the way they had come in. He stood there confused, and Roo felt bad for how she had acted. He was right. She was lording her superiority over him. She had brought him there so she could help him, not lecture him and show off, and that was just what she was going to do.

"Wait," she said. "I'm sorry. I— Maybe there is something else I can do. Do you— Or did your mom, rather, ever mention where she was going or anything like that? That would be the easiest way for me to find her."

"You think you can find her?" Mike was smiling now. He looked like he couldn't believe this change in luck.

"*Maybe*," Roo said. "I'm not making any promises. But if

you have something to get me started, I might be able to help. There aren't a lot of jumpers, especially in F, so she shouldn't be too hard to locate."

"Oh, well... She never really bragged about where she was going or anything," Mike said. "She mostly tried to keep it a secret."

"Yeah, okay. But I need *something* to work with, right? I can't go out there searching blindly. That would be pointless."

"What am I supposed to say?"

"*Ugh*. I don't know." This was getting to be too much. Maybe she shouldn't have agreed to help this fool after all. If he wasn't going to do something—anything—to help her, she wasn't going to be able to help him even if she wanted to. "Anything," she said. "Like, did she have a code word she uses when she was going out bending? Something like that."

"No." Mike shrugged. "Not really. She always just says she's gonna go hang out with the girls."

"That's exactly what I'm talking about!" Roo scoffed.

"Oh, well, yeah, then. She always says she's going out with the girls. That used to mean she was going to get a drink at the bar, but I've been checking there and she hasn't been going."

"What bar?" Roo asked, tapping and swiping on the touchscreen.

"*Uh*, I don't know. The one down the street from me. Do they even have names?"

Could this kid maybe think for himself for once? *Ugh*. "Well what street do you live on?"

"Banks and Corporate."

Roo typed it in. The map on the touchscreen zoomed in to that particular portion of F. "North, south, east, or west," she said.

"What?"

"What direction is the bar in? There's one a block away in every direction."

"*Uh*. I don't know. *To the right*."

Are you serious? "Okay, which building do you live in then? Exact address."

"4307 Banks St."

"Okay... Let me just..."

The world around Roo drifted away. There was nothing left but her and the computer screen. She was flying a bird's eye view over Banks street when a commotion caught her eye. Movement. Bending. Something on a grand scale. Not as grand as the walls themselves, but magnificent for FG. A bigger bending than Roo had ever seen in FG. Bigger even than any bending she herself had ever done. Her intention to help Mike disappeared in her curiosity to see what was producing so much change.

She zoomed in to get a closer look. It was made more beautiful with proximity. It was amazing the way all the paths swooped so close to FG then looped back around and braided themselves together, producing six connections so near one another. It seemed mind bogglingly impossible. To be able to hold each portal in place all at the same time without losing a single connection must have taken four or five benders at once.

She zoomed closer. The world was in constant flux now, the entire universe for all she could see. The paths were jumping and bouncing, but only between each portal. None escaped the home base in FG.

Roo's curiosity got the best of her. She couldn't help herself. The excitement was too much to handle. She reached out and touched one of the little paths, and with just that tiny nudge, everything crumbled.

She zoomed out fast, hoping not to be seen. The paths danced faster now. Their motion seemed panicked. One of them jumped to the alley outside of her lair and she gasped, almost breaking from the fourth dimension to see if they had found her.

No. No, no, no. She did not need this. Whoever these people were, she didn't want them outside of her door. She gave in to her desire entirely and started poking and prodding now, bending without remorse.

It was difficult at first. Whoever was doing the bending from the other side fought hard against her. Roo couldn't blame them. They must have thought that she was still interfering when all she wanted to do was make things right again. It took some goading on Roo's part to finally make them give in and accept her help, but eventually they did and finally Roo could sigh a deep breath of relief, sitting down on the metal grating in the hopes that everything was finally back to normal.

"*Fuck*," she said. "That was madness."

Mike scoffed. "You're telling me."

Roo looked back at him, finally aware of her immediate surroundings again, to find his eyes wide and forehead sweaty.

"I don't know what you were doing," he said, "but it seemed intense. I called your name a few times and nudged you, but you wouldn't respond."

Roo chuckled. "Sorry. When I get in the zone, there's nothing else in the worlds."

"Yeah. I could tell." Mike shook his head. "I guess that's probably how my mom gets with it, too. Huh? I guess that's why she can so easily forget about me and my brothers."

Roo blushed, breaking eye contact with him to slam the metal circuit box closed and restack the boxes in front of it. "Probably," she said, as she did.

"*Probably*? And I guess you didn't find my mom, either. Is that right?"

"*Uh...*" Roo shook her head.

"Alright, well, that's cool. I guess that's what I get for asking a *jumpie* for help. I'll just— I'll see you in class, or whatever. *Peace.*" He held out his hand first, to test the wall, but when it went straight through, he closed his eyes and half-jogged out of her secret lair.

Roo felt bad for letting him down—even though she owed him nothing in the first place. She stacked the rest of the boxes as quickly as she could then rushed out of the lair to try to catch up with him, yelling, "Mike, wait!"

She didn't have to yell, though. When she stepped out of the lair, Mike was still there, being held from behind by some dirty clothed person who was pointing a huge gun at his face. Roo stopped in her tracks and put her hands up.

"Freeze, fucker," the woman said, pointing the too big gun between Roo and Mike. "Don't move a muscle."

Roo didn't even move one to speak.

"Who are you?" the woman with the gun demanded. "Where the fuck am I?"

"You're in F," Roo said, raised hands trembling. "Or—*er*— FG. Who are you?"

"FG?" the woman repeated, getting flustered and waving the gun. Mike looked like he was going to piss himself. "What the fuck is FG?"

"You don't know?" Roo tried to smile so the woman would calm down but her lips only trembled. It wasn't the first time a gun had been pointed at her, but she had never even seen one this big.

"Who are you?" the woman demanded, pointing the bazooka—practically—at Roo now. "Don't push me. Now's not the time to piss me off."

"I'm Roo." She smiled without trembling this time. "I'm probably your only hope of ever getting home. You'll want to let my friend go or you'll never see it again."

The woman scoffed. "I don't think you're in the position to be giving orders. What do you think, boy?" She put the barrel of the gun right up to Mike's cheek and he shook his head, crying as he tried to get away from it.

"No," he begged. "Please." A little puddle formed in the front of his pants.

"I don't think you even know what position you're in," Roo said, chuckling, trying not to piss herself, too. "Where do you think you are?"

"I—" The woman hesitated. Roo thought she was going to shoot Mike right then and there, but to her relief, the woman dropped the gun and pushed him away instead. "I don't know. Where am I?" She let her gun dangle over her shoulder, and Roo let out a loud sigh of relief.

"In FG," Roo said after catching her breath. "Like I said. Which I believe is your world, too. In fact, I don't think we're too far from your home base right now."

"You know where the Family Home is?" the woman asked hopefully.

"If that's what you call it," Roo said.

"I don't find this funny," Mike said, stomping a foot. Roo had almost forgotten that he existed. "She pointed a gun at me!"

The woman raised her hands in defense, readjusting the gun's strap on her shoulder. "Hey," she said. "I'm sorry. You came out of nowhere and tackled me. What did you expect me to do?"

"Yeah, well..." Mike looked at his feet. "You pointed a gun at her, too," he said, pointing at Roo.

"Well she appeared like a ghost through the wall of that building," the woman said, pointing at Roo, too. "It was creepy. What do you expect?"

Roo chuckled. "She's got a point."

Mike scoffed, covering the pee stain on his pants. "Well, I still don't think it's funny."

"That's because you pissed yourself," the woman said, chuckling herself.

Mike's face turned a deep crimson. "Alright. Fuck y'all," he said, waving a hand and trying to leave.

Roo and the woman burst into laughter at the same time. Roo tried to control herself, though, saying, "No—Mike—*Ha ha*—Wait! Let me—*Ha ha ha*!"

He stopped to let them control their laughing even though he didn't turn to look at them. "And it better not be another joke," he said. "Or else I'm leaving for real this time."

"No," Roo said, controlling herself. "I think I know where your mom is. And I think I can help you, too," she added for the woman who was still wiping tears of laughter from her eyes.

"I just need to know how to get home," the woman said, composing herself.

"And I just want to get my mom back," Mike said, trying to cover the stain on his pants.

"And I think I can do both at the same time," Roo said. "If your mom's jumping in FG, she's probably doing it with whoever, *uh*... I'm sorry..."

"Oh, *uh*, Kara," the woman said, ticking off a weird salute. "Single name basis oughta be fine for now."

"Right," Roo said. "Your mom's probably jumping with the same people Kara here is jumping with."

"The Human Family," Kara said. "Y'all should think about joining up. Your abilities—well—" She stifled a chuckle at Mike. "—*your* abilities could be useful," she said, looking at Roo.

"*Human family*," Mike said, his eyes widening. "I think my mom did say something about that."

"If she's human, then that's the best thing for her," Kara said.

"*Right*," Roo said, with raised eyebrows. "Whatever. But you came through with a group, didn't you? You weren't alone?"

"What's that to you?" Kara asked suspiciously.

"You want to get back to your *family* don't you?"

"Yeah, well—"

"Then tell me. Did you come alone?"

"No. Of course not. We're a Family. We do nothing—"

"And do you know all your Family's names?" Roo asked.

"I—*uh*—well…"

"Mike, what's your mom's name?"

"Huh?" He looked like he hadn't been following the conversation. Roo was starting to wonder if either of them were.

"What is your mom's name?" she repeated, slowly.

"Oh, *uh*, Melody."

"Melody what?" Roo said, losing patience.

"*Uh*, Singer. Melody Singer."

"Melody Singer," Roo said. "Is she a part of your *family*?"

"I don't know." Kara shook her head, shrugging. "Maybe. Why?"

"Well I think it's time we find out."

ଓ ✖ ଓ

XLVII. Chelsea

She never could have imagined that protecting would be like this. Hell, she never could have imagined that she would be a protector in the first place, but here she was. It was all Tom's fault, too. Her becoming a protector and them sticking her in the shittiest of posts both. She was all too sure of that.

What had gotten into Tom anyway? Honestly, Chelsea was a little worried to have to leave Jonah home alone with him. Someone who thought it was a good idea to help Sixer trash by throwing his life away in an attempt to assassinate the Lord of Outland was probably not competent enough to raise a child, but they couldn't afford an outside housekeeper with a new recruit's pay—which amounted to not much more than food and boarding—and so Tom it was. Chelsea would have to climb through the ranks as quickly as she could if she wanted a proper caretaker for her son, and from the looks of it, her superiors weren't going to let her prove herself anytime soon. So far it seemed like the only thing they were going to do was sit Chelsea behind a desk, proofreading reports or signing weapons and evidence in and out of storage, a job which made her feel no more important than a housekeeper.

Chelsea scoffed, looking around the mostly empty room—empty except for one other Officer whose duty it was to sweep and vacuum the place like he was the protector force's actual housekeeper. That was a ridiculous saying, though, *no more important than a housekeeper*. No matter how often they had tried to beat it into her head since she was a child, it never seemed to stick. Even if she were on an actual protector's beat instead of sitting behind a desk, she would feel the same way. She couldn't help it. She enjoyed cooking, didn't hate sweeping, and loved nothing more than to see her son growing up with every new day, getting to be a part of his life as he did. No matter how many times anyone told her that the only fulfilling path in life was to become a protector and die in the course of duty, Chelsea knew they were wrong. She also knew she had no choice but to be a protector if she wanted what was best for Jonah, though, so there was no going back.

Chelsea groaned when *Officer Housekeeper*—she didn't know the man's actual name—left the room, pushing his cart of cleaning supplies and emptied garbage. She slammed her head on the desk a couple of times, trying to wake herself from the boredom, and when she looked up, *Sergeant Blowhard*—another protector whose name she had yet to learn—was standing at attention in front of her desk.

"Oh, *uh*, hello, sir," Chelsea said, blushing.

"*Good morning, Sergeant*," the Sergeant corrected her. "And salute when you're addressing a superior, Pardy. There's not much lower you can go from here, but there is something below you, and trust me when I say that you do not want to find out what that something is." He grinned an evil looking grin, imagining Chelsea in Officer Housekeeper's position no doubt.

"Yes, sir, Sergeant, sir," Chelsea said, saluting. As much as she enjoyed keeping her own house, she knew that nothing was more degrading than keeping the protectors' house for them. "What can I do for you, sir?"

"Well, why don't you start by telling me why you were hitting your head on your desk, Pardy. I don't remember seeing that maneuver anywhere in the regulation manual." He chuckled a big hearty belly laugh, holding onto his gut as he did.

"Oh. That, sir. Well… I just kind of do it to get my head straight sometimes."

"Get your head straight? *Ha*! Looks more to me like you were scrambling it. *Ha ha ha*!"

"Oh, well…" Chelsea didn't know what to say. No one was supposed to see that. No one was supposed to come back to her little dungeon until shift change. And Sergeant… *Fuck*. She really needed to figure out his name if she didn't want to make a fool of herself. But Sergeant whoever never came down there at all.

"Well, there, Pardy," *Sergeant What's-his-name* went on, seemingly ignoring Chelsea's embarrassment—she hoped. "I hope your brains aren't so scrambled you have trouble finding your way to the Captain's office. She sent me down here, personally, to fetch you so it must be urgent. I wouldn't want you making a fool of our little department down here so don't do anything that you might regret."

He didn't have to say that again. "No, sir," Chelsea said, shaking her head. "Or—*I mean*—Yes, sir. I won't, sir. I can find my way, sir. Any idea of why she'd be asking, sir?"

The Sergeant eyed her suspiciously. Chelsea wanted to blush, or look away, or cover her face, but she fought all her natural instincts. "You know I don't," he said, crossing around the desk and lifting her from her chair by her arm. "And even if I did, I wouldn't tell you." He took her seat, rocking back and forth as if to test its sturdiness. "Now hurry up, Pardy. I'm covering your post until you get back, and I don't have time for this shit work—pardon my French."

"Um—*uh*—yes, sir. *Er*—Sergeant, sir." Chelsea saluted, starting on her way out.

"And, Pardy!" the Sergeant called.

Chelsea stopped in her tracks, turning to face him.

"Don't embarrass me. You got that? Don't embarrass *us*."

"Sir, yes, sir," Chelsea said with a salute then marched out the door.

The Captain's office was far away from Chelsea's dank dungeon, no doubt, but with modern technology, even the furthest of distances was only an elevator ride away. Still, the short walk down the hall and the half-minute elevator ride felt like an eternity.

Her heart raced as she waited for the elevator to fall out from underneath her. Her palms slickened up so much she had to wipe them against her cargo pants.

Fuck!

She had forgotten her helmet in her haste to leave. It was probably sitting there at *Sergeant Know-nothing's* feet right now. She started breathing heavily just thinking about it, and soon the elevator doors dinged open.

Would the Captain care that Chelsea had forgotten her helmet? Maybe she should go back to get it. But, no. *Sergeant Angry-already* would be there, wondering what she was doing back, complaining that she had wasted too much of his time already. No. That wasn't an option anymore. She had t—

The elevator doors closed again.

"Shit," she said. "I mean, open!"

They dinged open then she took a deep breath and stepped out of the elevator. It couldn't be too bad, could it? Chelsea had been doing her best no matter how banal and inconsequential the job they had set before her actually was. Maybe the Captain had nothing at all to complain about, only praise in store. Chelsea took another deep breath, trying to hold that thought in her head as she marched into the Captain's office.

"Pardy, take a seat," the Captain said without standing from her own seat where she was staring out a long, tall window onto a snowy mountain scene. "And take your helmet off," she added.

"Oh—*uh*..." Chelsea hurried to the low stool in front of the Captain's desk—her knees bending up to her chest as she sat down—so she could hide the fact that she hadn't had a helmet on the entire time. "Yes, sir," she said as she did.

"Good," the Captain said, turning and folding her arms on the desk. "Now do you know why I asked you here today?"

"No, sir. No idea, sir," Chelsea said, shaking her head though she had a sneaking suspicion it was to talk about Tom. If Tom's failures were going to be the subject of discussion, though, the Captain was going to have to bring them up herself.

The Captain eyed Chelsea suspiciously, tapping her fingers on the desk. Chelsea tried not to blush or break eye contact, but it was getting harder with every second and it already seemed like the Captain had been silent for an eternity. Chelsea was about to burst out talking when the Captain sighed.

"No," she said, shaking her head. "I don't see how you could. You haven't had any communications from the outside worlds. I'm sure of that."

Chelsea held her tongue again. She didn't know why the Captain was bringing her communications up. She almost wanted to cry because of it. Not because of the breech of privacy—which was all but expected in the force—but because she missed Jonah so much and still had no idea why he hadn't even tried to contact her once since she joined up.

Then the Captain confirmed Chelsea's worst fear. "It's about your son," she said.

"Jonah!?" Tears came rolling down Chelsea's cheeks no matter how hard she fought them. "Wh—What happened?"

"Now calm down, Pardy." The Captain slammed her hand on the desk. "Get a hold of yourself. You're disrespecting the uniform."

"But— Wha—"

"*No buts*. Now listen to me. If you'll just let me speak, you'll see it isn't all that bad."

Chelsea sniffled and wiped her eyes, hating her job as a protector more than ever. If she were at home with Jonah instead of spending all her days behind a stupid desk, doing nothing useful, there would be no reason for the Captain to have this talk. Tom obviously couldn't handle being a protector—as easy as it had been for Chelsea so far—so why would she be naive enough to think that he would be capable of the infinitely more complicated task of caring for Jonah? She gathered herself, sobbed a few more times, then nodded silently. "Go ahead."

"Jonah's been arrested, Pardy."

"*Arrested*?" Chelsea gasped. "Is there anything worse than that?"

"Now settle down right now, Pardy!" The Captain slapped another hand on the desk. "You can still be demoted, you know. The storage desk is nowhere near the bottom of this Hellhole."

Chelsea composed herself. The Captain was right about that. *Sergeant Ignorant* had already warned her of as much.

"Now listen," the Captain said. "And keep cool because it gets worse before it gets better. Now he and his partner—"

"Liz? *No*." Chelsea held a hand to her mouth, shaking her head, and the Captain shot her a dirty look.

"They were both caught entering the holding cells from the Junior—*Now wait a minute. Let me finish*. They were with the Sixer, the little girl your husband helped, you know. What's her name again?"

Chelsea shook her head. How was she supposed to know the name of some Sixer trashling? Even if it was the same scum who had already ruined her life once, she wasn't going to learn the thing's name. And of course she already knew Tom was involved in this somehow before she even entered the Captain's office. Chelsea's face turned red. She wanted to stand up, knock the stupid tiny chair over, and quit the force right then and there so she could go home and take care of Jonah the right way. But she knew that wasn't an option. They needed a protector's income if they wanted to support the entire family, and she was the only one capable of being a protector.

"Anyway," the Captain went on. "Needless to say, they were

all apprehended as soon as they entered secure property. The trash was taken out, the girl was punished severely, and the boy—your Jonah—was given to me."

Chelsea sat up straighter in her seat. She regretted more than ever forgetting her helmet. She knew exactly what the Captain really meant under her veiled wording.

"Don't you want to know what I did with him?" the Captain asked with a smile. "With your baby boy?"

"Sir, no, sir," Chelsea said, saluting. "I'm sure you punished him accordingly, sir." She hoped that wasn't the case. The punishment for such a severe transgression would no doubt result in Jonah's expulsion from the Junior Academy, and as much as Chelsea hated being a protector, she knew it was Jonah's lifelong dream to become Chief of the force.

The Captain chuckled. "Pardy," she said, shaking her head. "You kill me. It's amazing how quickly your tone changes. You're so much more perceptive than your husband ever was. You know that?"

Chelsea didn't answer. She was perceptive enough to recognize a rhetorical question when she heard one. She let the Captain have her fun and waited on the edge of her seat for news of what punishment Jonah was suffered.

"Pardy," the Captain said. "That is the other Pardy, ex-Officer Pardy, your husband, seemed to be able to display a particular breed of denseness the likes of which I have never seen in my long years on this Force."

"I'm not my husband, sir," Chelsea said a little too sharply. She didn't mean for the words to come out sounding so harsh but she couldn't control her tone. She was tired of paying for Tom's sins already and the debt only kept getting deeper.

"No, Pardy." The Captain shook her head. "That's exactly my point, you see. You're not him. You're something entirely different. And that gives you a chance to make something better of yourself than he was ever able to. It gives you a chance to come out on top where he failed so miserably. You can do things the right way this time through, and I'm giving you the opportunity to do just that."

Chelsea shook her head. This was all fluff. It was densely packed with words, sure, but weightless words, wind. The Captain was hinting at something else, some grander plan, but Chelsea only cared about one thing. "My son," she said. "What punishment did you give him?"

"Now, I'm getting there, Pardy. Settle down. I'm trying to offer you an opportunity here. Or are you as blind as your husband was to that?"

Chelsea didn't respond. The Captain was going to take as long as she wanted to anyway. She only took a moment, though.

"No," the Captain said. "I didn't think so. You're perceptive. *As I've said.* Now, let's get back to your son—in a roundabout way, at least. What I've been trying to say is that I need you to accept a promotion to fieldworker."

"Yes, sir. Of course, sir. Don't know why I wouldn't, sir," Chelsea said, trying to hold back instinctual sarcasm. She really wouldn't have a choice but to accept the job even if the Captain wasn't holding her son hostage.

"No. Of course not," the Captain said. "There would be no reason for you to deny the job. There should be no reason why you won't agree to work Outland Five like I ask, either. Then again, you don't really have the option to request Six like your husband did, but you wouldn't do that to me even if you could, would you?" She smiled.

"Request?"

The smile got wider. "Oh," the Captain said, mocking surprise. "You didn't know?"

A tear welled up behind Chelsea's eye but she could fight this one. She had cried over Tom enough already. But still, it was hard to believe that even he could be so stupid as to *request* Outland Six. Though there really was no reason for the Captain to be lying to her about it now.

"Whatever," Chelsea said. "When do you need me in Five?"

"Oh, you don't care?" The Captain smiled. "I guess I see why. There's nothing *you* can do about it anymore. Is there? No. But you can still help your son. I had a nice little chat with the boy, you know. He's got a good head on his shoulders and a bright future. *If* you play your cards right."

"What do you want me to do?" Chelsea was getting tired of this Captain and her games. She wanted to stand up and rush out right then but she knew she couldn't.

"I want you to go back to your desk and take the rest of the day to think about what will happen to your son if you don't do exactly as I say. Then I want you to imagine something worse, and still, I promise you, you won't be close to what I have in mind for him." She grinned. "I *guarantee* it."

Chelsea sat on her hands so she couldn't swing at the Captain who chuckled at the sound of Chelsea's annoyed foot bouncing under the desk.

"Good," the Captain said. "You seem to be getting it. Go on back and mull it over now." She turned to look out the window again. "And be prepared tomorrow. You have a promotion ceremony to attend. You're the guest of honor."

Chelsea stormed out of the room before the Captain was done talking. She slammed the door closed behind her, not caring what the Captain thought, then stomped through the hall to the elevator and screamed at the top of her lungs while the floor fell out from underneath her. She had just enough time to take a deep breath and compose herself before the elevator stopped and its doors opened onto the surprised face of *Sergeant Blowhard*.

"Oh—*uh*—Officer Pardy," he said. "I was just coming to find you. I left Officer Janitor at your station."

Chelsea didn't care who was there. She just wanted to get back to her desk and be alone for a while—and maybe beat her head on it's hard surface a few times—but she couldn't even escape the elevator because *Sergeant Clueless* was blocking her way.

"Well, then, Officer," he said, not budging. "How did the meeting go? You didn't manage to embarrass me, did you?"

Chelsea shook her head, biting her tongue. "No, sir. I—"

"Well spit it out, then. What did the Captain say?"

"A promotion, sir. She offered me a—*uh*—a promotion."

"A promotion?" *Sergeant Disbelief* chuckled, holding his belly. "You've got to be kidding me. For what? All you do is sit behind that stupid desk all day."

Chelsea was pretty sure that all he did was sit behind his own desk all day—and a bigger, more comfortable desk at that—but she didn't want to draw the conversation out any longer. "I don't know, sir, but she told me I was being promoted."

"But, no." His face was turning red now. "I would— Someone would have told me if you, an inferior in my department, were getting a promotion. *I would have known.*"

Chelsea shrugged. Obviously not.

"What did she really say? You can't hide your punishment like this, you know. I'll talk to the Captain myself if I have to."

"Go right ahead, sir," Chelsea said, stepping to the side so he could get in the elevator and out of her way.

"Well—I—*uh*... I will, then." He stepped in and Chelsea hurried past him toward her office. "Just you wait and see."

Officer Janitor let out a huge sigh of relief when she came in. He looked utterly terrified to be sitting behind her desk. "Thank Amaru," he said, standing up and brushing off the seat behind him. "This is your job, right? I hope you don't need to check anything out because I don't have the slightest idea of what I'm supposed to be doing here." He scurried back to his supply cart and checked it to make sure everything was in order.

"Yes," Chelsea said, taking her seat. "You can go." And she didn't add, "please".

"Amaru serve you," Officer Janitor said with a little bow, pushing the cart out of the room. "I don't know how you stand such responsibility."

When he was finally gone, Chelsea slammed her head on the desk three times in quick succession. Why did her life continue to get worse?

No. She knew why. Tom was why. Even though his failures were so far away, they still rippled out to fuck her little world up.

All of a sudden her world literally shook. Her desk rattled, and not from her tapping feet or slamming head. Gun blasts went off in the hall outside, and Chelsea paused, frozen in place with shock.

Her heart beat faster and her hands slickened up. Her stomach gurgled. She had to react but how? Her muscles were ready before her mind was and they jumped into motion.

She scooped up her helmet and slammed it on her head first thing. She regretted forgetting it once already today and she wasn't about to let that happen again. As her eyes adjusted to the helmet's cameras, more gunshots rang from outside. It sounded like a war zone out there.

She ordered up a gun from the armory—she wasn't assigned one for normal duty but was almost certain that the gunfire outside was cause enough to implement emergency procedures. When she was sure her gun was loaded and ready, she pressed her back to the wall right next to the office door and took a deep breath. The gunfire had stopped but the assailants would no doubt still be out there. It was now or never.

She took one more deep breath and kicked the door open, pointing her gun out to look up and down the hall. The normally pristine white was marred with splatters of red, still bleeding bodies strewn across the hall. Here and there were a couple of dirty clothed pieces of trash who looked like they had come from Six. If anyone deserved to die, it was them, but Chelsea was remiss to see that the third body in the hall was clad in protector's white and lying next to a supply cart.

She ran to him and knelt at his side. Officer Janitor was still bleeding and having some trouble breathing, gasping for air with every breath. "It'll be alright," Chelsea whispered, brushing hair from his eyes.

Janitor coughed from deep inside his lungs. "I— They— Get them. *Kak kak*. Get... *Them*..." he managed to cough up before his lifeless head slumped to the ground.

Chelsea took a deep breath and tried to wipe away a tear but her helmet's face mask was in the way. Blinking the tear away instead, she stood in a rage. Scumbag Sixer trash had been responsible for enough misery in her life, it was about time they started paying for all they had done.

She sprinted down the hall, toward where she thought the gunfire had come from, and pressed her back against the wall. She took a deep breath then turned quickly around the corner, pointing her gun, to find no one, no bodies even. At the same time, two shots rang out from the other end of the hall and Chelsea only barely dove out of their path.

She crab crawled up to another wall—her back now to her office and the assailants—and took a few deep breaths, trying not to panic. There was no more gunfire. The Sixers were probably rifling through her stock already. Now was the time to make things right.

She jumped up and spun fast, pointing her gun down the hall that was still empty of any living person. She jogged to her office door, slammed her back on the wall next to it, then pointed her gun inside.

"Freeze fuckers!" she yelled, accidentally squeezing the

trigger and letting off a string of bullets into the room. One body fell to the ground as the others dove for cover. Realizing what she had done, Chelsea jumped to the other side of the door, taking cover herself. Good thing, too, because a barrage of bullets came flying back soon after. The Sixers had obviously gotten into the weapon stock, exactly what Chelsea was trying to prevent. She was pretty sure nothing could get worse when:

"Pardy!"

Chelsea turned to see the Captain—mustachioed helmet giving her away—yelling from down the hall.

"What the fuck are you doing? Don't you know what's going on?"

"Sir, yes, sir," Chelsea called back. Of course she fucking did. "We have intruders, sir."

"Intruders?" the Captain asked, moving closer. "Way down here? I thought they were all in the holding cells."

A round of shots rang out from Chelsea's office, embedding themselves in snug little holes in the wall across the hall. The Captain slid on her ass to put her back on the other wall, right next to Chelsea's.

"Intruders, sir," Chelsea repeated, smiling for some reason, though the Captain couldn't see it.

"I see. Well, take care of them, Pardy."

"Take care of them?" Chelsea chuckled. "Do you know how many there are? How many guns they have now? You take care of them."

"Now, Pardy, you listen to me. If you can't take care of a storage desk, then how can I promote you to street work? No, you'll take care of them yourself, and your son will thank you for it."

Chelsea scoffed. "You're not going to be able to hold this over me forever, you know. My son won't always be a student."

"But I'll always be his superior officer." The Captain smiled. "And yours. And I'll make both of your lives Hell if you don't do everything I say."

Chelsea shook her head. "This is only the beginning. You'll never let me out from underneath your thumb, will you?"

"Not at this rate I won't." The Captain laughed. "So get going or find yourself deeper in debt."

"I... *Fuck.*" Chelsea had no choice. She took a quick deep

breath, reassured her grip on her gun, then stood and fired blindly into the office, hoping for the best.

ଧ   �֍   ଧ

XLVIII. Ansel

The elevator doors slid closed behind her and she heaved a big sigh of relief. Finally. Without her mother and father she was alone in the world—in the worlds even—and it was about time she started acting that way.

She took a deep breath of the fresh wilderness air. It was warm—still afternoon—with plenty of light left to guide her far, far away from that stupid elevator to a place where no one would be able to find her. She'd leave them all behind. They were no one to her now anyway.

Leaves crackled under her feet as she made her way, weaving through the trees. She took the path that Pidgeon and her always took when hunting. Sure, they would search that way first if they came looking for her, but she'd be long out of their range by that time. Hell, Pidgeon probably couldn't even make it to the end of the game run by himself, and she didn't expect Rosalind or the Scientist to exert any effort at all in looking for her, so it was a safe bet she could get away.

She huffed, hefting her rucksack up higher on her back and shaking her head as she hiked. Poor useless Pidgeon. He would find out just how useless he was to them soon enough. Too late, probably. He was always too trusting. The orphanage, Rosa and Anna, and now *the Scientist* and crew. Ansel had trusted Tom, sure, and even tried to give him a second chance, but three strikes were too many, even for her. No, it was high time she started learning to trust herself so she didn't have to depend on anyone else for salvation. If anything, that was exactly what she was doing.

She smiled, a new spring in her step. The day seemed to brighten, whether from a moving cloud or her new sense of resolve, it didn't matter. The world was wide open before her now, and she was free to do whatever she pleased with it. So she was going to do just that.

In the short interlude between meeting the Scientist and leaving her, Ansel and Pidgeon had spent most of their time out in the wilderness, hunting. For Pidgeon, at least, it was just that, but for Ansel it had also been reconnaissance. Every time they went out there, she kept her eye on the mountain that towered over them—the same mountain which made the focal point of the Scientist's office window. This time, again, her eye was on that mountain because this time she was finally going to get the chance to climb it and see what was on the other side.

Her hike took her to the base of the mountain before she reached the end of the game trail. By this time in their previous journeys, Pidgeon would always be too hungry or tired to continue on, and they would inevitably turn back to go order something from the printer for him to gnaw on. Not this time, though. This time there was no Pidgeon to hold her back. Ansel's stomach was full and her feet were rested, and there was no turning back ever again.

The mountain was more of a hill from up close, as long as Ansel climbed it from the right angle. The face that was pointed toward the office window—and which seemed to be the mountain in its entirety—was a sheer, jagged cliff which would have required some sort of tools to climb, but Ansel hiked far enough around the edge of the thing to where it could be climbed on two feet instead of resorting to hands and knees.

The grade of the incline increased the higher she got, nonetheless, and slowly the trees disappeared as the grass gave way to gravel. It wasn't until about halfway up the mountain—maybe an hour and a half into hiking—that Ansel finally took a break, slouching down in a handy patch of grass that was hidden under a tall pine tree.

She took a few deep breaths and searched through her rucksack. There was the canned food, and the tent or whatever Rosalind had given her, but only one bottle of water. How could Ansel be so careless? She was still living with the mindset of a Street kid and she wasn't even on the Belt anymore. Fresh delicious meat was plentiful out here, but the only water she knew of was the pond she was leaving further behind with every step. She took a small sip from her bottle then closed the cap tight. She probably wouldn't find any other sources of water until she started going back downhill, and she was determined to make it to the top of the mountain before dark. She would just have to ration her water until she could make it down the other side.

The air got thinner with the trees as she continued her ascent. She walked slower because of it. What seemed to her like halfway before looked so much further now. She seemed somehow thirstier because she knew she had less water. Still she trudged on, heavy foot after heavier foot, one at a time, up the mountain.

She collapsed when she reached the top and cursed herself when she dribbled some of her precious water out onto her chin. When she had gathered enough strength to finally stand, she couldn't believe her eyes. The view was beautiful—no question—but oh so confusing to see.

She stood at the top of the mountain, a flattened plateau that was the perfect size for one person to stand on. On one side of her, the mountain dropped sheer down a cliff. This was the side that she was familiar with, the side she could see out the Scientist's window. The other side, the unfamiliar side, looked more like a rolling hill that went down and down almost forever. If she faced straight ahead in the direction of the cliff face—looking, she thought, at where the Scientist's window should be, though it or any other buildings were nowhere to be seen—there was another identical mountain, but this one as seen from the rolling hill side. If she turned directly around from there to look backwards, she saw again an identical mountain, but this time as viewed from the cliff side. Left and right? You guessed it. More identical mountains as seen from different perspectives. It was as if the whole world were made out of a pattern of the same mountain copied and pasted over and over again.

She sat there on the plateau peak, every now and then turning ninety degrees to stare at a different endless line of identical mountains, one infinite line of them going in every direction, until the sun went down, then she kept staring. Now, though, the black sky was patched with sparkly little white lights the likes of which she had never seen before. They kept distracting her from the endless mountains. The white spots were no more or less infinite or absurd than the mountains, but they were still somehow more novel to her.

What were they? Had they always been there, hiding in the almost dark? Why did they come out now when she was all alone?

She couldn't take her eyes off them. They were endless, sure, but they were patterned. Here was a shape and there something different. And—wait—did they repeat just there?

But no. Of course they didn't. It was just an illusion. She

could find patterns anywhere, even in the leaves of trees. With such a large pool to select from, of course she would find patterns in these strange white sky lights. She had to get her mind off of them for long enough to start thinking about what really mattered, though: water.

Her mouth went dry again at the thought of it. She smacked her lips together and they stuck. She had to pry them apart with her too dry tongue. She sipped the last little bits of water out of her one bottle, savoring every drop, before she packed it empty into her rucksack and hefted the bag up over her shoulder. She took one long look at the blinking, twinkling sky before dropping her eyes to the horizon, back down the mountain. She knew where a spring was behind her—one that Pidgeon and her had been to plenty of times—but she wasn't ready to go backwards just yet, even with her mouth as dry as it was, and she thought there had to be more than just one tiny spring to support all the animals and plants that were everywhere out there.

Her eyes spotted a small clearing in an extra green grove of trees in front of her and her feet took her toward it. The path was all downhill and the travelling was easier for that fact. The hardest part was making sure she didn't get going too fast and end up tripping over a root or losing her sense of direction. The ground started flattening out before she finally stopped to catch her breath and regain her bearings.

She took a few deep breaths, smacking her dry lips, and her stomach started to grumble. Hunger would have to wait until she found water, though. It was no good trying to digest on a dry stomach. She looked up at the trees and they all looked just the same as every tree she had already passed. All of them looked the same. It was nothing like traveling around the Streets with signs every few blocks and gridded pathways. She thought she was on the way to the clearing she had seen on the mountain top, but for all she knew, she could be walking in circles right back to where she had started. The only way to find out was to go forward, though, and so she did.

Each step she took brought her more worry. She could feel the water evaporating from every cell in her body. This was how she was going to die, stupid and alone, with no water, lost in the middle of nowhere.

What did it matter anyway? The protectors had killed her mom for doing her job. They had killed her dad for trying to protect his own daughter—for trying to do their job for them. And now they might as well be killing her. If they hadn't taken everything from her, she wouldn't be alone in the woods, dehydrating. She wouldn—

Ansel's left foot stepped lower than she had expected it to, splashing into knee deep water and sending the rest of her body tumbling in after. She came up for air, laughing and splashing, then brushed the wet hair out of her face, dunking her head under water and gulping in as much of it as her stomach could hold.

Now this was the life. She tossed her rucksack on the shore to dry then yanked off her shoes and tossed them next to it. The water wasn't deep, but she could crawl around in it and pretend like she was swimming—not that she actually knew how to swim anyway. This little pond looked exactly like the waterhole she and Pidgeon always stopped at near the elevator, but there was no Pidgeon here to interrupt the silence for her. There was only her, the trees, and the twinkling dark sky for the rest of forever.

She almost wished she was still up on the mountain, staring at those bright lights—the foliage overhead was too thick to see through—but she was happy to have water, and she had plenty of time to climb every mountain in sight. She had plenty of time to do whatever she wanted to from now on. She'd stock up on water, maybe eat some beans and find a way to use the empty can as extra storage, then she'd be ready to climb the next mountain in her way.

But not right now. First she needed some rest. She crawled out of the calm pond and laid in the grass next to her rucksack, using her hands behind her head as a pillow. Tomorrow was a new day and there were endless tomorrows after that. Tonight it was time for sleep.

℣   ✂   ℣

Ansel awoke with the first rays of sunlight. Even with all the noise she had made getting up, a big floppy-eared rat sat at the edge of the slowly rolling pond, sipping on the cool morning water. When Ansel remembered where she was and gathered herself, she jumped into hunter mode.

Every motion was performed without noise. Her muscles tightened. She slipped the sling out of her back pocket, fished a rock out of the pouch attached to her pants waist, and pulled the sling back, struggling a bit at first from the extra weight required by the new slingshot but soon holding her aim steady and on target.

Fwip.

The weird rat jumped, it's flopping ears flapping, and it landed upside down, half in the water and half out, back leg twitching with the last pangs of life.

Ansel pulled the rat out of the water by its ears and laid it out next to her shoes to dry before going to collect sticks and twigs to start a fire. With the fire roaring, she set to skinning the rat with the knife Rosalind had given her. She didn't see any use for all the other gadgets the thing came with, but the knife was worth having, especially without any other trash around to carve the rat with.

Ansel wondered at what exactly the animal could be as she removed it's skin. She had never seen a rat with such long ears before. Maybe it wasn't a rat at all. There were a lot of weird animals she had never seen before out in that wilderness with her. Hopefully they tasted as good as she already knew rats did.

This long-eared one did taste good, that was for sure. It was nothing like rat, sure, but more like a million times better. For starters, there was a lot more meat on this thing than there was on any of the rats that she had ever eaten. And secondly, all of this animal's meat was made of pure, delicious muscle. She chewed it down greedily, stacking the picked clean bones in a neat little pile behind her, then took another swim in the cool pond before laying out to dry and decide on what she wanted to do next.

Next was another mountain and she knew it. The mountains were everything to her now. She had climbed over one and she would climb over the next and the next and the next until she was as far away from the Scientist and everyone else in the worlds as she could be, however far that was.

She strapped on her shoes and filled up the empty water bottle—she hadn't opened a can yet so the bottle would have to do—then she dunked her head into the pond and drank as much as she could. When she felt like she was going to burst, she came up for a few breaths of air, then she dunked her head under again to drink some more.

She could hear the water swishing around in her stomach as she marched toward the next mountain, her rucksack on her back. She laughed and tried to skip along, but her stomach was too fat with liquid so she had to settle for a stroll, her mind set on the sheer cliff face of the next mountain in front of her.

The second climb didn't seem to take as long as the first. Probably because she was getting better at climbing through practice, but she felt like it was because she had already taken this path before and her muscles knew what to do by instinct. She was at the top of the mountain by mid day and she wasn't even thirsty— though her stomach did seem remarkably lighter to carry. She dropped her bag and stood at the summit, looking in all four directions at the world around her.

The mountains seemed equally endless from this new vantage point, forcing Ansel's throat to fall down into her newly emptied stomach. It was hard before, but without the twinkling blackness to distract her, all she could see was endless blue sky laying atop an equally endless repetition of the same green mountain she was standing on. She peered out at one of them, trying to figure out what that small little dot atop it was, going so far even as to wave in the hopes of getting its attention, but there was no use, the next mountain was too far away to see, and whatever it was it was probably just a figment of her imagination, anyway. There was no way anyone was out there climbing mountains at the same time she was.

Ansel huffed and sat down, fishing the still full water bottle out of her rucksack. She took a small sip then closed it tight and put it back. By this point in time yesterday, the entire bottle was empty, but yesterday she hadn't filled her stomach as full as it would go before setting off. She looked out toward the next valley in the line and thought she saw the same green clearing in the same place as the last one. Her next step would have to be finding another watering hole, anyway, so she started that way. Maybe if she could get down fast enough, she could get back up the next mountain by the time the sun went down and the sparkling lights in the sky came out.

Gravity took hold of her and Ansel ran with it, careening down the mountainside, becoming one with the universe. This was easy. This was fun. This was what she was supposed to be doing with her life, she could tell.

She wasn't even out of breath when the ground levelled out. The sun was falling but still high in the sky. She jogged along, not even needing to look down at her feet to dodge the roots and rocks.

Then she came upon the clearing.

No!

She threw her rucksack on the ground and kicked the pyramid of rat bones, sending them sprawling into the slightly perturbed watering hole.

No no no.

She fell to the ground and slammed her fists on the soft grassy soil.

Of course.

She gave up. She rolled over onto her back and sprawled out, stretching her body as far as it would go and screaming at the top of her lungs.

Of course. Of course. Of course.

No wonder Rosalind had let her go, no questions asked. No wonder there were so many mountains that all seemed to look exactly the same. No wonder she had no problem finding water even though she was on the other side of a mountain she had never climbed before.

Rosalind knew there was nowhere for Ansel to go. All the mountains were literally the same. No matter which side of the mountain Ansel climbed up from, it didn't matter. Water was forwards, backwards, left, and right. As long as she kept walking, she would hit it eventually. There was nothing more to this world than the one mountain and the one spring, repeating forever and ever, over and over again, so on and so on.

She sat up and held her knees between her arms, shaking her head.

No.

That couldn't be true. There had to be more. There was the sky, the twinkling night sky, something she had never seen before. There had to be more than that, too. She set her mind on seeing that sky and finding out what that *more* could possibly be.

First she refilled her water bottle and took a few more deep swigs from the spring. She wasn't too worried about water now that she knew it was everywhere, but she wanted to have enough in her system to be able to spend the entire night on the mountain's peak. She gathered some twigs and sticks, too, and tied them to her rucksack so she wouldn't have to search for kindling at higher altitudes where the trees were more scarce. The sun was almost halfway down in the sky when she started out on her trek, but she didn't care. She had climbed the same mountain so many times now she could probably do it blindfolded.

She went backwards this time, climbing it from the hill side because it seemed like a straighter shot. By the time she was at the top, the sun was long gone and the twinkling had started. Thankful to have the lighter, she started up a fire a little way down the hillside. That floppy eared rat she had eaten in the morning was big and meaty, but with all her climbing she was getting hungry so she opened a can of beans and fashioned a makeshift stand to hold it over the fire for her while she climbed back up to the mountain peak to sit with her knees hugged up close to her chest, staring at the twinkling sky.

She picked out the patterns she had found the night before and tried to find where they repeated themselves in the sky. She figured if the mountain and watering hole repeated themselves, why not the sky, too? And she wasn't wrong about that.

Right there she could see it. The same five bright stars—which if you connected the dots, looked like they formed an animal with a big, long neck, laying on its side up in the sky—could be found in every direction. Lines and lines of the same pattern emanated from one center point where Ansel was standing at the top of the mountain.

She stared at the pattern with dropped jaw for she didn't know how long. It seemed impossible. It was impossible. Of course it wasn't actually impossible because she was experiencing it for herself, but it still seemed that way, like her eyes were playing tricks on her.

The mountains and twinkling monsters in the sky couldn't really go on forever, though. They had to be the result of the same magic the Scientist used to create her window that looked out onto the mountain Ansel was sitting on even though Ansel still had no idea where that window was. It had to be there somewhere, though, probably with Pidgeon staring out of it while he ate something from the printer.

Ansel scoffed, wondering if Pidgeon knew anything about what he was staring at. Maybe he already had everything figured out. Maybe he already knew that the world out here was nothing more than an illusion. Maybe he stayed back because he knew it was pointless, knew that Ansel would just have to return soon anyway.

She scoffed again. That was giving Pidgeon too much credit, though. He had stayed back because he was afraid, nothing more. It was obvious in the way he acted. And if he expected her to go back there any time soon, he was going to be sorely disappointed. That was for sure.

A scent of burning reminded Ansel of her beans, and she ended up having to gag them down, drinking too much of her water supply just so she could swallow. She chided herself for being careless as she ate. She was letting thoughts of the past distract her from the needs of the present, and if she wanted to find her way out of this rat trap, she was going to have to stay focused on the task at hand.

She stared at the twinkling black sky as she forced the burnt beans down her throat, trying to figure the universe out. How did the Scientist do it? The entire world was like a giant quilt, stitched together at the seams, but each end of the quilt was attached back to the opposite end of the same square, making one long continuous universe. Still, there had to be seams somewhere, didn't there? Connections between the worlds?

The harder she stared the more certain she was that there were in fact seams and that she had found them. The fire had died down but there was still a lot of smoke, and without any wind that smoke went straight up and up and up, blocking her vision of the sky behind her. If she looked straight ahead, though, she could see as plain as day—or night, really, but the moon gave off so much light in the cloudless sky that it was plain nonetheless—the smoke rising from the hill side of the next mountain. Ansel would have been more upset to see it if she hadn't already come to the realization that this was a patchwork, repetitive world, or if the smoke in that direction had risen high enough to block out her entire view of the twinkling night sky, but she had and it didn't.

No, for some reason the smoke went up and up and up and then it just seemed to disappear. There was no wind to scatter it, not even that high up she was sure, and it didn't seem to dissipate in the slightest before it vanished. There was just a thick black pillar of smoke blotting out a giant portion of the sky, then all of a sudden, it was cut off in a long, slightly curved line, revealing the clear, twinkling sky behind the smoke. It reminded her of something she had seen before but she couldn't put her finger on it. She followed the arch of smoke down to where she imagined it would end on the ground, somewhere near the elevator by her eyeball estimate, and knew she had to go down there to investigate, but she hesitated. What did the smoke disappearing remind her of?

It hit her all at once. She had been in the Belt with Pidgeon, standing in the cat tree, and she looked up to find the clouds disappearing behind an invisibility cloak in the sky. Then she heard the gunshots—which she was only just realizing were probably the bullets that had killed her mother—and time flashed forward until Ansel was holding her father's lifeless body in her arms. She wept until the sun came up then strapped her rucksack on her back. She was going to find the seams, wherever they were, and get as far away from this world as she could, or she was going to die trying.

She took the straightest path she could find to get back to the elevator, which meant climbing down the steep side of the mountain, but she was going downhill so it didn't make much of a difference. Huffing and puffing and wishing she had stopped at the water hole to refill her now empty bottle before she went investigating, she found the elevator just as its doors slid open, forcing her to jump and hide in some bushes. She had no intention of going back to the stupid Scientist's lair, and she didn't care to talk to anyone that would come out of those doors, so she kept as still as possible, holding her breath as if she were hunting, and waited for whoever it was to go away.

It took a moment for Pidgeon to come stomping out of the elevator, announcing his presence to the entire wilderness. "I'll be fine, okay," she could hear him yelling. "I won't go far. Don't worry."

At the sound of it, Ansel was happy to not have him along with her. Where she was going, it was no doubt more dangerous than this little patch of green, and Pidgeon wasn't cut out for even the tiny amount of danger that could be found here. She stood as still as she could and listened to the sound of his crashing steps as they disappeared in the distance. When she was sure he was gone, she peeked her head out to get a second look then went to the elevator to inspect it.

The elevator had to be the key to the seams. Ansel slowly circled the wooden shack, touching every side through the thick vines growing all over it. That must be how the elevators worked, too. They could travel through the seams, from one quilt square to another, or something, but there had to be more to it than that. There had to be space for the elevators to travel through, right? There had to be something in between the worlds for the elevators to exist inside of.

Ansel must have circled the little shack ten times, lost in thought, searching for some way through without getting in, when she heard the approaching footsteps. She should have heard them sooner, they were so loud, but she was preoccupied. She only had time to duck behind the elevator's shack and hope Pidgeon didn't circle around it to find her.

The footsteps stopped a few feet from the elevator clearing. "Hello?" Pidgeon called, a hint of worry in his voice. "Ansel, is that you?"

Ansel held her breath, ducking down and putting her hands over her head as if that would hide her any more than she already was hidden. She was convinced she had already been seen, anyway, exactly what she didn't need when she was so close to finding the seam she was searching for.

"*Helloooo*," Pidgeon called again, and his voice hadn't moved. He was still in the clearing. He hadn't seen her at all.

"Well, anyway," Pidgeon said, raising his voice. "If you are out there, Ansel, I really miss you. Okay. I wish I would have come with you, even if it is a stupid, dangerous idea, and I hope you're not in trouble. You'll always have me, Ansel. I'll always be here for you when you need me. So… Well… *Bye*. Elevator open."

The doors slid open and closed, and it was so loud that Ansel could hear it through the silence left in the wake of Pidgeon's words. Did he really care about her as much as he said he did?

She shook herself out of it. No. He was lonely. A few old people and a cat could get boring quick, and Pidgeon just wanted someone his own age to play with. But Ansel didn't play anymore. She lived in the real world, and she was going to find those seams so she could make it to a different one.

She circled the elevator shack a few more times, searching every square inch of vine-covered wood for some sign of anything, but there was nothing. It was a wooden building with metal doors and there was nothing else to it.

Ansel took off her rucksack and flung it behind her in

despair, but the bag didn't make a sound when it landed. She turned, and where the bag should have hit a huge oak tree and crashed to the ground there was nothing. Kneeling down and reaching closer to investigate, her hand disappeared in a straight line at the wrist.

She pulled it back as quickly as she could then fell to the grass laughing. It was just like Anna and Rosa's door. She had found the seam. She gathered herself, took a deep breath, and plunged through the tree, only to crash into some person and fall to the floor on the other side.

"Who are you?" the formless mass demanded, standing fast.

"Who are you?" Ansel repeated back, up and ready to bolt herself.

And it took some time for either to answer.

ଛ   �֍   ৶

XLIX. Mr. Walker

Why him? Why did the universe always have to gang up on on little old Lor—er—*Mister* Walker? What did he ever do to deserve such bad luck?

The television across the room spat out stock numbers, but try as he might, Mr. Walker could not concentrate on them. Especially now, when his Lordship had only just slipped out of his grasp, was it more important than ever for him to make the most efficient trades possible, but the very same reason it was so important that he did concentrate on his business decisions was the reason he couldn't: because he wasn't Lord anymore.

He slammed his hand on the bed, sending his beautiful bulbous stomach jiggling in anger. That asshole Douglas—the Hand take him and all his holdings—would pay for this. With more than money, too. A simple wealth transfer wasn't enough. A wealth transfer would be necessary, of course, but not sufficient. If Mr. Walker was ever going to be Lord again, that went without question. All those years on top—an entire lifetime or two—had made Mr. Walker grow complacent, lazy. It was high time he shook things up, stirred the pot—so to speak—and Mr. Walker knew just the spoon to do it with.

A knock came at the bedroom door and Mr. Walker groaned. "Open it, you fool!" he called. "How many times do I have to tell you? Just open it already!"

The door swung open and in swept Haley, carrying a tray of breakfast over her shoulder. By the smell of it, at least, it seemed like she had finally remembered to hand prepare his food. How it could take a robot so long to learn something so simple he had no idea. He didn't remember it taking as much effort for the original Haley to get the task right, but then again, that was so long ago he couldn't really remember it at all.

"Here you are, sir," Haley said with a curtsy. "Fifth breakfast." She crossed around the bed to Mr. Walker's side table and lifted the empty tray off his lap to replace it with the newly filled one from her shoulder, knocking his empty mug to the floor as she did.

"Now you see what you did you clumsy fool?" Mr. Walker yelled as she bent to pick it up. "What if that cup had been full of hot coffee? What then, huh? Do you know how that would feel?"

"No, sir." Haley curtsied.

"It would burn, sweetheart. It would be painful. It would—*it would hurt*!" He shook his head. "What am I saying? You have no idea what I'm talking about. You're a simpleton, a robot. You know nothing of what it means to be human and you never will."

"No, sir." Haley shook her head.

"*No, sir. Yes, sir. Whatever you say, sir*," Mr. Walker mocked her. "You see what I mean? You have no independent thoughts. You are a dependent. So just listen to me when I tell you to be careful and do better next time."

"Yes, sir." Haley curtsied.

"Good. Now change the channel. I've had enough of work for this morning. It should be close to time for my infernal meeting anyway."

"Yes, sir," Haley said. "What channel, sir?"

"*Ugh.*" Mr. Walker sighed. "The reality network, dear. The same channel I watch every morning after breakfast. Honestly, honey, it's not that difficult, your job, and if you'd like to keep it, I suggest you get better at it fast."

"Yes, sir," Haley said, curtsying and changing the channel. "Is there anything else I can do for you, sir?"

"Leave me be so I can eat in peace," Mr. Walker huffed. "And get my tuxedo ready for the meeting. We'll be leaving soon."

"Yes, sir," Haley said, curtsying without leaving the room.

"Well? Get out! Leave me alone!"

"Sir, yes, sir." She scurried out and slammed the door behind her.

What incompetence. Mr. Walker stuffed his mouth with toast and almost gagged because it was burned black. Who had ever heard of a robot that couldn't even cook? It was just another sign of the universe's insistence on giving him the shit end of the stick. Still, no matter how much the Hand stacked the deck against him, Mr. Walker would come out on top. He always had and he always would.

The picture on the TV screen changed from lines of assembly

line workers to commercials, and Mr. Walker chewed his too crispy bacon. He had stopped paying attention for a bit, but something caught his eye. A tall dark actor, with bright red lips, was on screen, dressed in all black and leading a huge congregation of the most famous celebrities in a prayer to some god named Fortuna. They were all dressed in various shades of black, looking at the floor with teary eyes, and every word the tall man in front spoke elicited a new reaction from the crowd, as if his voice was the remote controlling the mass of robot actors, but robots they were not.

Then Mr. Walker realized what they were doing. They were mourning a death. Not just any death, either, but the death of Russ Logo, one more piece in the universe's conspiracy against Mr. Walker and probably the biggest reason why he was no longer the Lord of Outland. Mr. Walker had invested a lot of money in Logo and the life insurance payments alone were nowhere near the fortune he should have been worth. Still, it gave Mr. Walker an idea on how to accelerate his climb back to the top where he belonged. Maybe the old clown could be worth a little something even in death.

A knock came at the door but it cut itself short before Haley burst through, carrying Mr. Walker's pneumatic pants. "*Ahem.* Are you ready to be dressed, sir?" she asked with a curtsy.

Mr. Walker fumed. He wasn't even halfway through his meal. No, he was not ready to be dressed. But he contained himself, taking a few deep breaths before stuffing more bacon and eggs into his face. It was a happy mistake, this one. He did need her even though he wasn't quite ready to be dressed yet. He tried to convince himself that Haley had only come in because she knew he wanted something, even if she didn't know exactly what that something was.

"No, dear." he said through a full mouth. "As you can see, I'm still eating. But you can do something else for me. I need you to take a quick run to the market and open up bidding on Jorah Baldwin. We'll take all the stock at any price. You got that? If he's taking Logo's place in Three—which it looks to me like he is—we'll want him on our payroll. So go on and buy him up as soon as possible."

"Yes, sir," Haley said. "But the meeting, sir. Can't I just order the stocks remo—"

"Don't even say it!" Mr. Walker raised his hand to stop her, flinging some eggs onto his bedspread with the motion. "*Do not even speak those words.* We do things the old fashioned way around here. Just like cooking, you see. And if you leave right now instead of arguing with me, you'll be there and back with plenty of time to spare. Now get!"

"Yes, sir," Haley said, curtsying as she hurried away.

Mr. Walker sighed, stuffing his face fuller and fuller. It was never enough. Try as he might, he could never drown out the stupidity and jealousy of those around him. If they weren't against him in theory, everyone was against him in practice with their complete incompetence. It was a wonder he had managed to remain Lord for as long as he did.

He growled, throwing a mostly full plate of food against the wall and spilling it all over the bed and floor. It wasn't a wonder that he had been Lord for so long. He was surrounded by idiots. It was a wonder that one of them had somehow managed to surpass him. He had underestimated those little misters that surrounded him, and he had to keep on his toes if he ever wanted to be Lord again.

"Stock Market Report," Mr. Walker said and the TV changed channels. He stared, and studied, and did math in his head as he ate the last plate of fifth breakfast. There was no more time for entertainment. He was at war. He had forgotten that in his years of ease on the top of the food chain, but now that he remembered it, he knew exactly what he had to do to get back to the top of the economic pyramid. He ran a few more numbers in his head as he licked his last plate clean. It was going to be tight for sure, especially considering who owned the stocks he needed, but Mr. Walker was confident enough in his negotiating skills to believe that he could do it and come out on top in the long run.

A knock came at the door.

"Come in, come in. By the Invisible Hand, come in already!" Mr. Walker yelled.

"*Ahem*, yes, sir," Haley said, coming in with his pneumatic pants and tuxedo in hand. "I did as you asked, sir. We already own eighty-five percent of Jorah Baldwin shares."

"Good," Mr. Walker said, clapping his hands together and tossing his platinumware on his plate with a clatter. "*Great.* Then get this garbage out of my bed and get me dressed. We have an important meeting to attend."

"Yes, sir."

This was the worst part of breaking in a new robot. She was so slow and clumsy with the pneumatic pants. She could never get them up without pinching his skin, no matter how much he tried to wiggle and squirm to assist her. Then, when she finally did get them on, she took so long to button on his vest and tie his tie that he thought he would die of boredom.

"Okay, okay," he said, guiding his pants out to the garage. "I'll get my hat and monocle in the car. A cane, too, please." The pants carried him up into his white stretch hummer and sat him comfortably in the backseat.

Haley came in moments later, pushing the top hat and cane back to him. At least she knew enough to sit in the driver's seat instead of trying to ride like an honored passenger in the back with Mr. Walker. "Douglas Towers," Haley said and he groaned.

The Hummer pulled out of Mr. Walker's pristine garage and into the general parking garage for Douglas Towers, owned of course by Lord Douglas. The place was so cheap that it didn't even have designated parking for distinguished guests. Not to mention the fact that the parking spots were so small Haley had to drive them all the way out to the bus lot to find one that fit the Hummer. Mr. Walker groaned and griped the entire time his pneumatic pants carried him from the Hummer to the elevator. The sooner he became Lord again the better. Then the Fortune Five could resume meeting in style.

"Penthouse Conference Room," Haley said when the elevator doors slid closed. The floor fell out from underneath them, then the elevator doors opened onto a long gray hallway.

Ugh. Mr. Walker understood that this was a place of business, but a little class went a long way in making work more enjoyable.

The hall ended at a big rectangular room with a big rectangular wooden table. Mr.—*er*—*Lord* Douglas was already seated at the head of the table with Mr. Angrom at his right hand. Mr. Loch was late, as usual, and Mr. Smörgåsbord would no doubt be right on time but there were still a few minutes before the meeting was officially supposed to begin.

Mr. Walker took a seat on the far end of the table with a big smile, saying, "Well, boys. This is a *classy* venue, isn't it? No windows to distract us from each other's pretty faces. And what do you call that color? Industrial grey? I adore it. *Truly.*" He grinned, peering this way and that between Mr. Angrom's sneer and Lord Douglas's usual look of indifference.

"I'm glad you like it," Lord Douglas said. "I designed it specifically with your tastes in mind. Everything I thought you would love, I did the exact opposite." Mr. Angrom laughed. "In fact, that's how I make all my decisions in life," Lord Douglas went on, enjoying himself no doubt. "I figure, it's gotten me the Lordship, why stop now?" He laughed along with Mr. Angrom now.

"I'm glad to see I hold so much—" Mr. Walker started, but Mr. Smörgåsbord came in followed by a clearly drunk Mr. Loch whose ruckus sitting down cut any possibility of audible speech off. It was probably for the better, too. Fighting with Lord Douglas now would only make negotiations with him that much more difficult later on.

"Watch where you're going, sir," Mr. Smörgåsbord complained, taking his seat at Lord Douglas's left hand. "And please be sober for our next meeting. It's simply unprofessional."

"You *wash* where you're going," Mr. Loch slurred, plopping loudly into the last seat at the table, to the right of Mr. Angrom. "I do what I want."

"Okay, okay," Lord Douglas said, clapping his hands. "*Enough.* We're here to do business. Can we get on with it?"

"Precisely my point," Mr. Smörgåsbord said with a satisfied smile.

"Proceed," Mr. Loch said, raising a flask then tipping it back for a drink.

"Yes, Lord," Mr. Walker said with a grin. "Lead us, please. What did you bring us together for today, oh magnificent one?"

"Simmer down, Walkie Talkie," Lord Douglas said, raising a hand. Mr. Walker ignored the insult and let him continue. The negotiations to come were more important than the mundane showmanship of a general meeting so he could bite his tongue for now. "This is a routine meeting. We'll follow the same agenda we always follow—or the agenda we were supposed to follow, that is. You know, the one you ignored throughout your entire Lordship, Mr. Walker. Do you remember?" Lord Douglas chuckled and Mr. Angrom joined in.

Mr. Walker just held his breath, though, biding his time.

"Well then," Lord Douglas went on. "Smörgåsbaby. The floor is yours. Go ahead and give us your run down of the market numbers, if you'll please.

Mr. Smörgåsbord read off the net worth and major holdings of each member of the Fortune Five and the next five wealthiest owners in succession. These were the same numbers Mr. Walker had gone over for himself before coming to this stupid meeting. This type of thing was exactly why he preferred having these meetings at a restaurant or bar rather than some office building. That way he could at least have a drink in his hand while they presented him with information that could better be sent through email. Still, he used the time it did offer him to do a double check of his math from earlier and smiled, more than certain now that he could pull off his plan to become Lord again after all.

"Do you think that's funny?" Mr. Angrom asked, slamming a fist on the table and snapping Mr. Walker out of his daydream. "Let's see how funny you think it is when it's your companies that go dry first after the shortages hit."

"Woah there, Angry-Poo," Mr. Loch said, swinging his flask as he spoke and sloshing pungent alcohol everywhere. "I've got my own supply trains. You watch your mouth."

"So you and the Walrus are still colluding, huh?" Mr. Angrom shook his head. "I should have known."

"*Tuh*." Mr. Loch chuckled. "Okay, Mr. Right Hand Man. Why don't you—"

"Alright, alright, boys," Mr. Smörgåsbord said, raising his voice uncharacteristically loudly. "*That's enough.* And it's not the end of it. Now, Lord Douglas, if you don't mind, I think it's time for you to take the floor."

"*Ahem…* Yes," Lord Douglas said with a smile, fixing his tie. "I agree with Mr. Smörgåsbord. In fact, perhaps it's time for me to take more than just the floor."

Mr. Walker scoffed. Who did he think he was? Lord for a week and already so high and mighty.

"I'm sure you don't agree, Wally Boy," Lord Douglas went on, "but your opinion hardly matters these days. The world has gotten out of your control and now—"

"*Ahem.* Lord Douglas." Lord Douglas's secretary stepped up from behind him, interrupting the meeting. Mr. Walker would have taught her some respect right then and there if it was Haley that had interrupted him, but Lord Douglas just groaned.

"It's happening," the secretary said. "As we speak."

"Well," Lord Douglas said, shrugging her off. "It looks like our show is kicking off a little sooner than expected. Fellow owners, members of the Fortune Five, dare I say friends? Behold. This is what a world run by the former Lord Walrus Ass looks like. Video up."

A holographic video popped up in the middle of the table. Dirty clothed imps, carrying nothing more than two-by-fours with nails driven through one end, came spilling out of white walls and running, unimpeded, through the halls of what looked like a protector's precinct.

"Wha—where did you get this video?" Mr. Walker demanded, the only person there besides Lord Walker who was able to formulate a reaction beyond slack-jawed awe.

Lord Douglas laughed. "Security footage, Wally. Security footage from a protector's precinct under your ownership. Now what are you going to do about it?"

"No," Mr. Walker said, shaking his head. "It can't be my precinct." He saw his plans dissolving before his eyes. "That—I would know. It has to be one of yours. They were—"

"Mr. Walker," Haley said, stepping up from behind and putting a hand on his shoulder. "I'm getting messages from precinct zero seven five three, sir. They're saying—"

"*Enough*," Mr. Walker said, pushing her hand off his shoulder and slamming his own hands on the table. "You knew about this, Lord. You did nothing. You're complicit in this attack— if not responsible."

Lord Douglas laughed. Everyone else kept watching the video as the ragged imps went for an unguarded gun cache, taking everything their greedy, jealous hearts could force their tiny hands to haul away.

"No," Lord Douglas said. "I'm neither complicit nor responsible. I'm simply in the know. And we've already sent our response to pick up the pieces you left for us—*again*. Look. Here they come now."

A small crew of armed and armored protectors came into view of the camera, shooting into the armory as they approached.

One or two bodies fell, but most of the imp thieves scattered away, only to disappear back through the walls, exactly the reverse of how they had arrived.

"What the fuck was that?" Mr. Walker demanded. "What did you do?"

"You tell me, Wally," Lord Douglas said. "You saw it for yourself. You should know what's happening in your own precinct, shouldn't you?"

Mr. Walker looked to Haley then back at Lord Douglas with a sneer. "I know you had your hand in this," he said. "You're trying to kick me while I'm down, trying to make sure I stay down. You're scared."

"Kick you while you're down?" Lord Douglas laughed. "That's nonsense. You saw the video. Those were Sixers if I've ever seen them. Maybe some Fivers, too, now that there's not much of a difference between the two worlds. But either way, how could I have any hand in that? You think they'd listen to me? Have you ever tried talking to one?"

"I *shay* yous did it," Mr. Loch slurred.

"*I say you did it*," Mr. Angrom mocked him. "Prove it, then. Otherwise all I see is incompetence."

"Incompetence, yes," Mr. Walker said, grinning. "Our Lord Douglas's incompetence. What incompetence must it take to know the threat of an attack, even to go so far as to record it and set up a live stream, but yet still do nothing at all to prevent said robbery's success?"

"Right," Mr. Loch said, taking a swig from his flask. "*Incompetensh.*"

"Do nothing? *Ha*! You saw what I did. We all saw it. Those were my men bailing you out. My boots, my masks, and my guns, all saving your soil. The real incompetence is not knowing when there's going to be an attack on your own precinct, Wally. *That's incompetence.*"

"*Enough*," Mr. Smörgåsbord said, standing from his seat. "Pardon me, Lord, but that's enough. We're not here to argue whose fault this is. Are we? *No.* We're here to discuss the occurrence, tally up the damages, and figure out how to solve the already created problems. Now, if y'all don't mind, I've wasted enough of my precious time with your petty arguing, and I'd like to get this meeting on with."

"Well said," Lord Douglas said, clapping his hands. "Well said, Smörgy. Better than I could have ever put it. You see, it doesn't matter who's at fault here. No. What matters is who's in charge. How that person will respond. And—as standing Lord of the Fortune Five—I think there's a good case to say that person is me."

"Over my dead body," Mr. Loch said.

"That could be arranged," Mr. Angron muttered.

"Now now," Mr. Walker said, raising his hands in defense. "Slow down there, Lord. Last I checked, this was still a free market and I still owned a majority share in the protector force. Now, unless those facts have changed, or unless we've somehow become some sort of Fascist state which presumes to take control over the private property of owners, I think there's a better argument that *I* should be the one making the decision."

Mr. Angrom scoffed. "After you let them ransack your armory? As if."

"After *your* Lord let them ransack Lord Walker's armory," Mr. Loch said.

"I don't think so," Lord Douglas said, shaking his head. "You've made too many mistakes, Walker. There's precedent for me to take control of the entire protector force because of that. When the incompetence of one owner threatens the safety and wealth of the rest, as I think it's obvious this incompetence of yours has done, Lords throughout history have used their powers of eminent domain to put right what was wronged."

"Now wait—" Mr. Loch said.

"Hold on," Mr. Walker stopped him. "I've never heard anything like this before. Smörgåsbord?"

"It's true," Mr. Smörgåsbord said, nodding. "Though the circumstances were quite different than they are today. It was only done because one owner was using his protectors to—"

"*You see,*" Mr. Walker said, not caring about the rest of Mr. Smörgåsbord's boring speech because he had already gotten what he needed from it. "The circumstances were quite different. Right out of the mouth of a neutral party. Now, if you don't mind, I'll handle the protectors' response to this outrage myself. We can move on to other business now. Thank you, good sirs."

"Very well," Lord Douglas said, crossing his arms on the

table. "We'll table this issue for now. But I want all of you to mull this little episode over in your head and be ready to come back and vote on the issue at our next meeting. Maybe by then you'll all be able to see the consequences of Mr. Walker's blunder as well as I see them already."

Mr. Loch scoffed, standing from his chair and knocking it to the floor. "*Ish* that all then, *Lord*?"

Mr. Smörgåsbord looked to Lord Douglas expectantly. "I do have some work to tend to, Lord."

"Very well," Lord Douglas said, rubbing his hands together. "This meeting is adjourned. You can all get back to whatever is you think is so much more important than our economy. But remember what I said about the protectors response. And remember what has been done already—in both the present and the past. Think it all over well, comrades. This is your life on the line with this vote as well as it is anyone else's."

"Yeah, yeah, yeah," Mr. Loch muttered under his breath as he stumbled out of the room.

Mr. Smörgåsbord packed his notes and left close behind. "Very well, Lord," he said as he did. "See you next time."

Mr. Angrom sat staring at Mr. Walker who didn't move. Lord Douglas didn't move, either, it being his office building, but he was smiling instead of sneering.

"So, Wally Boy," Lord Douglas said. "Is there anything else, or have your pneumatic pants broken down on you? I can have Rosalind carry you out if that's the case." His impudent secretary scoffed behind him.

"I bet it was the pants," Mr. Angrom said with a grin. "Walker's fat ass finally wore them out." He chuckled alone to his own joke.

"No, Lord," Mr. Walker said, shaking his head and trying to put on his most respectful face. "My pants are just fine. I simply had some private business I wanted to discuss with you, and I was waiting for the rabble to clear out before I did." He sneered at Mr. Angrom.

"The only rabble here's you," Mr. Angrom snapped.

"Alright now," Lord Douglas said. "It's okay. Move along, Angry. I had some personal business I wanted to discuss with ol' Wally here anyway."

"But, sir," Mr. Angrom said, red faced. "We were supposed to— You said—"

"It can wait, Angrom," Lord Douglas snapped. "*Now git.*"

Mr. Angrom put on a sour look, standing slowly from his seat and eyeing Mr. Walker the whole way up. "Yes, sir," he said. "But I don't like it."

Mr. Walker chuckled as Angrom ambled out of the room.

"Well, then," Lord Douglas said, clapping his hands and rubbing them together. "What is it that you wanted to discuss, Wally Boy? Why do me the honor?"

For a second Mr. Walker considered spitting in Lord Douglas's smug face right there and leaving without even trying. His plan was probably pointless anyway. Any deal he could come up with would no doubt be shot down by Lord Douglas for the simple fact that it came out of the mouth of his arch nemesis and biggest competitor, Mr. Walker. But still, it was a good deal he was offering, and Mr. Walker had no choice but to try.

"Go on," Lord Douglas said. "I'm waiting…"

"Well—*uh*…" Mr. Walker said, gathering his thoughts and choosing a line of attack. "You see, Lord, I really just couldn't help noticing that you've taken quite a hit on your profit margins with your protetor costs as high as they are ever since all these shenanigans started."

Lord Douglas chuckled. "Yes, well, not quite as hard of a hit as you're taking, though. *Eh*, my boy?"

Mr. Walker shook his head in earnest. "No, no. That's true, Lord. I own a slightly larger percentage of the force so of course I take a slightly larger hit than you do. You're dead right on that point. But what if I told you that I could eat even more of those costs for you? Huh? How would you like that?"

Lord Douglas narrowed his eyes suspiciously. "What did you have in mind, Mr. Walker?"

Mr. Walker smiled, happy to hear the Lord use his formal name for once rather than the ridiculous nicknames he had become so fond of since taking his new title. It might mean that Lord Douglas was willing to play some ball after all. "Well, I thought I'd just go ahead and buy up some of your protector holdings so you wouldn't have to worry as much about all this hubbub," Mr. Walker said, shrugging. "That's all. A friendly gesture for my new Lord."

Lord Douglas chuckled. "I think I'd be *more* worried knowing it was you who was in charge of so much of my safety."

"Now, now." Mr. Walker shook his head. "You and I both know there's no way I could have figured out about your little attack before you pulled it off. That was no fault of my own."

Lord Douglas laughed heartily now, slapping his hand on the table. "You kill me, Walker. Even if that was true, even if I had orchestrated that little attack, it wouldn't excuse your continued failure to calm Two or determine the source of the Christmas attack. You're incompetent when it comes to security—among other talents you direly lack—and there's no arguing against that."

"Okay, enough," Mr. Walker said, standing from his seat in a huff. "You haven't even heard my offer and all you do is insult my character."

"I don't need to hear your offer. No amount of money would lead me to hand over further control of the protector force to you. You'll have to pry this force out of my cold dead hands."

"It's your funeral," Mr. Walker said as he stomped out of the room, down the hall, and to the elevator with Haley close in tow. He didn't wait for her when the elevator opened into the parking garage, and she had to jog to keep up with his furiously working pants.

"Hurry up!" Mr. Walker yelled from the backseat of the stretch Hummer as she climbed into the front, and at the same time his phone started to ring. "And answer that," he added with a huff

"I—yes—" It took Haley three rings to finally climb into the car and say, "Answer phone."

"It's about time sweetheart," Mr. Walker said to the air, knowing who would be on the other end of the line. Laura's portion of the plan was only important if Lord Douglas actually ended up cooperating, but Mr. Walker wasn't ready to give up on that just yet—negotiations had only just begun—so he would have to continue with the charade anyway.

"It's done," Laura said, her voice sounding cold all through the Hummer's heated air.

"Good," Mr. Walker said with a smile she couldn't see. "Very good."

"Yes," Laura said. "I'm calling about Loch Ness Studios Lot thirty seven. This is Laura Concierge." She was obviously speaking in code because others were there who she didn't want to overhear the conversation. A rather intelligent little operative, this one was.

"Yes," Mr. Walker said. "Very good, child. Keep up the charade. Tell me what happened."

"Yes, sir," she said. "Lot thirty seven, sir. We were filming a shoot when one of the studio lights fell on top of our star. He was knocked unconscious, sir. We're not sure he'll ever act again, and we only had the lot for a limited time at that. This is your responsibility, and we demand a refund and credit for more time in the studios as reparation."

"Very good, child. I assume you mean Emir when you say *star*, of course.."

"Yes, sir. He... He doesn't look good. We need a doctor. Someone to tell him just how bad it is, sir."

"I've sent someone already. My personal doctor. She'll give you the diagnosis you seek. And I expect to see you shortly, dear. In my office as soon as you're done there. You know the way."

"Yes, sir—" she said and he hung up the phone.

"Haley," Mr. Walker said. "Is Doctor Smith on standby?"

"Yes, sir," Haley said, holding the door to the now parked Hummer open for him to exit.

"Send her to Loch Ness Studios, lot thirty seven."

"Yes, sir."

"And get me Jorah Baldwin—in person. We have some business to tend to."

ଓ   ✄   ⅋

L. Nikola

Tillie burst through the building's tent flap doors—apparently no longer afraid of the guards—and ran down the dirt street, making Nikola sprint to catch up. Tillie was two blocks down the road and around a corner before Nikola finally grabbed her by the arm to stop her.

"W—Wait," Nikola said, hunched over and breathing heavily. "W—Where're you going?"

"I don't know," Tillie said, shrugging Nikola's hand off. "Does it matter? I've had enough of this place. I just want to go home."

"You heard my dad, Tillie. You can't go home. The protectors will—"

"*My dad* wouldn't let them do anything to me. He has a little more power than a protector, Nikola. *I'm a Manager.*"

Nikola scoffed despite her every effort to stifle it. She knew that Tillie couldn't help her ignorance. Tillie was a product of her experiences, just like every other human being in existence, and she had no control over what those experiences were. But it was all Nikola could do not to laugh in the face of such plain naivete.

"So what?" Nikola said. "That doesn't matter anymore. You're in the real world now. The real *worlds.* All of them. Things work a little differently outside of *America* and you're just going to have to get used to it."

"No, but..." Tillie turned to look at Nikola, a tear forming in her eye. "But my dad... Mr. Kitty... How am I supposed to..."

Of course. Nikola palmed her face then rearranged her glasses. Tillie missed her family. Nikola hadn't thought twice about it because her family was here, but no wonder Tillie wanted to go home.

"I know," Nikola said, trying to calm Tillie now. "I'm sorry. I wish you could go back to them, too, but there's no way. The protectors are after you now. They won't stop until they get you."

"And who's fault is that?" Tillie demanded, pushing herself

away. "They wouldn't be after me if I had served my sentence, would they?"

"Well, no. But you probably wouldn't even be alive if that were the case. Do you know what they would have done to you? You'd still be in that solitary drawer we saved you from—at the very best."

"*Probably wouldn't be alive.*" Tillie scoffed. "According to who? You're dad? He doesn't care about me. All he cares about is y'alls stupid country here—whatever you call it. I could tell that by the way he spoke to me."

"No." Nikola shook her head. "He does care about you. He cares about all the people of all the worlds."

Tillie scoffed again. "Yeah. Sure. What does he think he is, the Invisible Hand or something? As if."

"Far from it. As far as you can get. The *Invisible Hand* doesn't care about anyone. The *Invisible Hand* is the enemy we're fighting against. So, *no*. He is not, nor will he ever be, the Invisible Hand. My dad's something far greater than that."

"Fight against the Invisible Hand?" Tillie said backing away from Nikola and almost tripping over some rubble. "But tha—*that's blasphemous*."

"Of course we're fighting the Invisible Hand. What do you think Emma was doing? What do you think you've been doing this entire time? That's the whole reason you're here now. We've been fighting the Invisible Hand together."

"No—I..." Tillie looked like she was fighting back tears. "I wasn't. *We* weren't. Emma never said anything about *that* to me. We were fighting for the robot workers, not against the... *Invisible Hand*." She whispered the last two words as if the Hand had ears and was listening, as if it cared one bit about either one of them.

"Yes," Nikola said, trying to hide the annoyance in her voice. She kept reminding herself that Tillie had gone to American schools, that she couldn't possibly know any better, that Tillie had been raised in the religion of the Invisible Hand and she might not be willing to throw off its shackles so soon or all at once. "You were fighting for the robots and the assembly line workers against the will of the owners," Nikola tried to explain. "You were attempting to violate their property by freeing the androids. You were going against the will of the market by fighting for the rights of the assembly line workers who *voluntarily* chose those jobs. *You* did all of that, Tillie."

"I—But, no." Tillie gave up and plopped down onto a big piece of rubble then buried her face in her hands.

"Don't worry," Nikola said, taking a seat next to Tillie to try to comfort her. "It's not like the Hand struck you down on sight, is it?"

Nikola grinned, nudging Tillie who cracked a smile and chuckled, her head still buried in her hands. "I guess I'm still standing," she said with a muffled voice.

"Well, you're sitting in the dirt right now, but I get the point," Nikola said, standing and brushing her own dirty pants off. "C'mon," she added, holding out a hand to help Tillie up. "Let's go for a walk, clear your head. It should be nice after being cooped up in those boxes for so long."

"You've got that right," Tillie said, smiling as she followed Nikola through the rubbled streets to nowhere in particular. "Though I'm not sure how comfortable I am being around all these soldiers. It's like being surrounded by protectors." She shuddered as she said it.

"Oh, no, no," Nikola said, smiling and trying to sound cheerful. "It's nothing like that. You have to understand that you're in an entirely different country now. We're not capitalists here. Countries like this one are few and far between, and what few there are always seem to be under attack from one front or another. So, you see, this is all necessary. We're all revolutionaries in the People's France. There are no two ways about it. In America you separate your classes out, allowing the few to hoard property from the many, and you reserve military power for only a select group of people who are sworn to protect those property owners. That's why your protectors are so mean. They'll do anything and everything they have to do in order to preserve that unique monopoly they hold over the use of violence. Here in the People's France, though, you don't have to worry about all that. Here we all share the same power so here there's no unique monopoly to protect. Here we cooperate instead of compete, and as soon as all the worlds start acting the same way, we'll all be so much better off for it." Nikola was out of breath from the long winded speech, but she tried to be as reassuring as possible, smiling and nodding at Tillie as they walked.

"I don't know," Tillie said, shaking her head. "I still don't get it. It's all just so...*foreign* to me. I mean, how does your economy even work if you don't follow the Invisible Hand? Is it okay to steal things? What property can there be? What's stopping me from stealing your glasses right now?"

"Look," Nikola said, grabbing Tillie's hand and leading her toward her favorite food cart. "I'll show you. It's so much easier to see it in action than it is to try to explain the entire thing. Besides, you've got to be getting pretty hungry by now, anyway. I mean, I know I am, and I haven't been through half of what you have in the meantime."

"That I am," Tillie said, hurrying to keep up with Nikola who was getting excited at the prospect of food.

The food cart was only a few blocks away. It sat under a big khaki canopy which was filled with bodies—either waiting in line, or enjoying some meal at one of the numerous full tables in the canopy's shade. There were so many people they were even using the rubble on the side of the road as picnic tables, ignoring the glaring sun in their faces.

"This is probably not the best time to come here," Nikola said when they had gotten into the amorphous line behind a group of loudly talking camouflaged people. Before she went on talking the line had already grown longer behind them. "Lunch break is the busiest time for any eatery, and this particular cart is one of the most popular establishments on base. But it's worth the wait. I promise.

Tillie nodded, looking nervously around at the bustling crowd and the still growing line of people behind them. Her eyes were wide and she was fidgeting with the hem of her shirt.

"Is everything alright?" Nikola asked. Of course it wasn't with all Tillie had been through, but what else could she say?

"I—*uh*—yeah." Tillie nodded, eyes still dancing around the crowd. "I'm fine."

"It's gonna be okay," Nikola said. "I know dad seems like he's got a single track mind, but he'll do everything he can to help you. We'll get you back home as soon as we can. I promise."

"Oh, no." Tillie shook her head. "It's not that. Well—of course that doesn't help—but..."

"It's alright," Nikola said. "Tell me."

"Well," she said, stepping up in line and looking more and

more anxious the closer they got to ordering. "I don't know. I don't— How am I supposed to pay for this? How am I supposed to pay for anything? I can't live here, Nikola, this is crazy."

Nikola tried not to laugh, patting Tillie's back. "It's alright, girl. Don't worry. You'll see."

"Are you sure?" Tillie said, a look of relief washing over her face. "I mean. I'll pay you back when I can. I just—I wasn't really expecting to leave the country. I didn't even know you could." She managed a half grin.

"Of course I'm sure," Nikola said, stepping up to the counter. "And you won't have to pay me anything. Don't worry. Two of the usual, please," she added to the server, and within a moment, Nikola had the food in hand, giving one plate to Tillie. "There you are, girl. Now come on. Let's find a seat."

They navigated through the shaded maze of tables, in the hopes of catching someone at the end of their meal, with no luck. They ended up having to use some rubble as a picnic table but were lucky enough to find a nice spot in the shade of a building. Nikola set in on her food right away, eating as quickly as she normally did, but Tillie took her time, whether from habit or out of shock Nikola didn't know.

"So," Tillie said, taking a nibbling bite. "You get free meals there because of your parents or something? Do y'all own the place?"

Nikola shook her head, still stuffing her face with food. "Nope," she said through a full mouth.

"But you didn't pay," Tillie said. "Did you?"

"Nope." Nikola shook her head again, smiling with thick, food-filled cheeks.

"Well why didn't they stop you if you didn't pay?"

Nikola chuckled. "Well, technically, I do own the place."

"Well which is it?"

"We all own it," Nikola said. "Every worker in the People's France owns it. Any one of us can go up to that food cart and get our food for free, no questions asked. Not just you and me."

Tillie scoffed. "But how? How does that work? If everyone can just go down to the corner and get free food whenever they want, then why would anyone ever work?"

"Well, back home you could go to your dad's house any time

you wanted to and get free food there, couldn't you?"

"Well, yeah, but…"

"And you still worked, didn't you?" Nikola urged her on, nodding.

"Yeah, but—"

"So why'd you do it?"

"*Uh*… I don't know." Tillie thought about it for a second. "Well, first of all, my dad won't be there forever, you know. I won't always be able to go to his house and use his printer whenever I want—which, *by the way*, he works for the privilege to own. It's not really free, you know."

"It's free for you though."

"Not forever."

"No." Nikola nodded. "Not forever. But still. Is that the only reason you do anything? To make some money or earn a 3D printer?"

Tillie scoffed. "Well, no." She chuckled, shaking her head. "Of course not. There's more to the world than that."

"Like what?"

"Well…" Tillie hesitated. "I don't know. Like making something of yourself."

"Making your father proud?"

"Yeah, sure." Tillie nodded like she was getting into the conversation now. "That's a part of it. A *big* part with my dad, but it's still not everything."

"So what else, then?"

"I don't know." Tillie brushed her hair out of her face. "Like contributing to society, you know. Making the world a better place. That sort of thing."

"And that sort of thing is exactly why people still work, even though they can go down to the store and get a free meal any time they want. It's why we all still work when we get free rooms and clothes and everything. We know that society depends on our work, and we want to do everything we can to contribute, to make something of ourselves, to make our friends and family proud. And it's a lot more fulfilling than being materially rewarded while your comrades are held in artificial poverty, I'll tell you that much."

"I thought that's what *we* were doing, " Tillie said, breaking eye contact. "Me and you, and Emma…and even Rod. I thought we were contributing to society."

"We *were* contributing to society," Nikola said, getting heated again by trying to calm herself. "We were doing the best we could under the circumstances we were given. I still am doing the best I can. The only question is if you want to continue doing your best with me given your new circumstances or if you want to give up on everything you've been working so hard for this entire time."

"No," Tillie said, shaking her head and still not making eye contact. "But you said…" She mumbled something Nikola couldn't hear.

"What? I said we were doing good."

"You said we were fighting against the Invisible Hand!" Tillie held her mouth after she yelled it. "I'm sorry," she said more softly. "I—"

"No," Nikola said, shaking her head. "It's alright." She should have known better. She was attacking Tillie's religion, the root of her being, and she was being much too careless about how she was going about it. Still, there was no way left to go but forward. Retreating now would only make it worse for Tillie in the long run. "I understand," Nikola said. "You were raised by the Invisible Hand. It's all you know. Being told this about the Hand is just as jarring as finding out about the assembly line workers, sentient androids, and other countries, I'm sure, but I can't even really imagine what it's like to be you right now. That's a real shitstorm to deal with all at once after having been told so many lies for your entire life."

Tillie chuckled. "You can say that again."

"That again," Nikola said, chuckling herself.

Tillie smacked Nikola on the arm. "You know what I mean," she said, laughing.

"Sure I do," Nikola said. "But as hard as it is to accept, you have to understand that the Invisible Hand isn't a real thing. It doesn't care about you or anyone else. It doesn't care about anything. It doesn't have the capacity to care. It has no body, no heart, nothing. It's all just a fairy tale meant to keep you in line."

"No, but…" Tillie shook her head. "That's impossible. The Invisible Hand guides the markets toward our benefit. That's how the world works."

"That's how they tell you your world works, Tillie. That's how *most* of the worlds out there pretend to work. But it's not how this world works. That's not how the People's France works. You've seen it yourself. You're eating the products of it right now. There are no markets here—not in any sense of the word you would recognize, at least—and yet somehow we continue to manage."

"I don't know," Tillie said, shaking her head. "It doesn't seem sustainable. And you don't really have much, do you? I mean, your streets are all rubble and your buildings are half tents."

"Our buildings are rubble because your country and others like it make them that way. Do you think we blew them up ourselves? That we're too stupid to know how to repair buildings? Do you think we enjoy living like this?"

"I— No—" Tillie shook her head. "But—"

"No! Of course not. But we have to. Your country claims ownership over too many of the worlds' resources, so for as long as it and the others like it exist, cooperative countries like ours have to be as efficient as possible in using what little resources we have left to us after the imperialist countries suck the World dry. And that's World with a capital W, which stands for Earth, the one we all share no matter how high you build your walls or how *impenetrable* you try to make them. And sure it doesn't look like much from the outside, but every one of us gets enough, none of us goes wanting, and we'll only be getting more as we continue to reappropriate what's rightfully ours."

Tillie turned away, blushing. Her shoulders heaved slightly as if she were crying, or laughing, or trying not to do both. Nikola scooted closer, knocking her empty plate and Tillie's nearly full one to the ground, and patted Tillie's back.

"I'm sorry," she said. "I didn't mean to get so heated. It's not your fault and I didn't mean to imply that it is. It's like I said earlier, we—*you included*—were doing the best we could do to fight it from the inside. I know it's hard for you to see the Invisible Hand as anything but a source of good because that's all you've ever been taught about it, but you have to understand that the Hand is at fault. *It* is the reason your country claims the resources it claims. And for any of that to change, workers everywhere are going to have to see the true face of the Invisible Hand and realize how bad it is for the vast majority of people."

Tillie turned back to Nikola, wiping tears from her eyes. "I still don't get it," she said, shaking her head.

"Get what?"

"How the world could work without the Invisible Hand guiding it. It could only result in anarchy."

Nikola chuckled. "This is anarchy," she said with a big smirk. "Or on the way to it, at least."

"Well, okay then," Tillie said. "Why would you want that? There's nothing stopping anyone from doing anything. That's just chaos."

"Anarchy is not chaos. You've got that wrong. Did you see chaos when we got our *free* food?"

Tillie kicked some rubble. "It was kind of hectic in there," she said under her breath.

"But not chaotic. The line was orderly. Everyone knew who was up next. We chose seats based on availability and need. That's anarchy. No hierarchies. No chaos. Just cooperation."

"Yeah, okay," Tillie said, grasping at straws now. "Well, if there's no hierarchy, then no one tells anyone what to do, right?"

"Essentially." Nikola nodded.

"And there's no reason to do a shitty job, then, right? Like toilet scrubber or janitor or something. Especially if you get a room and food anyway. Right?"

"Well, I would—"

"So who does that crap work? Who cleans the toilets?"

"Who cleans your toilet at home?"

"I do, of course, but—"

"And no one pays you to do that, do they? No one tells you to do it. You do it because otherwise your house would stink and your toilet would get to be too disgusting to use. Well our house here is a little bigger. We own any toilet we use and take care of each of them accordingly. Not because we were told to do it by some superior. And not because we were paid to do it. There are no superiors. There is no money. We do it because it's our country, our house, our toilet, and we don't want any of the above to stink."

Tillie sighed. She stared at her feet for some time, and at the food on the ground which had been discovered by a troop of ants that was carrying it away on their backs, bit by tiny bit. Nikola let Tillie gather her thoughts and after a few silent minutes Tillie said, "I don't know why I'm arguing with you. You've probably been here your entire life, experiencing everything that I'm denying can even exist. Shit, I'm here living it myself. I'm harder to convince than Shelley."

Nikola chuckled. "It's alright, you know," she said. "I have a pretty good idea of what you're going through."

Tillie scoffed. "Yeah. Right. I'm sure. How could you have any idea?"

"Because I went through it myself. I had been living in America for some time before I met you and Emma, you know, but not forever. I was born here, in the People's France. I was raised here. And when I moved to America, I went through the same shock you're going through now, only mine was in reverse. I found myself faced with social relations which seemed too cruel to be anything more real than a horror story, and even though I was living inside of that all too real nightmare, I kept telling myself that it didn't exist, it was impossible, just too unfair, even if I was experiencing it with all my being."

Tillie smiled. Her eyes were red, and some moisture was welling up behind them, but she made no motion to wipe her tears away or hide them. "You do know what I'm going through," she said. "And I know what you went through. Well, we do and we don't."

"*Exactly*," Nikola said with a smile. "But I do know one thing for sure. You'll get through this alright, with or without the Hand by your side."

"I don't know," Tillie said, shrugging. "I sure hope so."

"I know so," Nikola said, standing and taking Tillie's hand to pull her up. "You've only just gotten here. The more time you take to experience it the less you'll have to argue with your senses about whether or not it's possible. Now help me clean this mess up and follow me. I've got something else I want you to see."

"*Oooh*," Tillie said, kneeling to pick up her plate but leaving a good bit of food for the ants. "Tell me it's another brother. With more guys like that, I could easily get used to living here."

Nikola scoffed. "You better not even joke about that," she said. "Now come on. You've got to see this."

She ran out ahead, leaving Tillie to catch up as they jogged through winding rubbled streets. Slowly, the lay of the land grew from flat to steeper and the crumbled buildings grew more dilapidated and sparser. They had slowed to a walk by the time the buildings all gave way to grass, trees, and the hill towering over them, but still neither said a word. They took in their surroundings in silence, Tillie paying extra attention to every detail of the beautiful wildlife scene, despite her heavy breathing, and Nikola paying extra attention to Tillie's every reaction. They were almost to the top of the hill, just at the point before they could see over it, when Nikola spoke again.

"I like to come here sometimes to get away from everything," she said.

"It's beautiful," Tillie said, not taking her eyes off the scenery.

"Isn't it? Just wait until we get to the top. You'll see what beauty can be."

"I can't imagine how it could get any better," Tillie said. "It's already so—" But she couldn't finish her sentence. Her jaw dropped and she stood in awe, looking at the entire base now revealed below them. They had gotten to the top of the hill, and from there, they could see this entire sector of the People's France, every last tent and brick of rubble.

"This is my home," Nikola said after some time of silence. "The People's France."

"It's— I..." A tear came to Tillie's eye.

They stared at the view for some time in silence, then Nikola started pointing things out. "I know it's not much," she said. "You can see pretty much all of it, too. You see that big green canopy down there, with all the tiny people around it?"

Tillie nodded. "They look like ants."

"That's where we got lunch. And we ate just over there." She pointed again. "And if you look a few blocks over and into the center a bit, you can see my parents' offices."

"The patched up building?" Tillie asked.

"Yep, that's the one. And the big tall one there in the middle of everything is where I came to rescue you from."

"Where they had me tied up."

Nikola shook her head, embarrassed. "I didn't think they would—"

"No," Tillie cut her off. "It's alright. It's not your fault. You did your best, right?"

Nikola nodded, not sure if she had actually done her best.

She could have gone to get Tillie out sooner. But how was she supposed to know they would keep her locked up like that? After some time of silence, thinking too much about it, Nikola pointed way off into the distance, out past the buildings and tents, to say, "You see that hill way over there on the other side of the base?"

Tillie shielded her eyes with her hand and gazed off in the direction Nikola was pointing. "Yeah." She nodded.

"That's the hill we're standing on right now. If we stood at the very peak of it with a pair of binoculars, we'd be able to see the back of our own heads, looking the other way off in the distance." Nikola paused to let Tillie understand what she had just heard. "That's how small this base is," she went on. "And this is the largest base in all of the People's France. Besides us there are maybe two or three bases that are half this size and countless micro cells. That's our entire country, and we're standing against giants. America, The European Union, East Asia, more countries than you could imagine, and they all claim ownership over more of our World and its resources than they could ever use in any of their lifetimes.

"I've been living in America for a while, you know. And it's great for the most part, sure. There are a lot of fun parties all the time, and it's liberating to be as wasteful as you want without worrying about the consequences because you always know you'll have more than you'll need, but that's not enough for me. It's too empty. *Heartless.* And if you spend some time here with us, I think you'll start to understand what I mean."

Tillie shook her head, still looking off into the distance, trying to see herself on the hill across the city. "And that's why you came to LSU," she said. "That's why you joined Emma's general assemblies or whatever. You were doing all this to turn America into the People's France?"

"No. I was doing it to help free the androids in your country. I was doing it to free the assembly line workers everywhere. Because I believe exploitation is wrong. Because it was the right thing to do. There are countless reasons why I was doing it, can't you see any of them?"

"So no one here uses robot workers then?"

Nikola shook her head. "Not like America does."

"And no one works on assembly lines?"

"We all work on assembly lines. We all work on farms. We

all join the military. Everything is so simplified, nothing requires specialization or training. We can all share in the burden of labor for the greater good."

Tillie scoffed. "So you've worked on an assembly line, then."

"I have. It's not like it's hard. It's just boring and mind numbing. But you get used to it. You can get used to anything. You'll see."

"And you would rather do that than live in America and never have to work on an assembly line?"

"I'd still be getting everything I need to live from assembly line workers, though, even if I didn't have to work on one personally. There's no choice in our World's economy. With that fact in mind, I'd rather do my own assembly line work than force some poor soul to do it for me. Wouldn't you?"

"I'm not forcing anyone," Tillie said, crossing her arms and getting defensive again. "It's voluntary. They choose to take those jobs."

"Voluntary?" Nikola scoffed. She was trying her hardest not to attack Tillie again when she was obviously vulnerable—fresh out of prison and in a foreign country she didn't even know existed only a few hours before—but Nikola couldn't hold back her passion for the argument. "Do you think they want to work on an assembly line any more than you do? Do you think they would be working on one if they had any better options?"

"Well, no, but—"

"Of course not. And the only difference between you and them is that you happened to be born in Outland Two while they were born in Outland Five. How does that make you any better than them?"

"It doesn't. I—"

"No. It doesn't. But that's how the world works when you live by the religion of the Invisible Hand. That's how the market works. There are only finite resources, and they all require labor to be made consumable. If one person takes more resources or does less labor—or, as is so often the case in your America, both—then someone else will receive less resources and do more labor to make up for it. It's like a law of physics, but instead of mass and energy it's called the Law of the Conservation of Resources and Effort."

Tillie sat down on the grass with her arms on her knees,

looking out over the base. She shook her head. "You know, I never thought of it like that."

Nikola took a seat next to her, unconsciously mimicking Tillie's posture.

"I guess I haven't really had the time to think about it at all." Tillie chuckled. "I only learned about the assembly line workers on Christmas break and life's been a bit hectic since then."

Nikola chuckled. "You can say that again."

"*The Hand—*" Tillie said. "Or—*er—fuck. Whatever.* I don't know." She shook her head. "What am I supposed to say now?"

"I think it makes a better expletive when you know the truth." Nikola chuckled. "You might as well keep using it."

"I can't believe I've been a part of that for so long," Tillie said. "I can't believe I've been forcing those people to do everything for me."

"You didn't know," Nikola said, patting Tillie's back. "And you had no choice, anyway. You were stuck in that system the same as everyone is."

"I guess." Tillie shrugged. "That doesn't make me feel any less guilty, though. Actually, it kind of makes me feel more guilty. Like I should have known, you know. Or maybe I could have known but I chose not to, chose to ignore it. It might even be worse that way."

"But how could you have known any different?" Nikola asked. "No one ever taught you. You've never met anyone who has even known the truth themselves unless they were in on keeping the secret. You're being too hard on yourself, expecting too much too soon. You're only human after all."

"I met you," Tillie said, shaking her head. "I met Emma. I lived with my dad, a high level manager, my entire life. The information has been right under my nose all this time, and I've only just now gotten to it."

"And as soon as you did, you did your best to change things," Nikola reassured her. "You joined Emma, and you protested, and you went so far as to get arrested for what you thought was right, and now you're here, with me, still fighting the injustice of it all." She smiled, standing up and brushing herself off.

Tillie scoffed, still seated. "I'm not doing anything."

"Oh, there's plenty to be done around here. New hands are

always welcome." Nikola chuckled.

"I don't know." Tillie shook her head. "What can I do?"

"As much as anyone else," Nikola said, pulling Tillie up. "Let's go ask my parents what they need. I'm sure they can find something for you. They're always finding work for me to do."

"*Hmmm*, well I guess. But I still want to go home."

"And my parents can get you there. So let's go."

ɞ ✶ Ɑ

LI. Laura

Laura did know the way to the voice's lair, but she had never had a reason to use it. She would be a much happier person, living a better life, if she never had a reason. She was okay with the way things were, never seeing the face that owned the voice on the other end of the phone, slowly, day by day, paying off her debt. But this? This was too much to ask

She stalled for time in her small apartment, staring at her reflection in the ancient battle station—so old it didn't even have makeup removing capabilities—despite the fact that she knew perfectly well she had no time to spare. ASAP meant as soon as possible, and to the voice on the other end of the phone that meant sooner than possible.

She cringed at the thought of what the voice's face would look like, at the power it held. That voice controlled every aspect of her life. That voice followed her every move thanks to the ankle bracelet she had been strapped with for longer than she cared to remember. That voice held the key to the same ankle monitor and that was reason enough not to keep the voice's owner waiting. She sighed and stood from the battle station, surveying her room one last time, surveying the life she had been chained to, imagining the life she would have been capable of living if it weren't for that anchor weighing her down at the ankle, and seized the moment. It was now or never and never was too late.

The public elevator was only a block away from her apartment complex, but she walked slowly. The end of her debt was supposed to be at the other end of the elevator ride, along with the voice's face, but Laura had been made promises before, and she was quite certain that she'd be coming home with her ankle monitor still attached. A little part of her couldn't help hoping she was wrong, that this was the day she was finally going to be set free, and it almost scared her to think about that freedom, so she forced herself back into the defeated cynicism that had been keeping her alive for so long now.

There was a short line at the elevator, but it was orderly and quick. Soon she stepped through the doors and they slid shut behind her. She took a deep breath of odorous air and sighed, hoping the password would work.

"I would tell him to shrug," she said and the floor fell out from underneath her.

It felt like her heart stopped for the entire thirty second ride, only jumping back into motion after the elevator ceased to move, like some cruel inertial joke. Her breath didn't start up again until the elevator doors opened, revealing a long, elegant hall lined with red carpet and hung with classical paintings and tapestries. She stood in awe for a moment and only just stepped out of the elevator as the doors slid closed behind her.

She looked around at the brightly lit hall, embarrassed. She didn't know whether to continue on her way to the big wooden door at the other end of it or to wait there until someone came to greet her. She really wanted to turn around, get back in the elevator, and go home, and she was about to do just that when the wooden door across from her opened and closed with a loud thud. A woman in a lacy, short black and white skirt came scurrying down the hall toward her, saying, "Hello. Hello." and curtsying every few steps as she walked. "I apologize, ma'am. I should have been here to greet you, but Mist—*er*—*Lord Walker* needed my assistance in his office. But I'm here now. So, *hello*." She curtsied one more time when she had finally crossed the long hall.

"Oh—*uh*…" Laura blushed. She didn't know what to say. This certainly wasn't the voice on the other end of the phone, but she couldn't just ask for a voice, could she? She would sound insane.

"Laura, I'm sorry," the woman in the black and white skirt said, blushing herself. "I'm so rude. I apologize again and again. Don't tell Mister Walker I said this, but I'm very new to this secretary business so you'll have to bear with me."

Laura nodded as if she knew what was going on. Whoever this person was seemed nice enough and it took some pressure off of meeting this Lord Walker—or whoever—who Laura assumed was the voice she had been talking to.

"My name's Haley," the woman went on, curtsying again. "We've been expecting you. Mister—*ooh*, shoot—*I mean Lord*. I'm sorry. I've got to stop doing that."

Laura chuckled, not sure what she was laughing at.

"*Lord* Walker is waiting in his office. He will receive you there. If you'll follow me, please." Haley made her way back up the red carpeted hall she had just come down.

Laura followed, but slowly, examining each picture, tapestry, and painting as best as she could with what little time she had. They all looked pretty much the same to her: fat, tuxedoed white men variously displaying their riches. She shook her head and caught up with Haley who had stopped at the big wooden door which only seemed larger with proximity.

"Now, when we get in there," Haley said, "be sure to address him as *Lord* Walker. He wouldn't want to be called by any other name. Trust me."

Laura smiled and nodded.. "And what's your name?" she asked.

"Oh, I'm Haley," the woman said, shaking her hand. "But that's not important. You won't need to address me at all. Only speak to Lord Walker and only after you've been spoken to. You got it?"

Laura nodded. It sounded about how she would expect the voice to act from what she knew about its owner already, but she wasn't sure how this Haley put up with being in such close proximity to the demanding beast for so long. "And you live like this everyday?" she asked.

Haley chuckled. "I get to," she said. "This is the best job a robot can have. You wouldn't believe what they'd have me doing if I wasn't here."

Laura's jaw dropped. She had seen androids before but nothing so lifelike as this one. She wasn't sure she believed Haley when she said she was a robot. She couldn't be. She looked so...*human*.

"Well, are you ready then?" Haley asked after a moment's silence. "Lord Walker doesn't like to wait."

Laura swallowed the dried up spit in her mouth. Her diaphragm and vocal chords couldn't coordinate themselves enough to make speech so she just nodded. Now or never.

Haley opened the door to reveal a room identical to the hall, only wider, and instead of being empty this one had a huge wooden desk with some chairs sitting across from it. Behind the desk, the largest person Laura had ever seen sat wearing a tuxedo and towering top hat. Laura chuckled internally at the sight of it. No offense to Steve, but the costumes they were using on set were nothing compared to the real thing.

"*Ho ho ho!*" the man behind the desk laughed in the voice that Laura recognized from all her phone conversations. The sound sent a chill up her spine. "Haley, dear. Be a good girl and show our company in, please. And Laura, my gem, don't be shy. *Ho ho ho!*"

Laura hesitated but Haley guided her in to sit at one of the chairs in front of the big desk. The chair was so puffy and soft that Laura felt like it would eat her up if she didn't sit right at the edge of it.

"There we are," the voice said, it's face fatter and more grotesque than Laura ever could have imagined. "I'm sorry I didn't stand to shake your hand, dear, but my pants have been acting up today. *Ho ho ho!*"

Laura smiled, nodding. She didn't find anything about this funny, but playing along would hopefully hasten the process.

"So," the voice went on "Laura. It's good to finally meet you face to face."

Laura nodded. "Yes—*uh*—Lord Walker. You, too."

The voice, Lord Walker, smiled. He chuckled a little then went into a full on guffaw. "Yes, dear," he said. "*Lord* Walker. How nice to hear it fall from your precious lips."

Laura didn't know how to respond to that. She just smiled and nodded along.

"So, then, girl." Lord Walker sneered and his face somehow became more grotesque—so much so that Laura had to stifle a gag at the sight of it. "Tell me again how it went."

"It went exactly as planned, sir," she said, trying not to vomit.

"Yes, yes. Of course. But humor me. Remind me of the plan. Bring me through it step by step. It's one of life's few pleasures, you know, a good story well told." He grinned.

Laura shook her head. Lord Walker already knew what she had done, why did she have to repeat it for him? It was just some sick show of power on his part. "I did what you asked," she said. "I knocked Emir out. He can't act anymore. What do I do next?"

"*Next*," Lord Walker said, his grin fading, "you bring me

through what happened, step by step. If you're not going to play along, then this isn't going to be any fun for anyone and I might just have to go find another convict grip who actually wants to live a life free of her ankle monitor. There are plenty of them out there, you know. And besides that, I own the protectors so I have the power to make more whenever I want to."

Laura swallowed down what she wanted to say—that she didn't believe Lord Walker would ever take the stupid monitor off her, whether she cooperated or not—because somewhere deep down inside of her she still had some hope that he would. Instead she said, "Well—I... *Uh*. Where should I start, si—*Lord*?"

"From the beginning," Lord Walker said, smiling again and tapping his fingers on the desk. "Go on."

"Well—-*uh*..." She still didn't know how far back he wanted her to go. "Three nights ago, as per your request, I went into Loch Ness Studios—which was unlocked and empty like you said it would be—to set up the rigging on the lights."

"Tell me," Lord Walker said, clapping his hands together like an eager child. "What kind of rigging?"

"Oh it was your simple laser disc," Laura said. "It's just a ring you can wrap around any object, then with the flick of a switch, red hot lasers instantly saw whatever it's attached to in half."

"*Ho ho ho!*" Lord Walker guffawed, throwing his head back to look at the ceiling as his heaving stomach jiggled. "And that's just what you did, right? Flicked a switch and *kerplow*!" He mimed an explosion with his ham hock hands.

"Yes, sir." Laura nodded. "As soon as he was in position I took the cue and set the effects in motion. I did exactly what you asked me to do and now Emir can't work for weeks. So please, how do I get rid of this stupid monitor?"

"*Ho ho ho!*" Lord Walker chuckled. "Slow down now, sweetheart. You're putting your cart in front of your horse. Do you know what that saying means?"

Laura shook her head. She didn't know what it meant, but whatever it did mean, she didn't like the sound of it. It sounded like Lord Walker was trying to weasel out of their deal—*again*.

"No, you probably wouldn't," Lord Walker said. "Not with your education, at least. You know nothing of history beyond the last hundred or so years of art history, and this saying comes from a time well before that."

Laura was tired of his games but she had no choice but to play along. "So what does it mean then?"

"It means you're getting things out of order. You've got it in reverse. You see, back before elevators, way back even before the automobile era, people used to get around by having horses pull them in carts. So you can see what a problem it would be to put your cart before your horse. It's not trained to push the thing. All it knows how to do is pull. So you're not gonna get anywhere that way. *Ho ho ho!*"

"What does this have to do with me?"

"Oh, not much, probably." Lord Walker shrugged. "Besides the fact that you're putting your cart before your horse by asking me to remove your ankle monitor before you've finished your services to me."

"No, but you said—"

"What did I say?"

"You said you would remove my ankle monitor if I—"

"*If you did something for me.*"

"Yes," Laura said. "Then you told me to rig the lights to fall on Emir and I did just that."

"And you did a very good job of it, too, dear. Dr. Smith told me you got him right on the head." He grinned from ear to ear, giving a thumbs up with his sausage finger.

"So you should hold up your end of the agreement, then," Laura said. What was his problem? This was no way to conduct business.

"I'm afraid not," Lord Walker said, leaning forward to cross his arms on the desk, getting serious about the conversation finally. "You see, that was only step one in the task I have in mind for you."

"*Ugh.*" Laura groaned. "And how many steps are there?"

Lord Walker tapped each of his chins with each of his plump fingers. "*Hmmm.* It's hard to break the plan into discrete steps like that. Each superstep includes various substeps. No, let's leave the step counting for later. For now let's get to step two."

Laura groaned. There was probably no end to the steps, but no matter how Sisyphean the task was, she had to push the boulder up the hill or be left with no hope at all. "So what do I do?"

"Oh, don't look so down." Lord Walker smiled wide. "This

step will be a lot easier for you than the last one. And dare I say fun?"

Laura scoffed. "Sure. Whatever."

"Oh, you don't believe me?" Lord Walker snapped his fingers, still smiling and staring at Laura. "Haley, dear. Bring our star in now, please. I think it's finally time for our employees to meet face to face. Maybe we'll do some ice breaker exercises or something. *Ho ho ho!*"

"Yes, sir," Haley said, curtsying and exiting through the heavy door.

"Who is it?" Laura asked.

"Oh, you'll see," Lord Walker said, pointing at the door. "Patience my dear. You'll see. *Ho ho ho!*"

The door opened and in came Haley followed by—

Laura shook her head. She blinked her eyes. She couldn't believe what she was seeing. She couldn't form words or move her legs to stand and greet him so she just sat there, shaking her head and chuckling in disbelief.

"Laura Concierge," Lord Walker said, "meet Jorah Baldwin."

The Jorah Baldwin, wearing a black paisley suit and his trademark red lipstick, bowed low and presented a hand to Laura. It took her a while to stand—her legs wouldn't work at first, like they had fallen asleep—but when she finally got the blood flowing again she managed to shake his hand and squeak out, "Nice to meet you, sir."

"Oh, *ho ho!*" Jorah laughed, taking her hand again and kissing the back of it. "Call me Jorah, please. Leave all this *sir* business for our great and powerful Lord Walker."

Lord Walker chuckled from behind the desk where he was still seated. "Now now, Jorah, my boy. Take a seat and leave all that flattery for a better time and place. Preferably somewhere more public where we're surrounded by owners. *Ho ho ho!*"

Jorah bowed low to Lord Walker before taking the seat that Laura had been sitting in. It took Laura some time to remember how to work her legs and sit in the seat next to him.

"Oh no, my Lord," Jorah said, shaking his head, stern-faced. "Don't get me wrong. It's not flattery. It's merely a statement of fact. Truths are not flatteries. Only embellishments can be."

"All the same," Lord walker said, smiling wider still. "Now

is not the time for truths. Now is the time for business. So, shall we get down to it, then?"

"Oh, yes. Of course. Go ahead," Jorah said, bowing his head.

Laura just nodded, still unable to think, much less to speak.

"Well, now," Lord Walker said, taking his time after asking everyone else to hurry. "What we have in front of us may *seem* like an odd decision at first glance, but I want to emphasize the word *seems*."

Laura nodded. Jorah nodded more emphatically.

"Let me assure you, however," Lord Walker went on, "that I have measured and weighed all the possibilities before us and this is the most profitable course of action."

"Good, My Lord," Jorah said, bowing his head with every other word. "I trust your judgement."

"It's good to hear that, Jorah," Lord Walker said, beaming. "Because I'm afraid this will seem much more absurd from your perspective than it will from our dear Laura's here, though I'm sure she never could have imagined this outcome in her wildest dreams."

"Oh, I'm ready, Lord," Jorah said, nodding and eager though Laura had some idea of what was coming next—an idea she couldn't believe, just as Lord Walker had said—and if she was right, Jorah was not going to like the plan.

"You, Jorah Baldwin," Lord Walker said proudly, "are going to star in the independent film being produced by Laura's company." He smiled wide.

Now it was Jorah who was caught speechless. "I—*uh*..." he stammered.

"He what?" Laura blurted out, covering her mouth after she had realized what she'd done.

"Yes," Lord Walker said, smiling and nodding. "He will take Emir's role as the robot in your film. I read through the script, you know. It pissed me off at first—being the inventor of the androids as I am, of course it did—but then it got me to thinking of how I could spin the story to my advantage. So, Jorah—the biggest star in existence—" Jorah acted embarrassed by the flattery, whether he was or not. "—will star in your movie, and I—the greatest owner in all of history—will back it as the executive producer. There's no way we don't have a blockbuster on our hands with names like Walker and Baldwin behind it."

"But why us?" Laura asked.

"Why me?" Jorah asked, shaking his head.

"Now listen here." Lord Walker slammed his hands on the desk. "You, girl, should be honored. You're going to have your name on the biggest film this year. Hell, the biggest film *ever*."

"But the script sucks," Laura complained.

"And you, Jorah, are going to be more famous than you thought possible under my ownership. I *guarantee* it. The only hitch is that you have to act in the roles that I tell you to act in or you'll end up as nothing more than another extra… *Or worse*. Got it?"

"But she said the script sucks," Jorah complained.

"*I* read the script," Lord Walker said, proudly. "And I found it to be quite entertaining. More importantly, I agreed with the message. And with the worlds' biggest star on the cast, we'll be able to spread that message all the way through Outland Six and back again."

"The message?" Laura scoffed. "That's the worst part of the script. Why would you want to spread that racist Luddite garbage?"

"Racist?" Jorah said, groaning. "What is she talking about, Lord?"

Lord Walker grinned and nodded at Laura, clearly impressed. "Well, well," he said, tipping his huge top hat. "It seems your education was a little more thorough than I imagined. Luddite garbage, huh? Now I wouldn't call it garbage, but I like where you're going with the Luddite bit."

"What are you two talking about?" Jorah complained.

"It's not gonna fix anything, though," Laura said. "All that *buy human-made only* crap. It doesn't change a thing. Everything just costs more so we get less anyway. That's never going to change unless the entire system changes."

"It might not solve any of *your* problems," Lord Walker said, chuckling. "Other than your little ankle monitor fiasco, of course. But it will certainly do wonders for mine."

"But, sir," Jorah said, looking confused. "Human-made only? I'm—I mean, aren't you— Don't you—"

"Yes, Jorah, my boy. You heard it right." Lord Walker laughed, clearly enjoying himself.

"But you own the vast majority of android production plants," Jorah said. "Why?"

"For now I do," Lord Walker said, serious faced again. "We haven't finished the movie yet, though. We haven't disseminated it to the masses. But I'll take care of my investments in due time, my boy. I assure you of that. Now you stop worrying about my finances and start preparing for your roll. Haley will make sure you have a copy of the script."

"I—but—" Jorah hunched over in his seat, giving up. He shook his head. "Yes, sir," he said, defeated. "When do I start?"

"Now that's the spirit," Lord Walker said, clapping his hands together. "I've booked a studio for you all starting tomorrow morning, bright and early. You'll get the shooting schedule along with your script. Is there anything else you need?"

"No, sir," Jorah said, shaking his head and missing the characteristic twinkle in his eye.

"Good. And as for you, sweetheart." Lord Walker turned to Laura. "I need you to go tell your crew that you found a replacement for Emir then give them the new shooting schedule. We have a deadline, you know."

"Yes, sir," Laura said, nodding. "I'll tell them, sir, but they may not like it. Especially Cohen and the shooting schedule."

"*Nonsense*," Lord Walker said, waving her concerns away. "I'm sure they'll love to have Jorah on board, and as for the rest, they'll like it or they'll never work in any business ever again. *Ho ho ho!*"

"I—*uh*… I'll tell them, sir." Laura shrugged. What else could she do?

"Good," Lord Walker said. "And while you're at it, get me in touch with that script writer of yours. Have him call me. I have some projects I'd like him to start working on right away."

Laura sighed. It was sounding more and more like Lord Walker was planning on stringing her along, never to remove her ankle monitor, just as she had expected. "I'll try," she said. "But we haven't been able to get in touch with him for some time now. And besides, he only really edited the script. Cohen's the only one of us who's met the original writer."

"*Interesting*," Lord Walker said, tapping his chins. "Well have this Cohen call me then. That way I can find the writer and straighten out any concerns your director has about the new shooting schedule in one fell swoop. Can you do that for me?"

"Yes, sir," Laura said. She'd love to lay some of this burden on that asshole Cohen. Maybe then he'd finally pull some of his own weight. "I'd be happy to. Anything else?"

"That's all, dear," Lord Walker said. "For both of you. Now go get some rest and prepare. You both have important work in front of you tomorrow."

"Yes, sir," Jorah and Laura said at the same time, standing to follow Haley out of the big oak door, down the hall, and to the elevator. Laura stepped aside to let Jorah into the elevator first.

"I can't believe I have to do this," he said, rolling his eyes. "Dressing room." The doors slid closed then opened half a minute later to an empty elevator.

"It was nice to meet you," Laura said when she had stepped into the elevator.

Haley blushed. "You, too," she said, curtsying. "Good luck."

The elevator doors slid closed and Laura said, "Indywood."

The floor fell out from underneath her and she shook her head, still unable to believe anything form the last few hours. First, she actually did rig the lights to fall on Emir, which she had never thought she would do, not even for freedom. Then she met the flabby fat face behind the voice that had been pulling her strings—and how many others'?—for so long. And finally, she met Jorah Baldwin, who—now that Russ Logo was out of the picture—was the biggest actor in all the worlds. Not only that, she found out that she would be working on a film with him.

The elevator doors opened and Laura pushed out past the line of people to vomit in an alley around the corner. Saying it all at once like that made her life almost unbearable to think about. She needed a strong drink—and fast—in order to get the taste of vomit out of her mouth and calm her nerves so she hurried to the bar.

Cohen, Jen, and even Emily were all at one of the normal tables. Guy was still nowhere to be found—she wondered if the protectors finally took him to be tortured like she had tried to warn him would happen—and Steve was presumably still taking care of Emir. Laura went straight to the bar without acknowledging the crew—who were deep in conversation and didn't seem to notice her anyway—to order a fireball and a Suburban. She took the shot at the bar—not taking it in one gulp but swishing it around in her mouth first to get rid of the barf aftertaste—and thanked the bartender. She needed that.

She carried the Suburban over to the crew's table and patted Cohen on the back as she sat down. "What's up?"

"Whoa!" Cohen screamed, jumping from his seat. "*Fuck.* You scared the shit out of me. Don't sneak around like that."

Emily giggled. "You might wanna change your underwear, then."

"Laura," Jen said. "When did you get here?"

Laura shrugged, taking a big gulp of her drink. "I don't know. Just now."

"And where the fuck have you been?" Cohen demanded, still fuming. "We've all been here furiously brainstorming some way to save this production. We've got a deadline, you know, and a shit ton of scenes Emir was supposed to lead."

"I know more than you could imagine," Laura said under her breath.

"What was that?" Cohen asked, holding a hand to his ear. "Why don't you speak the fuck up so everyone can hear you?"

Laura had had enough. What did it matter anyway? Cohen wasn't in charge anymore, whether he liked it or not—whether the entire crew liked it or not. That was just the way the world worked and they would all have to get used to it.

"*I said*, I know more than you could imagine," Laura repeated.

"*Daaaaamn,*" Emily said, snapping her fingers. "You tell him, girl."

"What the fuck is that supposed to mean?" Cohen demanded.

"It means we have a new shooting schedule," Laura said. "We have new deadlines to worry about that you don't know about. It means that I know more than you could imagine."

"*In yo face,*" Emily said.

"Wait, what?" Jen said.

"*I'm* the director," Cohen said. "I'll decide the shooting schedules. Nothing has changed until you consult me about it. You got that?"

Laura scoffed. "So y'all found a replacement for Emir, then?"

Cohen looked around the table at blank faces. "Well, no," he said. "But—"

"*I* have," Laura said, grinning. "And let me just say that the replacement will probably be better than the real thing."

"*Sure.*" Cohen scoffed. "You found someone better than Emir who will work for nothing. I doubt that."

Laura nodded, letting them stew a bit longer.

"Well, who is it?" Emily asked, unable to contain her excitement.

"Jorah Baldwin."

The entire table, save Laura, laughed.

"Yeah, right," Cohen said.

"Shit, girl." Emily chuckled. "You had me goin' for a minute there."

"*Sure,*" Jen said, giving a thumbs up. "Nice story. You trying to become a writer?"

"Laugh now if you want to," Laura said, "but you won't be tomorrow. You'll be stupefied probably. That's when we start shooting. The studio's booked and it's big enough for any scene. Look, I'll show you." She pulled out her phone and sent them all the shooting schedule.

"Well, this scheduling receipt looks legit," Cohen said after taking a moment to investigate it. "But you can't expect me to believe you got Jorah Baldwin to agree to work on this project for free."

"Has he even read the script?" Jen asked.

"No, I don't think he has," Laura said. "But he'll be there."

"But— But how?" Cohen asked, still searching through the schedule. "How could you schedule all this? When have you ever met Jorah Baldwin?"

"I didn't schedule it," Laura said. "The investor did. And I met Jorah today. He'll be there. I *guarantee.*"

"You're serious, aren't you?" Emily said, bouncing up and down in her seat. "We're actually going to get to work with Jorah Baldwin."

"An investor, huh?" Cohen said. "I'd like to meet this person."

"Well that's good," Laura said, sending him Lord Walker's contact information. "Because while you probably won't be able to meet with him in person, he does want to speak with you before tomorrow. I just sent you the number."

"Lord Walker?" Cohen said, checking the message again. "*The* Lord Walker? You can't be serious."

"Oh. My. *Fortuna*," Emily said. "He's like the richest producer in all of existence."

"Really?" Jen said.

"I'm serious," Laura said. "Give him a call and see for yourself, Cohen. He's how we got Jorah."

"Alright, one second." Cohen lifted a finger and went outside to make the call. He was only gone for a few minutes, in which Jen and Emily grilled Laura about Jorah's appearance and demeanor, before he came back in with a big smile on his face and sat at the table.

"So?" Jen said.

"Is it real?" Emily asked.

Laura just nodded.

"It's a go," Cohen said. "Six AM tomorrow. Expect Jorah. This is the real deal."

Emily squealed, Jen gasped, and Laura breathed a sigh of relief to have some of the burden off her shoulders.

⋈ ✄ ⌀

LII. Anna

They probably didn't need all six transporter rings for such a small operation in a low security area, but Anna had insisted. Once she had gotten a taste for the power that came from so much control over the universe, she couldn't get enough of it. They only used two of the rings for their search, but with six paths to choose from she could ensure the paths they did use were spot on. The humming of the rings died down, and when she looked up from the consoles they were still only six. No Kara had been found.

"It looks like Five to me," Rosa said, dropping the huge protector rifle she was holding to hang from her shoulder. Anna was still a little uneasy at the sight of all those guns dangling from her Family members like black misshapen shadows, but she couldn't argue with why they had taken them and she wasn't about to try. "You were right about that."

"There's more than that, though," Anna said, shaking her head. "There are tiny disturbances I can barely see, maybe some holes in the wall or something. Did you search thoroughly? What did you see?"

Rosa scoffed. "We searched every brick of both alley walls. If there were holes, we couldn't get through them."

"She has to be there somewhere," Anna said, shaking her head. Maybe if she hooked up another console or two, she could get a better picture of what was going on, a higher resolution image. She was getting so good at controlling two consoles that she could almost do it with one hand tied behind her back, so why not try to control three or more? Then she might be able to find the holes herself without anyone having to leave the basement at all. It was a—

"Anna!" Rosa said, breaking her from her thoughts. "Did you hear me?"

"Huh? What was that?" Anna hadn't heard anything outside of her own head.

"I said fire them up again. We're gonna station a lookout.

Two at a time, switching up every six hours. Crake, Janice, you're on first watch. Everyone else go get some rest. We may have won the battle, but the war's nowhere near over."

Anna didn't hear the rest of Rosa's orders or see the others leaving. She went back into her own little universe, setting the pathways and imagining new and better methods of finding Kara by herself. When the rings stopped humming and she looked up from the consoles again, she was alone with Rosa smiling at her.

"What?" Anna asked, blushing and feeling self conscious, as if she had just woken up to someone watching her sleep.

"Nothing," Rosa said, grinning from ear to ear. "You look so beautiful when you're working, lost in your own world like that. That's all."

Anna's face got hotter. "I was just thinking."

"I know," Rosa said. "You always stick your tongue out like that when you're thinking, and you're always thinking. That's why I fell in love with you. For your brains."

Anna giggled. "Stop that."

"What?" Rosa said, coming closer to embrace her. "Stop complimenting you? Stop stating the facts as I see them? Why?"

"Why?" Anna said, kissing Rosa's cheek. "Because I don't want—"

The door slammed open and a pair of boots stomped down the stairs at top speed. Anna wasn't sure whether she gasped because of the sound of it or the sight of another gun.

"I'm sorry, ma'am," the owner of the boots said, looking at their feet as Anna and Rosa broke apart. "There's a call for Rosa."

"A call?" Rosa said, confused.

"A message," the boots said. "A messenger. She demanded to see you. Said you wouldn't want to miss this investment opportunity. It was about a movie or something."

"My movie?" Rosa said, interested now and a little less confused. "How did they get here?"

"I don't know, ma'am," the boots replied, shrugging. "But she's waiting for you in your office." Then the boots stomped back upstairs and disappeared.

"A messenger?" Anna said, raising her eyebrows.

"One of the Threes working on our movie, from the sound of it," Rosa said, shrugging. "Though I didn't think they were capable of interworld travel."

"Well there's only one way to find out," Anna said, taking Rosa's hand and leading her upstairs. "Let's go."

The "messenger" was standing behind one of the office chairs when they arrived. She stood as straight as a statue, staring at nothing across the desk and wearing a mostly black, skimpy skirted outfit with white lacy frills. She looked like she could maybe be from Three—she was certainly tall enough—but that's only because a Three could look like anyone or anything, that being their entire purpose in life, acting like someone else.

"Hello," Rosa said, crossing the room first and extending a hand to the messenger. "I don't think we've met."

So if it was a Three, it wasn't one Rosa knew. Mark that in the previously empty column of things that Anna knew about this messenger.

"Hello, sir," the woman said, curtsying instead of taking Rosa's hand then trying to reach for it after Rosa had already taken it back. "I'm Haley. It's a pleasure to make your acquaintance."

"*It's a pleasure to make your acquaintance*, too, Haley," Anna said, trying not to sound ironic. "My name's Anna and this is my partner Rosa. Please, take a seat." She indicated the chair that Haley was standing behind.

"Oh, no," the woman said, shaking her head. "There's no time for that. We should be leaving as soon as we can. Mist—*er*—*Lord* Walker doesn't like to be kept waiting."

"Lord Walker?" Rosa said. "I was under the impression that you had some message about our movie. Am I wrong?"

"Oh, no, ma'am. Not at all. It's about the movie alright. There are some exciting new directions Lord Walker has planned. He'll tell you all—"

"New directions?" Rosa said, and Anna could tell she didn't like the sound of that.

"Lord Walker can explain everything better than I can," Haley said. "Please. Come with me and I'll take you to him." She started out the door as if they would follow her.

"But where do you expect us to go?" Rosa asked, her voice getting angrier and angrier. "And how?"

"To Lord Walker's compound," Haley said, stepping back into the office. "We would have called first, but—well... You know.

You have no phones to call here."

"And what makes your Lord Walker think I want to speak to him?" Rosa demanded.

Haley laughed. She shook her head then paused when Rosa and Anna didn't laugh along. "Wait," she said. "You're kidding, right? This is a joke? I still don't understand humor very well so you'll have to humor me."

Rosa shook her head and groaned. Anna tapped her foot. Neither said a word.

"Well, he's an owner," Haley said, as if it should be obvious to them with that information alone. "Like pretty much the richest owner in all of existence."

"Is that supposed to impress us?" Anna asked, a little impressed.

"It doesn't?" Haley asked. "Well, either way, he loves your movie, and he thinks he can provide further investments which would serve to boost your message."

"He loves my movie?" Rosa asked, confused.

"Our message?" Anna said, equally so.

"Yes," Haley said. "Both. But you'll have to come meet with him for any of that to happen. So what do you say? Let's go."

Rosa turned to Anna with that *I know you're going to think it's crazy but I want to do this anyway* look and said, "What do you think?"

"I don't know." Anna shook her head. The owners were exactly the people who were holding their Family down, exactly the people they had sent a protector to assassinate, and now they were thinking about getting into business with one? It didn't seem right. "We don't even know who this guy is. How can we trust him?"

"It couldn't hurt to see what he has to say, though," Rosa said, unrelenting. "Right?"

"I guess." Anna shrugged. It was no use arguing when Rosa had her mind set, especially about this movie of hers. "But if you go, I'm coming with you this time. I'm not going to sit here and wait anymore."

"We may need someone to—" Rosa tried to say but Anna held a finger to her lips to stop her.

"No. Either we both go or neither does. You decide."

Rosa smiled, kissing Anna's finger. She turned to Haley.

"You heard the woman. Let's go. Lead the way."

They followed Haley out of the Family Home, through the streets and alleys of Five/Six, to the nearest elevator where she opened the doors and showed them in. "Right this way, m'ladies." When they stepped in and the doors closed she added, "The office." and the elevator fell into motion.

The elevator opened onto a long hall lined with red carpet and hung with tacky, overly rich paintings and tapestries. Anna tried not to gag at the sight of it even though she knew it was meant to impress. It looked like some poor person's sick idea of what a rich person's house should look like.

Haley led them to the other end of the hall and through huge oak doors into a similarly decorated office with a giant oak desk populated by the fattest person that Anna had ever seen. The man chuckled with a deep "*Ho ho ho!*" not getting up from his seat as Haley showed Rosa and Anna to the two chairs across the sea of desk from him.

"*Ho ho ho!*" he was still chuckling once they were seated. "It's so good to finally meet you, though I must say that I expected an individual not a pair. *Ho ho ho!*"

"We're a Family," Rosa said, and Anna smiled. "There are no secrets between us."

"*Ho ho ho!* A family. Of course. Just like your script, huh? It wasn't all fiction, then. Was it?"

"Not in the least," Rosa said.

"*Good*," Lord Walker said, slamming a ham fist on the desk. "That's exactly what I wanted to hear. You see, I'm more interested in your message than I am in your medium. Though I do think you have some gumption. *Ho ho ho!*"

"And what do you think the message is?" Anna asked.

"Well," Lord Walker said, staring at Anna for a moment in silence. "I would say the message is made quite obvious in the script."

"Humor me," Anna said. "Pretend I haven't read it." She actually hadn't but she knew what the message was anyway. She didn't have to read it to know. She knew Rosa well enough to know what it would say.

"Read it?" Lord Walker said. "I thought you had written it, my dear."

"*I* wrote it," Rosa said, proudly—and deservedly so.

"Answer the question," Anna said. She couldn't quite put her finger on why she disliked this jiggling, black clothed man in the tall hat, but she knew that she did.

"*Ho ho ho!*" Lord Walker chuckled. "She's a feisty one, isn't she?" he said to Rosa. "Like an angry cat or something. I see why you brought her along. *Ho ho ho!*"

"I'd like to know the answer to her question as well," Rosa said.

"Of course, dear. Why wouldn't you? Your message is an obvious one, and one I'm afraid I've only recently come to understand the true profundity of. It's an old fashioned message, if I've ever heard one, and I mean that with all due respect. Old fashioned is my motto, you see. I live by it. And, yeah, though I may have been lost, I now am found." He grinned, nodding his head and sending his chins jiggling.

"And..." Anna said. For all his words the big man hadn't said a thing.

"And a sturdy dose of old fashioned capitalism is exactly what we need. For too long now we've been lulled into a false sense of lazy security by the ever present and ever popular robot service force, but I'm afraid the jig is up. The worlds are crashing down around us. You've experienced it for yourself first hand, I'm sure. And the only way to prevent that disease from spreading to the rest of the worlds and beyond is to return to our roots. We are not meant to have social relations with things, tools, objects. Instead we should be hiring people, human beings. And in that human—we might even say *familial*—interaction we will return to the glory days when there was enough work to go around. As soon as we get rid of the robot menace, all our worlds will be made right again. I assure you of that, my dears. I assure you of that. *Ho ho ho!*"

"Well," Rosa said, "I can't argue with that."

Anna only shook her head, though. She still wasn't sure about this *Lord* Walker. He seemed to understand their message, but there was something a little off in his delivery. The words he used were a little too perfect, a little too planned, as if he had been rehearsing them for some time before delivering them, and from the look of him—so richly dressed and overweight, sitting in his opulent palace while messengers fetched his visitors for him—he was getting more out of this—or any—relationship than he was putting into it.

"So what did you have in mind?" Anna asked.

"Ah, yes," Lord Walker said, grinning. "Finally. To the business. First and foremost, since we've already been discussing it, the movie. As I said, I thought it was brilliant. I mean, I loved every bit of the script. It was full of top notch symbolism and simple enough for even the dullest of Sixers to understand."

Anna scoffed. Who did this pompous whale think he was?

"Yes," Rosa said. "I really tried to make it accessible and entertaining. I think those are the keys when you want to spread your message as far as it can go."

"Oh, yes," Lord Walker said. "There's no doubt that those are two of the keys—and very important keys at that—but as you'll come to see, my keychain is full to the brim. One thing, for instance, that I find you're lacking in is a proper crew and the right actors."

Rosa scoffed. "No doubt. But I don't really have much control over that. I was forced to take what I could get on such short notice, I'm afraid."

"Yes," Lord Walker said. "I realize this. That's where my keys come into play. I've already selected an actor to play the robot. He's a real star, too, top of the line, and he should give us the name power we need to get this movie seen throughout all the worlds."

"And the rest of the crew?" Rosa asked. "I was scraping the bottom of the barrel to get them. They're prolly not any better themselves."

"Independent's big right now," Lord Walker said, waving her concerns away. "Don't you worry about that. I'll ensure they have the studio space and equipment they need, and they should do just fine."

"Good," Rosa said. "Great. What do you think Anna?"

Anna shook her head. "I don't know. What's in it for you?"

"*Ho ho ho!*" Lord Walker laughed. "Spreading the word, my dear. That's all. And it doesn't matter if you agree anyway because I'll be helping whether y'all ask for it or not. I just wanted to meet you to get a feel for you. And I'll tell you, I like what I see."

"So that's it then?" Anna asked. "You don't want anything else?"

"Well..." Lord Walker tapped his sausage fingers on the desk. "There is one other thing."

Of course. Anna sighed. There was the matter of what he wanted from them out of all of this. There was always that.

"What is it?" Rosa asked, smiling. "Anything we can do to help our new friend."

Lord Walker chuckled. "Yes. *Friends*. I'd like to think of you that way. And in turn I'd like for you two to think the same of me." He eyed Anna as he said it. She had to suppress a groan. Now she remembered why she never went to any of these meetings with Rosa. She couldn't play the fake kissy kissy suck up game that Rosa was so good at.

"And can your friends serve you in any way?" Rosa asked, proving again she thought nothing of this man—if he even was human. If Rosa held any regard for him at all, she would have called him brother—or son at the worst, but she would have brought him into the Family in some way nonetheless. *Friend* was something else to Rosa, something lower, and the funniest part was that Lord Walker didn't understand that fact one bit. He thought she was being nice when she called him friend, and Anna wanted to laugh out loud at him for it.

"Well, you see..." Lord Walker paused for a moment, taking the monocle out of his eye and setting it on the table. His neck must have been tired from carrying his already massive head, not to mention the towering top hat with it. "This is a touchy subject. I don't want to offend." He spoke as if he had already gained their confidence.

"Please," Rosa said. "Go on. We know you have no ill intent."

Anna did scoff at that one. She couldn't help it. If anything, Lord Walker's intent was entirely ill. She regretted the scoff as soon as she had let it out, though, and held her hand to her mouth in embarrassment.

Lord Walker sneered at her. "Yes, well... I don't want to make any assumptions about your intent, either," he said, focusing all attention on Rosa alone now, practically acting as if Anna wasn't there. Anna didn't care, though. She didn't want him talking to her anyway. She wanted to leave. She never should have been there in the first place. "Which is why I will try to be as elegant and proper as I can when I tiptoe around this one."

"Please, Lord," Rosa said, bowing her head a bit. "No

tiptoeing."

"Well, you see," Lord Walker said, still tiptoeing nonetheless, an amazing feat for such a wide frame—it probably would have been havoc on his pants if he were doing it in real life rather than with words. "There was a slight disturbance in Outland One recently. A group of terrorists—as what they did can only be described as an act of terror—attacked one of the protector precincts under my ownership." He paused, waiting for a response, but he got none. Ann and Rosa both knew how to control their emotions when it was essential.

"And the only reason I bring it up," Lord Walker went on when he was sure he wasn't getting the response he wanted, "is because it just so happens that one of my protectors found the source of that disturbance. It took them some time, yes. Whoever these people were had to be very clever in order to break into my precinct. They knew how to cover their tracks, you see, but not well enough. There's always some trail left behind, I'm afraid, and my bloodhounds never fail to sniff it out."

"I'm not sure I understand what this has to do with us, sir," Rosa said.

"*Hmmm.*" Lord Walker frowned. "I thought you would by now. You're smarter than that, aren't you? No." He shook his head. "That's not it. You're not stupid. That's for certain. You act this way because you're afraid. You shouldn't be, though. This affects nothing about the deal we've already made. In fact, if anything, it makes me more eager to work with you. You'll fit in better with my new business model this way." He smiled.

"What are you saying?" Rosa asked.

"I'm saying, my dear, that I know it was you who attacked my protectors and stole my guns. I'm not as stupid as you're making yourselves out to be." Rosa tried to speak but Lord Walker cut her off. "*But,* as a gesture of friendship, and as a way to get our new business relationship started off on a good foot, I'm willing to overlook your transgressions without recompense. *Furthermore,*" he went on, cutting Rosa off again. "I'll see to it that an arsenal twice the size of what you've already taken ends up in your hands, with the promise of more weapons to come as you prove to me that I can trust you." He smiled, finally relinquishing the floor, but Rosa nor Anna said anything in response.

"Well," Lord Walker said. "What do you think?"

"Work together toward what?" Anna asked.

"Toward our common interest, sweetheart. What else? Toward the destruction of the robot industry. Toward the benefit of myself and yours. Toward whatever we can agree on, including this movie we've already begun. What's it matter to you if you're doing what you already would be doing and getting some extra benefit from it on top?"

"*Some* benefit." Anna scoffed. "Some benefit much smaller in proportion than our input, I'm sure."

"Your input?" This time it was Lord Walker's turn to scoff, unable to control his own emotions. "And what exactly do you think that is, sweetheart? You're nothing more than bodies. Anyone can be a body. Everybody's some body. I can pick up anyone off any corner in any world and they can contribute exactly the same thing as you. Any benefit you get is more than proportional to your input. If anything, it's charity on my part. The only reason I chose you is so I didn't have to meet with any other disgusting low worlders or deal with the headache of punishing you for your hilariously inadequate crimes. Now. You can take what I offer you, which is more than you can ever expect otherwise, or you can turn around right now, leave my office, and face the wrath of Lord Walker." His nose was flaring and all of his chins had gone red by the end of his heavy breathed speech.

"You can f—" Anna started to say but Rosa stopped her. She turned to Anna and nodded with a straight face. That's all it took. Rosa would handle this. Anna wouldn't like how she did it, but that was how the world worked. Anna fumed under her skin about that fact, hiding it well, as Rosa spoke.

"I'm sorry if we've offended you," Rosa said and Anna took special notice that she used "we've" instead of "she's". "It was not our intention. You must understand that we would be stupid not to ensure that we get a fair deal out of this relationship."

Lord Walker nodded. "Yes, of course, but—"

"And you must also realize," Rosa went on, taking control of the conversation finally, "that when you talk about a future relationship it implies future demands on our time which we may not be prepared to put up with. Given zero knowledge of your future plans, we would essentially be handing you a blank check by accepting your offer."

Lord Walker grinned. "It's funny you should say that," he said, "*a blank check*. It's such an archaic term, especially for a Sixer."

"I've made it a point to remember my Family's history," Rosa said, nodding once.

Lord Walker nodded back. "Yes," he said. "It's important to remember history if you want to know how to come out on top when it repeats itself. But how about I offer you a blank check in return then?"

"How so?" Rosa said.

"Well, I'll simply send you one of the armories. They're essentially 3D printers capable of creating all the guns and armor you have time to ask for. That'd be about the same as a blank check, and it would serve to show just how much I trust you and value our new relationship."

Rosa looked to Anna who shook her head. She didn't like this idea. He was giving them a blank check, technically, but it was limited and Lord Walker could cut off the supply whenever he wanted. And besides that, there was no telling what he would ask of them in return.

"And this is a once in a lifetime offer," Lord Walker added, anticipating their reluctance. "If you leave here without saying yes, then you've said no and you're responsible for whatever happens to you and your family as a consequence."

Anna shook her head again. She still didn't want to get in bed with this flabby monster, but she knew what Rosa was going to say before she said it.

"We'll take the armory," Rosa said. "And we'll see where we go from there."

"Good," Lord Walker said. "*Great*. That's all I needed to hear. Haley will show you home and carry the armory for you, but I'm afraid that's all I have time for today, ladies. I'll get you a phone, too, so we won't have to meet in person all the time. You heard that Haley? Get them a phone, too. Now, *ta ta!*" He turned in his seat so his back was facing them and they couldn't respond if they wanted to.

Anna and Rosa followed Haley out through the elaborate hall to the elevator where the armory was waiting for them.

"He's so pompous," Anna said when she saw it.

Rosa grabbed her arm. "We need this."

"Sorry for the tight fit, Haley said, squeezing into the elevator with them. "Sector US1Q84." The doors slid closed and the elevator fell into motion. When they opened again Haley pushed the armory out, following them in silence to the Family Home.

"All the way in the basement, please," Rosa said when they had arrived, and Haley obliged.

"It was a pleasure to meet you," Haley said when she had climbed back upstairs.

"And you," Rosa said, extending a hand to Haley who took some time to shake it before curtsying and leaving.

"I can't believe you did that," Anna said, slapping Rosa on the arm and stomping to the kitchen. "And all for some more guns." She had to cook something and get some food in her stomach to forget how gross everything about what had just happened was.

"I didn't hear you speaking up," Rosa said, following her into the kitchen and sitting at the bar. "I did what needed to be done."

"*Ha!*" Anna set to cooking, not even knowing what she planned on making. "I didn't have to speak because you knew how I felt already. I don't like all these guns around here, and I certainly don't want any more in the House."

"Technically, there aren't any more, just a printer that can make some." Rosa grinned, trying to lighten the mood.

"You know what I mean," Anna said, dicing harder and faster. "There will be because of that thing. And more deaths, you can count on that. I don't like one bit about this Lord Walker business, and I don't understand how you could."

Rosa chuckled. "Oh, don't worry. I don't trust that fat old man as far as I can throw his gigantic top hat, but what did you want me to do? Say no and piss him off from the get go? At worst, we get some guns out of it so we can defend ourselves better when we inevitably do piss him off by not bowing to his every demand."

"Unless he cuts off the pipeline," Anna said, tossing the diced vegetables into the frying pan.

"Then we'll just have to be sure we get the guns before we piss him off. Won't we?"

"*Exactly*," Anna said, throwing a can of beans in with the vegetables. She hated using the cans, but she was too hungry to wait for the real thing. "Which means more guns in the House, exactly what I said I didn't want in the first place."

"Well, I'm sorry," Rosa said, shaking her head and letting her hands flop on the table, not quite slamming them. "I know you don't want violence. I don't either. But that's the only way that they know how to respond so we have to be prepared when they do."

"I don't know." Anna shook her head. "It's almost like we're asking for it if we stock up on weapons like this."

"It would be asking for it if we didn't," Rosa said. "We have to protect ourselves. No one else will."

"Well, I hope you're right," Anna said. "And I hope *Lord* Walker doesn't ask us to do something we don't want to do in the meantime—like maybe start the violence instead of defending against it. What do we do then?"

"We say no."

"And deal with his wrath?" Anna said with a laugh, setting a full bowl of food in front of Rosa and sitting next to her to start in on her own.

"Exactly," Rosa said with a smile, taking a bite. "*Mmmm. Delicious.*" She took another. "And exactly why we'd be dumb not to arm ourselves in preparation. You met the guy."

"Which is why I don't trust—" Anna turned to say but Kara came rushing into the kitchen to cut her off.

ॐ ✳ ॐ

LIII. Roo

Roo had lost herself again in the fourth dimension. Although there was no longer a beautiful tapestry of timespace to act as her guidepost, it was easy enough to retrace her path back to the place where the tapestry had originally been produced. This, Roo thought, was where the woman with the gun who was now sitting in Roo's secret lair had come from. Roo changed the exit path from her lair to the *family home*—or whatever Kara was calling it—and returned to Earth to see once and for all where exactly that was.

"I still don't see why I have to come," Mike said, obviously uncomfortable in his still wet pants.

"Nor do I," Kara said. "Just open the door and send me home."

Roo scoffed. "You need me," she said to Kara. "That's why you're taking us with you. And you're the only one who can identify your mom," she said to Mike. "Which is why you're coming. It's quite simple, really."

"You can't talk to me like that, girl," the woman said, grabbing her gun again as if she would use it.

"And you can't force me to go with you," Mike said, crossing his arms.

"I can, and I can, actually. In fact, I already have. There's no way for you to go home home now so you'll join us or you'll wait right here until I get back."

"You opened it?" the woman asked, dropping her gun to her side and stepping through the wall.

Roo followed close behind while Mike hesitated, still trying to decide if going or staying would be worse, then called, "Wait up!" before chasing out after them.

What they stepped into didn't look like a house. It was one big room, with cement walls and floor, that was lined with electronic rings—one of which they had just stepped through—leading Roo to believe that this was where some serious bending took place. The spacetime tapestry she couldn't stop picturing in her head was probably woven right here at these two consoles.

Two consoles? Roo couldn't believe her eyes. She thought it would take at least four benders to hold together something so complex as what she had seen, but taking a step closer to get a good look, she could see that no more than two people at a time could possibly control these six portals with the way they were wired up. That couldn't be right, though. Whoever these benders were must have some sort of remote console system set up so more than two people could work on the transporters without having them all in the same room. That had to be it.

"*Uh*, Roo," Mike said, tapping her on the shoulder to break her away from her intense investigation of the console and ring system. She turned around to find Kara gone and the room empty save Mike, her, and the transporter system. "I don't like the feeling of this place," Mike went on. "Maybe we should go back home."

"But we haven't even looked for your mom, yet," Roo said, though she wasn't in the least bit concerned about that. All she wanted was to figure out who operated this system and how they had done what she had seen them do. She couldn't come outright and ask that, though, bending being so frowned upon—not to mention illegal—but the search for Mike's mom served as perfect cover—which is why she couldn't really let him leave just yet either. "You came to me asking for help," she reminded him. "Well, here it is. I'm helping."

"Yeah, okay," Mike said. "Well, what do we do now, then? If you're so confident my mom's actually here."

"We follow Kara upstairs and go look for her. That's what. Now come on." Roo waved for him to follow and started up the stairs.

"No, wait," Mike called. "But what if they—" But Roo didn't stop to listen. She climbed the stairs, and as soon as she got to the door, it swung open to reveal two old ladies looking down on her. Roo almost fell down the stairs, jumping in surprise at the sight of them.

"Woah now, child," one of them said. "We won't hurt you."

"What are you kids doing down there?" the other asked, sounding angry where the first was only surprised. "And how did you even get in?"

"I—*uh*—" Roo's heart beat faster and faster. She couldn't

remember why she was there.

Luckily, Mike found some courage for once, climbing up the stairs behind her to say, "My *mother*." His voice cracked as he spoke, but he still somehow managed to sound resolute in his words. "We came to find my mother and bring her home."

"They're just looking for family," the nicer woman said. "I told you."

"And who might your mother be?" the angry one asked.

"Melody Singer," Mike said.

"And what makes you think she's here?" the angry woman asked.

"Well, I—*uh*—" Mike looked to Roo, losing his cool, but it was okay because he had stalled long enough to let Roo regain hers.

"She said something about a family, or a home—or something—when she left last. She was very vague," Roo said, smiling a little but trying not to grin—she always got the two mixed up when she was trying to be sneaky.

The angry woman eyed Roo suspiciously. "Is that so, child?"

"Now now," the nicer woman said. "Enough of this stairway interview. Let us at least take this to the office. Or—*better, yet*—the kitchen. I'm sure our guests here wouldn't mind a little bite to eat while we speak. Am I wrong?" She looked down at Roo and Mike, expecting an answer.

"Oh, well, I guess I could eat," Mike said, unsure of himself.

"I'm not hungry," Roo said. Then she smiled and added, "Though a seat might be nice. Thanks."

"There're seats in the kitchen," the nicer woman said, shepherding them the rest of the way up the stairs and past the angry woman who eyed them as they passed. "And you'll be hungry once you smell the food. I promise."

"I guess so," Roo said, letting the woman push her through a short hall into a large kitchen where she sat Roo and Mike on stools at the bar and set to cooking something up. The angry woman followed in last and stood off to a corner, staring in Roo and Mike's direction.

"So," the nice woman said as she chopped some bell peppers. "Your mother has told you about the Human Family, then?"

"The human family?" Mike repeated.

"She's not my mom," Roo said.

"But I thought you said—" the angry woman tried to say from her far corner of the kitchen but the nice lady shot her a look that shut her up.

"I'm helping him find his mom," Roo explained. "I'm just doing him a favor. His mom mentioned some family home so we came here to see if we could find her."

"Is that right?" the woman said, turning her back to toss some bell peppers into the pan and grab an onion to chop. "Your mom mentioned it?" she asked Mike who nodded.

"This is the place, right?" Roo asked.

The woman nodded. "This is the Family Home. Yes."

"Then have you seen my mom?" Mike asked, hopefully.

The woman nodded again, adding the onions to the pan. "She's been here. Yes. You haven't seen her recently, though? I don't think she's been on duty for some time."

"On duty?" Mike said.

The woman nodded. "For the Family, child. For all Humankind. It's a noble thing your mother's doing."

"And what exactly is that?" Roo asked.

"Fighting the robot menace," the woman said, stirring the vegetables to send them sizzling then adding some sausage to the mix. "Destroying the walls between our human brethren. Protecting the Human Family."

"Robot menace?" Mike said.

"Destroying the walls?" Roo said.

The woman smiled, adding canned beans to the pan and letting it simmer in silence. When it was set and cooking, she crossed to the bar and stood across from Roo and Mike, smiling. "I think it's time I ask a question."

"I—*uh*…" Mike said.

Roo just nodded. Sometimes questions revealed more information than answers.

"How did you get into the basement?"

Mike looked to Roo who didn't break eye contact with the woman, Roo who didn't respond to the woman's words in any way, when it became clear to everyone there that no answer was forthcoming, the woman spoke on.

"Let me venture a guess," she said, back turned again to stir the pan once more and let it simmer. "You jumped in."

Mike sounded like he had choked on his own spit with his gagged coughing. Roo still didn't respond.

"Oh, don't worry," the woman said, crossing back to the bar to stare into Roo's eyes. "I'm not even mad about it. In fact, I'm kind of impressed. For two children to jump back into my Home, carrying the very same Family member we've been searching for without success—why that can only be a blessing from above."

"Who are you?" Roo asked, not impressed by the woman's obviously insincere attempt at flattery.

"My name's Anna," the woman said, extending a hand across the counter. "And you are?"

Roo hesitated then took the woman's hand. "Roo."

"Hello, Roo. So nice to meet you."

"Is that your transport system in the basement?" Roo asked, ready to get down to business now that all the subterfuge was uncovered.

"So you did jump in then," Anna said, laughing and dishing out two bowls of red beans, one for Roo and one for Mike. "You admit to that."

"So who besides the two of you controls the consoles?" Roo asked, ignoring Anna's statement. Of course they had jumped in. How else could they have gotten into that basement? "Or do you have some remote units hooked up somehow? I'd like to see them, too."

The angry woman in the corner scoffed while Anna chuckled. "Remote units?" she said "What makes you think that?"

"I saw the bending you were doing," Roo said as a matter of fact. "Complexity of that level is too much to handle for two benders alone, especially for as tiny of a space as you were holding those wormhole exits inside of."

Anna smiled wide, almost blushing, then let out a short burst of laughter. "Oh? Well, there weren't two of us. I'll tell you that much."

"Then there were remote units," Roo said, confident she had figured it out without having to be told. "I knew it."

"No," Anna said, straight faced. "No remote units, either."

"Then how did you get more than two people to control the transporters? You only have two consoles down there."

"There weren't more than two, either," Anna said. "There

weren't even as many as two."

Roo shook her head in disbelief while the angry woman chuckled in her corner. Mike went on eating, oblivious to the world around him now that he had been assured that his mother was safe and at home.

"Then that means…" Roo said.

"That I created the symphony you witnessed all by myself." Anna laughed.

Roo couldn't believe it. It was impossible. No one person could maintain that all by themselves. This woman was obviously a liar. "Prove it," Roo said.

Anna chuckled. "Now? But you haven't even touched your beans."

The angry lady cackled behind her. "I'm out of here," she said, kissing Anna on the cheek. "I trust you can take care of this, my dear."

"I didn't come here to eat," Roo said, standing from her stool, and the angry old lady ruffled Roo's hair as she passed to leave.

"Nor to find your friend's mom," Anna said, "from the sound of it."

"Hey!" Mike said, finally back in the conversation at the mention of his mother.

Roo shrugged. "We've already found her. You said she was here before and hasn't been on duty since. Is there any reason I should disbelieve your word? I don't know. Maybe there is. Maybe demonstrating that you actually are capable of holding six transporter paths together on two consoles—*by yourself*—will help me believe you. What does it matter what I came here for anyway? We're here now so let's move forward. Shall we?" She stood as if to go toward the basement and waved for them to follow along behind her.

Anna smiled and nodded, clearing Mike's empty bowl and Roo's untouched one. "You know, I don't mind showing you because you seem to have a rather advanced knowledge of the system, but in the future, you'd do better for yourself to be less pushy in your demands when made upon a complete stranger. I don't have to show you anything if I don't want to. I have nothing to prove and others might not be as accommodating as I am. That being said,"

Anna went on, rinsing her hands and drying them on her apron. "I'm curious to see how much you would actually understand about a demonstration so, please, lead the way"

Roo started to protest before she realized what Anna had said. When she did, it took her some time to process the information and get her feet moving toward the basement for the others to follow. Downstairs, Anna went straight to the consoles and Roo stood looking over her shoulder. Mike sat on one of the bottom steps, bored and uninterested in a beauty he had no way of deciphering.

"So, *uh*, what about my mom?" he called from the stairs as Anna booted the consoles up. "How am I supposed to get home?"

"I'll send you along presently, dear," Anna said, pressing the consoles' various buttons and levers to get them going. "And with six paths to choose from. That ought to satisfy your curiosity. *Eh*, girl?" She smiled at Roo who nodded, staring in awe as the woman's hands flicked unconsciously across the screens, buttons, and levers of the consoles, untangling the universe even as the old woman spoke. "Now, what can you see me doing here, child?"

"I—" Roo gulped down spit. "*Uh*—You— You're not even looking. How could you be using two separate consoles if you're not even looking at the screens?"

"How could I be using both consoles at once if I had to look at the screens?" the woman asked, still swipping and swiping, sending space into flux, and forcing it back down into submission. Not at two points alone, though, creating one path between them, but at twelve points along six separate and nearly intersecting paths. Roo couldn't imagine the sheer feeling of power emanating through Anna's body at being able to exert so much control over the universe. "Which screen would I look at?" Anna continued. "No. You see, I could do this with my eyes closed if I had to. In fact, I will." She closed her eyes and kept swiping and typing.

The transporter rings hummed into action. The noise was loud but Roo welcomed it. It drowned out the rest of the world so she could focus more entirely on the masterpiece being created in front of her eyes, a masterpiece on the scale of the one she had witnessed earlier, and this tapestry was clearly created by a lone bender using two consoles at once—*with her eyes closed!*

Roo was falling headlong into the four dimensional

masterwork when a cold hand grabbed her from behind and jerked her back down into 3D reality.

She flailed her arms and legs and screamed in protest, but there was no response to her fighting. Before she knew it, she was no longer in the basement of the Family Home. Instead she was lying on a cold, hard floor, watching the hole she had been pulled in through disappear behind her. She climbed to her feet and slammed her fists on the elevator doors which took the place of the hole in spacetime.

"Where am I?" she demanded, turning to find a big metal arm with a too human hand waving at her as it rolled back and forth on thick treaded metal tires. "W—What are you?" She backed up to the elevator doors and the door across the hall opened. An old white lady in an old white coat came through, smiling and nodding.

"Very good, Popeye," she said. "Thank you so much. That'll be all for now."

The metal arm waved and went out through the door that the white coated woman had come in through.

"Who are you?" Roo demanded, trying to back closer to the elevator doors she was already pressed flat against. "Where am I?"

The woman chuckled. "Settle down, dear. There's no need to be alarmed. You're safe here."

"Where am I?"

"You're in my lab, dear. My home. Now, please. Come with me. We have so much to discuss."

"No." Roo stood her ground. "I'm not going anywhere until you tell me why I'm here."

The woman stopped crossing the hall and turned back to Roo with a smile. "And what if I didn't answer?" she asked. "You could be standing there for quite a while, you know."

Roo shook her head. She hadn't thought about that possibility. She turned to the metal, handle-less elevator doors behind her and tried to pry them open with her fingers but it was useless.

"You see," the woman said with a chuckle behind her. "There's no point in trying to escape. And you have nothing to worry about, anyway. I'll tell you everything you want to know, but I'd rather do it in a more comfortable setting. Could you agree to that much at least?"

Roo gave up on trying to open the elevator doors and turned slowly to face the woman. Roo didn't like the lady's white hair or coat, or the wrinkles on her face, or anything about her really—especially the whole kidnapping thing—but she didn't really have a choice in the matter, either, and maybe if they went somewhere else, Roo'd be able to find an escape.

"Well, come on, then," the woman said, waving for Roo to follow her down the hall. "Let's have a seat and chat." She opened the door and Roo went in.

There were no more exits on the other side of the door than there were in the hall. In fact, there were less, only one, the door she had come in from. Other than that there was a big desk and some puffy chairs around side tables that were next to a giant window that looked out onto a huge wilderness scene—probably a video played on a fake window, or something like that, because nothing so beautiful could possibly exist in real life.

"So, what do you think of the place?" the woman in the white coat asked, taking a seat in one of the puffy chairs and indicating for Roo to sit in the chair across from her.

"Pretty cool graphics," Roo said, nodding at the window as she sat down.

The woman chuckled. "Oh, it's pretty cool alright, but they're not graphics. That's the real world out that window. I assure you of that."

"No way," Roo said. "That kind of wilderness doesn't exist anywhere but stories."

"It does," the woman said, pointing out the window. "There it is." She smiled.

Roo scoffed. "Yeah, right. So I could just walk out there right now and see it for myself? Show me."

"You would have to take the elevator there," the woman said, "*if you decided that was what you wanted*. But we'll get to that later. Didn't you have some questions you wanted answered first?"

Roo shook her head. She had more and more questions the more she experienced. At this rate it seemed like none of them would get answered. "Yeah," she said. "So what?"

"So how about we play a game? Would you like that?"

Roo shrugged. "Depends on the game."

"This is a game of questions. I ask you a question and you

answer it, then you ask me a question and I answer it. Simple as that."

"Any question?" Roo asked.

"Any question."

"And you have to answer it?"

"As do you."

Roo nodded, thinking about it. "And why can't I go first?"

"Well my first question will be simple, an opener. So essentially you will be first after you answer it." Roo tried to protest but the woman went on speaking anyway. "What's your name?"

"*Uh*—" Roo hesitated. "Roo," she said. "What's yours?" And she held her hands to her mouth, regretting the wasted question.

"The Scientist," the woman said. "Nice to meet you, Roo."

"The Scientist?" Roo scoffed. "What kind of name is that?"

"It's one I've chosen," the woman said. "And I didn't have to answer that question because it's my turn, but I'll let it slide this once. You should be more careful in the future. Think about what you're going to say before you open your mouth."

Roo nodded solemnly.

"Okay." The Scientist nodded. "Good. Then question two: What were you doing with those women I found you with?"

Roo frowned, shaking her head. "What? Those human family jerks? Nothing. I don't even know them."

"That doesn't answer my question."

"I—*uh*—I don't know. I was helping a friend look for his mother."

The Scientist eyed Roo suspiciously. "Is that right?"

Roo nodded. "Yes," she said. "She got addicted to jumping, and she was doing it with that family—or whatever—so we went there to look for her."

"How did you know she was there?"

"It's my turn," Roo said. "I don't have to answer that."

The Scientist nodded with a smile. "Go on."

Roo thought hard about what to say next. She wasn't going to waste another question on something stupid like she had done with her previous turns. When she was satisfied she had formulated something vague enough to extend her turn as long as possible, she said, "Why me?"

"Why you?" the Scientist repeated.

"That's what I said. Why me?"

"Why you what?"

"Just why me?"

After a moment's thought, the Scientist said, "Because you know about the walls."

"The walls?"

"Yes, the walls, the elevators, the other worlds. Because you know about jumping, or whatever you want to call it. That's why."

"I—*uh*..." Roo hesitated, not sure how much it was safe for her to reveal to this woman.

"Am I wrong?"

Roo knew she couldn't lie, not about this at least. "No," she said, shaking her head. "But how do you know?"

The Scientist laughed. "I control the walls, dear. I have my eyes everywhere. I know about every little thing that happens on either side of my babies."

"So why did you bring me here then?"

"Technically it's my turn," the Scientist said. "But answering this leads into my next question, so in answer, I'm impressed by the knowledge you've gained through self study. Yes, I've seen your work, and yes, I'm impressed by it. How couldn't I be?"

"*Ummm.*" Roo tried not to blush. She had never been complimented on her bending before. "Thanks... *I guess*. But I'm still not sure what all this means."

"It means I want to train you, dear. I think you've got what it takes. I want to teach you all the secrets of the fourth dimension."

Roo scoffed. "You don't know all the secrets."

"I know a good deal of them—more than anyone, I'd venture to say. I certainly know more than that Anna who I'm sure you were quite impressed by."

Roo's eyes grew wide. "You know about her?"

"Everything on either side of my walls," the Scientist reminded her, nodding.

"And you know what she can do, then? All alone, operating two consoles at once, six paths with one brain."

The Scientist chuckled. "Yes. It's quite impressive with her limited technology. I'll give you that much. But what if I told you that I could control every single wall in existence, all by myself, using only a single computer?"

Roo scoffed, shaking her head. "*Impossible.*"

"Not impossible," the Scientist said. "That's how the worlds work. That's what I can teach you. That's my question for you, dear. Are you willing to learn?"

Roo shook her head. "I don't believe you."

"You don't think any human created the walls? Maybe you think they were always there. Or is just that you think they're beyond human powers to control?"

Roo shook her head. "No, I didn't say that."

"You think it takes more than one person, then?"

No response.

"Well, dear, I have the technology, you see. I have everything you would ever need to reshape the universe on the scale that I do, and I'm offering you the opportunity to use it."

Roo shook her head. She didn't know anything about this woman. She still didn't know where she was or why, not to mention how she was supposed to get home, so she didn't respond at all.

"You have nothing to say, then?" the Scientist asked.

Roo shook her head, lips held in a straight line.

"You do understand what I'm offering, don't you? With my equipment here you'll be able to do things you could never imagine. Haven't you ever dreamed of having this level of technology at your disposal?"

"No," Roo said. "I bend just fine with what I've got. I never even knew this level of technology existed until you just told me about it, so how could I have dreamed of having it?"

"But you do know now," the Scientist said. "And you can use the technology for yourself if you want to. I'll even teach you how. Don't you want that?"

"That would be fine," Roo said, nodding.

"Then what's the problem? I don't understand."

"Well, ma'am." Roo paused, trying to formulate her thoughts into something that could be translated into words. Honestly, she didn't have a particularly logical reason why she distrusted this scientist, but Roo knew that something was off about the conversation that had been going on between them so far. "I can't accept your offer when I don't know what it will cost me," she said. "I don't— I just don't like to owe someone like that."

The Scientist chuckled, shaking her head. "No, dear. It won't cost you anything. This isn't a deal. It's an offer."

"No, ma'am." Roo shook her head. She had been taught better than that. "There's no such thing. It'll cost me something. You're just not telling me what that something is yet. That's why I can't take the deal, ma'am. I'm sorry."

The Scientist smiled, standing from her chair. "You're a clever girl, you know."

"I ain't stupid," Roo said.

"No." The Scientist shook her head. "You're not that. And you deserve to know the truth, what this would actually cost you. Though I'll say now that it's not me who you'll be paying, it's yourself. But come along. You'll see. I'll show you." She extended a hand for Roo to grasp.

Roo looked at it for a second, hesitating. "I'll pay myself?" she asked, standing but not accepting the Scientist's assistance.

"You alone will have to deal with the knowledge I'm giving you," the Scientist said. "You'll pay in your responsibility to your own conscience, the most miserly fee collector you'll ever encounter."

"My conscience?" Roo tried to say, but the Scientist had already left the room. Roo followed her, and the Scientist closed the door behind them.

"Do not speak when I open this door again," the Scientist said, looking deep into Roo's eyes. "These people cannot know that we're watching them. If they see you, even I may not be able to keep them from punishing you."

Roo nodded. What was this crazy woman talking about?

"And don't try to step through the door," the Scientist added. "It's a long fall from up here, and I'd hate to lose such a promising young prodigy to their glitz and glamour."

Glitz and glamour? The more she spoke the less sense the Scientist made. Roo shrugged. She didn't see herself stepping off a cliff any time soon, and she didn't really need anyone warning her not to.

"Well, then, dear," the Scientist said, opening the door. "Open your eyes to the worlds."

Roo looked down into a steep drop off over a mass of the biggest, fattest people she had ever seen, all dressed in the same black and white outfits and wearing too tall hats. They were seated at massive tables, stuffing their faces with mounds of food, and laughing, joking, and drinking as they did it—mouths full or not. Roo almost wanted to barf watching them. Why was this woman showing her these disgusting beasts?

"Disgusting, isn't it?" the Scientist said, chuckling and shaking her head.

"What does this have to do with me?"

"Look at them down there, oblivious, all enjoying the food that you and your family grew, shipped, and prepared for them."

"Is this some more of that human family shit?"

"Oh, no no. I mean your nuclear family. Your mom and dad and brothers and sisters."

"So what?"

"So now you know. Now you have to live your life with the knowledge that they take everything you produce so they can live like this, like the disgusting fat beasts you see down there devouring everything you've ever created."

Roo looked down at them one more time then slammed the door. "So what? What do you want me to do about it?"

"Do you think you could do anything?"

Roo scoffed. "I am the greatest bender any of the worlds have ever seen. I can do whatever I want."

"Then prove it," the Scientist said. "Show the worlds that you can master the fourth dimension. Use the technology you so want to use. Use it to shape the universe into the image of what you think it should look like."

"And if I just want to bend for the sake of bending?"

"Then be my guest. But I'm sure you'll think of something more creative to do with your time and newfound power than tinkering with wormholes."

Roo shook her head, chuckling. She still didn't trust this woman, but she did like the possibilities presented by what she was offering.

ଓ �֍ ⚘

LIV. Chelsea

Her heart stopped. The world spun around her. There was one body left at her feet. The others had fled, chased by the backup that arrived all too late, but Chelsea was proud of herself. She had done her duty. She had protected. She plopped down onto her seat, let her gun fall to the floor, and slammed her head on the desk three times in quick succession.

After some time alone in silence, punctuated sporadically by the sound of her head hitting the desk, an Officer she didn't recognize rolled a cleaning cart in and set to disposing of the body which was still lying, breathless and dead, on the once white floor behind her. Chelsea didn't react to his presence. She simply laid her head on the desk, trying to catch her breath and listening to the Officer as he struggled clumsily with the still warm body until the cart creaked away again, quieter under the new weight of Chelsea's first kill.

She gagged, grabbing the wire mesh trash can at her feet as fast she could, but only managed to dry heave. Luckily she hadn't been eating much lately or the can and the floor would have been covered in whatever meal came before murder. She stood to stare at the bloodstains on the floor, which would no doubt take some effort to wash away and would thus remain for a long time to come, reminding her of just what she had lived through. She looked down at her hands and thought for a second that she saw blood on them then tried to laugh the vision away. That was nonsense, insane, true metaphorically—perhaps—but when one started hallucinating metaphors it was high time to seek out psychological assistance.

She turned to look away from the blood, her entire body trembling. She had done her duty. That's all. They were trespassers with cruel intentions, and they deserved what they had gotten. But why did she still feel so guilty about it?

She was standing there, staring off into the nothingness behind the bloodstains on the floor, when a hand grasped her by the shoulder and jerked her back into reality.

"Pardy!" the hand's voice said, the Captain's voice. "Don't you go all Pardy on me, now. I know it's your name, but unlike your husband, you can handle a little violence in the course of duty, can't you?"

Chelsea shook her head, still not fully back to reality or completely able to understand what the Captain was saying. "Go all Pardy, sir?" She squinted, trying to be sure it was actually the Captain she was talking to and not some metaphorical hallucination.

"Like your husband, the former Officer Tom Pardy. He couldn't handle his first kill, either. A lot of people think that's what made him do what he did. A lot of people hope so, at least, but they'll probably never get the chance to find out the truth now."

"What are you talking about?"

"It doesn't matter, kid," the Captain said, patting Chelsea on the back. "You did good."

Chelsea flinched away from her touch. "I don't think so," she said, shaking her head. "I never should have left my post to chase after them. They never should have made it into this room in the first place."

"That was one little mistake," the Captain said, chuckling. "We can sweep it under the rug with ease. No problem."

"I—*uh*—"

"Now let me finish," the Captain said, adding a hint of harshness to her tone which betrayed the gaiety she had obviously been struggling to maintain. "The important part is that you understand that you didn't have a choice. You were forced to kill those intruders. Killing them was the only regulation course of action. They don't call it a Protector Force for nothing, you know. You were *forced* into it." The Captain tried chuckling again, but it did nothing to lighten the mood.

"I should have killed more," Chelsea said, shaking her head. "I should have killed all of them." Tears welled up behind her eyes but she fought them back without wiping them. She didn't want the Captain to see her weakness.

"You did what you could, kid. You're a rookie at a desk job who doesn't even carry an assigned weapon. Another Officer was killed, you know. At least you fared better than he did."

Chelsea cringed at the thought of Officer Janitor's lifeless body.

"And you did me proud," the Captain said. "Which should be bountiful for your career—as long as you're willing to keep it up. You are willing to keep it up, aren't you?"

"I—*uh*…" Chelsea wasn't sure about killing another person, no matter how much they deserved it, but she also knew that it was probably the only way to keep her son safe under the Captain's custody. "Yes, sir, Captain, sir," Chelsea said, ticking off a weak and lazy salute.

"Very good, Pardy," the Captain said, slapping Chelsea on the back. "Then follow me to my office. I have some good news and some bad news we need to discuss, and they might just be the same thing. *Ha ha!*"

"I—What?" Chelsea tried to say but the Captain had already left the office.

In the hall, Chelsea picked her way carefully around the blood she knew belonged to Officer Janitor while the Captain marched unceremoniously through the still sticky puddles, leaving red boot prints in her wake. Chelsea breathed a sigh of relief when the elevator doors closed and she didn't have to look at the blood any longer.

"Oh, I know. You must be tired, kid," the Captain said in response to the sigh which she must have mistaken for a yawn. "But I'm afraid this bit of information can't wait. You'll get an opportunity for rest after this meeting. I swear it."

The doors slid open and the Captain marched out fast, leaving Chelsea to play catch up. When the Captain swung her office door open and burst through it, Chelsea stopped dead in the doorway with dropped jaw. Sitting there, bent kneed and clearly nervous, staring out the window across the desk, was Tom. All Chelsea could do was wonder who was taking care of Jonah if Tom was there.

"*Ah*, Pardy," the Captain said, crossing around the desk to take her seat. "You're already here. Perfect. And I'm sure you know Pardy." The Captain smiled at her own joke.

Tom stood and stepped toward Chelsea to hug her then awkwardly tried to tick off a salute toward the Captain when Chelsea didn't reciprocate, unable to decide who in the room he should be looking at. "I—*uh*. Yes, sir," he said. "*Chelsea—I—*"

"Yes, Chelsea Pardy," the Captain said, "but let's keep this professional, please. While you're on the Force you have no spouse, you have no family, you have no one but your fellow Officers, and I am your superior. Do you understand me?"

"Sir, yes, sir," Tom and Chelsea sang in unison.

"Good." The Captain smiled. "Now take a seat, both of you. We have so much to discuss."

Tom sat straight back in the seat he had been occupying, and when Chelsea tried to cross to the other side, he made it more awkward than it had to be by clumsily standing up, bumping into her, and switching seats instead of simply moving his legs out of the way so she could get by. When the scene was finally over, Chelsea sat on the stool red faced with embarrassment and starting to get angry.

"Well, now that we've been through all that," the Captain said, crossing her arms on the desk, "let's talk about your son."

"Who's taking care of him?" Chelsea demanded, looking first at Tom then the Captain and back again. "*Who*?"

"I don't—" Tom started.

"He's being taken care of," the Captain said. "You can trust me on that. And he will continue to be taken care of for as long as you two continue to do what it is that I ask of you."

Chelsea nodded, not wanting to say anything to endanger Jonah.

"And if we don't do what you ask?" Tom asked, all too confidently. Chelsea could have killed him for using "we" instead of "I". He was trying to drag her into his sins again.

"If you decide to disobey me, *your superior officer*," the Captain emphasized to remind Tom as she had only recently reminded Chelsea, "then maybe I'll be less able to ensure your son's safety. He *was* caught committing a serious crime, you know. Him and his girlfriend together. They both got off easy if you ask me."

"You wouldn't—" Tom said.

"How could you let him do that?" Chelsea demanded of Tom. "You were supposed to be his caretaker."

"I didn't *let* him do anything," Tom said defensively, holding his hands up like Chelsea was going to hit him—she was getting so furious she was actually starting to think about doing it, too. "There was no way I could have stopped him. It's not like he told me what he was planning on doing."

"*I* would have known. I should be taking care of him now."

Chelsea reared back her hand to actually hit him before she remembered where she was and gathered herself, apologizing. "I—uh—I'm sorry, Captain. I—

"Shut up, both of you," the Captain said, pushing herself up from the desk with both hands. "*Enough.* I told you we need to keep this professional."

"You're the one who brought Jonah up," Chelsea snapped, regretting it right away.

"*Yes.*" The Captain smiled, much to Chelsea's relief, and retook her seat. "That's true. But only as insurance that you two will remain professional. As long as you do, I do. You don't want this world here to start affecting your personal life. Believe me. It always seems to get ugly when business and the personal cross paths in One."

Chelsea shook her head, trying not to cry. She knew Tom was going to fuck this up for her somehow. She had to do everything in her power to make sure he didn't.

"Yes, sir," Tom said. "I understand."

"And you agree to follow orders like a good protector?" the Captain asked.

Chelsea stared at Tom, dreading the answer.

"I would never do anything to hurt Jonah," he finally said, not making eye contact with either of them.

"Good," the Captain said, smiling. "That's all I needed to know. I'm guessing you can't wait to hear what I have in store for you, then. Am I right?"

Neither Tom nor Chelsea answered, both tired of her games, no doubt.

"Well, it's pretty simple, really. We've found the masterminds behind the terrorist attacks—including the latest, Pardy, the one you were instrumental in putting an end to."

Chelsea nodded.

"What does that have to do with us?" Tom asked.

"I'm getting there, Pardy," the Captain said, hesitating. "Uh—*er*, Pardy Two. That's going to get confusing, isn't it? Either way, you two, Pardy and Pardy Two, are going to go undercover to apprehend or assassinate—your choice—the Sixer trash that was responsible."

"Assassinate?" Chelsea said. That was escalating things

rather quickly considering this was only her first day out of the desk job.

"Your choice," the Captain repeated, shrugging. "That's why I said *or*. Apprehend *or* assassinate. Though assassination's not as expensive, assuming you are successful. None of those storage fees, you know. *Ha ha*!"

"But why us?" Tom asked.

"*You*," the Captain said, looking at Tom, "because you already know the targets."

"Anna and Rosa," he said, shaking his head.

"The very same," the Captain said with a big smile. "They are responsible for your attempted assassination of then Lord Walker. They orchestrated the attack which you, Pardy One, just helped to foil. And they no doubt had a hand in the Christmas bombing of the walls between Five and Six."

"But why *us*?" Chelsea complained, still unable to believe how far Tom was pulling her into paying for his mistakes. "I've been sitting behind a desk for the entirety of my very short career and *he's* been dishonorably discharged once already. There has to be somebody better you could choose for this job."

The Captain chuckled. "Oh, there are plenty of protectors who are better trained or more experienced, and they could no doubt perform much better under the given circumstances. That's not a question. But sadly, they're all preoccupied with other—more above board, shall we say—missions. If I had the luxury of going to them, then trust me, I wouldn't be here arguing with you two to do it."

"And how are we supposed to trust you when you killed Rabbit?" Tom asked, and Chelsea cringed again at his use of the royal "we".

The Captain laughed. "Alright now, Pardy Two. It's not the time to be bringing up nonsense like that. You're in no position to say anything about Rabbit—or anything else that went on that day, as a matter of fact."

"They didn't have any guns," Tom said and Chelsea was on the verge of hitting him again. Didn't he care at all about Jonah? If he did, he wouldn't be arguing with the Captain after the threats she had made.

"If they didn't have guns then, they do by now, boy," the Captain snapped, sneering. "You keep bringing up ancient history that it would be in your best interest for everyone to forget. The less we remember about it the less we're reminded of *your* traitorous and unforgivable actions which we have yet to sufficiently punish you for. Do you understand me, Pardy Two?"

"Then why am I here if my actions are—" Tom started to say, but Chelsea couldn't take any more.

"Shut up, Tom!" she yelled, slapping his arm. "Fuck! Don't you care about your son at all?"

"I—*uh*—" Tom looked hurt. "Of course I do. I—"

"Then act like it and shut the fuck up. It's that simple."

The Captain chuckled, shaking her head. At least she seemed to be enjoying this. "You know, Pardy One's giving you some good advice there, boy. You'd do right to listen to her."

"But—" Tom protested.

"*No buts*," Chelsea said, shooting him one last look which he finally acquiesced to.

"Well, do you two lovebirds finally have that out of your system?" the Captain asked to no response. "Good. You've had a rough day—the both of you—so I'll try not to get too angry over your insolence. For now you two need to go ahead back to your quarters and get some rest. We'll be expecting you bright and bushy tailed at oh six hundred hours tomorrow morning. Your mission can't wait any longer than that, I'm afraid."

Chelsea nodded. "Sir, yes, sir." She could definitely use the rest and some time alone to process the day's occurrences.

"And what about you, Pardy Two? Can you handle that?"

"I haven't been assigned any quarters, sir," Tom said, trying to avoid eye contact with Chelsea who did not like the sound of what was coming next.

"No, Pardy," the Captain said. "You haven't. And you won't be. You'll be staying with Pardy. There's limited space with all our new recruits, and this is the best we can do for you—all things considered."

Chelsea scoffed, shaking her head. So much for having no family when you were on the force. "I won't—"

"You will do as I order," the Captain cut her off, slamming a hand on the desk. "I thought we've been over this already. Or do you not care about your Jonah either?"

The way the Captain said "Jonah" sparked a fire inside of

Chelsea which took all of her willpower to contain. She didn't dare speak for fear that opening her mouth would let it all out in one burning, explosive burst. Instead she just nodded.

"Good," the Captain said, turning to look out her window. "Then get out of my sight. I need my own rest. I don't want to see another Pardy's face again until the mission tomorrow. You got that?"

Chelsea stood and stomped out of the room without waiting for Tom to follow. She had taken care of enough of his problems for him, he could find his own way in the worlds from now on. The elevator doors were sliding closed between them when he stuck his arm inside, just in time to pry them open.

Tom stood in the now open doors sheepishly, not making eye contact, trying to put on that puppy dog face he always used when he knew he was in trouble, but being cute wasn't going to get him out of this one. "Well, are you getting in or do you plan on standing there all night?" Chelsea snapped.

Tom stepped in, still avoiding eye contact, still making puppy dog eyes, still without a word.

"*Quarters*," Chelsea said, staring straight ahead at the closed too late elevator doors while the floor fell out from underneath them.

Neither Pardy said a word before the freefall stopped and the elevator doors dinged open. Chelsea marched down into her door near the end of the hall, slamming it shut before Tom could catch up. She went to order a meal out of the printer in the kitchen—one continuous room along with the entryway/living room—and Tom came in to take a seat on the couch.

"I don't see why you're so mad at me," Tom said after a short time of silence, only filled by Chelsea's ordering from the printer.

Chelsea scoffed as she took her food out of the printer and into the living room to sit behind her dinner tray, in her favorite chair, and watch some TV while she ate.

"It's not like I wanted any of this to happen," Tom said. "I only did what I thought was best for Jonah."

Chelsea dropped her fork on her plate and stared at Tom, shaking her head. "You've got to be kidding me."

"Of course I'm not kidding you. I did what I thought was best for Jonah. What else—"

"What else?" Chelsea scoffed. *"Let's see...* What else, besides throwing your life away by attempting to assassinate a Lord and retainer, could you have done to keep your son safe? Well, *Amaru,* Tom. I don't know. That's a hard one." She tapped her chin and crossed her eyes to drive the sarcasm home. Even Tom couldn't be dense enough to miss that.

"Well, of course it sounds stupid when you put it like that," Tom said, looking genuinely hurt. "But it wasn't like that at the time. You weren't there. It jus—I—It seemed like the right thing to do, the best thing to do at the time."

Chelsea scoffed. "And does it still?"

Tom shook his head. "I can't answer that, you know. I mean, I'm different now. I've seen how things turn out if I attempt the assassination, but that's not to say that things couldn't be worse right now if I hadn't done what I did in the first place."

Chelsea chuckled despite her anger. "I don't see how they could be much worse than they are now, Tom." She went back to eating her food and half-watching the TV.

"It's not that bad is it?" Tom asked. "At least we're together, you and me." He smiled an unconvincing smile.

"And what about our son?" Chelsea asked, standing and throwing her mostly untouched meal down the trash chute. "Jonah is the most important thing in my life, the only thing that matters to me at all anymore. Don't you understand that?"

"Of course I do. He's all that matters to me, too. It's not like I asked to come back here. If I had a choice, I'd be back at home with him."

Chelsea shook her head, not sure of the implications of what she was hearing. Had he had a choice before then? Did he throw his life away on purpose, so he could get out of the Force? Who was this person she was talking to, and where was the Tom she had married? "Then why are you here?" she demanded, getting heated. "You've been able to do a pretty good job of keeping yourself off the force up until now."

"None of this was on purpose, okay. I made some stupid decisions, and I got kicked out, and now they installed a draft so I'm back in. They kick me out when I want to be here and they bring me back in when I want to leave. What am I supposed to do, huh? I'm just a lowly Officer with no say in the matter."

Chelsea shook her head. "You're supposed to protect your family," she said. "*Your son.*" But with as little agency as she had been able to enact for herself since she'd become a protector, Chelsea was starting to understand where Tom was coming from—even if she still wasn't ready to forgive him for his actions.

"There's no use in arguing about it, anyway," Tom said. "We're here now and we can't do anything about that. We might as well try to make the best of what we do have."

"Which isn't much," Chelsea said.

"Which is each other."

Chelsea really looked at Tom for what must have been the first time since she had left home to become a protector. She pictured him as he was back then on that day, standing next to Jonah, shaking his head, pleading with her to stay, trying to lie to himself that they could make a good life for Jonah on a two housekeeper income. He had taken it worse than Jonah who just stood there, still as a toy soldier, and when she went to hug her boy and say goodbye, he stepped back and ticked off a salute. She almost lost it then. Back then, when Jonah had saluted, leaving her no choice but to salute back then turn around and leave him, and just then, when the look of Tom's puppy dog eyes sent the memory of it all rushing back to her in pictures and sounds. She fought the tears off both times, though, this second time staring coldly into Tom's eyes to say, "We don't have anyone, Tom. You heard the Captain. We have no family now, only the Force."

"Well that didn't stop her from holding Jonah hostage to blackmail us with, though, did it?"

"No," she said, shaking her head. "You're right about that."

"That's because we do have a family, no matter what they say. And no matter how hard they try to split us apart, we'll always stick together." He paused, waiting for a response, but Chelsea didn't have one. She still didn't know how much she could trust Tom after what she had been through because of his mistakes. "For Jonah," Tom added and the tears finally won out on Chelsea.

She stood and walked away from Tom, hiding in her bathroom to keep her weeping secret. Tom would just try to comfort her if he saw her crying, and she didn't want to feel his comforting touch just as much she did want to. She still wasn't ready to forgive him, though, so didn't won out over did. Her crying under control, she fixed her hair in the bathroom mirror, tying her ponytail tighter, then went back to sit in the living room and watch TV, avoiding eye contact with Tom again.

"What do you think she did with him?" Chelsea asked after a few minute's silence, turning off the TV but still staring at the black mirror that was left in place of whatever police procedural was on the screen before.

"I don't know." Tom shook his head, shrugging. "Nothing yet. I hope. She seemed to have treated him well when he was arrested."

Chelsea cringed. She had almost forgotten about the arrest with Jonah's new danger. "How could you let him do that?" she demanded again, still not satisfied with the conclusion of their earlier, more public, argument.

"How could I stop him?" Tom asked. "His partner was out there, too, you know. Are you calling her father a bad parent, or are you just calling me one?"

"No, well, but I—"

"You would have been asleep the same as me," Tom went on over her. "You would have been left to wait and react the same as I was. It wasn't my fault. Children will be children, and there's no changing that."

"No, well—" Chelsea hesitated. Tom almost had a point. *Almost*. "If you hadn't gotten mixed up with that Sixer trash in the first place, Jonah never would have had a reason to go to the holding cells. So the situation might not have been the result of bad parenting directly, but it was your fault in the end anyway."

Chelsea braced for a response but none ever came. Tom just sat staring at his feet and shaking his head. Chelsea felt guilty for hurting him like that, but only for a moment, then she remembered that he deserved it. "Well," she said. "What do you have to say for yourself?"

"Nothing," Tom said, still staring at his feet. "There's nothing I can say. You're right about that."

Chelsea should have been happy to finally hear him admit to being wrong, but for some reason, it only made her feel worse, more guilty, as if she were kicking him while he were down. "Then what were you thinking when you did it?" she asked.

"I thought I was protecting Jonah," Tom said, his voice on

the verge of breaking. "I thought it was for the best."

Chelsea couldn't stay mad at him any longer. She crossed to take a seat on the couch next to Tom and pat his back. "You had no choice," she said, trying to reassure him. "They take control of your entire life here. It was the Protector Force that made you do it. That's why they call it a *force*." She tried to chuckle even though she thought the joke was even stupider the second time around.

"The Force may have been the reason I killed that girl's mom, but they had nothing to do with the rest of it. That was all me."

"No, but—" It was true. It was all Tom's fault, but she didn't want to rub that fact in his face any further than she already had. Tom had suffered enough for it already, just as she had. "But you wouldn't have ever met that girl if you weren't forced to kill her mother, right? So maybe they did kind of forced you into it."

Tom shook his head, staring at the floor, and Chelsea found herself grasping for anything she could say that would make him feel better. Nothing seemed adequate. Then she remembered the rest of her day. She remembered all she had been through, even before the Captain had brought up the danger her son was in, before Jonah's danger wiped every other concern from her mind, and she knew what she had to say. She let go of Tom's hand and tried to stare at the same point on the white vinyl floor that he was staring at. "I killed someone today," she said.

Out of her peripheral vision she saw Tom staring at her in horror. "No," he said.

She nodded. "Yes."

She had expected a barrage of questions to avoid, but Tom just shook his head in silence. After some time of it, mulling the incident over in her head, she finally said, "How did it feel when you…"

"When I killed her?" Tom finished Chelsea's sentence for her. "When I killed Ansel's mom?"

Chelsea only nodded. They didn't need many words after so long together.

"What was it like for you?" Tom asked.

Chelsea thought back to the scene at the precinct. It seemed like it was a million miles away and eons ago. It probably was, even though it was only an elevator ride away and earlier that day. She looked down at her hands and could almost see the blood that was never really there. She felt the gun recoiling and remembered the euphoria as the bullet she had fired ended one of those scumbag's reign of terror once and for all.

Euphoria? No. She couldn't have.

She had just killed someone. Human beings weren't supposed to feel euphoria at—

"Well?" Tom urged her on.

"I asked you first," Chelsea said, trying to deflect the attention from herself.

"I felt like I wanted to throw up," Tom said, shaking his head with a disgusted look on his face—the one he always used to wear when he was changing Jonah's diapers. "It was the most horrible experience in my entire life, and I will never do it again. No matter what the Force threatens."

"You'd even risk our son?" Chelsea asked, trying to ignore the fact that Tom had reacted to killing the way that she had thought she would have before she knew better, the way she thought she should have even though she hadn't.

"Of course not," Tom said. "Why do you think I'm here right now? But I'll do everything in my power to make sure I never have to kill again. You've done it yourself. You know what it feels like to kill someone. Don't you think the same?"

Chelsea pictured the scene. The adrenaline rushed through her body from even replaying it in her brain. She was there again, firing those same shots, and she didn't feel the same way he did. She would go back and do it again if she had the chance. Again and again, even. She longed for a gun in her hand. She couldn't wait for tomorrow when she could put her newfound joy into practice.

"No," Tom said, standing from the couch and backing away from Chelsea into the kitchen. "You've got to be kidding me."

Chelsea realized she was smiling and wiped it off. "What?"

"You—you enjoyed it, didn't you? You would do it again if they asked you to."

"*I* did what was best for Jonah," Chelsea snapped. She didn't know why she felt the need to defend herself against the worst parent and protector in the history of existence, but she went on anyway. "I did what was best for the Force."

"*You killed someone.*"

"Someone who deserved it. I killed someone who would

have killed me if they had the chance. I did what I had to do."

Tom shook his head. "There had to have been a better way."

Chelsea scoffed. "Says the failed assassin. You've got to be kidding me. Who are you to give me lessons on morality?"

"But I know that what I did was wrong. I've admitted to that. You, you're—"

"I'm protecting our son," Chelsea said, stomping a foot. "I'm doing what you should have been doing all along. You can shut up about it and sleep on the couch, but I'm tired of listening to you. Good night."

Tom tried to protest, but Chelsea wasn't having any more. She stormed into her bedroom and slammed the door behind her. He'd just have to wait until after the mission if he wanted to discuss the matter further.

ଧ   ✄   ଥ

LV. Ansel

"I asked you first," the boy said, standing from where he had been knocked down by Ansel and brushing himself off. She could see that he was a boy now and that he was wearing a long white coat just like the Scientist's.

"So," Ansel said, picking up her rucksack and wishing she had come up with a better response than "So".

"So?" The boy scoffed. "So you should answer first, that's what. It's common courtesy."

"And what if I don't answer you at all?" Ansel asked, crossing her arms, stuck in this ridiculous line of reasoning because of her earlier one word response. "What if I don't trust that you'll answer my question in return?"

The boy laughed now, but when Ansel gave him a look he stopped. "Wait," he said. "You're serious? Why wouldn't I? Sharing information costs me nothing and maybe you could do something useful with the knowledge. As to why you wouldn't give me your name, I don't see any good reason for you not to. I mean, our conversation would certainly be more productive if we knew each other's names. Don't you think?"

Ansel couldn't argue with that. She wasn't quite sure why she was arguing in the first place. Maybe she just didn't want to trust anybody anymore. "I'm Ansel," she said with a shrug.

"Hello, Ansel," the boy said, holding out a gloved hand for her to shake. "I'm Ashley."

Ansel scoffed. "Ashley?"

"Yes, well, I answered your question, didn't I? That's my name. So what's the problem?"

"Well, that's a..." Ansel didn't know how to else to say it so she just put it bluntly. "That's a girl's name and you're a boy."

"I'm not a boy!" Ashley insisted, crossing his arms and tapping one foot.

Ansel couldn't argue with that, either. She knew how much she hated it when people tried to tell her she was a girl when she knew she wasn't one, and now here she was doing the same exact thing to this bo—*eh*—*er*—Ashley. "I'm—*uh*—I'm sorry," she stuttered. "I didn't mean to... *I'm just sorry.*"

"Good," Ashley said, nodding and uncrossing his arms. "And in the future don't go around assuming things when you only have limited evidence. You'll end up making a bigger fool of yourself than you already have." He picked up a heavy bag and strapped it over one shoulder, making to lug it away and leave Ansel behind without another word.

"*Uh*, wait," Ansel said, stopping him. He looked pretty irritated to be standing there with the heavy bag over his shoulder. "Where are you going?" she asked. "Where are we now?" She hadn't taken the time to look around before, but now that she did, she was a little unsettled by the place. They were standing in a long, dark, slightly curved tunnel with cement walls and metal grating for a floor. Maybe going through that seam wasn't such a good idea after all. It didn't look like she'd be able to find food or water anywhere near this tunneled labyrinth of caves, and her minimal supplies were only enough to last a day or so at most.

"I'm going home," Ashley said, his voice straining against the weight on his shoulder. "My shift's over and you're here to relieve me. So on that note, goodbye." He started to walk again, his feet clanging on the metal grating with every heavy step.

"Wait, relieve you?" Ansel said, rushing over and taking his bag off his shoulder to let it fall with an echoing bang on the metal floor. "What are you talking about?"

Ashley groaned. "You've got to be kidding me. You have been through training, haven't you? Let me guess, you don't even have your own interface."

"I have no idea what you're talking about." Ansel shrugged. "I don't even know what an interface is."

"*Great.*" Ashley sighed, bending over to open his bag and fish a big heavy computer tablet out of it. "Just what I needed. You know, I don't get enough credit to waste my time training newbies. I have other shit to do."

"I don't need any—"

"Look. It's okay. You can use mine this once, but you have to bring it back to me right after your shift. You got it?"

"Would you listen to me?" Ansel said, stomping her foot with a loud clang. "I don't have any shift. I don't need any training.

And I'm *not* here to relieve you. I just need you to tell me where I am and how I can get out of this stupid tunnel."

Ashley stared at her, blank faced, taken aback by Ansel's aggressiveness and finally at a loss for words.

"Well..." Ansel said. "You had answers for everything else. Why not this?"

"I—*uh*— Who are you now?" Ashley asked, taking a step back from her.

"I'm Ansel. I already told you that. Now it's your turn. *Where* am I?"

"How did you get here if you don't know where you are?" Ashley asked, taking another step back. "Who are you?"

"*I'm Ansel,*" Ansel repeated. "How many times do I have to tell you? I came through the seams the elevators travel through and now I'm here. Where is here, and how do I get out of this stupid cement tunnel?"

"*The seams.*" Ashley said, excited, stepping forward now and apparently over his initial fears. "What seams? What are you talking about?"

"I don't know how to explain it," Ansel said. "The seams between the edges of the worlds. I think it's the same sort of way an elevator travels between them."

"But you didn't take the elevator?" He was putting the interface, or whatever, into his bag now and fishing some other foreign tool out of it. "You walked through the fields without any protection?" He waved a little beeping and flashing wand in front of her, apparently communicating some meaning to Ashley who was staring at it rather than Ansel as he spoke.

"No elevator," Ansel said. "Not this time. I hate those things. And besides, do you see any elevator doors around here?"

"Of course not," Ashley said, still scanning her with the wand. "But you could have ridden an elevator near here then walked the rest of the way."

"Hey, cut that out!" Ansel pushed the wand away and stepped back from Ashley now. "All I need to know is how to get out of these stupid tunnels, alright. Leave your little beeping scanner doohickies for someone else."

Ashley chuckled. "Doohickies? Hardly. If you came through the fields unprotected, there's no telling what you passed through—

or for that matter, what passed through you. This here little *doohickey* might just save your life. Now, can you read this?" He held the wand too close to her face for her to see anything.

Ansel snatched it out of his hand to get a better look. "Sonic Scanner," she read.

"Good. Very good," Ashley said, snatching the scanner back. "That means you have no spatial distortions. You came out facing the same way as you were when you went in. Getting flipped around's not a fatal outcome, of course, but it would be rather annoying to deal with if you ask me."

"Whatever." Ansel sighed. "I've had about enough of this examination. If you're not going to show me which way is out, I'll just find it on my own. Good bye and good riddance." She stomped loudly down the dark tunnel, picking a direction at random.

"*Uh*, I wouldn't go that way," Ashley said, re-packing his bag and hefting it up over his shoulder. "The security bots will stop you if you try. I'm surprised they haven't noticed you yet as it is. Come on. Let's go this way. I'll show you."

Ansel hesitated, not sure if she wanted to trust this guy just yet—she had made plenty of judgement errors in deciding who to trust lately and she didn't need to add another mistake to that list—but in the end she didn't really have a choice either way.

"We'll get something to eat, too," Ashley said, starting his slow trudge up the tunnel and limping from the weight of his bag over one shoulder. "Come on. We have so much to talk about."

Ansel hesitated again but only for show this time. She knew he was her best bet in finding out where she was, whether she trusted him or not. After a moment's wait to let him think she wasn't too eager to join him, she jogged to catch up and followed him to an elevator.

"I hate these things," Ansel said as the doors slid closed.

"I love them," Ashley said, dropping his bag with a thud. "Dorms, please."

"Dorms?" Ansel said, and her stomach grumbled—she wasn't sure if it was out of hunger or because the floor falling out from underneath her made the butterflies in her stomach scatter.

"Don't worry," Ashley said. "It's not like I'm inviting you up to my room or anything. You can wait in the lobby. I just have to drop this bag off. It's too—*ugh*—heavy." He lifted it up on his shoulders with a huff as the doors slid open.

Ansel tried to say that she could take care of herself whether it was in the lobby, in his bedroom, or anywhere else in all the worlds, but she couldn't form words when she saw what the elevator doors opened onto. This was no lobby. It couldn't be. It was outside. It looked like the wilderness with the endless mountains she had just escaped from, like a tiny patch of the green belt without the skyscraper walls closing it in on either side.

"Well, come on," Ashley said, already on his way through the grass. "There's a bench by the bubble. You can wait for me there if you don't want to come up to my room. Let's go."

Ansel forced her jaw shut and hurried to catch up. "This is the lobby?" she asked, stupidly, regretting it instantly.

"That it is. Pretty lame, huh? But it could be worse."

"Worse?" What was this guy talking about? He didn't know how good he had it. "Are there any animals?"

"*Ugh*. Yes. Tons of squirrels and rabbits. And beware, they *will* charge at you for any little crumb of food. They've gotten pretty mean lately, but they usually stick by the pond so as long you stay away from there, you should be safe."

"There's a pond?"

"Well, duh," Ashley chuckled, setting his bag on a little bench under a huge oak tree that was hung with ivy. "This isn't Pennbrook. We have some class here. Though—what am I saying?—there's no telling where you come from. You probably have no idea at all what I'm blathering on about, do you? Here. You wait right here and I'll be right back." He hefted up his bag one more time and carried it into a little glass bubble near the bench. The doors of the bubble slid closed and the translucent thing carried Ashley up into the sky to disappear behind the fluffy white clouds.

Ansel set her rucksack on the bench then sat beside it to take in this new wilderness. It seemed larger than the one she had come from, but maybe that was only because there was no mountain to give her perspective. There were no hills at all, in fact, only flat ground and trees too thick to see through in every direction. It didn't really seem like a forest, though. It was more like a bunch of trees.

Ansel stood and paced in front of the bench, getting anxious. What was taking this kid so long and when was someone going to figure out that she didn't belong there? There weren't many people around, sure, and plenty of space for them to spread out into, but the few that Ansel did see were all wearing the same long white coat that Ashley was—like it was some kind of uniform or something. It made Ansel feel self-conscious about the new jeans and t-shirt that had so shortly ago made her feel more comfortable than she'd ever felt wearing clothes.

Where was she anyway? *Ugh.*

Maybe she shouldn't wait for this Ashley kid to come back, after all. She had promised herself to be more careful about trusting strangers, and here she was waiting for one to come and take her who knows where. Maybe she should just go find that pond he was talking about and hunt those squirrels and rabbits, whatever they were. They probably tasted good. Why else would someone stock this wilderness with them?

She had gathered her rucksack and decided to go do just that when the bubble came back down out of the sky, carrying Ashley in his long white coat. "You're not planning on ditching me, are you?" he asked as the pod doors slid open. "I've got so many questions I need to ask you before you go."

Well, she *was* planning on ditching him, but it was too late for that now. "Nah," she lied. "I saw you coming. I was just getting ready."

"Let's go, then," Ashley said. "You said you were hungry, right? Well come on." He waved her on back toward the elevator they had ridden in on. Getting into it after him, Ansel noticed the elevator was in a wooden shack just like the elevator in the wilderness outside of the Scientist's window. In fact, the shack looked like an exact replica. "Dining Hall," Ashley said as the doors closed, and his stomach grumbled while the elevator fell into motion. "I guess I'm pretty hungry myself," he said with a blush.

The elevator stopped and the doors opened onto a huge dining room filled with long tables that were half empty. The floor was white vinyl, the tables and chairs were silvery and metallic, and every single person besides Ansel was wearing a long white coat.

"Well, come on," Ashley said after some time of Ansel staring at the scene from the safety of the elevator. "Let's get some food, then we can talk."

"I don't know," Ansel said, hesitating, still standing in the elevator door and preventing it from closing. "I don't feel right. I wish I had one of those white coats. I look like a Street orphan trying to pass herself off as a Day Schooler."

Ashley looked at her as if he hadn't even known she were wearing clothes until she mentioned them. "Well, I don't know," he said. "I didn't even notice they were different." But now that she had pointed it out, Ansel could tell that he couldn't stop noticing.

"Well, someone will notice," Ansel said. "And when they do, it won't be hard to figure out that I don't belong here. Then what would they do with me? I don't need any protectors ruining my plans."

"Protectors?" Ashley chuckled. "Protectors haven't existed since 3D printers were invented. There's no need for them anymore. They're ancient history. I promise. You don't have anything to worry about. Now come on out of that elevator, someone's probably trying to use it."

Ansel scoffed. "Then the 3D printer hasn't been invented yet," she said. "I've seen protectors and I know they exist. You can fuck with them if you want to, but I'm getting out of here so I don't get caught. Doors close."

The elevator doors tried to close but Ashley stuck his arm inside to stop them before they could. "Wait," he said. "Hold on a second. You see, that kind of information is exactly what I want to talk to you about. You can't leave."

"Well I'm not going in there looking like this," Ansel said, crossing her arms. "I won't do it. That would be stupid and dangerous."

"*Hmmm.*" Ashley thought about it for a moment. "Okay, well, here." He started to take off his jacket. "Take mine. You'll look like you belong here so no one will mess with you, and I actually do so it won't matter if they try messing with me." He held out the jacket with a smile.

Ansel hesitated. She wasn't sure his logic was sound, but she was getting pretty hungry and she still had no idea where she was or where she was trying to get to. "Alright. *I guess,*" she said, begrudgingly taking the coat and slipping it on. It fit her perfectly and smelled like something attached to a distant memory she couldn't quite put her finger on. "But if anyone starts acting suspicious, I'm out of here."

"And I won't stop you," Ashley said with a big smile. "You

say the word and I'll show you back to the seam where I found you—or you found me—whatever."

Ansel nodded. "Good. Let's go get some food then."

He led her between the tables, and at first Ansel was still worried that she was going to be found out, but she came to recognize that no one there was paying any attention to her. They were all too busy with their own lives, doing their own things. Some were arguing with one another—across tables and up and down them—about a subject matter that must have been important from the tones of their voices. Peppered among the debaters, sitting at tables all alone even if sitting right next to one another in body, were others who furiously clicked and typed on tiny computer screens, working on something equally as important as the debates going on around them. None of them from either group were really even eating, it seemed, and those who were only did it with one hand or through a mouth full of words, more worried about subjects far beyond basic human needs for nourishment.

The line they waited in for food was short and quick. Each person ordered the same thing without thinking, and the printer dashed it off, no questions asked. When it was their turn to order, Ashley said, "One special, and a—*uh*…" and he looked to Ansel.

She froze. She didn't know what she wanted to eat. She never knew. There were always way too many things to choose from, and she had no way of knowing what this Ashley might think was weird food to order. Before she went into full meltdown mode, agonizing over the decision, Ansel went with the only thing she could think of, the same choice she usually made during anxiety breakdowns, following the crowd. "Same," she said.

"And one special," Ashley said with a grin. The printer hummed into motion and soon Ashley was handing Ansel a tray and leading the way to a table. He started to sit at one that was already filled with people until Ansel urged him to move to a more secluded area. Even with the jacket she didn't really feel comfortable being out there in the open like that.

"So," Ashley said through a bite of his sandwich, the same sandwich Ansel was chewing on. The special was apparently the same meal she had gotten for lunch when she let the 3D printer order for her in the Scientist's kitchen: soup and a sandwich. "I have so much to ask you I don't even know where to start."

Ansel scoffed, poking at her sandwich. She should have ordered wild game, that was what she really wanted to eat, not this sliced, pre-made cold sandwich. "How about you start by answering some of my questions," she said.

"Splendid idea," Ashley said, spitting a little half-chewed bit of food across the table in his excitement. "Your questions should be as informative as my answers. Even more so, probably."

"Well, okay," Ansel said, stirring her soup. She didn't really believe what he said, but she didn't mind the flattery. "So where am I?"

"Where are you? *Hmmm.*" Ashley dropped his sandwich, really thinking about the question. "That all depends on how you mean."

"*Ugh.*" This wasn't getting anywhere fast. "What do you mean how I mean? I mean where am I?"

"Well, you're sitting right there aren't you? But that isn't a very useful answer."

"No. It's not. It's a little too obvious."

"*Exactly,*" Ashley said, clapping his hands. "Too specific. Already known. I could say you're in the dining hall of Tulane Advanced STEM Academy, too, but that would be equally useless for you."

"What's the Tulane Advanced Stem Academy?"

"You hit the nail on the head again." Ashley laughed. "Though technically true, the statement relies on knowledge inaccessible to you, rendering the truth it holds once again moot."

"Oh my God," Ansel said, putting her head down on the table, almost in her soup. "Can you tell me anything useful?"

"God?" Ashley grinned. "Now that's an archaic term. And finally we find some small illumination of the matter at hand. May I ask you a question now? Have you ever heard the word of *Sic bo?*"

Ansel groaned, raising her head to look at him and actually spilling some of her soup with the motion. "I don't know. Is it something useful?"

Ashley chuckled. "About as useful as God most of the time, if you ask me, but in this instance rather useful as it appears to be a key to your origins."

"My origins?"

"Your origins. From the Latin *oriri* meaning to rise, become visible, or appear, sometimes used to mean zero on the Cartesian coordinate plane. Your origin is thus the center or your world, where you came from. So, have you ever heard of *Sic bo*?"

Ansel shook her head.

"And Mother Maria, ruler of fate?"

"What does this have to do with anything?" Ansel complained. "I thought I was supposed to be asking the questions."

"I'll take that as a no, and I'm not surprised by the fact, either. It's further evidence in support of the hypothesis that you, Ansel, are not from this world at all—maybe not even from this country or time period for all I know, but more evidence is required before making further inferences."

"I'm from the Streets," Ansel said, fighting back unexpected tears from the memory of them. "I don't know what world you're from, and I don't know what a country is, but I do know that *I'm* from the Streets."

"The streets? You see? I mean, is that even in America?"

"What's America?"

Ashley made to speak then stopped. He put a hand to his chin and shook his head. "I— Well, it's— You know... *our country*."

"Whose country?"

"*Us*. The people who live here. The people who think and create here, moving America's technology forward. Who else is there?"

Ansel chuckled. She had no idea what this guy was talking about anymore, and the only way she could respond without lashing out or crying was with laughter. "Who are you even?" she asked.

Ashley had to think about that one, too. "You know," he said after some time. "I've never really pondered that one, either. You ask a lot of questions I've never even thought of. This is amazing."

"Well while you do *ponder* it, maybe you can figure out how to tell me where I am, then more importantly, how to get out of here. I think I'm done with this place."

"*No*," Ashley said without hesitation. "You can't go yet. I have so much to learn."

"Well I'm not learning anything, Ash. So what's the point?"

He smiled wide. "I know how I can explain where you are and maybe find out where you're from at the same time."

Ansel shook her head, not believing him. "And what about

where I want to go?"

"That, too. All of it." He stood fast from his seat, knocking it over with a clang. "Come on. I'll show you." He grabbed Ansel's hand and pulled her to the elevator, leaving her just enough time to grab her rucksack in the process. "Lab," he said when the doors closed behind them.

"Lab?" Ansel said. "No, I'm not going back there."

"Back?" Ashley scoffed. "You've never been to my lab before."

Ansel calmed down, blushing. All this time she had thought that there was only the one lab, the Scientist's Lab, she had no idea it was a general word like kitchen or bedroom.

The elevator doors opened onto a short hall that looked just like the Scientist's. Ansel fought her urge to push Ashley out of the elevator and ride it back to the wilderness lobby where she could live in peace and instead followed him through the hall to the door at the other end.

"Are you ready?" he asked, holding his hand on the doorknob.

Ansel nodded

Ashley opened the door to reveal a room that looked exactly like the Scientist's office—the smaller one Ansel had only been in a few times—but instead of looking out onto a line of assembly line workers, the window here looked out onto the same scene as the window in Rosalind's giant office—the wilderness scene with the endless mountains which Ansel had climbed over and over and over before travelling through the seams to literally run into Ashley.

"So what do you think?" Ashley asked, scurrying to the desk where he flipped on the big bank of monitors—just like the Scientist's only a little smaller.

"I've seen better," Ansel said, casually strolling to stand behind him and drop her bag. "That view's kind of played out, isn't it?"

"I like the mountain," Ashley said, defensively, still typing and clicking at the computer. "It reminds me of Sisyphus. I could only imagine what it would look like to stand atop that mountain."

Ansel scoffed. "I don't know what Sisyphus is, but it's not that great of a view up there. It's kind of annoying, really, to see all those mountains and know that you'll never be able to climb them all. And I'm telling you that from experience."

Ashley stopped typing to turn and stare at her. "No," he said, jaw dropped. "You haven't. You couldn't have. That would mean that you—"

"*I did*," Ansel said, smiling and nodding, proud of herself. "That's where I came from when I ran into you." She pointed out the window. "I stood on that mountaintop before I traveled unprotected through the elevator seams into your tunnels."

"No way. *Uh uh*. Impossible," Ashley said, clicking and typing away again. "Look at this." A complicated diagram came up on the bank of screens. Ansel wasn't sure, but it looked kind of like a three dimensional map. "There's only one way into that sector and it's too heavily guarded for anyone to get into or out of, much less both."

"Well I did," Ansel said, beaming—and blushing a little bit, becoming a little full of herself for some reason. "Now how do I get back?"

"You don't." Ashley scoffed. "I don't even know how you claim to have gotten in there in the first place, but it's out of the question to go back."

"That's shit," Ansel complained. "You told me you could help me find where I wanted to go. I want to go back there, to where I can at least hunt for my own food. So are you going to help me do it or what?"

"Hunt for food? Now you're really crazy."

"I am not, and I don't care what you think. I'm leaving." Ansel stormed out of the room but she didn't emerge into the hallway. She would have complained about how hard those stupid doors were to operate, but she was distracted by what she saw. The room she had gone into was filled with the same type of glassware she had seen in the Scientist's big lab, these vials and beakers filled with variously colored chemicals in different states of matter— Rosalind had already taught Ansel a little bit about chemistry in her short stay with them. Ansel rushed over to get a closer look at a particularly bright red concoction that was boiling, steaming, and mixing with a colorless gas to form a new green liquid, when Ashley rushed up and pulled her back from the table. "Be careful," he said. "I've been working on that set up for weeks. Don't mess it up."

"What is it?"

"Chemistry homework. I *hate* chemistry." He grimaced. "I don't see how it's ever supposed to be useful for a spatial physics major, but they make us all take the basic science classes and that includes the worst of them, chemistry."

Ansel scoffed. "This is basic?"

Ashley blushed. "Yeah, well, I got held back in my first few attempts. *None of those being my fault, of course.*"

"But what are you doing?" Ansel asked, ignoring his embarrassment.

"Making some inorganic something or other. *Ugh.* I can't even remember anymore. Does it matter?"

"*Uh... Yeah,*" Ansel said. "It's pretty much the coolest thing you've shown me since I've been here."

"My homework? Wow. You know, there's a lot cooler stuff around here. You should see the zoo. We have actual four dimensional animals, though all you can really see are their projections on our 3D space, of course."

"Zoo?"

Ashley laughed. "Yeah, you know, a place where they keep animals to look at. It's much better than stupid chemistry, and it'll help me explain where you are. Come on. It's not going to make sense until I show you."

Ansel didn't want to leave the shimmering colorful glass paradise, but she would like to see some strange new animals—and maybe even figure out what that long eared rat she had eaten in the shade of the endless mountain was. She followed Ashley down the hall and into the elevator where he said, "Zoo."

"So you just keep the animals caged up or something?" Ansel asked. "Is it so they're easier to eat?"

"Eat?" Ashley chuckled. "Mother Maria, no. Of course not. It's so we can study them. And preserve most of them, really. There aren't many species that aren't endangered these days."

Ansel nodded, not entirely sure what he meant, but at the same time not wanting to make a fool of herself. She thought she could understand the word species from context clues—it was a type of animal—but endangered was a little more difficult. Ansel knew what danger was—probably a lot more so than this white coated kid would ever understand it—but she still had no idea what it meant to be endangered. Was she endangered every time she was in danger? It was better she didn't ask so she could save herself from sounding like an idiot. She'd try to pick up more clues as to what the word meant when they got to this *zoo*.

The elevator doors slid open to reveal another wilderness scene but this one packed denser with dark leaved trees all hung with vines. Ansel stepped out onto the soft soil of a dirt path and stared up at the canopy where the sun burst through in tiny clumps of rays, giving the canopy the appearance of a green night sky similar to the black one she had seen twinkling over the endless mountain.

"They always bring you to Africa first," Ashley said, leading Ansel along the tiny dirt path that seemed to go on forever in front them. "Every zoo I've ever been to, I swear. They want to hit you with the big stuff right when you enter so you'll be hooked from the start for the rest of a mediocre ride to the grand finale."

"Africa?" Ansel asked, not really interested in his response because she was too distracted by the endless trees and echoing noises which must have belonged to some strange creatures.

Ashley chuckled, stopping in Ansel's way and pointing out to guide her vision through a small clearing in the trees. "*Africa*," he said. "Another country, one with animals like you've never seen before."

There in the clearing was a black cat that looked almost exactly the same as that Mr. Kitty that Ansel had chased ages ago, but this cat was twenty times Mr. Kitty's size. It stood in a hunter's stance, muscles tense and twitching, ears pointed backward, long black tail held flat, and green eyes staring through Ansel's skin to the meat and bones it so wanted to taste underneath. Ansel's muscles tensed up along with the big black cat's, her own hunter's reflexes kicking in, while Ashley didn't seem to care that the thing was staring at them, ready to pounce, when it did.

Ansel let out a shrill scream that didn't make sense—she had meant to yell "Look out!" but the words came out jumbled and unintelligible—and dove to push Ashley out of the hungry beast's way, dreading those sharp, deadly claws which were angling for her jugular.

✄   ✄   ✄

LVI. Mr. Walker

"Waltronics Unlimited is seeing profits rise sky high as riots around the worlds increase demand for friendlier, more compliant employees at an exponential rate," recited the big bald face on the television screen, beads of sweat glistening in the camera lights. "The cost of food and other amenities continues to plummet as cheaper robotic labor drives down profit margins at the benefit of preventing shortages in the luxuries we all need to live."

Mr. Walker chuckled in his bed, the springs bouncing up and down with his behemoth movement. This newscaster knew nothing about the inner workings of the Free Market. He—like all journalists and most owners—was stuck in the fetishism of numbers. He and people like him had a money fetish, but Mr. Walker knew better. Mr. Walker could see beyond the glamour of the gold and green to the true source of money's power: Power.

A bit redundant, sure. He chuckled again. But that's why it was such a powerful realization when he had finally come to it. It was hidden in plain view. He could tell any owner in existence the secret to his success, and each and every one of them would no doubt laugh him off. *The source of money's power is power?* they would say with a wry grin on their faces, not sure if good ol' Mr. Walker was having a jest with them, making a fool, taking the piss. *That's ridiculous. It's a tautology.*

At which point Mr. Walker would smile and nod, still not letting on to whichever owner it was whether he were joking or not. Would he really give his secret away like that? But after all he would decide that it didn't matter if any of them knew the secret because none of them were man enough to wield it anyway, and Mr. Walker would say, "Yes, my boy." Maybe patting him on the back—because it would undoubtedly be a him, the owners were almost invariably men as the secretaries were almost invariably women—but Mr. Walker would pat whoever he was on the back to encourage him on a bit then say, "The source of money's power is power. That is what's truly important in life and in business. That's my secret to success."

Then Mr. Walker's student would mull it over for a bit, unable to tease out the very truth which was so simply and plainly staring him in the face, only to laugh and pat Mr. Walker on the back, saying, *Good one, old Lord. You had me going there for a second.* At which time the poor boy would walk away to the next conversation, forever to be haunted by the spectre of lost opportunity and missed information.

"The Market as a whole is in a steep decline," the sweating bald face on the television droned on mechanically, obviously reading from some eye implant. "Not since the historic rise and crash of the last century have we seen such steep and bracing freefalls in stock prices all across the board."

Mr. Walker laughed out loud now. The fetish was blinding our dear newscaster again, only this time it wasn't simply a fetishism of money but a fetishism of the Market itself. This particular fetish was probably more prevalent and harder to get past than the money fetish. Owners especially loved to hold the Market on high as a separate being worthy of being kept alive for the sake of principal. The Market should exist because it always had existed, was their motto, and who could blame them? For all intents and purposes it was the Market—and money—which gave these owners their power. Or so it appeared.

Mr. Walker knew better, though. He knew better than this idiot newscaster, of course, but better even than any other owner in Inland. That was how he had remained on top for as long as he had. Forever, really, until a minor lapse of attention on his part and one lucky decision—along with some mildly clever colluding with Mr. Angrom, he had to admit—made by the now Lord Douglas. But Mr. Walker was back in the survival mode which had made him Lord, the survival mode which he should have maintained even while on top of the food chain and which he would never come out of again— even when he finally and inevitably did regain his Lordship from the Standing Lord Dougy.

Mr. Walker understood that the Market was nothing more than a means to an end. That was it. It was no magical force. It was no independent actor. It was simply the culmination of billions and billions of tiny independent social interactions, all expressing themselves at the same time in a similar place. Each of countless billions of actors did what they themselves thought would get them most of what they wanted in life, and it was that exact selfishness that was the embodiment of the Market, its driving force.

So what if there were less economic exchanges occurring today than there were yesterday? So what if less wealth changed hands? Mr. Walker still ate fifteen square meals a day—more on weekends—and drank his old fashioneds to top off the night. So what?

It made no difference, but only as long as you hadn't been caught up in the money fetish. Money isn't power. Mr. Walker knew that. Money's only power when it's in style. That's when it can best perform its magic trick illusion. And money's only in style when times are good. When times are rough—when the worlds are rioting and there are plenty of robots to make all the commodities but no humans to buy them up—that's when money loses its flair, the glamour fades, the fetish is revealed. Owners finally see what Fives and Sixes live through their entire lives: money is nothing but symbols. People, food, and electricity form real wealth. Those are the three basics any economy will always need: People, food, electricity. Power, power, power.

"The power went out in one Three neighborhood and they were not pleased," a new voice said on the TV screen and Mr. Walker groaned. The propaganda sector was his least favorite section of Outland and he hated hearing their news. Still, he was deep into Three with this movie business—and only getting deeper as things progressed—so he would have to bear through it.

"We have with us live the one and only Jorah Baldwin—most viewed living actor—for an exclusive interview. So, Jorah, your building is at the heart of the affected area, you're right in the middle of this brown out, is that correct?"

"Brown out?" Jorah said, frowning. Even Mr. Walker, with as little experience as he had in PR, could tell that Jorah's makeup was off, like it had been put on by a broken robot. "What is that supposed to mean? You mean blackout?"

The camera cut to the news caster whose face had turned red, embarrassed. "Oh—*Uh*. I'm sorry. I thought that was— I didn't want to offend you."

Jorah scoffed and the camera cut to him. "Well, the *black*out sucks, and there isn't anything offensive about that, girl. My makeup is likely much more offensive. I had to put it on by hand, *in the dark.* So you can imagine how tough that was. I mean… damn."

"Oh no, you look great," the newscaster said, smiling and nodding—and maybe even flirting a little. Pretty creepy if you asked Mr. Walker. Jorah was *his* property after all. "Tell me, have you been able to get food or water? What about the elevators? Are they running? Are you trapped?"

"Oh, well…" Jorah bit his lip. "I'm afraid I haven't tried the elevator, or gotten hungry for that matter. In fact, all I've done since the blackout is get dressed and prepped for this interview. Which was pretty hard, you know. Did I mention that I had to put my makeup on in the dark?"

"You heard it here fans," the newscaster said, a serious look on his face as he stared into the camera. "They're putting their makeup on manually and in the dark. And in case you were unaware, that is a difficult and annoying task. More in thirty minutes as the story progresses."

Mr. Walker chuckled, wishing he had an old fashioned to sip after that story but not wanting to call Haley for it—really he shouldn't have to call her, she should just predict his every need like a robot was supposed to do. He shook his head, ignoring Haley's incompetence and bouncing up and down in his bed with more laughter. Putting on their makeup in the dark? *Ho ho ho!* That was an apt metaphor for his fellow owners if there ever was one. Mr. Walker, on the other hand, created his own light by which to see. *Power, power, power.* And he was ready to leverage himself into more of it.

Haley came in—*finally*—carrying an old fashioned. Mr. Walker sighed in relief at the sight of the drink but growled in anger at her tardiness. Robots, it seemed, were going out of style, and Mr. Walker needed to get himself positioned on the right side of that divide before anyone else did.

"I thought you might like a drink, sir," Haley said, curtsying by his side table.

"I would have liked a drink five minutes ago," Mr. Walker grumbled. "Now I absolutely need one. *Gimme.*" He snatched the drink out of her hand, spilling some on his nightshirt and the comforter in the process. "Now look what you've done," he snapped, sipping the drink. "Clean it up!"

Haley was already cleaning it. "Yes, sir."

"And you get out of here until it's time for my meeting. I'm not to be disturbed. Do you understand me? I need to prepare."

"Yes, sir." Haley curtsied and left, slamming the door too loudly as she went.

If only Mr. Walker could fire her right then and there. He was so mad he wanted to chuck his glass at the TV but the drink's soothing insobriety and the television's priceless information were both worth too much to him and it would no doubt take Haley far too long to replace them both as it took her far too long to do anything these days. Mr. Walker would simply have to continue biding his time as he had been doing since that fateful day on which he had lost his crown as Lord of Outland.

He was no longer Mr. Walker at all, in fact. Instead becoming Mr. Red Queen, the Sisyphus of playing cards, always running faster and faster just to keep up—not to mention getting ahead—and he would find his way to the top of the deck again no matter what it took.

"The power went out in one Three neighborhood and they were not pleased," the newscaster repeated, and Mr. Walker groaned as they played the same "live" interview with the same poorly made up Jorah. The power was out. Mr. Walker had gotten the point the first time around. This wasn't a news story that needed repeating.

"Haley!" Mr. Walker called. "Haley, dear. Get in here!"

It took her much too long to open the door in a fluster and say, "Yes, sir." with a clumsy curtsy.

"Get my pants, dear. I'm not waiting any longer. We'll take the old boy by surprise. Chop chop, now. Hop to it." He clapped his hands together, jiggling his belly with genuine mirth.

"Yes, sir."

Getting dressed was the same struggle it had been ever since he had gotten this new model of Haley. Mr. Walker couldn't wait until he could finally get rid of the ignorant, useless thing. Perhaps if this meeting went well enough, he could set that process into motion sooner than later. Not before getting the android to find her own human replacement, of course, but soon. He laughed then yelped as the idiot machine pinched his thigh in the restricting pants.

"*Damnit*," he snapped. "Be careful!"

"Yes, sir." Haley curtsied as she worked, pinching him again.

"Sorry, sir."

By the time he was fully dressed Mr. Walker was happy to have summoned Haley as early as he had. If he had waited any longer, her incompetence might have made them late. As it was they were almost five minutes early, which to Mr. Walker was right on time.

They parked in the cheap parking garage—the one that didn't even have reserved owner parking—and Mr. Walker didn't gripe once on the long walk all the way from the bus parking spots to the elevator. In fact, Mr. Walker had even insisted that they hold this meeting at Douglas Towers. He wanted Lord Douglas to feel comfortable on his own turf as they made the negotiations. The more comfortable Lord Douglas was the more likely he was to go along with Mr. Walker's offers. That was Salesmanship 101. If it took parking in bum fuck Egypt with the busses and meeting in an austere conference room, then that was exactly what Mr. Walker was going to do.

Haley made an incessant tapping noise with her feet on the floor of the elevator as they rode it down to the conference room. Mr. Walker was about to yell at her to stop when the elevator doors slid open to reveal Lord Douglas's grinning face waiting in the hall for them. Mr. Walker almost scoffed though he was able to hold it in. If he wasn't mistaken, Lord Douglas's hat had grown noticeably taller since they had last met.

"Wally the Walrus," Lord Douglas said with a smile. "You're just on time, five minutes early. As predictable as a secretary, you are." He chuckled.

"Sometimes I'd wish they were more predictable." Mr. Walker tipped his hat and bowed as low as his pneumatic pants would allow. "But you know that I prefer to treat my business associates with respect, Lord Douglas. Early is on time, on time is late, and late is unforgivable in my book."

"Yes, well in that case, you were early so you were on time so you were late, and that, my friend, is unforgivable in your very own book." Lord Douglas laughed, looking at Haley to join in but Haley only blushed and broke eye contact.

Mr. Walker fumed. What was his robot doing blushing at a single glance from his arch nemesis? What was he doing trying to make a deal with that very same enemy? Why hadn't he spit in the insolent fool's face, marched out of those shabby wannabe towers, and been done with this toxic relationship once and for all?

He smiled, regaining his cool, remembering why he was there, and said, "Of course, Lord." bowing again, but this time not as low and without the hat flourish. "The contradictions are there for anyone to see. It's just wordplay, though. You know what I mean."

"Is it though?" Lord Douglas smiled. "Just word play, I mean. You honestly believe that someone who is not early is not on time, don't you?"

Mr. Walker fiddled with the knob of his cane. He didn't like this line of questioning one bit. He was losing control of the conversation already and they hadn't even started the negotiations. This was going to be a long meeting if it continued on like this, but Mr. Walker had no choice. He had to answer in appeasement if he wanted to keep Lord Douglas on the line. He only wished he had ever actually fished before—rather than seeing it in old movies—so he could better understand the metaphor.

"Yes, well, that's my personal motto," Mr. Walker said with a smile. "I can't hold everyone to it though, of course."

"Yes, so if you're early, you're on time, right?"

"Yes," Mr. Walker said, groaning in his mind. And if I'm on time, I'm late. You've been there already. Get on with it so we can get to where I want to go.

"Then I'm sure you can see where I'm going from here," Lord Douglas said, stepping into the elevator with Mr. Walker who stepped back in surprise to let him on. "But I'm not sure you'll be able to predict where we're going now." Lord Douglas smiled.

The doors slid closed and the elevator fell into motion without another command from Lord Douglas. When the doors reopened Mr. Walker was speechless.

This wasn't the drab gray conference room he had expected. No, this wasn't Lord Douglas's style at all. It couldn't be. It was too grand, too beautiful, too...

The room was a giant office, at least twice as big as Mr. Walker's own. There was a big desk—twice again the size of the desk in Mr. Walker's office—and some fluffy looking chairs that surrounded a side table, all looking out onto a wilderness mountain scene.

"I see you like this office much better than my usual

conference room," Lord Douglas said, already seated in one of the fluffy chairs by the windowwall and indicating for Mr. Walker to take the seat across from him. "I thought it might be a bit more your style."

Mr. Walker tried not to react as he took his seat, but he knew that not reacting was reaction enough for Lord Douglas to discern. "I didn't know you had any taste," Mr. Walker said with a smile. "Even this little," he added, trying to play some small amount of offense in what had become a defensive game for him.

"Well." Lord Douglas shook his head. "I'm afraid I can't take much credit for the decor in here—if any. I pay people to worry about such minor details for me. You know how it goes."

Mr. Walker chuckled, fidgeting in his seat. "Oh, I don't now. I like to do things the old fashioned way myself."

"Oh, I'm sorry," Lord Douglas said, standing from his chair. "Did you need something to drink? I'm such an ungracious host. An old fashioned, though, right? That is your preferred beverage."

"An old fashioned would be just fine," Mr. Walker said.

"Very good, then." Lord Douglas smiled and bowed. "I'll return shortly."

Mr. Walker couldn't believe that Lord Douglas actually left the room to get the drinks himself after showing off with this magnificent office. What kind of madness was he getting at? Lord Douglas had a secretary who Mr. Walker had seen on many occasions, so where was she in all this? Mr. Walker turned around and Haley was still standing there, staring at one of the blank walls instead of out the window. She smiled and feigned a curtsy, conscious of Mr. Walker's gaze, while Mr. Walker just went on wondering what kind of play Lord Douglas was making.

Lord Douglas returned with drinks in hand and gave one to Mr. Walker—who didn't leave his seat to accept it, wanting to reappropriate some control of the situation. "There you are. One old fashioned for you and one for myself. Let us drink together to the Invisible Hand's rule over all our fates." Lord Douglas raised his glass.

Mr. Walker clinked his glass to Lord Douglas's with a smirk. "To the Hand's infinite wisdom," he said

The old fashioned burned hot all the way down Mr. Walker's throat and into his stomach, like nothing he had tasted since

Christmas when the new Haley had come into his life and fucked everything up for him. She wouldn't be in it for much longer, though. Not much longer at all.

"So," Lord Douglas said, setting his empty glass on one of the side tables, unphased by the fire of his own drink. "You came here for a reason, Wally Boy. Let's get down to it."

Mr. Walker chuckled, trying to cover up the burning that was still going on inside his own mouth and stomach. "Of course I did, Douggy. It's always business between us, isn't it?"

Lord Douglas frowned. "Is it, Walrus? You don't consider me a close personal friend?" Even Lord Douglas couldn't keep a straight face saying something as ridiculous as that.

"Am I?" Mr. Walker asked, chuckling himself. "Is that what you're looking for here, a friend?"

"No—*Ha ha*! No, Wally." Lord Douglas put on a straight face again, abruptly halting his laughter. "Not exactly. I'm looking for something more than that."

Mr. Walker felt like he was on the defensive again. He had initiated these negotiations, how had they gotten so far out of hand so quickly? He needed to retake control of the conversation and fast.

"But this isn't about me," Lord Douglas said, as if laying down his arms for the time being, giving up his advantage and letting Mr. Walker speak for some unknown and supremely suspicious reason. "You initiated this meeting, Walker, so you tell me what it is you want and I'll decide where we go from there."

"Yes, well..." Mr. Walker fixed his bow tie through his grizzly beard. "I hate to tread ground already walked upon, but I'm afraid we never made it to the end of the particular path in question. That is to say that I called this meeting to finish what we've already started."

Lord Douglas didn't smile or nod, but his eyes twinkled. "I assumed as much," he said. "I also assume—forgive my presumptiveness—that you are talking about your desire to relieve me of my shares in the protector force. Correct me if I'm wrong."

Mr. Walker smiled. Now they were getting into territory he had prepared for. Finally he could retake control of the negotiations. "No, you're not often wrong. Are you Lord Douglas?" He diverted his eyes, being as earnest as he possibly could, feigning a sacrifice of position but only setting himself up for success in the long run.

Lord Douglas couldn't help but grin, as Mr. Walker knew he would. "Go on, Walrus," he said. "This flattery gets you nowhere."

"It's not flattery when it's true," Mr. Walker said, taking a page from Jorah's book. "Only embellishments can be flattery. But let's continue anyway. Stating common knowledge is no use to either of us. No, what's most useful to both parties is for us to discuss the benefit that would accrue to you by consolidating ownership over the android and AI industry."

Here Lord Douglas was caught speechless. His jaw didn't drop but the subtle twitch of his eyes expressed his complete and utter awe at the prospect. "Slow down there, Walton my boy," Lord Douglas said, fidgeting in his seat. "I thought you were here to talk about the protectors."

"Oh, yes, yes." Mr. Walker laughed. "Of course the protectors factor into this, but that's exactly the ground we've already tread upon."

"I see." Lord Douglas nodded.

"Do you though? Can you honestly see the possibilities? Have you been following the news at all, Lord Douglas? The numbers? The more the people riot the more the robots are worth and the the more the protectors cost. These are basic axioms of economics."

"Sure." Lord Douglas laughed. "That's why you're so eager to rid yourself of Waltronics for a bigger share of the protectorship. Right? Because androids are becoming more profitable and protectors are becoming less. That makes a whole lot of sense."

"That's where you get me wrong, Doug." Mr. Walker smiled a tense smile. This was the hail mary, the lynchpin of his entire plan. It was all or nothing, full force or no force, and so he went into it with everything he had. "I'm not in it for the money, my Lord. I'm in it for something more than that."

Lord Douglas scoffed. "Oh yeah? What more could there be besides money?"

"*Principle*," Mr. Walker said, slamming his ham fist on a side table and nearly crumbling the fragile thing under his brute strength. "The rule of law. The sanctity of private property and the Free Market. What more could there be in the worlds than that?"

Lord Douglas tapped his chin, thinking about how to answer—or at least wanting to look the part. He took his monocle out of his eye and blew some warm breath on it to rub it clean with his pocket square. "Principle, you say," he said. "I think I understand all too well the principles on which you stand, and I'm not sure I would like those to be the driving force behind the protectors."

"But they already are." Mr. Walker laughed. "Ignoring the fact that I already own a majority share—however slight that majority might be—the principles I stand for are the principles we all stand for. They are the principles of the Free Market, foremost among those being the absolute utility of private property rights and the complete freedom of discretion with regards to one's own property. What could you find to argue against in that?"

"I could argue with your performance, Wally Boy. That's what. Talk all you want about ideals, the fact of the matter remains that you have yet to solve the two largest terrorist attacks in recent history, one of which occurred under your Lordship."

"I'm afraid your information's a little dated." Mr. Walker smiled. "Both cases have been solved and the terrorists responsible are being held accountable."

"Oh. Well then." Lord Douglas gave a slow, sarcastic, palm clap. "Bravo. It's only taken you this long. Do you want a cookie cake?"

"No," Mr. Walker answered without hesitation. "I'm not proud of the time it took. I should have done better. I *can* do better. And I would have, but I didn't have the proper resources. We're running low in One, as you know. We're pulling rookies up before they're properly trained. Furthermore, the force is too fractured for it to be as effective as it needs to be in these particularly trying times— as evidenced by our little armory attack last afternoon."

"*Your* little armory attack, Mr. Walker."

"Exactly my point, dear Lord. This is *our* protector force, meant to protect *all* of us, not just the ones who own them. If we had shared information instead of hoarding it, we could have prevented the attack instead of letting that scum get away with the guns. Now hold on a second there, Lord. Let me finish, please. You see, I know you'll never work that close with me, sharing all the secrets you gain, and I don't blame you for it. Information is too valuable to be sharing it like that. So the way I see it, for the good of every owner of Inland, I believe we should consolidate ownership of the protector force under one head so—whoever that head is—he will be able to properly utilize the resources and manpower that are needed to completely and thoroughly protect our economy in these dire times in which we find ourselves." Mr. Walker was breathing hard by the end of his speech. He had to get it all out in one breath so as not to leave any spaces for Lord Douglas to interject. Now that Mr. Walker wanted him to respond, though, Lord Douglas was taking his time.

After what seemed like an eternity, Lord Douglas, with raised eyebrows, finally asked, "And why, then, should it be you at the helm of the protectors and not me?"

"Well, Lord Douglas." Mr. Walker bowed as low as he could without losing his top hat—not far because the hat was so tall. "Do you really want to be at the helm of a sinking ship? The protector force is hemorrhaging money. Life would be so much easier taking advantage of the riots by selling robot replacement workers than it would be paying for the protectors who are supposed to put those riots to an end. Don't you think?"

"Which brings us back to the question of why you would be volunteering to do the harder job in my place."

"I've already told you. Honor, my boy." Mr. Walker puffed out his chest. "*Respect*. I'm no longer Lord, you know, and it's starting to sink in. Not only that, I keep falling further and further behind every day. I'm sure you know that. You watch the markets as close as any good owner."

Lord Douglas smiled and gave a slight nod.

"I'm not catching up to you any time soon—even with complete control of Waltronics Llc.—and I know that. You know that. Every owner who can read a stock quote knows that because it's a fact. I'm just trying to find another way to do something worth being remembered for, and I think stopping this riot might be the best course of action for me. You're beyond all this protecting now. You're Lord. Everything you do is honorable and destined for the history books. I, on the other hand, am forced to find other avenues through which to make my life a fulfilling one, and protecting is what I've chosen."

Lord Douglas nodded. "And what exactly is it that you're offering?" he asked. "What is it that you want?"

"I propose a one for one trade. I own ninety percent of Waltronics android facilities while you own ten percent of the same. I own fifty-one percent of the protector force while you own forty-nine percent of the same. I suggest an even exchange, my Waltronics holdings for your protector stocks. Straight up. Now, I know they're not exactly—"

"Deal."

"Wait a second. You can have some time to— What?"

Lord Douglas stood and extended his white gloved hand across the desk. "I agree to trade all my protector stocks for all your robotics stocks. *Deal.*"

Mr. Walker looked at the hand. This was way too easy. How was it so easy? Still, it was what Mr. Walker had wanted. He stood and shook Lord Douglas's hand vigorously. "Deal, then Douggy," he said. "I'm glad you could finally see it my way. You won't regret this, now. Haley, my dear, you got that, right? You witnessed it?"

"The transaction has been processed, sir," Haley said with a curtsy.

"Very good. *Ho ho ho!*" Mr. Walker said, still shaking Lord Douglas's hand. "It was so good doing business with you, Lord."

"And you, my friend," Lord Douglas said with a wry smile. "Better than you could imagine. But—and only if you don't mind, of course—there is one last piece of business I'd like to share with you. If you would, please, sit down."

"*Ho ho ho!*" Mr. Walker retook his seat, his stomach jiggling in glee. "Anything, my Lord," he said. "After a deal like that, I'll do anything you ask of me."

"Don't get ahead of yourself," Lord Douglas said, leaving the room. "There's someone I'd like you to see."

Mr. Walker didn't care who it was. He had gotten what he wanted out of these negotiations, and they were a success no matter who came through that door behind Lord Dug Bot. The fool had no doubt fallen into the same sense of ease that Mr. Walker had when he was Lord, and Mr. Walker was going to make him pay for it.

The door opened and Mr. Walker did a double take, looking back at Haley then forward to Haley again. No. It couldn't be.

"I believe you know Haley," Lord Douglas said with a grin, stepping behind her. "And I hope you don't regret our deal, after all."

ʕ ✄ ⋈

LVII. Nikola

"Uh, that's not really what I had in mind, Dad," Nikola said, looking to her mom for help. "I don't know, I thought maybe we'd start on the assembly lines, or in the farms, or something. You know, something a bit more suited to someone without any basic training— no offense Tillie."

Tillie didn't respond. She was still staring blankly across the desk at Nikola's dad.

"Give your American friend some credit," Nikola's mom said. "She looks strong and healthy from here. She seems to have put up with capture by those vicious protectors. You can handle it, right, dear?"

Tillie nodded.

"*Ugh*, Mom." Nikola sighed, looking back to her dad for help now. "Can't you to just leave her alone for like a day. She's only just gotten out of that prison. You can't expect her to have gotten over it already."

"None of us can say whether she has or not," Nikola's dad said. "Only she can decide that for herself. She doesn't need you speaking for her, you know. Now, American, do you understand what we're asking of you?"

Tillie still just stared blankly across the desk.

Nikola scoffed. "Her name's Tillie, Dad. *Not American*. And no one understands what you're asking of her. Not even me."

"We've found the linchpin in America's walls, dear," Nikola's mom said. "They've centralized control of them so much that we can shut down all transportation in one fell swoop. That includes 3D printers."

"How would they eat?" Tillie finally spoke up, in a quiet, almost croaking voice.

"Excuse me, soldier?" Nikola's dad said.

"Without printers how will they eat?" Tillie repeated, louder this time.

"The printers won't be off for too long," Nikola's mom said.

"You can be sure of that. But by the time they get turned back on, we'll have a foothold on the inside. We'll remain there, controlling and monitoring everything, long after they think we've gone." She smiled.

"How long is too long?" Tillie asked. "My dad needs printers to eat, printers to get dressed, printers to feed Mr. Kitty, Hell, he needs printers for everything required to sustain his life. How long will they be off?"

"All of fifteen seconds is what we need," Nikola's dad said. "In and out just like that. And you're gonna give it to us."

"But why us?" Nikola demanded. "Isn't there someone else who's better for the job?"

"Why Tillie, you mean," Nikola's mom said. "She's the key. I'm not so sure it's a good idea to let you go along, in fact. What do you think, honey?"

"I'm not letting her go without me," Nikola said.

"If it convinces the American to help," her dad said, "it might be worth the risk."

"Yes, but only the—" her mom started.

"Why me?" Tillie demanded.

Everyone turned to stare at her. Maybe she was ready for the mission after all.

"The Scientist, dear," Nikola's mom said. "We've been following her for some time, actually, trying to find our opening. It wasn't easy, you know. She practices tight security. But what's important is that we've been following the Scientist, and we've found that she's been following you. Now since she's already looking for you she won't be surprised to find you on her doorstep. When she let's you in you just have to garner enough trust to get near a computer then we can do the rest."

"That's it?" Nikola scoffed. "Get near a computer? She doesn't even have to use it?"

"It doesn't even have to be turned on," Nikola's dad said with a big smile. "Just wear this transceiver and get near the thing." He held up a silver bracelet, grinning wide and proud of the little gadget—he always did love his electronic gadgets. "No one will even know you've done a thing."

Nikola took the bracelet out of his hands so her dad would sit down and stop pushing it on Tillie who seemed to be lost in her own little world.

"So how do we get there?" Nikola asked, stalling for time since Tillie obviously needed more to work out how she felt about the situation. "To the Scientist."

"That's the tricky part," Nikola's dad said.

"And it's not *we* yet," her mom added.

"Why don't you tell them, honey," her dad said. "This is more of your area."

"As I said," her mom went on, "we've been following the Scientist following your Tillie ever since we helped her escape from that prison."

Nikola couldn't tell whether it was a cough or a scoff, but Tillie made a noise.

"Beyond that," Nikola's mom went on, not noticing the noise or ignoring it—probably the latter. "We've been leading the Scientist on a wild goose chase—if you'll forgive the archaic saying."

"She means we're making the Scientist think we took you someplace where we didn't," Nikola's dad clarified.

"The plan is to let her actually find you," Nikola's mom went on. "She'll take you back to her lab, and then it'd be up to you to find the computer."

"And if she doesn't take us to her lab?" Nikola asked, not confident in this flimsy plan even though she was definitely going along with it if Tillie decided that she wanted to. "What if the protectors greet us instead?"

"They won't," her dad said. "And the Scientist will. She's smarter and faster than those protectors, and she'll want to protect your American from them. She's got something in store for you, girl." He chuckled, nodding at Tillie.

Nikola scoffed. "Dad!"

"And when are we supposed to do this?" Tillie asked.

Nikola's mom smiled. "As soon as you can, dear. The sooner the better. We have an operation set up at fourteen hundred hours— that's...two hours from now—but any later than that and we'll have to find another suitable transfer point in the next two weeks or so."

Tillie took the bracelet from Nikola's hand and strapped it on her wrist. "And I just stand close to the computer?" she asked. "I don't have to turn this on or anything?"

Nikola's dad chuckled. "That's my girl. And no. We'll

control everything from here. You just get us in range."

"I'll do it," Tillie said. "Just tell me when and where."

"Great!" Nikola's dad stood and clapped his hands together. "Nikola, take our American friend to get some proper mission attire then meet us in the Central Depot at fourteen hundred hours. You're doing a great service to all the World's beings, dear girl. We thank you for that." He grabbed Tillie by the hand to shake it vigorously while pulling her up out of her seat.

"Alright, Dad. We'll be there," Nikola said, prying Tillie's hand away from his and showing her out the door. "Don't worry."

They didn't talk again until they had traversed the halls and stairwells to Nikola's room where she said, "You know you don't have to do this if you don't want to, right?"

"What? Wear *proper mission attire*?" Tillie asked with a little chuckle. "Good. Because I wasn't planning on doing that anyway."

"No," Nikola said, shaking her head. "I mean you don't have to go on this mission at all if you don't want to. My parents can't make you do it. No one can make you do anything here."

"I want to," Tillie said. "Trust me. It'll be good to get back home anyway. Even if I won't really be home for good."

"Yeah, *sure*," Nikola said. "I guess." Though she wasn't sure.

"Trust me, Nikola. I'll be alright. There's nothing to worry about. Now let's go get some more of that free food before we go on this *mission*. I'm starving."

"Yeah, I bet." Nikola laughed. "The ants ate all yours earlier."

⚮ ✳ ⚯

They met Nikola's parents in the Central Hub. Not really, though. After riding the bullet proof glass elevator down into nowhere they were probably far far away from the People's France. They were in a tiny room with cement walls and a linoleum floor. Nothing else. Just the four of them staring at each other.

"Now you're sure you want to do this," Nikola said. "They have no control over you. You can still say no if you want to."

Tillie nodded.

"And you have the transceiver?" Nikola's dad asked.

Tillie held up her arm with the bracelet still attached.

"The Scientist might not take you directly to the world with her computer in it," Nikola's mom said. "She probably won't. That's likely to be a heavily secured area. So you two are going to have to do whatever you can to get her to bring you there."

Nikola scoffed. "Like what?"

"Ask her about the walls," Nikola's dad said. "How they work and all that. Pretend like you don't believe in them. She's a scientist, she'll want to teach you, prove them to you. She won't be able to resist. I promise."

"And what if she never takes us to the right place?" Nikola asked. "How are we supposed to get back home if you don't have control over the system?"

"We'll get you back," her mom said. "We've done it once before, haven't we?"

Nikola scoffed. "*Barely.*"

"With perfect timing is how I like to think of it," her dad said with a smile. "How are you feeling, American?"

Tillie hadn't spoken since they had left the food cart for the Central Hub. She fidgeted now, looking for the right thing to say. "Ready," she finally did.

"Good," Nikola's mom said with a smile. "Your ride's almost here. We'll send you along to the alley then you wait for our signal there. Good luck, girls. The solidarity of our people rides with you."

Nikola and Tillie stepped onto the elevator in silence. This was a different elevator than the one they had ridden in on. It was all steel—walls, ceiling, and floor—instead of glass and linoleum. The doors slid closed, hiding her parents from view, and Nikola breathed a sigh of anticipation. "Are you sure you want to do this?" she asked again. She hated sounding like a broken record, but she had to be sure they weren't taking advantage of Tillie.

"There's no turning back now," Tillie said, and the floor fell out from underneath them.

When the elevator stopped and the doors slid open Nikola took a deep whiff of the world around her. She could smell America. There was something in the air that made it different. A camouflaged French revolutionary waved them out of the elevator and into an alley where they were left to wait for the next leg of the trip. Nikola paced back and forth from wall to wall as they did while Tillie stood still, staring off into the distance at nothing, lost in thought again.

"This is the last chance to turn back," Nikola interrupted her revery. "Are you sure you want to do this?"

The revolutionary—who Nikola didn't recognize somehow, she thought she knew everyone on the base if not anyone who'd be on this mission—shushed Nikola and waved for her to get closer to where he was hiding behind a dumpster. "Fat chance," he said. "No turning back now. So shut up and get over here. You're endangering the mission."

Nikola stopped pacing. "Endangering how?" she asked, looking up and down the alley then back at the pushy soldier. "There's no one even out here."

"Not now there isn't," the soldier said in a whisperyell. "But someone could walk by at any minute. Now get over here." He waved to her again.

"You have no control over me," Nikola said, standing her ground. "I don't even know your name."

"I'm not trying to control you," the soldier said, getting flustered. "I just want to ensure—" He held a hand to his ear. "Never mind. It doesn't matter anymore. Your ride's here. Follow me." He jumped up onto the balls of his feet and made his way down the alley in a crouch.

Nikola tried to make a joke about it as they followed the *crouching tiger*, but Tillie wasn't interested. She didn't look when Nikola tried to tap her on the arm to get her attention, and she didn't even grin or crack a smile, much less chuckle or laugh, when Tillie told the joke anyway. Maybe it was time to get serious after all. Nikola set her mind on doing just that, falling into line behind the solemn parade led by a crouching madman.

The soldier stopped in front of a public elevator a block and a half away and looked surprised when he turned to find Tillie and Nikola walking with a normal stride, not trying to hide themselves at all. "Get down," he demanded, waving them toward the elevator. "Do you want to be seen?"

"I thought we were trying to get caught," Nikola said, looking around to find the streets as empty as they had been the entire time. "Isn't that the whole point of this operation?"

"You have to get caught by the right person. If the protectors get you, we're fucked. Now get in." The elevator doors slid open and the soldier pushed Nikola in.

"Alright, shit," Nikola said, regaining her balance. "I'll remember that."

Tillie stepped into the elevator. "Door closed," she said.

"You don't even know my name," the soldier said as the doors slid closed between them. "Or the code!" he added, trying, but failing, to get his fingers inside and pry the door open.

"Shows him," Nikola said, chuckling. "We should let him stew for a while before we open them up again."

"We don't need the code," Tillie said, staring straight ahead at the closed doors.

"What do you mean? How are we supposed to get to the Scientist?"

"I already know the Scientist," Tillie said. "Well, I know of her. Emma knew her."

"Emma?"

"Yes, Emma." Tillie turned to Nikola and smiled. It was an eerie smile, more of a smirk, like no grin Nikola had ever seen on Tillie's face before. She looked almost mad. "Emma was working with the Scientist. The Scientist gave us the keys we needed to destroy the walls between Five and Six. *We* did that, Nikola."

"*No*." Nikola shook her head. It couldn't be true. She had seen the intelligence reports on the operation. It was a false flag attack put on by the Scientist in order to distract the masses from her true plan. It had nothing to do with Outland Two. It—

"Yes. Emma, the Scientist, and I were all working together. There's no way I'm about to sabotage everything we've worked so hard to build. And I'm not about to let you sabotage it, either."

"No—but— She isn't working with us," Nikola pleaded, trying to knock some sense into the ignorant American before it was too late. "She holds their walls up for them. Without her the walls would crumble and our job would be so much easier. You can't be working with her. It goes against your interests."

"Without her Five and Six would still be separated," Tillie said, sneering. "Without her I wouldn't be in this fight to help you at all. Without her none of this would be possible, and I won't let you ruin it now."

"No. Tillie, listen—"

"The struggle itself is enough to fill one's heart," Tillie said and the floor fell out from underneath them.

"Tillie, please," Nikola begged. "You can still do the right thing. Or if you want, give me the bracelet. I'll do it and you won't have to feel any guilt at all. But don't ruin this opportunity for us. *Please.*"

Tillie scoffed. "Giving you the gun to shoot for me would be exactly the same as pulling the trigger myself." The elevator stopped. "We're here anyway. Let's see what the Scientist has to say about it."

The elevator doors slid open to reveal a short empty hall. Tillie stepped into it right away but Nikola hesitated. Maybe she should just stay in the elevator and leave Tillie to deal with the Scientist, after all. By the sounds of it, Tillie wasn't going to cooperate and Nikola would have a hard time finding a way back to the People's France as a result. She knew she couldn't do that, though, that she still had to try to complete her mission no matter how hopeless it looked, so she followed Tillie out into the hall and the elevator doors slid closed behind her.

"Now what?" Nikola asked Tillie who was slowing down, looking a little less sure of herself.

"Well there's only one door," Tillie said, pointing. "So there's really no choice, is there?"

As she said it, the door opened and in stepped a tall, dark faced woman with a severe look about her. She was wearing a pinstripe pantsuit which only seemed to make her legs look longer as she took a few strides to cross the short hall and stand in front of them with a sneer. This couldn't be the Scientist, could it? She didn't look like she'd be willing to cooperate at all if she was, so Nikola certainly hoped not.

"Are you the Scientist?" Tillie asked her outright, seeming to stand taller as she said the words.

The woman didn't answer, though. She just stared blankly down at Tillie, not even sparing a second glance for Nikola who didn't regret that fact.

"We're looking for the Scientist," Tillie persisted. "It's urgent. Can you take us to her?"

"Urgent, huh?" the woman finally said, and the deep baritone of her voice took Nikola off guard. Nikola almost let out a gasp but managed to hold her silence as the woman went on. "I'll be the judge of that."

"W—We— Who are you?" Tillie stammered.

The woman chuckled and it sounded eerier than her voice. "I'll be asking the questions here, girl. You trespassed on my property. Now who are you?"

"Tillie Manager, ma'am." Tillie swallowed some spit, making enough noise for Nikola to hear it. "I need to—"

"And your friend, *Tillie Manager*, does she have a name, too?"

"Nikkie—" Tillie started but Nikola elbowed her to shut her up.

"Nikkie Manager," Nikola said. "Who are you?"

The woman chuckled. "She's a feisty one, isn't she? No wonder you brought her along with you."

"We need to see the Scientist," Tillie said, a hint of anxiety slipping into her voice. "Where is she?"

"And what do you *need* to see the Scientist for? She's a busy woman, you know."

"We—*I* have information," Tillie corrected herself. "It's about an attack. I'm with Emma."

"Emma who?"

Tillie tried to speak but nothing would come out. Nikola didn't know Emma's last name and she wouldn't be surprised if Tillie didn't know it either. Neither of them knew what to say now. At least Tillie hadn't given away their mission yet. There was still a chance it could be a success.

"And you expect me to trust you?" the woman said, chuckling. "I'd be in my right mind to kick the both of—" The door opened behind her—interrupting her speech—and a big metal arm with a too human hand rolled out into the hall on giant tires. "Popeye," the woman said, "not now. Can't you see I'm busy?"

The hand waved then turned this way and that, as if it were trying to communicate something.

"Yes, they're here," the woman said. "Can't you see them right there?"

The arm did another, slightly different, dance in response.

"I'll bring them in shortly," the woman said. "I'm just having a little bit of fun before I do. I am still allowed to have fun, aren't I?"

The mechanical arm waved her away and rolled back into the room it had come out of.

"W—Was that—" Tillie said. "The Scientist?"

The woman chuckled. "Creator, no," she said, shaking her head and wiping a tear from her eye. "We'd all be in a lot worse position if that no brains arm was the Scientist. Now come on. It looks like she's ready for you."

They followed the woman through the door at the end of the hall and into a huge office room with a giant oak desk, a circle of big fluffy chairs around a few side tables, and a wall-sized window looking out onto a vast, green wilderness scene. There were no computers, of course—just Nikola's luck—only a white haired old woman in a white coat sitting in one of the puffy chairs and the big mechanical arm washing the giant window.

"Come in, come in," the woman in the white coat said, standing from her seat and showing Tillie and Nikola to two of their own before retaking hers. "Have a seat, please. We have so much to talk about."

"Are— Are you the Scientist?" Tillie asked, taking her seat. Nikola took a second to stare out the window at the rolling hills before sitting, too.

"I am, dear," the woman in the white coat said. "And you already met Rosalind." She indicated the tall scary woman who had received them at the elevator. "And of course Popeye." The big mechanical arm waved then went back to washing the window. "And you two are?"

"I'm Tillie," Tillie said, not choosing to speak for Nikola this time.

"Yes, Tillie," the Scientist said. "I know that one already, actually. Your friend here, however..." She lowered her eyes at Nikola.

"I'm just a friend," Nikola said. "No names needed."

"Ah. I see," the Scientist said, tapping her chin. "I can't make you do anything, now, but I'm afraid I'd be more comfortable if I had a name I could call you by." The Scientist waited for a response, but when it became clear to everyone that Nikola wasn't giving any the Scientist said, "Have it your way, then. Friend it is. So, Tillie and Friend, how can I help y'all?"

"I need to—" Tillie started, but Nikola knew it was her last chance to interject before Tillie ruined everything.

"You could stop propping up the ownership class for starters," she blurted out without thinking.

The Scientist gave Nikola a death stare. Rosalind, or whatever her name was—sitting at the desk and playing cards with herself—scoffed. The sound of it made Nikola feel a little more confident and seemed to perturb the Scientist who shot a glance in Rosalind's direction. "Friend," the Scientist went on, "if you're going to talk to me like that, I'd rather we were on a first name basis."

Nikola scoffed, almost perfectly mimicking the sound of Rosalind's and surprising herself because of it. "Sure thing, *the Scientist*." She held up air quotes around the woman's "name". "My name's Friend, the Friend. Nice to meet you." She stood and held out a hand for the Scientist to shake.

Rosalind chuckled at the desk, and this time the Scientist did more than shoot her a glance. "Don't you think there's a better place for you to play your cards," she snapped.

"Not if I want to hear what y'all are talking about," Rosalind said with a snicker.

"That's exactly my point," the Scientist said, turning back to Nikola and composing herself. "Now, Friend, where were we?"

"Alright, alright. I get it." Rosalind grumbled, making an effort to take a long time picking up the cards. "C'mon, Popeye. We're not wanted here." She waved the arm along to follow her slowly out of the room.

"Well…" the Scientist said, raising an eyebrow and trying to ignore Rosalind's loud exit. "Go on, Friend."

Nikola hesitated. She had lost track of the conversation. It wasn't her turn to talk, was it? The ball was in the Scientist's court. She took too long and Tillie ended up picking it up and running with it, "We wanted to tell you something."

"No, that's not it," Nikola said, cutting the Scientist off before she could respond. "You were about to tell us your name. It's your turn to offer up some information. You got Tillie's name first, now you give us yours. Tit for tat. Your move."

The Scientist smiled. She seemed to be enjoying this now, which didn't sit well with Nikola. "I already knew Tillie's name," she said. "No new information was exchanged there." Nikola tried to speak up but the Scientist raised a hand to stop her. "*But*. I will give you the benefit of the doubt by going first in an exchange of names, Friend."

"*Fine*," Nikola said. "Go ahead then. I'm waiting..."

The Scientist made her wait just a little bit longer, that wry wrinkly grin on her face. After a few more moments of silence, letting Nikola stew in it, she said, "My name is Dr. Haley."

"And..." Nikola said, motioning her on. "Dr. Haley... What? Not just a first name basis. A full name basis."

The Scientist started to squirm in her seat a bit. Nikola scooted up to the edge of hers. Tillie did, too, apparently not as set on thwarting the mission as she had first seemed. "Now that wasn't part of the deal," the Scientist said, fidgeting still. "A name for a name, Friend. Now what's yours?"

"You have my last name already," Tillie cut in, and Nikola knew she had won the conversation. "You apparently knew it before I even told you."

"Yes, well..." the Scientist said, looking for some escape, but she was trapped.

"Well what is your last name?" Nikola asked, confident the game was done.

"I—Well... Dr. Haley Walker," the Scientist said—Dr. Walker said.

"Walker?" Tillie said, eyes wide. She looked to Nikola. "You knew, didn't you? Why didn't you tell me?"

"I didn't know you were working with her," Nikola said. "*We* didn't know. We didn't know Emma was, either. If we had known, we wouldn't have gone through all this. I promise you that."

"Who are you, Friend?" the Scientist asked, standing up. "And how do you know so much?"

Nikola laughed. "It's not so great being on the other side of the information divide, is it?"

"You're related to Lord Walker, aren't you?" Tillie said, her attention turned to the Scientist still. "That's why you keep his walls up for him."

"The former Lord," the Scientist said. "Huey's Lord now. But, no. I keep the walls up because we need them, child. How else would we eat? Our population is just too big. The 3D printers are necessary. That's how you've gotten everything you need to live since you were a baby, you know. That's how your father lives. None of us would be here now without those fields, and the second they go down is the second society crumbles."

"*No.*" Tillie shook her head. "But you— Emma told me that you gave us the entry code. You helped us tear down the walls between Five and Six."

"One wall between two worlds," the Scientist said. "That puny thing was causing more harm than good. If we could only get these riots under control, the economy would be running better than ever without it."

"You hear that?" Nikola said to Tillie rather than the Scientist. "*The economy.* That's the only thing she cares about. *The Invisible Hand.*"

"Oh, no." The Scientist shook her head. "This hand won't be invisible. It will be the rubber gloved hand of a scientist. *My hand.*" She held one up to underline the point. "With the help of the robots, of course, thanks to the very generous Mr. Walker who was cooperative enough to trade all control over the production of androids to me. Now all that remains to be seen is how cooperative you, my new friends, are willing to be?"

"Y—You're one of them," Tillie said, shaking her head and standing from her seat. "You're no different from the people you sent us to fight."

"That's where you're wrong, dear," the Scientist said, standing to meet her gaze. "I'm very different from them. I'll be able to use the walls and the robots together to provide goods and services more efficiently than ever. We've done it, Tillie. We're finally in control. Everything you and Emma worked so hard for is finally coming true."

Tillie scoffed, stepping away from the Scientist. Nikola stood and stepped between them, as if her physical presence could maintain the mental rift she had seeded with her words. "Don't listen to her," Nikola said.

"You're no different," Tillie said. "More of the same. You sit here benefitting from our exploitation just as much as those fat owners do, comfortable in your too big office with your too big view, literally mending their walls for your profit. If anything, you're worse than they are. Without you, they wouldn't know how to put the walls that keep us apart back together again."

"No." The Scientist shook her head. "Those walls do more than keep us apart," she said. "Much more. You can't see that yet—which is why you want to tear them all down at once—but the unintended consequences would be disastrous. You're too young, too inexperienced to make a decision of this caliber, and you have no idea what you'd be in for if you tried."

Nikola scoffed. "And you're too old to change your mind. You've shown us nothing, told us nothing to convince us. What evidence do you have? Why should we believe you? We shouldn't even be here listening to you right now. This is ridiculous. C'mon Tillie. Let's go." She grabbed Tillie's surprisingly compliant arm and dragged her toward the door. While Tillie didn't resist—she seemed too shocked to even think, by the look on her face—-the Scientist did everything she could, short of grabbing Tillie's other arm and having a tug of war, to stop them. They were out in the hall—the Scientist still begging them to stay—when Tillie finally woke up to the world around her and shrugged Nikola off.

"You're a bad person," she said, turning to the Scientist. "You should have told us what we were really fighting for instead of keeping us in the dark like that."

The Scientist shook her head. "I told you all I could, child. I'll show you more now if you'll stay."

"No," Tillie said, and she turned to get on the elevator.

Nikola got on, too, and told the doors to close behind her so the Scientist couldn't beg anymore. "Take us home," she said, happy with the outcome of the mission even if her parents would call it a failure, and when the elevator fell and stopped and the doors opened, they were not in the People's France. They were nowhere Nikola had ever seen before in a world that seemed impossible.

LVIII. Laura

The assembly line ran and none other than Adam Torrence slip, snap, clicked furiously at Fortuna knows what. He was much faster than Emir—there was no doubt about that—and the post-production editing would be easier because of it. That was at least one thing made easier by this whole messed up situation.

Alice Walton came on camera to say, "No. *You.*" holding her trembling hands to her mouth, on the verge of crying.

Adam peeled his eyes away from the work, losing no speed on his slip, snap, clicking, and grinned a wide, evil-looking grin. He didn't have to make a sound to elicit a deep feeling of discomfort in the audience—or in Laura, at least.

"It can't be," Alice went on. "What about my coworkers? What about our families?"

Adam chuckled. It's the only word Laura could think of to describe what Adam did, but the term didn't do the acting justice. It was more like a half chuckle, half cackle which turned out entirely spine tingling. So this was what it felt like to work with a true professional. Laura could get used to it.

"I am a robot," Adam said, still cackling. "I don't care."

"No, but…"

Adam stood from the assembly line, finally stopping his slip, snap, clicking. He crossed to Alice in two long strides and grasped her by her shoulders, holding her face close to his. "I am a robot," he repeated. "I don't care."

He jerked her closer and Alice leaned in to kiss him.

"Cut!" Cohen yelled. "What the fuck was that, Jen?"

Jorah—now Jorah again, no longer in character as Adam and seemingly an entirely different person because of it—pushed Jen—formerly Alice—away in disgust. *"Please, people,"* Jorah complained. "This is serious business. Do you think I enjoy being here with you no name nothings?"

Jen blushed. "I—I'm sorry. I don't know what came over me. I'll—"

"I'll be in my dressing room," Jorah said, storming out. "Get this under control before I return."

Cohen waited until the studio exit door slammed closed behind Jorah to scoff. "Or else what?" he said, chuckling to himself and looking to Jen and Laura for support, neither of whom were offering any. "He's just an actor. I don't care how big of a star he is, he has no power on my set."

"He has more power than you do." Laura scoffed.

"I'm so sorry," Jen said, still flushed crimson. "I didn't mean to— I don't know what came over me."

Cohen scoffed again. "Oh, I know what came over you." He chuckled. "Just don't let it happen again. Lord Walker wouldn't want anything to happen to his Jorah. Laura's right about that much."

Laura scoffed again, too. It seemed like they were all doing so much scoffing ever since Jorah joined the crew. "Alright there, Cohen ol' pal. We know how buddy buddy you and Lord Walker are now that you've had an all of five minute conversation with him, so why don't you tell us exactly what it is that your Lord Walker *would* want?"

"I—well…" Cohen didn't know what to say. He rubbed his thighs with probably sweaty hands and fidgeted in his uncomfortable director's seat.

"It won't happen again," Jen said. "I swear." She crossed her heart.

Laura was still laughing at Cohen's lack of spine when Jorah returned from his dressing room. "Does everyone have their libidos under control?" he asked, standing in the door still, apparently not wanting to enter until he was sure the answer was yes.

Jen blushed, trying to sneak off set without being noticed, but Laura could still see her—and the camera always saw everything.

"Everything's under control," Cohen assured Jorah, moving closer to try to grab his arm and guide him on set while Jorah dodged all Cohen's advances to walk on unassisted. "I've had a speaking to with the girl, like any proper director would, and she'll be good and ready for the next take. It'll be the best yet. I assure you of that."

"I hope so." Jorah scoffed, taking his place at the assembly line. "The sooner we're done with this stupid shoot the better."

"Alright, alright," Cohen yelled, clapping his hands and

retaking his director's chair. "Everyone to your places," he added, though everyone was already in their places. "Roll the line, please."

Laura flicked a switch and the assembly line started moving. Jorah started putting pieces together automatically—even without the cameras on—and all of a sudden he turned into Adam Torrence again.

"Lights!" Cohen called.

Laura flipped another switch and the lights changed, producing a bright white halo aura around Adam's head.

"Cameras rolling!"

Laura flipped the cameras on. She didn't have to look through the viewfinder to know that the shot was perfect. They had already gone through this scene once before and the camera hadn't been moved since. All she had left to do was wait and watch.

Adam Torrence slip, snap, clicked furiously at Fortuna knows what. Alice Walton came on camera, holding trembling hands to her mouth, on the verge of crying, to say, "No. *You.*"

Adam peeled his eyes from the line, not stopping his slip, snap, clicking. He grinned an evil grin and didn't have to make a sound to communicate—

Laura's pants vibrated to the horribly loud sound of her once favorite song—which after this instance, would no doubt lose that high pedestal in her mind. Jorah was pissed—made obvious by the fact that he had so quickly slipped out of Adam—Jen seemed happy that it wasn't her making a fool of herself this time, and Cohen yelled, "What the fuck is that and why is it interrupting my perfect take?"

Laura slipped the phone out of her pocket and groaned at its glowing face—she was sure she had turned the damn thing off. "I'm sorry," she said. "I have to take this." and she answered it.

"Laura Concierge, you fucking degenerate," Cohen said. "You hang up that goddamn phone right now."

"What is this?" Jorah demanded, offended by another interruption.

At the same time Laura said, "Hello, Lord Walker. How can I help you?" loud enough for everyone to hear.

"You tell Lord Walker how much we appreciate his support," Cohen added, trying to cover for himself. Jorah just nodded, keeping silent.

"How's the shoot going?" the voice on the other end of the line asked, Lord Walker's voice. "I'm sure Jorah's working out for you. Am I right?"

Laura nodded then realized she was on the phone and Lord Walker couldn't see her. "Yes, sir," she said. "He's right here next to me. Do you want to talk to him?" Why was he calling her anyway?

"No, no," Lord Walker's voice said. "Not now. No need. All I needed to say is that I'm coming to see you on the set."

"You're coming here?" Laura asked, more for the benefit of Cohen, Jen, and Jorah—who were all trying to eavesdrop without appearing to be listening—than because she couldn't understand what Lord Walker had said.

A low deep groan emitted from Laura's phone's speaker "I'm almost as surprised as you are," Lord Walker grumbled. "I want to be there much less than you want to have me, trust me, but it just cannot be avoided, I'm afraid. I've promised the writer—the real writer, that is, I knew no kook from Three could be capable of writing such a brilliant manuscript—but anyway, she wants to personally observe the progress of shooting. To dispense with the long story and finally end this tedious conversation, suffice it to say that we'll be there shortly."

"How shortly?" Laura asked.

Lord Walker grumbled and groaned through the phone. "I'm getting into a car now. Haley! Don't forget my hat!"

"Yes, sir," Laura said, but Lord Walker had already hung up. "Well," she added for the room, making extra certain that her phone was silenced before pocketing it again, "they're on their way."

"No shit," Cohen snapped, hurrying here and there to adjust, re-adjust, and un-adjust every tiny detail of the set design. "We need to get this place in order."

Jorah scoffed, plopping down onto the stool he was supposed to start the scene from.

"They?" Jen asked, fixing her appearance even though she was dressed and made up to look like a dirty assembly line worker. "There's more than one of them?"

"I don't know," Laura said, following Cohen around and fixing everything he had messed up in tampering with the set. "He said he found the writer or something."

"Guy?" Jen asked. "Where has he been anyway?"

"No, not Guy," Laura said. "The original writer or whatever."

Cohen stopped moving around everywhere, finally taking his clumsy hands off of Laura's perfectly set rigs. "The original writer?" he asked, swallowing hard.

"Yeah, the investor or whatever, I guess. You've met them before, haven't you?"

But Cohen didn't have time to answer because in came Haley, wearing her black and white maid uniform and calling everyone to attention. "Hear ye, hear ye," she sang. "Now entering is the distinguished and unique Lord Walker, treasure trove of efficiency and master of self-reliance, accompanied by honored guest, denizen of the lowest of worlds, and your writer for the present production in progress, Rosa Chandelier." Haley curtsied.

Jorah stood from his stool and applauded, staring at the door in eager anticipation of the honored guests' arrival. Jen blushed and tried to fix herself up one more time before joining in the applause with a demure clap of her own. Cohen seemed to try to hide behind the camera, afraid of someone more powerful than he was. And Laura just stood there waiting. She knew what to expect from Lord Walker, and she just wanted to get it on and over with.

In waddled mushroom shaped Lord Walker, flabby body folding and rolling over his tuxedo pants, in the same top hat and monocle that seemed to be a part of his body, attached to his head since birth. He was followed by one of the shortest, tiniest, frailest old ladies Laura had ever seen. Laura thought at first that she only looked so small in comparison to Lord Walker's massive girth, but when the woman came in and stood next to anyone or anything else in the room she still looked like the world was too big for her.

"*Ho ho ho*! I say," Lord Walker said, holding his stomach as he laughed. "This is a rather fine set up you have here."

The frail old lady tutted, scurrying around the room with the same haste that Cohen had exhibited earlier, investigating every tiny detail of Laura's set.

"What do you think, Rosa dear?" Lord Walker asked her as she scurried around touching everything. "Does it live up to your standards?"

She just tutted again in answer and kept on with her tedious investigation of the set.

"And Jorah, my boy." Lord Walker crossed to Jorah who bowed low before him.

"Ever in your service, my Lord and master," Jorah said, kissing Lord Walker's hands then flashing his twinkling teeth.

"Now now, my boy," Lord Walker said, grabbing Jorah's hand and pulling him in for an unexpected—by the look on Jorah's face—embrace. "We're good friends here, all of us. No need for that Lord and master bit you always find so funny. Got it?"

"I—*uh*—Yes, sir," Jorah said, struggling to free himself from the too long embrace. "I mean." Suddenly he transformed into another character entirely. "I mean, yeah, buddy. We go way back, don't we?"

"Alright, alright." Lord Walker finally let go of his bear like grip—if only he would do the same for the metaphorical grip he had on Laura's life. "And you, Laura," he said to her, as if he had read her very thoughts. "Is everything up to schedule? I'm counting on you to ensure this production gets underway in a timely manner. It's in *everyone's* best interests that you do."

"I—*uh*—*ahem*," Cohen said, coming out from behind the machinery and cameras to finally speak up for himself now that Laura was getting a little bit of attention. "I think you meant to say that to me, sir," he said, raising a finger in the air like he were a school child who wasn't quite sure whether or not he had the correct answer to the teacher's question. "I'm Cohen, sir. The—*uh*—the director of this project."

"*Ho ho ho!*" Lord Walker laughed, turning on Cohen who shrunk back towards his safe hiding space behind the machines. "Cohen, my boy. I recognize your voice from the phone. You're having no troubles with our new arrangement, are you? If so, speak up now or forever hold your peace. We can always find another eager young director who's capable of handling a platinum platter when served to them. I assure you of that, dear boy. *Ho ho ho!*"

Cohen shook his head. "No, sir. I mean, yes, sir. No problem, sir. I am capable, sir—or—*Lord.* I just—"

"Good. Good. Very good, my boy." Lord Walker turned to Laura again. "He is telling the truth, isn't he?" he asked.

Laura glanced at Cohen, trembling in his too expensive loafers, payed for no doubt by his inheritance from a famous director in the family long since dead. Cohen got more visibly nervous at her pause—wiping his hands on his pants and pulling his collar in the universal sign language motion for "Is it hot in here?" He probably would have pissed himself if Laura had taken any longer to nod and say, "It's been fine so far. *I guess*." Then she added less confidently, "Though this visit might put us a little off schedule."

Lord Walker grinned at her, a much better—though nonetheless grotesque with his face—reaction than she could have hoped for. "Well, dear, don't let us get in the way," Lord Walker said, looking around at his tiny companion. "In fact, I rather think we would like to see your work in progress. Isn't that right, Rosa?"

Rosa scurried off set and into Lord Walker's shadow to say, "Show us what you've got."

"Well then, get on with it," Lord Walker demanded.

Jorah jumped into his first position without hesitation. Jen took her cue from him and went to her first position, too. Only Cohen still stood dumbfounded by the presence of such a very fat—very demanding—man and his tiny friend.

"Well..." Lord Walker said, tapping his cane and urging them on.

"*Cohen*," Laura snapped. "You're supposed to be a director. Direct."

All of a sudden Cohen snapped out of his haze and jumped back into the director they all knew and hated. "Okay, okay," he said, clapping his hands and taking his position behind Laura's back. "Everyone to their places, please," he called, though everyone already was. "Lights!"

Laura flicked a switch. Everything disappeared into darkness—Lord Walker and his tiny friend, judging every motion, Cohen, too proud of himself, Jen, unfixing herself for the start of the scene—except for Jorah now Adam, surrounded by a halo and slip, snap, clicking air because the belt wasn't rolling yet.

"Cue the belts!" Cohen called.

Laura flipped a switch and Adam's hands, though maintaining their exact pace, picked up bits and pieced them together.

"Cameras!" Cohen called.

Laura flipped a switch and the cameras rolled right along with the conveyor belt and Adam's fluid motions.

"*Aaaaand action!*"

The room held its breath. Adam slip, snap, clicked. Jen, slightly off cue and not quite Alice, entered. "No." She gasped, holding a hand to her mouth. "Not you."

Adam slip, snap, clicked, not paying attention to her, intent solely on his work, as a good robot could only ever be.

"But—but—" Jen stammered, having some trouble getting into it still—perhaps because of the added pressure of their new audience. "But what about my coworkers? What about their families?"

"I am a robot," Adam said, turning to smile at Jen. "I don't—"

"Wait, cut!" a voice called, but it wasn't Cohen's. It wasn't Lord Walker's, either—Laura knew that voice all too well from their phone conversations. Instead it was the tiny old lady, Rosa. "Cut, cut, cut!" She waved her arms, storming out to the center of the set and blocking the cameras. "This isn't right. *Cut!*"

Jen blushed, not sure whether to look to Cohen or Laura for help. "I—but—" she stammered. "Those were my lines, right? I didn't mess them up."

"Those might be your lines, but they're not mine," Rosa said, shaking her head and pacing up and down the conveyor belt. "You see, this is exactly why I requested this visit, to be sure you're making the right movie, *my movie*, which by the looks of it, you're apparently not."

"*Ho ho ho*, now," Lord Walker said, jiggling and looking to Laura for confirmation. "Is this right, girl? You're not shooting her script?"

Laura shook her head, not wanting to get involved. Whatever deal they had made was between Rosa, Cohen, and Guy. Laura had nothing to do with that part of it. "This is the script you read," Laura said. "We've been using these lines since day one."

"They're not my lines!" Rosa stomped her tiny foot. She almost looked like a child except for her wrinkles and curly white hair. "The assembly line worker is worried about *her* Family, the Human Family as a whole, not about the separate individual families of her coworkers. Your line says what about *their* families. My line says what about *our Family*. Do you understand the difference?"

"*Um*, Alice, ma'am," Jen said, almost too quietly to be heard.

"Who?" Rosa demanded.

"The assembly line worker's name is Alice," Jen said, even more quietly than the first time.

"No. It isn't." The woman was getting angrier as she paced the line again. "The assembly line worker doesn't have a name. She is no one and everyone at the same time. To give her a name is to humanize her. To give her a name is to compartmentalize her and separate her from the Human Family as a whole. She is not you, or me, or Sally Fae down the street, she's all of us together as one, and to feign some fatal attempt at putting a name onto something so grand and holy as that is to defile the very reason that this film is being created in the first place."

Two hands in applause and Lord Walker's voice, the voice Laura so detested, came whooping and hollering as if this were a bar show. "Bravo, my dear Rosa. Bravo! I dare say you should take our incompetent Cohen's position as director of this film, but I'm afraid you're much too busy for such base work—if I can assume without making an ass out of us."

Cohen's face went white and it looked to Laura like he might pass out. Rosa smiled for a moment before going stern faced again. "If you want a job done right," she said, "you have to give up everything else in your life so you can spend enough time to do it the right way yourself. Isn't that what they say?"

"Oh, that might be what they say in your neck of the woods," Lord Walker said, chuckling, "but where I come from the saying's a little different. We say, if you want something done right, you just have to pay the right person the right price. *Ho ho ho!*"

"Tell me, then, Lord Walker," Rosa said, shooting him a look that stopped his laughter. "Did I find the right people for this job? Because the price seems astronomical."

"Well now," Lord Walker said, turning an angry eye on Laura. "Don't ask me. You're the one who found them. Laura, dear, are you and your crew going to be able to live up to your requirements, or are you going to remain shackled to your past blunders forever?"

"We can get it right," Laura replied fast. They had to get it right. She couldn't live like this forever. "We just need the right script. Like I said, this is the one we've been working with since day one. I thought Cohen and the investors had already agreed on this one or else we wouldn't have started shooting with it in the first place."

"I never agreed to any edits," Rosa said, staring at Cohen who cowered further behind the camera equipment. "Not these one's for sure."

"You did agree to some edits," Cohen croaked and ducked behind the camera again.

"What was that, boy?" Lord Walker demanded, waving Cohen out of his hiding spot. "Come on out here and take responsibility for your actions like a man. And speak up, I can't hardly hear you."

"Um. I said she did agree to some edits—*uh*, Lord, sir," Cohen said, creeping into the light. "When I gave her our demand list."

"Demand list?" Lord Walker looked to Rosa with a furrowed brow. "What demand list?"

"The investment," Rosa said. "And the script *I* approved said *our Family*."

"And what do you say to that, my boy?" Lord Walker asked Cohen who stuttered and stammered his response.

"I—*uh*—well—we were— There were deadlines, you see— And I had to do what—or I had to make sure we got what we needed— We made the movie— And Guy— He—*well*..."

"So," Lord Walker said, tapping his cane in annoyance. "What you're saying is that you failed me, boy. You failed our dear old Rosa here. You failed the entire Human Family for that matter." Rosa smiled at that last part, and Laura didn't like the prospect of the fresh new Hell she would face shackled by the ankle to what was now becoming a two-headed beast. "And how should I make you pay for your mistake?"

"I—what?" Cohen begged. "No. It wasn't a—a mistake. This version's better. It— I— You read it. You—"

"That doesn't matter," Lord Walker said, shaking his head. "If the customer demands an inferior product, you give them an inferior product. It's the law of the market, good business practice. In this instance Rosa and I are your customers, and you will do as we say or you'll go elsewhere with your pretentious *demand list*. Do you understand me?"

Cohen tried to choke out words but he couldn't. Laura pitied him a bit—knowing the wrath of Lord Walker from first hand experience—so she stepped in to try to save him a little face. Even if he was a huge jerk most the time, not even Cohen deserved Lord Walker's wrath. "We'll get you whatever you want," she said. "Just get us a script we can work with. This movie is gonna be crap with or without the edits, anyway." And she could tell she had gone too far by the reactions of her audience.

Jorah grinned a little, which showed enough because he was such a master of his emotions that he shouldn't have reacted at all. Jen gasped and panted and fanned her face, the epitome of old-world *feminine*, deserving an A+ in any college level performance. Cohen stared at Laura blankly, unbelieving. How could Laura have the guts to say exactly what he wanted to when he didn't even have them to do it for himself? Lord Walker looked like he was trying to hold back a laugh himself, though he was doing a much poorer job of it than Jorah was. Then there was the little old lady, Rosa. She fumed, no doubt pissed that Laura had called her precious script shit, which Laura couldn't really blame her for even though the script was still shit.

"*Ho ho ho!*" Lord Walker bellowed. "I like your style, girl. However much I disagree with your substance. But I won't have you insulting our writers to their faces any which way about it. The script's not that bad, now. Is it?"

"Guy's isn't," Laura said, ignoring Rosa's anger and Cohen's pleas for her to shutup alike. "It's not entire shit, at least. It's the best way to handle the theme you want covered—if there can be said to be a good way to handle it at all."

"My script's not shit," Rosa complained. "*This* is shit. What you're doing here now is shit. It's lying, blasphemous, putrid bile, and you'll get nothing out of me for producing it. Mark my words."

"Now, now, now," Lord Walker said, gesturing to calm the old woman down. "Settle down, old girl. First of all, I don't see that much of a difference between what our lovely actor here—" Jen curtsied as he indicated her with a slight nod of his tall hatted head. "—said and what you say you believe should have been. It's just semantics. "

"There's a big differ—" Rosa started.

"Now, now, now," Lord Walker cut her off. "Let me finish. Where was I? That's right. The big business. Second of all, your investment is nothing compared to mine. As a result, your power over this production has declined in proportion. I provide the studio. I provide the equipment now. I provide the star of the show." He indicated Jorah who bowed low on cue. "*I* am the director, producer, and Lord of this entire gig, and as sole master of its fate, *I* will be the one to decide whether or not your script is shit."

"And *I* decide whether or not the Family works with you," Rosa said. "*I* decide if the Family fights for you or against you. If you don't make the movie I asked for, the movie that's best for the Family, then what point is there in us working with you at all?"

Lord Walker grinned, twirling his cane. "There is the little matter of that blank check, dear. Let us not forget its existence in all this excitement."

"The blank check which we were reluctant to accept in the first place," Rosa said. "The one you practically forced on us, as I recall."

Lord Walker chuckled. "Everything was done voluntarily, my dear. You chose to accept the deal, now you must deal with the consequences of that decision. You're not backing out on me now, are you? I have an army with or without your stupid Family, you know, and they will punish you for breaking a contract."

"You have—" Rosa started, but taking everybody by surprise—Laura at least, though it was mostly because of the relief she felt at him finally taking some responsibility for this production—Cohen stepped up to interject.

"Now I—" he squeaked, stopping himself to cough and clear his throat before going on more clearly in his usual annoying deep voice. "I may have a solution to both of your problems."

Lord Walker looked as surprised as Laura felt. He couldn't think of anything to say before Rosa said, "Spit it out then, crook, and don't you let it be a lie. You already have one strike in my book and this is not baseball."

"Oh, well... I don't know anything about baseball," Cohen said. "But I do know a good bit about hammering out a script, and if we can have—forgive me, Lord—just a little more time and the ability to work face to face for a day or two, I think we can get something workable for both parties. I mean, her demand isn't too difficult to work into Guy's script, and I imagine that, other than minor details which can just as easily be changed, she'd be okay with the rest of the script as is.

"Who is this guy y'all keep talking about?" Lord Walker asked.

"What exactly are you proposing?" Rosa demanded.

Laura laughed internally, happy it wasn't her under the spotlight anymore, but fearing the heat would turn on her again.

"Guy's our writer," Cohen explained. "He can't be found right now but that doesn't matter. You and I—uh—*Rosa*, can sit down together with the script we have and fix any problems you have with its content, starting with changing the *their families* to *our family* as per your request."

"*Our Family*," Rosa corrected him. "It has to be capitalized."

"That sounds reasonable," Lord Walker said, nodding. "What do you think, dear?"

Rosa shook her head. She looked like she didn't want to go along but had no other choice. Laura had been in that position for so long, making those same faces, she knew exactly how to spot them in someone else. "I get final veto on every word," she relented.

"*I* get final veto on every word," Lord Walker corrected her.

"And if you're veto doesn't match with mine, then I—and the entire Human Family with me—will have something to say about it."

Lord Walker chuckled. "*Ho ho ho*, dear. We'll ride that elevator when we come to it. For now, though, there's one more stipulation I'd like to make. Instead of your Cohen boy *hammering out* the script, like he so eloquently put it, I'd like my girl Laura to work with you. No offense to you Ice Cream Cohen—well maybe a little—" Lord Walker winked. "—but I trust her as much as I can trust a Three—*not much*—and I'd be more comfortable with her at the table than with you at it."

"But, sir. I came up with the—" Cohen said, unable to finish what he had started.

"I don't care who it is," Rosa said. "As long a someone fixes it before we move on. You all decide for yourselves and send whoever you pick my way with a script."

"*Ho ho ho!*" Lord Walker chortled as Rosa stormed out of the room.

"Well," Jorah said, clapping his hands and exuding a deep sigh. "I guess that means we're done here for the day. I'll be in my dressing room until further notice."

Lord Walker stopped Jorah midway to the door so he could shake the star's hand and hug him. "Good show today, Jorah, my boy. You prove your worth more with every new second. I'll have Haley contact you when shooting resumes."

"Please do, sir," Jorah said, bowing low. "And please get me a better part soon. I play to the level of the role I'm given, and too much of this trash will wreak havoc on my acting abilities."

"Will do, sir. Will do. *Ho ho ho.*" Lord Walker laughed and Jorah disappeared through the halls toward the elevators.

"Lord Walker, sir," Cohen stammered. "But, I—"

"*Enough,*" Lord Walker cut him off. "You've come too close to embarrassing me already. I'm not risking anything else on trusting you, boy. Now shut your mouth. Laura, dear. I expect updates on this. Get it right or you'll never be rid of your past mistakes. Got me?"

Laura nodded.

"Good bye, then. All of you. I hope you do better in the future, for all of your sake."

Lord Walker rode his pneumatic pants out of the studio and Laura could only imagine that she'd never rid herself of her past mistakes no matter how the stupid movie turned out.

໒ ✳ ஃ

LIX. Anna

That was her. That was the Scientist who had told Rosa that she was watching the Family. She had enough power to steal Rosa en route through the fields, and she had enough power to hack into Anna's pathways, bending them to the Scientist's own will. It had to have been her. Anna knew it. But what was she supposed to do about it?

"What the fuck was that?" the little boy who had come looking for his mom said, cowering at the foot of the stairs where he had been sitting when the doors opened and the monstrous mechanical arm came storming in to snatch the little girl away and disappear with her. "Wh—Where's Roo?"

"Roo?" Anna shook her head. Who was Roo? She couldn't think of anything but the Scientist's cold grip on the universe, her power to bend and shape it, not only to her own will but against Anna's.

"Um... Miss, *uh*...ma'am," the boy squeaked in a cracking, trembling voice that was ready to break down into full on sobs at any second. Anna almost felt a tear in her eye at the sound of it. "Where's my mom?" the boy asked, crying now. "I want to go home."

And Anna's tears came, too. She couldn't stop them. The universe, and bending, and the Scientist's control over every aspect of every tiny detail of every single human's life evaporated from her mind. Anna had lost sight of what truly mattered. She had forgone Family and Home for power and influence, and now she was on the verge of forgetting this little boy who was standing in front of her— this little boy whose name she couldn't even recall, only driving Anna to further tears—this little boy who had just lost his best friend in their search for his missing mother, and all he was asking for was to go home.

"Oh, child, no," Anna said, still weeping as she moved to embrace the boy who backed away, crab crawling up a few stairs, before giving in to her hug and sobbing in rhythm with Anna's sobs, comforted in the knowledge of being unjudged. "You are Home,"

Anna went on in a soft voice. "I'm your Mother now. One of them at least. You can call me Anna." She soon controlled her own tears and comforted the boy until he stopped weeping himself.

"W—What happened?" the boy asked, done sobbing now but still wiping tears from his eyes.

"Someone kidnapped your friend," Anna said, patting him on the back. "Did you say her name was Roo?"

The boy nodded, looking like he could break down into tears again at any moment. "Who would do that?"

"I think I know the answer to your question, and I have a way to find out for sure. I might even be able to get your friend back. But first we need to take care of you."

The boy shook his head, eyes welling up with tears again. "No, but— Roo, she..."

"No buts," Anna said, standing from the stairs and pulling the boy up with her. "You look hungry. I know you just ate, but wouldn't some dessert sound perfect?"

The boy grinned a little despite the tears still tumbling from his eyes and the rush of red blood still flushing his face. "I like ice cream," he said. "Though Mom never buys it."

"Of course," Anna said, leading him upstairs to a seat at the bar in the kitchen. "That's why you were here in the first place, wasn't it? You were searching for your mother. What was her name again?"

"Melody Singer," the boy said, climbing up into the stool to cross his arms and lay them on the counter. "Chocolate, please."

"*Hmmm*. Melody Singer," Anna said, searching the freezer for ice cream—Rosa usually liked to keep a little around when they could find it, and she had stocked up with the printers in use. "And your name is?"

"Mike, ma'am," the boy said with a grin. "Mike Singer. What's yours?"

"Anna Chandelier," Anna said, plopping a bucket of ice cream, chocolate—Rosa's favorite, too—on the counter between them. "It's very nice to meet you, Mike."

The boy laughed and sniffled, wiping a big glob of snot onto his sleeve. "And you, ma'am." He grabbed the spoon and swallowed a scoop of ice cream that looked too big to fit in his mouth.

"I only wish we could have met under better conditions,"

Anna said, still standing across the bar from the boy and watching the poor child as he ate, taking each heaping spoonful straight out of the bucket. His mother was Melody Singer. She was one of the bodies who had been taken by the scum protectors, probably to be desecrated for kicks. This little boy had been through so much Hell already and it was only looking to get worse for him. Anna pitied the boy's tiny face as he teared up again, sobbing through a big bite of ice cream because he somehow knew what Anna was about to say.

"Better conditions?" the boy asked, his trembling lips sending slops of chocolate ice cream all of the counter. "Y—You mean, my mother. She's not at home, is she?"

Anna grabbed a towel to wipe up the mess then hurried around the counter to comfort the sobbing boy. "She was an honorable woman, your mother," Anna said, because it was true. "She died fighting to give you a better life."

"*Dead?*" The boy dropped his spoon now, creating another mess which Anna ignored in order to pull him up out of the stool and into a hug. "She can't be!" he demanded, as he fought against her, crying in anger and pain.

"No, no, no. *Shhhhh.* It's okay." Anna patted his back and rocked him like a baby, reassuring him until he settled to the occasional sob and a trickle of tears—not to mention a lot of sniffling. "She was a good woman, your mother. She was doing what she thought was best for you. She was doing what *was* in your best interests. She deserves our respect for that much, for everything she did for you and the Human Family in general. She was a good woman."

"*Hah.*" The boy scoffed, gaining enough composure finally to wriggle away from Anna and stand up, wiping the tears from his eyes and sniffling. "Yeah, right. We must be talking about different people then. Maybe my mom isn't dead after all."

Anna's heart broke just a little bit at the sound of this little boy's beautiful, tragic hope. She shook her head, fighting to hold back more tears of her own. "I wish that were true," she forced through them.

"It is!" the boy yelled, stomping a foot. "That's not my mom! My mom wasn't honorable. She was an addict jumpie who forgot about her kids because she needed to... *Oh my God.*" The boy crumpled to his knees on the kitchen floor, bawling again. "My—

What am—I— *My brothers*—" And his day became worse than Anna had already imagined it to be.

"W—We'll take care of your brothers," she said, only barely controlling her own sobs and having more trouble the more she tried to speak. "And you. But you can't talk about your mother like that. She loved her Family."

"You know nothing about our family!" the boy screamed. "You didn't even know I had brothers! You're the reason my mom's dead. Why would I trust you to take care of us?" He looked around as if he were searching for an escape.

"Because I *am* your family, dear. Me and Rosa are the Family your mom's been coming to help. She's no jumpie." Though she also never mentioned having any kids, but Anna wasn't about to tell the boy that. "She was helping us, helping build a better world for you and your brothers to live in."

The boy scoffed. "*You're* a jumpie. Of course you wouldn't admit that she was. You're a jumpie, my mom who you got killed was, and Roo who you got kidnapped was. Now I'm getting out of here before you try to turn me into one, too, and something equally as bad happens to me." He made for a door but it went to the office, deeper into the Family Home instead of out of it.

Anna followed him, blocking the doorway so he couldn't escape. "*I'm not a jumpie*," she said. "And neither was your mom. I'm telling you. Why won't you listen to me?"

"Listen to you?" the boy said, still searching for an escape that Anna wasn't going to give to him. "I am listening, but you aren't saying anything. You keep talking about some family I've never even heard of, acting like it's my family, too, when you didn't even know I had brothers. You don't even know their names. You probably don't even remember my name, either, and I just told you."

Anna tried to go back in her mind to when he had introduced himself but his name still wouldn't come to her. Her mind was still filled with the problem of the Scientist and where she took that girl to. The only name Anna could think of was the boy's last name so she said that. "Singer."

"Yeah," the boy urged her on. "That's the easy part. What's my first name?" He waited for an answer but Anna just couldn't think of one. "Exactly my point," he said. "You don't know the rest. You don't know me at all. I'm not who you think I am and you better let me go." He rushed at her, trying to push through her arms to the other side of the door, and he did in a way, but only inasmuch as he and Anna fell in a tangle to the ground, both struggling to their feet and ending up in the position they had begun in, the boy searching for some way out of the office and Anna blocking his every exit.

"Hold on, hold on, now. Wait a second," Anna said, breathing heavily. The fall and ensuing struggle had taken more out of her than she'd care to acknowledge. It made her feel so old next to this tiny young thing who would never give up fighting by the looks of him. "You're right. Okay. You're right. Settle down."

The boy stopped searching for an escape for just a moment, taken aback by this admission of ignorance from so old and decayed a woman as Anna herself. Anna took his momentary lapse as a point of entry and continued her speech.

"I've come too far and lost my way," she said. "But I was pushed here, Lord. I was pushed here. And you..." She paused, shaking her head and letting one tear fall from her eye, just one. "Yes, dear child of the one true Family, you are correct when you say that I know nothing about you and your maternal brothers. You are correct when you say that I have lost sight of your names. But child, sweet, innocent, pure, and living human child, you are wrong about why I have lost that sight."

The boy made to speak but the weight of Anna's words, and her heavy eyes staring, kept him quiet.

"You, sweet child, say that I do not care about you, that I am not your *real* family," Anna went on in his silence. "You think I forgot your name because I don't care to remember it. I say, no. No! Your face is forever in my memory after this day. Your love is forever in my heart. Your infinite potential as a free and autonomous human being is forever in my mind. But forgive me your name. Please. Name's pile up with the years. There are too many countless whose flames have gone extinguished and whose light we must continue to reflect in order to keep them alive. Your mother: Melody Singer. Who died protecting you and your brothers from evils she hoped you would never have to face. Yujin Moon and Isha Tender, two of our Family members who died on the same day as your mother and in the same manner. The countless brothers and sisters taken from our lives on the day the *protectors* invaded our homes and murdered our Family for sharing our food with one another. Do you want me to list the names? I can: Billy Serkin, Rwanda Driver, Audrey Baker, John Ryder, Jason Garifo, Treyvon Baker, Aneesha Holmes. I can go on and on and on, but I won't. I assume you get the picture. Names upon names upon names of people I personally knew and cared for. My Family. *Our* Family, yours and mine. And all dead for what?"

The boy just shook his head, tears all dry by now. "How am I supposed to know?" he asked. "You tell me."

"All for you, precious child. All for you and your brothers. Your mother hid you from us because it was the only way she could hide you from the truth of the worlds, but the truth of the worlds took her so now there's nothing left but reality from here on out. You are still a child, though. You're vulnerable. I mean, I'm sure you could take care of yourself if it was only you who you had to worry about, but you have your brothers, too."

"Ron and Bob." The boy shook his head.

"You have Ron and Bob to worry about," Anna said, sensing the boy's interest intensify at the mere mention of solid names he recognized and could grasp onto. "You would never dream of leaving them to fend for themselves, they're too young."

The boy was still shaking his head. "Never," he said. "They're my brothers. I'm the oldest now so I'm the one who has to take responsibility for them. That's how it works."

Anna didn't know whether to chuckle or to cry. The boy looked so earnest in what he said, and he probably truly believed it—and that was probably how the worlds should work—but he was oh so wrong. It was never the oldest, the humans who had been there the longest, giving them the most time to make a mess of things, who paid for all the fun and foley the Family inevitably fell into. No, it was always the youth, the next generation, the ones who had nothing do with anything, who only inherited a mess that no one could teach them how to handle because no one knew how to handle it in the first place, it was always the youngest and most vulnerable who faced the ultimate consequences of all the sins of every human who came before them.

"That is how it should go, my son," Anna said, kind of chuckling and tearing up at the same time. "And that's how it will go in the future that we're building. But you're not the oldest, you hear me? You're too young to be taking on that much responsibility. One life is too many for you to take care of, not to mention three. No. I told you. You're a part of the Family now. You always have been, even when we didn't know you existed. Your mother was a dear good friend of mine, and I swear on her grave and the grave of my own mother that I'll do everything in my power—which is a lot if you'll excuse a momentary lapse of humbleness—to ensure that you and your brothers will have everything you need to continue your life as usual, if not more than that."

The boy scoffed. "What?" he asked. "Like two moms?"

Anna had to suppress a grin. He had played into her hand so perfectly. "On the face of it," she said, "yes. You will have two moms directly in myself and my partner Rosa—that is if you would like to stay here, we have more room than ever and more than enough to accommodate you—but even more than that, you'll be gaining every single mother in the Human Family. Your mother was one of us when—God rest her soul—she was still alive, and now you will meet and be loved by the rest of us."

"I don't know." The boy shook his head. "I don't know. How do I trust you?"

"How do you trust anyone? Why did you trust your mother?"

The boy laughed. "She was always there for me. She's my mom. Why wouldn't I?"

"I thought you said she forgot about you and your brothers."

"Yeah, well…" The boy was looking bashful now. "Not really, you know. Like she always came back just in time or whatever. You know. I mean, we're still alive aren't we?"

"You are." Anna smiled. "More alive than ever. And your mother did everything she could to keep you that way, including working with us and making connections in the Human Family. It was her insurance. I know you don't know what insurance is, but that's what it was. She was making sure you and your brothers would be protected in case anything ever happened to her."

"No, but…" The boy was fighting two sides of a lose lose battle in his head. The cognitive dissonance was visible on his face. "I don't even know you. She would have told us something about you if she wanted this, anything."

"She was protecting you, son. Not from us, but from everything we're fighting against. But now, I'm afraid, the fight has come to your doorstep and you're left only with two options. You can give up and run away, try to make it on your own protecting your two brothers by yourself, or you can join the Family that's waiting for you, choose the option that's best for yourself, and more importantly, choose the option that's best for your brothers."

"No, but..." He shook his head.

"But what? Where else do you have to go?"

He looked like he was going to burst again. This time, though, not into tears, into something else entirely, something which Anna couldn't predict, only wait to unfold. "But—"

The front doors burst open instead, and Anna could hear it even though it was a few rooms away. Feet stomped from the door, through the conference room and kitchen, until they were stomping up behind Anna who turned to see Rosa as pissed as she had ever been. "Anna! Anna!" she called as she stormed through the Home. "You'll never believe what the—" She stopped in her tracks when she saw the kid, still trying to decide what his future would be. "Who's this?"

"Oh, I..." Anna said, glancing between them.

"Mike," the boy said, saving Anna from the embarrassment of still not remembering. "Mike Singer, newest member of the Family—apparently."

"Mike Singer?" Rosa said.

"*Mike*," Anna said, embracing him. "Really?"

"You said so yourself," he said, squirming away a little but not trying too hard. "I can't take care of my brothers myself, can I? I need a family. I need you."

"Yes, yes, oh yes," Anna said, kissing him on the head then turning to Rosa. "Did you hear that, Rosa dear? You'll never believe it. We have three new children."

"*Great*," Rosa said, rolling her eyes. Obviously the meeting about the movie didn't go too well or else she would be in a better mood. "Just what we need. some kids running around the House with all the new guns we have."

"Guns?" Mike said, wide eyed and excited by the prospect.

"I told you I didn't want them in the House," Anna said. She had forgotten about that little discussion in her need to overpower the Scientist, but now that she remembered it, she would have to be sure to take extra precautionary measures in storing the armory away so the kids couldn't get to it.

"And I told you we had no other choice," Rosa said. "We've talked about this already and I don't have time to go over it again. *Any arguments?*" She shot a look at the kid which Anna thought didn't bode well for the future of their growing nuclear family. "No? Then if you'll excuse me," she stepped between them into the office and gently showed them out, "I have some planning to get underway and there's no time to waste. Good day." And she slammed the door behind her.

"Shit," Mike said, holding a hand to his mouth as if Anna would chastise him for using the word. "I mean, she was cranky."

"You must forgive her," Anna said, showing Mike back to the kitchen. "It's been a rough day on her—a rough few weeks, as a matter of fact. She's not always like this, though. I promise that, *cross my heart*. She'll warm up to you and your brothers. You'll see."

"Um, yeah. About that," Mike said, playing with the hem of his shirt. "So does that mean we're supposed to move in here or what? We wouldn't be able to stay in our own place, would we?"

"Oh, no." Anna shook her head. "I'm afraid that's impossible. There's no telling what would happen when the owners of the apartment found you boys living there without paying rent, but I can tell you for sure that, whatever it is, it won't be good. No, you're going to have to go get your brothers right now and pack all your things up then come back here where we can set you up with a room of your own."

"I get my own bed, though, right?" Mike asked, holding up a finger as if his question were a demand and this conversation some kind of negotiation. "I'm not sharing again after I only just got my own. Waking up in a puddle of pee every night is no way to live."

"Of course, dear. Each of you can have your own bed. Bunk beds, as a matter of fact. Three stacked on top of each other. You hurry up and get your brothers, then I'll show you."

"Bunk beds?" Mike said, excited, scurrying for the front door now that he knew which it was. "I call top!" he said and he slammed the door behind him, off to bring two other new children back into the Family. Oh how it continued to grow.

Anna groaned. All she wanted to do was get back on the consoles to hunt the Scientist and the missing girl, but she knew she had to see what was bothering Rosa first—problems with the execution of her precious movie, no doubt. Anna had tried to tell her that Threes couldn't be trusted, their entire profession was lying, but Rosa insisted that they needed professionals to do the job if they wanted it done right.

Rosa was sitting behind her desk, scribbling in one of the many notebooks that were strewn all around the office, when Anna entered. Rosa didn't look up at the sound of the door opening or closing, or even at the feel of Anna's hands massaging her too tense shoulders. She only looked up when the thought in her head was all out on the paper, and then she did it with a sigh. "You won't believe what I just went through," she said, shaking her head and getting into the massage now. Finally her muscles started to loosen. "Though it sounds like you've had an adventure of your own today."

Anna chuckled, shaking her head though Rosa couldn't see the gesture. "Besides the three kids we just adopted," Rosa groaned, "another one was kidnapped right out of our basement."

"Out of our basement?" Rosa asked, turning to look at Anna. "How? By who?"

"The Scientist," Anna said, crossing around to take a seat on the other side of the desk so Rosa wouldn't have to crane her already tense neck. "And some giant robot arm. I'm pretty sure I can find where she took the girl to, though—and get us there, which might be even harder."

"Great." Rosa sighed. "Just what we need on top of everything we're already facing."

"So how'd your meeting go, then?" Anna asked, trying to change the subject even though she could already predict the answer to her own question based on Rosa's mood.

"Horrible. Terrible. No good. Very bad. Worse than I could have imagined. Worse still because of our dear *Lord* Walker's involvement. I'm not sure we can rely on this project to spread our message at all anymore. It may be time to abort the mission entirely and start over at a more opportune time."

"That bad, huh?" There weren't likely to be any more opportune times than this one. Now was the moment they had been waiting their entire lives for.

"Worse. They're not following the script we agreed on."

"I told you we shouldn't have given them their equipment

until after they shot the movie for us."

"But then they couldn't have shot the movie at all." Rosa sighed. "We had no choice."

"So how different can it be, though?" Anna asked. "Can't we just make them change it back?"

"Too different." Rosa scoffed. "It's still anti-robot, but that's only half the message—the less important half, at that. All mention of the Family and its supreme importance: *Whoosh*." She made a gesture with her hands as if they were flying out the window.

"But we had an agreement." That was worse than Anna had thought it could be. She didn't care nearly as much about the anti-robot message as the pro-Family one. To her, that was pretty much the entire message, not just half of it. "We'll make them change it or take back everything we've given them. It's the only way we can respond."

"Oh, I've thought of that already," Rosa said, chuckling and shaking her head. "That was my first thought, in fact. But I'm afraid it's impossible. Our great and powerful *Lord* Walker has taken control of things, and anything we took from those no good Threes would simply be returned to them from Lord Walker's own stores. In the end it means nothing to any of them who they're working for or which of our printers their equipment comes out of, they just want to work."

"*Great*." No wonder Rosa was ready to scrap the project altogether. Anna would have no problem scrapping it, either, if the pro-Family message wasn't going to be included, but, "Wouldn't Lord Walker just continue filming without us anyway? So what's the point in scrapping the project?"

"That's the exact point," Rosa said with a big smile. "We sacrifice this project because we're not going to be able to change their minds, and they'll still make half our message without us doing any work. This way we can direct our time and attention toward tactics with a higher chance of success and revisit this one if it becomes feasible again in the future." She leaned back in her chair, satisfied with her assessment of the situation but not looking happy about it.

"And what tactics did you have in mind, exactly?"

"I've been waiting for you to ask just that," Rosa said, leaning forward again and putting her arms on the desk. "I think we should leave our *Lord* to his play acting—never alerting him to our exit from the project, of course—while we get back to reality."

"I wish you'd stop calling him *Lord*," Anna complained, smacking her lips like she had a disgusting taste in her mouth. "It sounds so blasphemous."

"Whatever," Rosa said, waving her hands. "That's not the point. He's nothing compared to *our* Lord, and he has nothing to do with what I plan next, anyway."

"Which is..." Anna said, slightly comforted by Rosa's words.

"Which is to bring the fight to the people who deserve it the most, to bring it to the *things* that cause all our problems in the first place. I've had enough of dealing with flabby, fat tuxedoed owners and slippery, sly, lying Threes. It's time for us to take our fate into our own hands by taking the fight to the robots' front door."

"The robots' front door?" Anna scoffed. "Do you even know where that is?"

Rosa twiddled her thumbs on the desk and put on her puppy dog—I'm innocent of any evil ever—face that Anna knew all too well. "Well, darling." Rosa smiled, a twinkle in her eye. "That's where you come in."

"Of course." Anna sighed. "And do you have any idea how hard it is to do something like that? Do you know how much work it takes? The energy?"

"I know that my Nanna is the greatest four dimensional composer known to all of Humankind. I know you can do it." She smiled wider. "I know I love you."

Anna scoffed despite her blushing grin. "And how do you know all that when you don't even know the work it takes?"

"Because I know my Nanna Banana," Rosa said, coming around the desk to sit on Anna's lap and kiss her all over her face. "She can do anything in that fourth dimension of hers. She's the Queen of it, master and commander." Kiss, kiss, kiss, kiss, kiss. "You are, though, aren't you? You can do it," Rosa said, standing and going around to massage Anna's back. "You *can* do it."

Anna groaned in pleasure as her muscles gave way to Rosa's touch. "Well, yes," she said. "That is," she added, correcting herself so as to not sound too pretentious. "I think I can find your robots for you—not that I think I'm the Queen of the Fourth Dimension, or whatever you called me."

Rosa laughed. "I call 'em like I see 'em." She retook her seat behind the desk. "So you really think you can find them?"

"Yes." Anna nodded. "I do. On two conditions."

"Go ahead." Rosa smiled.

"One: You have to come down there in the basement with me while I do it so you can see just how much work it takes. Maybe then you won't be so willy nilly about how you throw the fourth dimension into your plans in the future."

Rosa chuckled. "I can do that. What's number two?"

"We talk about the kids before we do anything."

Rosa groaned. Anna knew this would be the only way to get her to discuss the matter, though, so she pressed on. "They need us," she said. "They need a Family, Rosa, and their mother died helping ours."

"And why them?" Rosa asked, shrugging. "Why not one of the countless other human children across Six—and beyond—who all need the same exact thing?"

Anna hadn't exactly thought about that. How many other Mikes were there out there? How many orphans were created on the day the protectors came storming through their streets, guns ablazing and looking for a target? Too many, Anna was sure, but they would have to wait. First she would take care of these three who were right in front of her, then she would take care of the Scientist who had created the androids and promoted the killing of her Family, then she'd take care of the rest of the needy children after all of that. "Because these three landed on our doorstep," Anna finally said. "Because their mother was killed in our assault on the protector's facilities and that makes us more culpable in their situation than the situations of the other orphans in Six. Because I already told the boy we'd give him and his brothers a place to stay. And because we have more than enough food and room to accommodate them with our countless transporter rings and printers."

"Well, when you put it that way," Rosa said, giving in. She had fought too many battles already that day to keep arguing this unwinnable one. "What about the guns?"

"I'll keep the armory on lockdown," Anna said. "And you'll make sure everyone else keeps close track of theirs. In the meantime, we'll teach the kids proper safety precautions. Everything will be fine as long as we're not stupid about it."

"And maybe we can get a few more little soldiers out of it." Rosa chuckled.

Anna frowned, even if it was just a joke.

"Alright, alright. I was just kidding," Rosa said. "Can we go find those robots now? I want to set the battle plans as soon as I can."

"So that's it?" Anna asked. "You agree just like that, now on to what you wanted to talk about in the first place?"

"Well, did you want me to argue further?"

"No. Of course not. But I do want you to actually consider what you're agreeing to, Rosa. We'll be their parents for the rest of their lives. There's no turning our back on that responsibility once we've agree to bear it."

"Which you already did," Rosa said.

"Yeah, but—"

"So there's nothing more to discuss until the kids actually get here, right?"

"I guess, but—"

"Then let's do what's best for the Family and find those robots."

Anna cracked a smile despite her annoyance with Rosa's flippancy. "You know, you're lucky I want to find that Scientist so bad," she said.

"Oh yeah?" Rosa asked, crossing her eyes. "Why's that?"

"Because I think we'll find her and the robots in the same place. Now come on." Anna grabbed Rosa by the hand and led her down to the basement.

"Well, then," Rosa said. "Demonstrate, my Queen of the Fourth Dimension."

"Stop that," Anna said, chuckling and slapping Rosa on the arm. "Now look. You see this?" She flipped both consoles on at once and set them into motion.

"Yeah, so?" Rosa shrugged.

"This is the solution to all your problems. Look at this." She tapped and swiped a few times, one hand on each console, to bring up a map of all seven worlds spanning both the screens. "This is the universe as you know it."

"I don't see anything," Rosa said, but Anna didn't hear her.

She wasn't paying attention anymore. Something was going on in the fourth dimension that she had never seen before. She swiped and typed and clicked and tapped. The notes of the universe arranged themselves into patterns so complex as to be impossible. She searched for a source, expecting to find the Scientist in control of this symphony, but it came from somewhere else, somewhere familiar. Then she knew where it was.

Anna looked up from the consoles, calling, "The girl!" but even though Rosa was there to hear her, it was too late. The basement had vanished around them and they were in a new world entirely. A world like nothing Anna had ever seen before.

ಓ ✄ ✑

LX. Roo

All Roo wanted to do was bend, but life kept getting in the way.

First of all, she would have been happy in her closet—*er*—secret lair, though it was hard to keep calling it that after she had seen what other benders were working with, but she would have been happy there, bending one path at a time, hacking into the system from the outside, if it weren't for Anna and the Scientist. Anna had shown Roo the true art of bending. She set the bar for what one person with limited equipment could possibly accomplish by themselves. While the Scientist, on the other hand, had bending down to a science. Instead of the warm creativity of a gut feeling, the Scientist relied on cold hard data fed through intricate algorithms until it was gobbledy-gook that only robots could understand. Both methods offered their unique benefits and drawbacks. Going Anna's way, Roo could remain the free, independent outsider she had relished being for so long now, while going the Scientist's way meant she could command control of a wider sweeping stretch of the universe than she ever even knew existed. It was an almost impossible decision to make, made actually impossible for the moment thanks to point number two, which was that, second of all, Roo still had to go to school.

"You can't be serious," she complained to her mom when she had finally got home from being with the Scientist. Though she hadn't agreed to anything yet, Roo still took the system out for a test drive and she didn't leave the Scientist's lab until early in the morning. Roo would still be there bending, too, if the Scientist hadn't forced her to leave and go make her decision. Well how was she supposed to decide anything now with stupid school getting in her way? "It's just one day, Mom," Roo begged. "*Please.* I haven't taken a sick day in weeks."

"That's because you haven't been sick for weeks," her mom said, shaking her head. "And you're not sick now. So, no. You're going to school and that's final." She handed Roo her backpack.

"But, Mom, I—"

"*No buts*. You can make your decision—or play your bending game—or whatever it is you're so eager to do after class. Now go on. You don't want to be late."

"But—"

"*Go*."

Roo heaved a big sigh as she grabbed her bag and strapped it on her back. "*Fine*," she said. "Whatever." And she stomped out of the house, towards her secret lair rather than towards school despite her mom's demands. Roo never should have asked for the day off in the first place. It was always easier to ask for forgiveness than it was to ask for permission, anyway.

She was walking by instinct, giving no thought to the path she had traveled so many times before, trying to find some way to decide between the art and the science of bending, when she ran into Mike—literally—and tumbled to the ground in a heap with him.

"Oh—*uh*—I'm sorry," he said, standing to help her up. "Oh, Roo! It's you. Just the jumpie I was looking for."

"I'm not a jumpie," Roo groaned, wiping the dirt off her pants.

"Yeah, yeah, *whatever*." Mike rolled his eyes. "But I just had to find you, okay. You're never gonna believe what happened after you left."

Roo scoffed. "I wouldn't really call what happened to me leaving. It was more like I was kidnapped."

"Oh, yeah," Mike said. "I guess you can call it that. Where'd you end up going anyway?

Roo gritted her teeth. She kind of wanted to punch this annoying kid in the face. He was just another in a long line of distractions that were trying to prevent her from deciding her future. "Do you really care?" she asked.

"What? Yeah, of course I do." Mike almost looked offended. "You're my friend. Especially after you—well—at least you *tried* to help me find my mom."

"Tried? What do you mean tried? We did find her. Anna said—"

Mike shook his head. Roo was afraid he was going to cry for a second—she had no idea how to comfort sad people and didn't have time to learn—but he quickly snapped out of it and half smiled. "No, well, Anna was protecting us. Her and my mom both were.

And, technically, you did help me find her, though there was no her left to be found."

Roo held her hand to her mouth. "You mean..." she said.

Mike nodded. He made a motion like a knife slitting his throat so he didn't have to say the words, and Roo wasn't sure which would have been worse. She noticed her jaw was open—and probably had been for some time—then forced it closed only to fail at opening it again to spit out words.

"You don't have to say anything," Mike said after Roo had tried to talk and failed at it for long enough to be embarrassed. "You know, it's kind of for the better, actually. I know, I know, it would obviously be better if she weren't dead, but at least I know who she really was now."

"Who was she?" Roo asked, happy her vocal chords were able to sound at least three short words.

"*Not a jumpie*," Mike said, stomping a foot as if he were crushing the idea of it like a bug. "She wasn't addicted to anything. She was protecting us. You saw what those people were capable of."

"What who was capable of?"

"Oh, well, you know. The people who took you or whatever, for starters. And the one's who killed my mom, right? Especially them."

"But who killed your mom, Mike?" Roo was getting worried. Mike's ideas didn't seem to connect. It was like he was reciting taught information that he didn't quite understand yet. "I never saw them."

"Well, no. Me neither." He shook his head, looking more confused than ever. "But Anna did. She told me it was the protectors, or whatever. That's who Mom was protecting us from."

Of course. Anna and the Human Family were behind this. No wonder it was like arguing with a student instead of a master. "The protectors?" Roo asked. "That's why your mother left you all those times? To protect you from the protectors?"

Mike nodded emphatically, like he was trying to convince himself, too. "That's right. She was fighting to keep us safe. All of us humans. You, too."

"*Right.*" Roo nodded, not really believing the kid's story but not wanting to burst his bubble about his dead mom either. "So who's supposed to take care of your brothers now? Just you?"

"No." Mike scoffed. "*Ugh*. I couldn't handle that. As a matter of fact, for the first time ever, I won't have to. I'm free, Roo. I'm finally free to live my own life."

"But who if not you?" Roo asked, dreading the answer.

"*The Family*. That's who. That's what I've been trying to tell you. Anna and Rosa said I—said *we* could come live with them. Isn't that awesome?"

"You're going to live with Anna?"

"And Rosa." Mike nodded. "She's not supposed to be that cranky all the time, by the way."

"And all because they told you that your mom was working with them? Because they told you that she was fighting to protect their Human Family, or whatever."

"*Exactly*," Mike said, smiling. "So now the Human Family is going to take care of us. Isn't it great?"

"And the Scientist already knew about Anna and her capabilities a long time ago. She wasn't afraid at all, otherwise she would have done something about them."

"The what? What are you talking about now?"

"There has to be some connection between the two, some reason the Scientist continues to let Anna's transport system exist. Some thing is holding those two together, and I'm going to figure out what it is."

"What are you talking about? I don't understand."

"You said they were letting you live at their house, right? Or the Home, or whatever. Did they give you a room yet?"

"Oh my God, *yes*. You wouldn't believe it. I get my own bed, okay, my own desk, my own toy box. I don't have to share any of it. It's insane."

"You know, I'd really like to see it," Roo said, grabbing him by the collar and pulling him toward the Family Home. "How about we skip class and go take a tour instead?"

"I—but—" Mike complained, pretending to fight but not really trying to stop her from taking him wherever she wanted to go—no one ever really wanted to go to school. "What if the teacher get's mad at..."

The *Family Home* was a few blocks away. They made quick time of it as soon as Mike stopped pretending to want to go to class and carried his own weight. When they got to the block the building was on Roo pulled Mike into the shadow of an alley.

"So you have your keys, right?" she asked him.

"Oh, it's never locked." Mike chuckled. *"The doors to the Family Home are always open to any human in need,"* he recited as if he were mocking someone's voice—probably Rosa's or Anna's.

"So is anyone gonna be there?" Roo asked.

"Yeah, prolly. I don't know." He shrugged. "What's it matter, anyway? I live here now."

"But Anna, is she going to be there?"

"I don't know. Why do you care? We're just going to see my room. I'm allowed to have friends over."

"Alright, alright," Rosa said, turning him around to face the house and patting him on the back to calm him. "Settle down now, cowboy. I was just asking. Let's go see it already."

"Wait," Mike said, stopping and turning back around to her. "I'm not as stupid as you think I am, you know. Just because I don't know about the fourth dimension—or whatever—and just because I don't know about jumping and all that doesn't mean I was born yesterday. You got that?"

"Woah, now," Roo said, waving her hands in mock defense. "I don't think you're stupid."

Mike scoffed. "You sure treat me like it."

Roo felt a little ashamed. He was right about that, but she wasn't ready to admit it. It wasn't that she thought he was stupid, per se, just that he wasn't as smart as she was. No one was. So if she thought he was stupid, she thought everyone everywhere was stupid, and Mike really had no reason to complain anyway because he wasn't unique in that aspect. "I don't think you're stupid," she repeated trying to placate him. "I'm sorry if I made you feel that way. So, please, can we go see your room now?"

"Then prove it," Mike said, crossing his arms. "Tell me what you really want to do here. I know you're not interested in seeing my bedroom."

"I—well…" There was no hiding it now. She would just have to convince him to go along with her plan—or at the very least not to spoil it. "I did have a little something else in mind. Yes." She nodded.

"Well…" Mike tapped his feet.

"Well, I just wanted to get another look at Anna's transport system, you know," Roo said, unable to think of a lie even if she wanted to tell one. "Her consoles are more intricate than anything I've ever seen, and I thought I might find some inspiration for the design of my own secret lair."

Mike scoffed. "Your janitor's closet?" he said. "You'll never be able to—"

Roo slapped him on the arm. "My *secret lair* needs work, I know, but that's why I want to look at Anna's. She's bending the walls without even being tapped directly into them, and I want to know how she does it. It's almost like she's creating her own walls right there in her basement."

Mike scoffed, shaking his head. "That's just a bunch of jumpie jargon," he said. "It means nothing to me. You know, maybe I shouldn't let you in after all. I don't want to ruin a good thing for myself on the first day of living here. C'mon. Let's go back to class." He took a few steps in that direction but stopped when he saw that Roo wasn't following.

"Never call me a jumpie again," she said. "I'm a bender."

"*Fine*," Mike said. "Then it was bender jargon. There's no difference. You're addicted, and I'm not going to enable you. Now c'mon. We're already late for class."

"I'm *not* your mother," Roo said.

Mike scoffed. "Leave her out of this. She wasn't a jumpie. Anna told me the truth about her."

"Lies. Anna told you lies and she's gonna keep telling them to you to keep you in her stupid family. It's a trap, Mike, and now's the time to get out while you still can."

"You're wrong." Mike looked like he was going to cry again. Roo felt a little bad that she had to talk about his late mother like that, but it was too late for pity. Pity would only put him in further danger. "My mom believed in the Family, too," he said. "She gave her life for it."

"She gave her life for Anna's benefit and the benefit of her cranky partner. No one else. Not you, not your brothers, not some mythological Family which doesn't even exist. She was trapped just like you are, and if you don't get out now, you'll end up dead just like your mom."

"Fuck you, jumpie!" Mike was crying now, and spitting while he screamed, "I never should have come to you for help in the first place. You're toxic! You can find your own fucking way in. I'm leaving." He stomped away toward school, whether he was going there or not.

Roo stood in the alley, shaking her head in silence. She hated to piss Mike off like that—on some level—but he needed to see the truth despite his denials of its verifiability. Hopefully he'd wake up to it before the trap was sprung—that is if it hadn't been sprung already.

She turned to face the family home, that central hub of evil with its tendrils emanating through all four dimensions. Her mission would be more difficult without the bedroom tour as cover, but if anyone questioned her as to why she was there, she could just say that she was looking for Mike, was he home? She watched the door from her alley corner for some time—no one entering or leaving—before she cautiously slunk over and extended a trembling hand to the door knob.

She took a deep breath, opened the door to an empty entryway, and blew all the air out of her lungs in a too loud huff. Grinning at her luck, she made her way to the basement door and pulled it open to reveal stairs she didn't recognize. Climbing down them she found stacks of supplies rather than the transporter system she was sure was there before.

"*Ugh.*" She groaned as she climbed back up the stairs. This had to be the place. She knew it was. She closed the door and scanned the still empty—thank God—halls but her reconnaissance only proved to her that she had gone in the right door. She opened it again and ran down to groan at the empty supply room before running back upstairs and slamming the door closed behind her.

She huffed, leaning her back on the stupid door. What did this all mean? This was the door, the transport system was supposed to be down there, what was she to do now?

The door tried to open behind her, but by reflex, she braced against it, shutting it tight. She only had a split second to decide what to do next and ended up diving into an office instead of the kitchen. The door swung open again and out came Anna and her cranky partner who was complaining loudly.

"I can't believe that stupid door got stuck again. I can't take it anymore."

"It was probably just someone going to the supply closet,"

Anna said, her voice moving toward the kitchen—thank God. "You can't have two doors in the same place like that at not expect to get some crossover."

"Yeah, whatever," her cranky partner said as Roo dove into the basement door they had just come out of right before it closed.

The stairs were different now. They were the stairs Roo recognized. She climbed down them to find the two consoles and six transporter rings she had been looking for. It was now or never.

She only booted up one of the consoles. Two would be too many to control and more to shut off if someone found her out. She got distracted playing with the thing for a while before she remembered where she was and what she was there for, then she started searching through the console's recent history.

A lot of it was random. Another lot of it directed at the protector's world where *the Family* must have been doing some type of thing. Then there was the anomaly. It was a place that had been searched often but never visited. It seemed more like it was being surveilled. Roo zoomed in on that spot and there weren't a lot of paths in or out, maybe two or three: printing, disposal, and a single entrance—a single entrance for now.

Roo's hands flew over the console's touchscreen, levers, and keys. The universe unravelled before her. A path opened up and she put it into place. Soon the transport ring was humming and she knew someone would hear the sound, but whoever it was would be too late. The secret was found out. She stepped through the door just as it fwipped closed behind her, silencing the voices that were calling for her to stop as they ran down into the family's basement.

She was in a giant office now. The carpet was red and soft, and there were paintings of big fat people dressed up in black and white costumes all over the walls. Behind a gargantuan desk sat a flabby fat man who was wearing the same costume as the people in the paintings. At Roo's appearance, he coughed and choked on something from the huge pile of food he was eating in front of him. It reminded Roo of the scene she had seen from above when lines of similarly clothed fatties ate from similarly giant piles of food. She was disgusted and wanted leave already, but she stood her ground despite that.

"Who—*Ho ho*—" The big fat man in black and white said through his coughing. "Who are you? Wh—What are you doing here?"

"Who are you?" Roo demanded, walking straight up to his desk, which was too high so she had to push a chair close to it and jump up to be seen.

"I am Lord Walker, master of everything you see and have ever seen," he said, sweeping his hands in a grand gesture over the vast desk. "I demand to know who intrudes on my private time."

"How do you know Anna?" Roo asked, ignoring his demands.

"The Sixer? She's Rosa's partner. I'd be rid of your Anna if I could, though."

Roo nodded. "So you do know them, then."

"*Enough.*" Lord Walker slammed a fat fist on the desk and the sound of it rang in Roo's ears. "Who are you? I demand to know."

"And the Scientist? You know her, too. Don't you?" Roo went on.

The fat man scoffed. "That's about enough," he said. "Haley! Come get this child out of here. How did it even get in here in the first place?"

"*Wait.*" Roo had to think fast. "Wait, wait. I'm just kidding, okay. I—"

"Who are you?" the fat man demanded. "Stop toying with me. Are you—*ooooohhh*—of course, you're the director I've been talking to. Is that it? Aronostly is it? I didn't expect anyone so... So..."

"Stop right there," Roo said, about to pee herself she was so nervous but continuing her show of confidence nonetheless. "Just tell me, why are you working with Anna?"

"That's exactly what I asked you here for, old boy. I'm working on a movie with her. She's hired a director, but he's not living up to my standards. I need someone with more vision. Someone like you. I've got a big project for you, now. Bigger than anything you've ever worked on. What do you say?"

Roo didn't have anything to say. She didn't really know what she had gotten herself into or how she was supposed to get out of it.

A door opened somewhere behind her. In walked a woman who was wearing black and white, too, but her costume was a short, lacy skirt with no top hat. She strutted up to the side of the desk, between Roo and Lord Walker, and curtsied. "Yes, Lord," she said in a quiet voice.

"Why didn't you tell me our guest had arrived?" he chided her. "We need refreshments, dear. I'll take an old-fashioned and our guest will have…"

"Guest, sir?" the woman looked confusedly at Roo.

"What would you like?" the fat man asked her. "Any drink you can think of, we have it."

"Oh—*uh*…" What was she supposed to say? "I'll have a milk, please."

"Milk?" the fat man said, a strange look on his face. Roo's body wanted to run away at the sight of it, but before it could, the fat man started laughing. "*Ho ho ho*. You heard the man. Milk it is. A real old fashioned drink, that one. *Ho ho ho*!"

"Yes, sir." The woman curtsied and left through the only door in the room.

"So," the fat man said. "Your milk's coming. *Ho ho ho*. And you've heard my offer. Now tell me, what do you think?"

"I, *uh*— Well, sir… I'm still not entirely sure what it is you're offering," Roo stalled.

"A job, my boy. *Ho ho ho*! You're not truly so dense are you? No, of course not. I've seen your body of work. I know better. You're just pulling my leg, aren't you? This is an act. *Ho ho ho*. Good one, my boy. You Threes never quit entertaining, do you?"

Roo groaned, hoping the gesture wasn't audible, but what was this fatso going on about? Directors and movies had nothing to do with Anna and her transport system for as far as Roo could tell, while this Lord Walker, whoever he was, kept going on about some sort of job. He thought that Roo was someone else, someone who could probably still walk into the office at any minute and blow her cover, so she'd have to get what little information she could out of the fat man as fast as she could then get out of there soon after—if she could even find an escape when the time came.

The door opened behind her and Roo almost jumped out of her seat at the sound of it. Luckily it wasn't the director she was impersonating but the servant woman in the short skirt with their drinks. She set a brownish liquid in front of Lord Walker and a tall glass of milk in front of Roo.

"Is that all, sir?" she asked with a curtsy.

Lord Walker downed his drink in one loud gulp. "I'll have another of these," he said, slamming the empty glass on the desk with a loud clang. "What about you, old boy? Do you need anything else?"

Roo shook her head. She didn't even want the milk she already had, but she took a sip of it anyway so she didn't have to speak.

"Then just the old fashioned, dear. Move along." He waved the woman out of the room and she left with a curtsy.

"What do you think of that one, eh?" Lord Walker asked, winking at Roo and pointing at the door the woman had just left through. "Legs that go on for miles, if you know what I mean. *Ho ho ho!*"

Roo nodded and laughed even though she had no idea what he meant.

"Yeah, I know you do, old boy," Lord Walker said in a conspiratorial tone. "I saw you oogling her."

Roo blushed. "I—"

"*Ho ho ho!*" Lord Walker slammed a fat fist on the desk. "No need to worry, my boy. You've done nothing wrong. I won't chastise you. She's nothing more than an object, after all—another one of my possessions. She's meant to be looked at, designed to like it even. She likes you looking at her, boy, and I do, too, so go right ahead and do it. *Ho ho ho!*"

Roo nodded and smiled. She had met boys who thought the same about girls before, but never one who thought that she was a boy, too, and as such, revealed to her what was truly on his mind. No matter how much she disagreed with it, though, she had to play along or blow her cover. She needed to get out of there sooner than ever.

"*Oh ho ho!*" Lord Walker went on. "I know, my boy. It leaves you speechless, doesn't it? All that concentrated beauty in one single package, and all at my beck and call. I snap my fingers and she's there. My stomach grumbles and she's already making me breakfast. Time to take my pants off and she's by my side." He winked and Roo almost choked on the milk she was sipping. "Oh you ol' sport." Lord Walker grinned. "You heard that right. She's next to my bed, under it, or in it, however I require. *Ho ho ho!*"

The conversation had already gone too far and Lord Walker

just kept taking it further. Roo had to say something to put an end to it, but what?

"*Uh*—Right, sir—*er*—Lord." Roo smiled, trying her hardest not to look as disgusted as she felt. "But I'm not sure what this has to do with me or the job you're offering."

"*Ho ho ho*," Lord Walker chuckled. "Don't play sly with me now. You know good and well what I'm getting at. I'm sure you have fantasies of your own, the perfect woman lifted from the best attributes of characters in the movies you've made. Well, my boy, it's not just a fantasy anymore. I can make all your dreams come true, *no matter how depraved they might be*." Lord Walker grinned and winked his monocled eye.

Roo couldn't take it anymore. She wanted to gag, or to spit out some insult and run away, but she choked down both urges. "And if my fantasies can't be fulfilled with a woman?" she asked. "What then?"

"*Ho ho ho*! Really, my boy? I know things are different in Three, but I never took you for the type. And *yes*, we have men, too, if that better suits your desire. *Ho ho ho*."

"*No*," Roo snapped. "I mean, no, sir—*uh*—Lord, sir," she went on more calmly. "What if no slave at all could fulfill my desires, man or woman?"

"I take offense to that term, *slave*," Lord Walker huffed. "She's no more a slave to me than your camera is to you, or the elevator you rode in on is to anyone else. She's a robot, not a human. She can't be a slave."

A robot? That was impossible. Something so lifelike couldn't be anything but human. Lord Walker was just making excuses for his abhorrent behavior. He was a sexist pig—almost literally a pig at his size—of a slave master, and Roo had seen enough. As if on cue, the woman—who was clearly a human after looking at her again—came back in and put another drink in front of Lord Walker with a curtsy.

"There you are, sir," she said with a smile—a *human* smile. "Can I get you anything else?"

"No, sweetheart. Not right now," Lord Walker said, shooing her away. "We're trying to have a conversation here. Be gone."

"Actually, sir," Roo said before the woman could curtsy and leave. "It's a little embarrassing, but I could really use the bathroom right now." She did a little dance in her seat like she really had to go.

Lord Walker looked shocked for a moment, like Roo had started speaking a foreign language all of a sudden. "The bathroo— *Oh*. Of course. *Ho ho ho*." He slammed his ham fist on the desk with his bellowing laughter. "*The restroom*. I thought you meant to take a bath. I wasn't going to say anything about your stench, but I didn't think you needed to go so far as request a bath mid meeting. *Ho ho ho!*"

"Yes, well..." Roo said, still dancing and actually getting an urge to pee as she pretended to have one. "Do you mind?"

"*Oh ho ho!* Of course not, sport. Forgive me. With these pants I never think twice about it, you know. *Ho ho ho.* You heard the man, Haley, dear. Show him to the restroom, please. *Ho ho ho!*"

"Sir, yes, sir." Haley curtsied and turned to Roo. "Follow me, please, sir."

Roo scooped up her backpack and followed Haley out of the door and into a long hall. Roo kept going toward the metal doors at the other end of the hall, but after after Haley had closed the wooden door they had just left, she called Roo back. "This way, please, sir."

"Oh," Roo said, crossing back. "I'm sorry, I thought—"

"Yes, sir. We only use the one door here, though. So if you'll please." She opened the door and instead of the office there was the biggest bathroom Roo had ever seen, with too many toilets and just as many gold plated sinks. "I'll be out here to escort you back to the office when you're done."

"Oh—*uh*, thanks," Roo said, stepping into the bathroom as Haley closed the door behind her.

Roo dropped her bag on the ceramic tile and rushed over to vomit in the toilet. She didn't know if it was all the adrenaline from almost being caught or the disgusting combination of Lord Walker's sloppy face and creepy words, but she had to get everything inside of her out. After she had eradicated it all from her body—including her mouth by washing it with water from the faucet a few times—she sat on the toilet to take the pee she had faked needing and figure a way out of this Hell hole.

She could just try to finish the meeting then leave like she was always supposed to be there, but that came with plenty of risks. First, she'd have to sit through more conversation with the disgusting Lord Walker. Second, the person who she was impersonating could walk in at any minute—then she'd really be screwed. And third, when she did get to leave, there would be no telling where they would send her. Three, by the sound of it, almost certainly wasn't the world she wanted to go to, her world, home. So that was pretty much out of the question.

What else was there, though? She could burst out of the door and make a break for it. But that Haley would be outside waiting, and even if Roo could get past her, she wouldn't know how to use the crazy doors they have which obviously relied on some advanced automatic remote bending system of some kind that Roo had never seen the likes of—except maybe at the Scientist's lab.

Which brought her back to the real crux of the situation, back to the problem that was eating at her mind even more than her need to escape the rat trap she was caught in, the fact that her future, her entire universe even, was being controlled by three old fogies she had never met before in her life. Anna had her transport system, capable of forming new walls in remote locations and run by the most competent bender Roo had ever witnessed, Anna herself. Lord Walker here had his magic doors and elevators, and no doubt countless other secret control systems hidden away in his labyrinth of pompous, fat, sexist slave mongering. And the Scientist had the most technologically advanced four dimensional bending system possible with the current standards of technology. All three of them were stuck in their old fashioned ways, all three had too much control over Roo's universe, and all three lacked one vital attribute which alone could save them from collapsing in on themselves: foresight.

Roo finished, flushed, and washed her hands then set to pulling her handheld transporter console out of her backpack. The bathroom door had to be connected to the walls, it was the only way it could work the way it did, opening onto different rooms like that. She looked around for something hard, found a plunger under the sink, and used the wooden end to bust open the drywall next to the door jamb. She worried at first about the noise but gave in and smashed without reserve. Hopefully Haley was worlds away, not just on the other side of the drywall.

Behind the filthy white wall she found exactly what she needed, a mash of multicolored wires almost teeming with electricity. She ripped one out, careful not to shock herself—not that she hadn't felt that pain a million times before already—and jacked her portable console in. In the next second it was on and she fell deep into the fourth dimension. Every one of them were going to come face to face and admit what they had done, admit what they had colluded to keep alive, Anna, Lord Walker, the Scientist, and anyone else who stood in Roo's way. It was time for them all to see that their grip on the universe was slipping and the era of a new generation of bender was dawning.

ß   ✼   ∂

LXI. Chelsea

The alarm that morning must have been the most grating, terrible sound that Chelsea had ever heard in her entire life. It didn't sound any different than it did on any other day of the week—she had been woken up by the same alarm since she joined the Academy—but still, the noise was worse than ever with the weight of what she was expected to do that day bearing down on her.

She took her time getting out of bed, enjoying the warmth of the comforter and the solitude of her bedroom. Finally, she knew who she was. She was a protector and she was ready to put right the wrongs which had been allowed to exist in the worlds for too long. That was what was best for Jonah. It was the only thing she could do.

When she eventually did get out of bed, she filled out all her paperwork in her bedroom, eschewing the bathroom and a shower—one day without wouldn't be too bad—because she wasn't ready to face Tom just yet. Her hair pulled into a ponytail, her protector's suit on, and her helmet lodged up under her arm, Chelsea took a deep breath in preparation and opened her bedroom door.

She let all the air out in one loud breath when she saw that Tom wasn't even there. He must have gone ahead to the meeting without her. Hopefully so. She didn't need him to be late. The Captain would probably end up making her pay for that, too.

Chelsea's stomach grumbled on the way to the elevator. She was hungry, sure, but that would have to wait along with her shower. The mission came first, and if assassination was on the plate, she already knew what her reaction would be and an empty stomach was for the best. She stepped onto the elevator, said, "Captain's office." not knowing where else to go—she didn't need the locker room because she was avoiding Tom—and the floor fell out from underneath her.

She held her breath and counted her heartbeats as the elevator moved. Twenty beats, a good indication she was calm and ready for what was to come. The elevator stopped, the doors slid open, and

Chelsea's heart skipped a beat, speeding up. There was Tom, standing in the hall, in full uniform except for his helmet which was tucked up underneath his armpit.

She must have registered her surprise—and hopefully only the surprise and not also the disgust which had seemed to build up over night with all her time alone to imagine what dangers exactly it was that Tom had put her Jonah into—because his voice was already defensive, if not his words, as he said, "*Uh*, hey." kicking dust like a scolded child. "I thought you'd be in the locker room. I tried to clear out so I wouldn't bother you."

"Oh, yeah?" Chelsea shrugged. What did he want, a medal of honor for being able to discern her obvious feelings for once in a lifetime? "I hadn't noticed."

"So, about last night... Well—"

"Just forget about it," Chelsea cut him off. Now was not the time to be arguing again. Now was the time to be cool and collected and ready for a mission. Why couldn't Tom understand that? "We should be going in," she said, trying to pass him, but Tom stopped her.

"No, wait," he said, and Chelsea jerked her arm out of his grip. "I'm sorry, I—"

"No!" Chelsea snapped, losing her temper despite her every effort to control it before such an important mission. "Not now, Tom. You lost your opportunity to explain yourself when you put our son in danger—and on multiple occasions at that. *No*—Stop! Listen to me. Let me finish. Now we're going to get in there and do whatever the Captain asks us to do no matter how much you object. And—*I'm not finished*. Just shut up for a minute. *And* we're going to do it all while keeping the fact that the safety of *our* son, Tom, the safety of *our* Jonah is on the line and we cannot forget that. I'll do *anything* to protect him, okay. It doesn't matter what the Captain asks me to do, I'm going to do it for Jonah. You got that?"

Tom nodded. "Of course. I would, too. But—"

"*No buts*. We just do it. Anything she says, Tom. Now come on." Chelsea stormed past him, toward the Captain's office. She knocked twice on the door then burst through it without waiting for an answer and groaned when the Captain wasn't there. She heard Tom come in behind her and blurted out, "I told you not to—" before she blushed, slapping her hand to her mouth, and said, "Oh, *uh*, Captain, sir. I'm sorry, sir. I— I thought you were—"

"*Can it*," the Captain said, brushing Chelsea off and marching around to sit in the chair behind the desk. "There's no time, Pardy. I've got much more important shit to take care of. So please, let's just get this over with. Sit down. Both of you."

"*Uh*, yes, sir," Chelsea said, ticking off a salute and taking one of the low seats in front of the Captain's desk, thankful not to have to explain herself.

Tom took the seat next to Chelsea and the Captain got straight to business. "So I gave you some generalities about your mission yesterday, but no specifics. Mostly because we didn't have them. But now we do, and I'll tell you, there's not a lot of subtlety to this one. We'll be sending you straight to your targets. That's it."

Tom fidgeted in his seat and Chelsea swallowed some spit.

"Tom, you've been there before, but not like this. The world's become a much different place since you were a protector last, and you may not recognize as much as you expect to, but you should have no trouble recognizing your targets. They haven't changed. I assure you of that. Chelsea, you studied the maps in bootcamp—or whatever facsimile thereof they're giving you new recruits with as fast as we're pulling you in these days—but you can fill in the holes of what Tom remembers and ensure y'all get to the right place."

"Yes, sir," Chelsea nodded.

"Anything else, sir?" Tom asked.

"Not really, Pardys. I'm afraid you won't have much support out there beyond the normal patrolling officers, and they'll, by necessity, be stationed as far away from your position as possible when we send you over there. It's just you two, your guns, and the entire Force that's counting on you—despite the fact that none of them actually know you're even on this mission."

"Sir, yes, sir." Chelsea said, saluting. "We won't let you down, sir."

"I hope not," the Captain said, standing and saluting back. "Now get out of my sight. I have other business to tend to."

Even Tom got the message on that one and scurried out close behind Chelsea.

"Did she say where we're supposed to be going?" Tom asked, trying to keep up with Chelsea who was hurrying to the elevator. She wanted to get this done with as soon as possible.

"She said you're supposed to know the place." Chelsea shrugged. "It'll come up in our viewports. Come on."

They got on the elevator and the doors slid closed. Chelsea waited but the thing didn't move and no directions came up in her mask's viewport. She was starting to get a little nervous.

"Well..." Tom said, nervous himself from the sound of it.

"Well, you know the place, don't you?" Chelsea snapped. Did she have to do all the thinking? "Take us there."

"Oh—I guess... Well, Outland Six Sector F, then," Tom said and the elevator fell into motion.

When it stopped and the doors slid open, Chelsea stepped out but Tom didn't follow. "Well," Chelsea said. "C'mon. This is the place, isn't it?"

"I—*uh*... I don't know," Tom said, stepping out of the elevator and surveying the buildings all around them. "This— It didn't look like this before."

Chelsea scoffed. "Of course not. You do recall that the walls between Five and Six were destroyed, don't you? It did happen on your watch. Seems like something I'd remember."

Tom ignored her, still staring at the new world in awe. "No, but... This used to be a long strip of green surrounded by buildings. Now it's just a patch. Where'd it all go?"

"You really have no idea how the worlds work, do you?" Chelsea chuckled. "That's how the walls function, Tom. This is the world now. Just show me where to go so we can get this over with."

"Why are you so eager?" Tom asked, finally breaking his eyes away from the towering buildings that surrounded them to address her. "Why do you *want* to do this?"

"I *want* to protect our son," Chelsea said with a sigh. "We've been over this so many times already. Just leave it at that for now and let's do what we came here to do: protect Jonah."

"It's almost like you—like you're looking forward to killing them," Tom said, breaking eye contact again but this time to stare at his feet.

Chelsea swallowed the spit that had gathered in her throat. She shook her head slowly, trying not to show any emotion. "I'm doing what's best for our son," she said in the steadiest voice she could muster. "I'm doing what you should have been doing all along, what you should be doing now. So please. *Let's go.*"

Tom bowed his head and shuffled down the sidewalk, hopefully in the direction of their targets. Chelsea followed close behind, observing her surroundings and noticing that there was no one in the streets, no one anywhere, it seemed. Her school lessons had taught her that Six was packed to the brim and overflowing with criminals, hooligans, and harlots—the real scum of the earth—and she wondered where they were all hiding. Probably under a rock somewhere where they belonged.

After a few blocks of walking it was starting to seem like Tom didn't actually know where he was going at all. That or he was taking her off course for a reason, trying to protect his trash friends. Probably the former, though. Chelsea saw a lot more ignorance in Tom than malice, and she still held some small hope that he would do what was best for Jonah in the long run.

"Wasn't there a closer elevator?" Chelsea asked when the walking had grown to be too much and they still weren't where they were supposed to be.

"I don't know," Tom said, turning to Chelsea and looking genuinely concerned. "I mean, no. This was the closest elevator before the walls came down, but I'm a little lost now."

"*Great.*" Chelsea scoffed. "Perfect. Now what?" She was on the verge of calling back on her radio when Tom gasped.

"Wait a second. *Wait.*" He pulled Chelsea by the arm to hide in an alley. "That's it," he said, poking his head around the corner of the building.

"Are you sure?" Chelsea asked, moving him aside so she could look. "Let me see." She poked her head around, too, but didn't know what she was looking for so all she saw was more of the same buildings and streets they had been passing already. "Which one?" she asked.

"A few buildings down. Right in front of that patch of grass," Tom said and she could tell the one he was talking about. "That's the one for sure. It was in a different place the last time I was here, but that is the one."

"You're sure?" Chelsea asked him again, looking into his eyes. "Jonah can't afford any mistakes."

"I'm sure." Tom nodded. "Though I'm still not sure how you want to go about this."

Chelsea thought about it for a second. The Captain hadn't been specific. Chelsea had assumed they would just go in and get the job done then get out. How hard could it really be in Six? But maybe Tom was right this time. Maybe a little more finesse was in order. "Did you have anything in mind?" she asked him, because she sure didn't.

"Well..." Tom didn't look very sure of what he was about to say. "The Captain chose me because I already know the targets, right. Maybe she thinks they'll just let me in."

Chelsea scoffed. "Do you think so?"

"Well not like this, obviously," Tom said, taking off his helmet and vest. "Come on. You, too, if you're coming in with me. They don't trust protectors."

Chelsea scoffed again. "Well, we are here to kill them. I mean, you don't think they'll be able to tell? I thought they already knew you, anyway. They know you're a protector."

"So?" Tom said, down to his undershirt and cargo pants. "They don't know you. And we don't need to rub it in their face, anyway. And say we come to someone else before we find our targets? They might not recognize me, and what do you think they'd do if they saw a protector?"

"Try to kill us," Chelsea said. "Exactly why we should keep our armor on. I'm not taking mine off."

Tom chuckled. "C'mon," he said. "These people are tiny. You've never seen them before. They'll be no match for the two of us. I'm leaving my gun, too, but you can bring yours if you want to."

"*Tom.*" Chelsea scoffed. "This is ridiculous. You don't have to be tall or strong to shoot someone. You're not listening to me. We're here to get something done and we can't do it without our guns."

"Well I'm not taking mine with me," Tom said, tossing it onto the pile with the rest of his uniform. "You can do whatever you want to." He looked at her like she was going to take off her armor and throw her weapon down, too, and when she picked his gun up to strap it over her back instead, he let out a big sigh. "*Fine.* Whatever. C'mon. Follow me."

They snuck, hugging their backs to the wall, from the alley to the doorway despite the sheer emptiness of the entire world. Tom crossed to the other side of the door and made the hand signal that indicated he was going to kick it in. Chelsea held up a finger, stopping him just before he did, and tried the handle—which, of course, was unlocked. She pushed the door open with a grin on her face, then got serious again and pointed her gun up and down the entrance hallway. When she saw it was all clear, she waved for Tom to follow her.

While Chelsea snuck from wall to wall, hall to hall, in perfect reconnaissance procedure, Tom didn't even try to hide or protect himself at all. Chelsea was getting the feeling that he might not be as dedicated to Jonah's safety as he claimed to be. She cleared a big conference room, kitchen, and office, leaving only one closed door left in the place, when she finally spoke.

"What the fuck are you doing, Tom?"

"Searching the premises." He shrugged. "It looks like no one's home."

Chelsea's hands started to tremble and her palms slicked up. If she wasn't wearing gloves, she might have dropped her gun, but instead, she raised it, aiming the barrel at Tom despite her brain's confusion as to exactly why. "You're not taking this seriously at all," her mouth said. Why was it being so harsh on him? "This is our son's life at stake, Tom. *Jonah's* life. And you're willing to throw it all away?"

"Woah, now. Settle down," Tom said, raising his hands in defense. Chelsea was glad she had her helmet on so he couldn't see the disgust she couldn't keep off her face. "I'm not the bad guy here. No need to point that thing at me."

Chelsea held the gun steady, still pointing it at him. "Aren't you, though, Tom? You're the one who said you'd do anything so you didn't have to kill someone else. Is that what you're doing now? Sabotaging the mission? Putting our son in danger for your own selfish desires?"

"No." Tom chuckled nervously, hands trembling in the air now. "Of course not. I— I wouldn't... Jonah would— The Captain—"

"Now your tune changes." Chelsea laughed and she didn't know why. She felt like she was losing control of herself. She couldn't stop. "Now that you see the gun pointing at *your* head it means something to you, but when you can't see it and it's pointing at our son's head this is all a game."

"No, I—"

"It's *not* a game, Tom. I'm not playing it anymore." She shook her head, her arms trembling and grip on the gun loosening. "You can take this mission seriously, or I'll—"

Bang.

The front door of the house swung open and in pointed five or six guns.

Pow.

Chelsea's trigger finger slipped. Her arm recoiled. Tom made his puppy dog eyes one last time before, gripping his stomach, he fell to his knees.

Pow pow pow.

Shots rang out from the pile of guns in the doorway, whizzing past Chelsea and setting her feet into motion. She dove into the kitchen, back braced against the counter, her only protection, and shots still rang.

No. She shook her head, blinking tears away as the shots still fired over and around her. No, no, no. Not like this. Not my Tom. Not by—

Crack crack.

Their aim was getting better. Their guns were more powerful than the standard Sixer fare, too. Those were probably the same terrorists who had attacked the precinct. They were firing the protectors' own guns at Chelsea. Her inherited instinct and training kicked in. She knew what she had to do.

Pop pop pop.

She jumped up from behind the counter like a protector in a box and dropped three of the five bodies with three well placed shots. Her kill count was steadily rising, and the more she did it the more she wanted to.

Pop pop.

Two more shooters dead with two more shots, and Chelsea plopped back down, hidden behind the counter despite the room being empty of anything living but her. She was getting better at this killing thing, she told herself over and over, trying to get her heartbeat under control. Maybe she would make a good protector after all.

Her heart rate calmed and most of the adrenaline absorbed into her body, Chelsea stood on shaky legs, using what was left of the counter as a balance, to survey the room. By the looks of the tattered mass of splinters that the counter she had been using for cover had become, a few more seconds of indecision on her part and she'd be just another body dying in that room. She shook her head. Thank Amaru she wasn't.

There were six lifeless bodies on the blood-stained floor, but only one that Chelsea crossed to kneel by. His whole undershirt was puddled with blood all up under his limp arm and on his stomach while his face was twisted into a grotesque smile, as if he welcomed the fate that had finally come to him. Chelsea didn't want to throw up this time, but she did want to cry, and cry she did until her tears were dried up.

She stood and surveyed the room again only to find the same six bodies and all dead thanks to her. Had she done the right thing? Of course not when it came to Tom, but tha—that was an accident.

That was an accident. *That* was an accident. That *was* an accident.

The more she repeated it to herself the more she believed it was true. She was pointing the gun at him, yes, but she never would have pulled the trigger if that pile of trash didn't storm in with their guns blazing. She had never meant to hurt him, her Tom. Of course she didn't. She was simply trying to get his attention, to make him take this mission seriously, and it worked. It worked until…

What had she done? What was she to do next?

She couldn't just stand there and wait for someone else to come. Another troop of Sixers would be on their way soon, no doubt, and then there'd be an even larger mass of bodies to explain. No, she had to get out of there and fast. But she couldn't just leave Tom's body behind. Not after she had…

She had to call for backup. It was her only option. Even if it took the local patrol forever to get there. She ran back to the alley to strap Tom's vest back on him and lay his helmet by his side then make the call.

"Emergency line open," she said, finding it surprisingly easy to keep her voice steady. "This is Officer Pardy reporting a four three nine in progress. We have an Officer down in Sector F of Outland Six. Send medical unit and backup as soon as possible. Over."

"Loud and clear, Officer Pardy," a voice replied over the

headphones in her helmet. "Repeat. That's a four three nine in progress?"

"Affirmative. I repeat, we have a four three nine in progres. Send backup immediately. Over."

"The closest Officers are on their way. Over and out."

The comm link shut off with a barely perceptible blip and Chelsea let out a sigh of frustration. Maybe Tom wasn't so incompetent after all. Maybe the entire Force and the rest of the worlds beside that were just as ignorant, naive, and incapable. She had seen enough idiots getting ahead in the Force to think that stupidity was the norm rather than an anomaly.

What those protectors might have thought when they first saw Chelsea, standing over a mass of lifeless bodies, staring through the blood-stained vinyl at a universe far away and only accessible to her, she may never know. If they were less trained in reacting to violence or more loving of the scum that inhabited World Six, those Officers might have seen her as a crazed murderous psychopath, bent on admiring the ghastly product of her horrible profession. These two protectors, though—Officers and rookies though they were—had been through a particular upbringing, the same one Chelsea had gone through as a kid. Violence was a part and parcel of life in Outland One. Surviving violence and inflicting it on those who would inflict it on you before they had the chance to displayed the epitome of prowess. Murdering Sixers made one venerable, put one's picture in the school books next to the mythological heroes of society, recorded your biography so generations yet to be born could read it forevermore. These protectors saw not a psychopath in Chelsea, but a heroic protector, doing her duty in the defense of property, liberty, and life, and she would no doubt go down in history for avenging the death of her husband on duty.

Hands patted her back. There were still only two other officers there, but it seemed like so many more. They asked her how it felt to finally get to destroy some of the scum from Six. They congratulated her on her kills. They apologized for her loss, even if it was an honorable loss, even if Tom had found the perfect way for a protector to die. And she?

She smiled and nodded, playing along with the other protectors. She told them it was exhilarating to finally take justice into her own hands, exciting to dispense it to those who so direly needed their fair share. She thanked them, assuring them that this was not the end of her kill list, that she would do her best and damndest—excuse the word in such a heat of excitement—to dish out the same justice to all Sixer trash. She nodded, letting a single tear fall from her eye, and agreed with them that this was indeed the best way for a protector to die, as a martyr for property, liberty, and life. She only worried about how to tell her son.

Then there were more of them. Protectors flooded the room. Chelsea was lost in a sea of them. How long she had been reminiscing and congratulating herself with the other two she didn't know, but she was glad it was finally over. It was all over now. No more mission to Scumland to kill scumbags. No more of Tom's exploits to endanger Jonah. No more of Tom at all.

Her control over herself was breaking and she was on the verge of bursting into tears when a gloved hand grasped her by the shoulder and turned her to stare into a masked and mustachioed face. "Officer Pardy," the Captain said in a modulated voice, hiding any emotion underneath those blinking neon teeth. "To my office. Now. I'll meet you there."

"But, sir—" Chelsea started.

"Now!"

"Sir, yes, sir," Chelsea said, ticking off a salute in automatic response to the volume of the Captain's voice—even modulated she could hear it. "Right away, sir." She marched out, bumping shoulders with the crowd of protectors left in her wake, and stood at attention until the elevator doors closed, cutting her off again from the rest of the world.

The elevator ride was infinite. The solitude was welcome and it elicited a sobbing, sloppy, teary-eyed scene which Chelsea was glad no other human witnessed. She enveloped herself in the cold misery of a life alone, responsible for the life of another. She was out of Hell into a new one, out of the pit and into the frying pan, and yet somehow she managed to bottle it all up inside again by the time the elevator stopped and the doors reopened.

The hall was empty, thank Amaru, and there was no one to question her about what she had done—what *she* had done. She found solitude in the Captain's office, too—staring out the wall sized window onto the snowy mountain scene—but she didn't let her sadness overtake her this time. She maintained control of herself.

The Captain could walk in at any moment and Chelsea didn't need her to see what only the elevator had witnessed.

When the Captain did walk in, a single tear had broken through Chelsea's defenses. She wiped it away as she turned to salute, and the Captain didn't even acknowledge the salute—much less the tear, to Chelsea's relief.

"Fucking shit, Pardy. Fuck—*king*—shit," the Captain said, throwing her helmet at the wall and plopping into her desk chair. "What do I have to do?" she yelled out the still closed window at no one.

Chelsea didn't say a word. She didn't want to make things worse. The Captain was obviously pissed at what Chelsea had done, and with good reason, too. They had lost an officer in the line of duty on an operation that was supposed to be hush hush. Chelsea was responsible for that and her punishment would no doubt be severe. Hopefully a little less so for the fact that she knew not to defend her heinous failures.

"You have no idea what's going on out there, Pardy," the Captain said, turning in her chair to look into Chelsea's eyes. "Do you?"

"I—*uh*... No, sir." Chelsea shook her head. She really didn't, and now was not the time to pretend like she did.

The Captain grinned, nodding her head slowly. The way her teeth reflected as white as the walls and the snow on the mountain outside seemed to want to impose some meaning on Chelsea but she didn't know what it was. "Pardy, you're a good Officer. I hope you know that. That's why I hate for this to happen to someone such as yourself."

Chelsea braced herself. Here it came, her punishment for killing Tom and starting the shootout. Even if the Captain never found out it was actually Chelsea who had killed Tom and not the trash that died with him, this was karma taking its due. "I understand, sir," Chelsea said. "You do what you have to do. As did I."

The Captain broke into laughter. "I do— Wait— *Ho ho ho.* Me, Pardy? What did I do besides send you on an impossible mission?"

"I— What, sir? I meant your punishment, sir."

"Punishment?" The Captain was really laughing now. "*Ho ho*

ho. Pardy. Now— Pardy— *Ho ho ho*. Punishment for what?"

"Well, for my failed mission, sir. Tom—*er*—Officer Pardy, sir... *He's dead*. I killed— I killed all those Sixers. I—"

"*Oh ho ho*! You kill me, Pardy. Sorry for the ill timed figure of speech, but there's no better way to say it. What do you think this is, huh? So you killed some Sixers? So what? They had guns, Pardy. You performed your duty and eliminated the threat. The only one who failed is Pardy Two for dying, but how could we punish a dead man? *Ho ho ho*!"

Chelsea gritted her teeth. Even though it was her who had pulled the trigger that ended Tom's life—an accident she reminded herself—she didn't like the flippant manner with which the Captain was treating his demise. Who was she, even as a Captain, to put such little value on Chelsea's husband's life?

"If anything, we'll be giving you a medal of honor, Pardy," the Captain went on. "And we'll be giving Pardy Two a posthumous one at that. No, you've done well for yourself—and for your son, whose future is looking brighter than ever. But that's not what I asked you here for."

Chelsea was speechless. This couldn't be happening. She wasn't even sure if they had killed the right Sixers, Tom was gone forever, and more than anything, she had a deep sense that the mission was an abject failure. There was no way in this world—or any of them for that matter—that she should be getting praise for what was probably a fireable offence.

"Although there was one little snag in your performance," the Captain said.

Chelsea scoffed, as if Tom's death wasn't snag enough.

"You didn't get the targets I tasked you with specifically. Though you did manage to take out most of their closest staff. So we got that going for us. Which is nice."

"I—*uh*. I don't understand."

"Your targets weren't there, Pardy. You know, the people you were supposed to kill."

"O—or apprehend, sir."

The Captain chuckled. "Sure, Pardy. But we see the choice you made, don't we? *Ha ha ho*!"

Chelsea didn't know what to say. She had failed and failed and failed, and the Captain didn't care one bit.

"No, Pardy, but that's not what we're here about. I admire your decision. It was the correct one, the profitable one, and if you stick with me, you'll see some of those profits. But only if you stick with me."

"I—sir..." Chelsea didn't understand. Any of it. She felt worse now for doing what she had done than she had felt when she was actually doing it. Why? What was different? "But Tom— I didn't get the targets— I—"

"You did your best, Pardy. You did what you could and what you had to do. There's no question about that. *From anyone.* You did good well, and I want to ensure that you're in a position to do it even better in the future. Are you feeling me? It's a war out there, Pardy. A big one. We're tight on bodies here in the Force, and you've shown us that you have what it takes. So what do you say?"

"I—*uh*—" Chelsea's lips stuck together as she tried to speak. Her palms should have been slick but they seemed to dry and crack. The whole world was evaporating around her. "I don't know, sir. I don't understand."

"I'm offering you a promotion, Pardy. I'm offering you a team under your command under my command. I'm offering you the ensured safety of your career here and your Jonah at home. I'm offering you the world on a platinum platter. So, Officer Pardy, what do you say?"

What could she say? "Sir, yes, sir."

ƍ   ✳   ǝ

LXII. Ansel

The claws never came. Nor the jaws. Only the laughter of Ashley who couldn't even speak he was so doubled over. Ansel crawled to her feet, picking up her rucksack and brushing herself off, and the huge cat was no longer in front of her. She turned to find it inside another clearing behind her, across the dirt path they had come in on, looking out the other way and ready to pounce on some unseen thing.

"Oh. *Oh ho ho!*" Ashley laughed, trying to get control of himself. "Don't worry. He can't get you. *Ho ho ho!*"

Ansel reached out toward the cat and her hand disappeared in a straight line at the wrist, just like it had done when she had tried to open Anna and Rosa's door what seemed like ages ago.

"You see," Ashley said behind her, and Ansel turned to see her disembodied hand floating on the other side of the dirt path. "We can't get to it, either. The only difference is that we can see the jaguar's side of the wall and the jaguar can't see ours. It's kind of like a one-way mirror in that sense."

Ansel waved her arm and the floating hand waved in unison. What kind of world was she living in?

"Pretty nifty, isn't it?" Ashley asked

"I thought it was going to kill you," Ansel said, pulling her arm out of the—whatever it was in—so it looked like her body was all in one piece again. "I don't really find that funny."

Ashley grinned, laughter trying to burst out of him again. "Well, I did. And there was no danger, anyway. *And* you acted heroically, trying to push me out of the way like that." He giggled. "*My saviour.*"

"Alright," Ansel said, walking down the path the way they had been going before Ashley stopped her to see the big cat. She wondered what other animals she might see on the way. "Enough funny business. Why'd you bring me here, anyway?"

Ashley followed along behind her, keeping good pace and walking more quietly than Pidgeon would have ever been able to.

"Well, a few reasons," he said. "First, to show you that my chemistry homework is far from the coolest thing in this world."

Ansel nodded, not really hearing what Ashley was saying. Out in a clearing to the right of her was a giant hairy human-like thing with bigger muscles and a bigger head than she had ever seen—except for maybe on those fat tuxedoed babies at the dinner party. The hairy human thing was scratching itself in the sun and chewing on a pile of fruits. Ansel's knees shook a little. She would have bolted out of there already if she hadn't experienced the embarrassment of the giant cat incident earlier. Why was everything so much bigger and scarier here? "What is that?" she asked.

Ashley had to look again, as if he hadn't noticed the thing the first time because it was an everyday occurrence to him. "Oh, a gorilla," he said. "A rather big one, too. They've been bred to be larger and more ferocious for the show value. Thank our Holy Mother for the Walker-Haley fields between us or this guy here would be more dangerous than that jaguar we saw earlier."

"A gorilla," Ansel said, mesmerized by its huge bulging muscles and chomping jaws. "These things just live out in the wild?"

"*Ho ho ho*, not anymore." Ashley chuckled. "A long long time ago this guy's great, great, great times a bunch ancestors lived in the wild, but like I said, they were a lot smaller back then. Now they're an endangered species. Pretty much completely extinct, actually. Like most of the animals in here, they only exist in captivity."

Here came that word again: endangered. "So that's what makes them endangered?" Ansel asked. "Because they only live in captivity?" She had been held captive her entire life, kept ignorant of these worlds and the many others she had discovered in so little time since finding the first new one. Maybe she was endangered, too.

"Well, not exactly," Ashley said. "But yes. We hold them here because they're endangered, they're not endangered because we hold them here."

"*Pshh*. What's the difference?"

Ashley had to think long and hard about that. Ansel just let him. She was happy enough to stare at the magnificent gorilla as it ate. Who would endanger such a beautiful beast?

"You know," Ashley said after some time of silence, breaking Ansel away from her reverie. "I'm not entirely sure there is a difference anymore, the more I think about it. It's like, in the beginning we built walls to keep everything out for our own protection, and now we have to build walls that keep them in for their protection. I'm not sure when that changed, but when it did, it rendered any differences there might have once been entirely meaningless."

Ansel didn't know exactly what he was saying. She wasn't sure she cared, either. She didn't respond. Instead she just walked on along the dirt path in search of whatever new creature she might find in the next clearing. Ashley followed behind her, seemingly content to explore his own thoughts in silence while Ansel explored the real world.

It was a long walk before she came to the next animal, but Ansel didn't mind. The anticipation was part of the fun, and there were plenty of exotic plants everywhere—not to mention birds of various bright colors flying around. But then the giant towered over her with its long yellow and brown spotted neck, chewing leaves it ripped from the trees with a finger-like tongue. Ansel didn't ask what this one was, it didn't need a name. She just stared up at its towering figure, plucking leaves from the trees, and tried to imagine what it saw through its elevated eyes.

"That's a giraffe," Ashley said, giving Ansel a name for the beast anyway. "It's my favorite 3D animal, personally. They're so tall and graceful, and such perfect pieces of evidence in support of evolution by natural selection. The way their laryngeal nerve goes all the way down and back up the neck again instead of taking the short route..."

Ashley kept going but Ansel didn't hear a word he said beyond giraffe. She kept repeating it in her head. Giraffe, giraffe, giraffe. Who would endanger the giraffe? How could you trap such a strong looking gorilla? What kind of person would hurt a big black jaguar? She wasn't sure she could take any more of this zoo if it meant seeing more caged and endangered beauties like this one.

"*Alright, enough.*" Ansel snapped, cutting off Ashley's lecture on giraffes which was still going on despite her ignoring it. "Why did you bring me here? Tell me."

"I—*uh*... I thought you might like to see it. I don't know. And I thought it might help explain where you are. I just— I, *uh*..." He shrugged.

"How is this supposed to help? Just tell me where we are."

"*Uh*, well, it's—you know—like a model, really. Or maybe a metaphor. It's meant to illuminate—"

"Get to the point."

"Okay. Well. You know how the jaguar couldn't pounce on you, right?"

"Of course."

"Well, we couldn't really touch it and it couldn't eat us, right. I mean, the cat couldn't even see us, okay. So you could essentially say that we are in two separate worlds, right? Us and the jaguar, I mean. The jaguar in their own world, and they can't see into ours, but we can see into their world even if we can't physically go there. Right? Not by walking off the path here where it looks like the jaguar's world should be, at least."

"Okay," Ansel said still having a hard time following him. "So what?"

"Well essentially, the wider world—or worlds you might say—are split up the same way. Okay. They're all right next each other like we are with the jaguar, but there's no line of sight going either way. It would be more like if we couldn't see into the jaguar's habitat either, just like it couldn't see out to us."

"We wouldn't even know they were there," Ansel said, starting to understand now.

"Exactly." Ashley smiled. "But those other worlds *would* be there, with all those people in them, living their own lives, oblivious to everything going on in our world, acting as if we didn't exist either. Do you see where I'm going?"

Ansel nodded. She saw exactly where he was going. She wasn't quite sure if she could believe what he was saying, but he had given her plenty of evidence to support his story with the way this zoo worked, and what he said seemed to explain some of the stranger experiences she had been going through ever since she moved to the Belt and beyond. "You're saying that the world works exactly like this zoo," she said. "You're telling me that humans live in these same sort of cages that y'all have endangered all these animals with."

"Yes, well, I'm not sure I would call the worlds cages," Ashley said with a chuckle. "I'm not even sure I'd call what these animals are in cages, either. I mean, besides there being no bars, this is all the wilderness any of their ancestors have known for generations. These...*protected habitats*, let's call them, make up the entire universe that these animals can ever experience, sure, but they're not caged in, really, and they don't know any better anyway."

"Because they can't know any better," Ansel said. "They're just animals. But you're trying to say that humans are caged up like this, too. Would that be okay with you as long as the humans didn't know any better?"

"First of all, they're not cages," Ashley said. "*Habitats.*"

"Whatever."

"And second of all, you don't give enough credit to these animals—or maybe you give too much credit to humans, I'm not sure. But take the gorillas, okay. They started out smart, of course, but you should see how intelligent they are now that they've been bred for it." He nodded over at the long necked giant that was still munching on leaves. "That giraffe over there can figure out a lot more about the worlds than you might think. I promise you."

"Wait, I don't understand," Ansel said. "Are you saying you would be okay with humans being caged, or *put in habitats,* or whatever you want to call it, as long as they didn't know any better?"

"I'm not saying that exactly," Ashley said, tapping his chin. "How can I communicate this in a way that you'll understand? I could see how it might be for the best. That's it. Just like the reserve here—let's get that nasty word zoo out of our mind for the sake of objectivity. Without this reserve, where else could these animals go?"

"To the wilderness," Ansel said. "Where they would be free to roam wherever they want to without being sent back to the beginning every time they finally get to the end."

"What wilderness?" Ashley scoffed. "You're looking at all the wilderness there is left that isn't already owned and in use. And if there was any more, that would only broaden their playing field. The animals would still be sent to the beginning every time they got to the end because that's how a round planet works."

"And the humans?" Ansel asked, feeling her control over her temper loosen. "It's best for them, too? You think it was best for me to be caged in the Streets, surrounded by cement and concrete, without any source of food or support of any kind for as far as I could possibly go in my little world? What kind of habitat is that? What was *I* being protected from?"

"I don't know what you're talking about," Ashley said, looking like he was getting a little angry himself. "You've given me no information about where you're from so I can't speculate as to whether it was for your best or not. I can see how it's for the animals' best because I've studied them thoroughly, but I have yet to come to a conclusion on humans. If you were a little more cooperative in answering my questions, maybe I could figure out how I felt about your situation sooner than later."

"I—*uh…*" He was right even if he was being an ass about it. Ansel had been too harsh on him herself, though. He probably knew as little about her world as she knew about his. "I'm sorry," she said. "I'm just— I'm a long way from home, I think, and I've been through a whole lot of Hell to get here. I miss my family and friends, and I never should have come all the way out here on my own in the first place." She shook her head, fighting tears. "We do nothing alone."

"It's okay," Ashley said, looking terrified at the prospect that Ansel might start crying—which made her chuckle a little. "You're— You're not alone, okay. I want to help you, you know. I will help you."

"You don't just want to study me?" Ansel smiled.

"Oh, I could study you all day." Ashley held a hand to his mouth, blushing. "I mean— You know what I mean. But that's not the only thing I want to do. I want to help you, too. We can help each other, I think."

"*Psssh*. Yeah right. How could I help you? You don't need any hunting done, do you?"

"Well, no." He shook his head.

"Then I prolly won't be much help. Sorry." Ansel shrugged.

"I doubt that." Ashley chuckled. "The mere fact that you've brought my attention to the possibility of worlds beyond those that are known and mapped has been help enough. I always knew there were way more lines of tunnel than the maps showed us, and now I might just understand why."

"Wait, so you didn't know about the other worlds either?"

"I knew of one," Ashley said. "We call it Never Never Land.

It's where all the celebrities live. But I imagine it's not the world you come from, is it?"

Ansel shook her head. "I'm not really sure what a celebrity is."

"*Exactly*. Pointing further to the fact that you hail from a third, separate world and implying the possibility of further worlds after that."

"All because I don't know what a celebrity is?"

"All because you came through the seams," Ashley said, smiling. "Now come on. Let's get to my lab so we can try to find your world." He grabbed her by the hand and pulled her running back the way they had come from.

Ansel forgot herself in the wind whipping against her face and the flying branches all around her. The giraffe, gorilla, and jaguar were nothing more than blurs in her peripheral vision, along with the long smudge of dark jungle green. It wasn't until the world stopped moving again and the elevator doors slid closed behind them that either of them spoke.

"They still weren't as cool as chemistry," Ansel said at the same time that Ashley said, "I think I know how to find your world."

"Oh, sorry," they said at the same time.

"And chemistry? You're way off," Ashley said while Ansel said, "Oh, cool."

"Animals are much cooler than chemistry," Ashley said when they were done apologizing for talking over each other.

"But those animals were so far away," Ansel said.

"Luckily for us. Lab."

The elevator fell into motion.

"Well, I'd still like to know more about chemistry," Ansel said.

"Maybe I'll show you after we search for your world."

Ansel shrugged. She didn't really care about finding her world, more so she just wanted to find a new one to live in. The elevator stopped, the doors slid open, and she stepped into a long hall but Ashley didn't follow. Ansel turned to look at him and found him shaking his head, looking afraid. "What's wrong?" she asked.

"Th—This isn't my lab," Ashely said, still shaking his head. "This is wrong. We should go. Come here. Get back in the elevator." He waved to hurry her up.

Before Ansel could respond, though, the door at the other end of the hall opened and in came Rosalind, followed by Popeye. Ansel groaned. She knew she recognized this hall, but she had thought it was because all those white-coated people's buildings looked the same.

"*So*," Rosalind said with a grin, "the prodigal child returns."

Popeye waved emphatically, like the tail of a dog who was happy to see its owner, but Popeye was all tail and no dog.

"I didn't return," Ansel said, crossing her arms. "This isn't where we were trying to go."

"Oh, then what are you doing here?" Rosalind laughed a cackling laugh.

"*Um*, I'm sorry, ma'am," Ashley said, finally coming out of the elevator and putting a hand on Ansel's shoulder—which she shrugged away. "It was some sort of malfunction in the elevator. We were supposed to go to my lab. We'll just be leaving now." He tried to pull Ansel back into the elevator but she wouldn't budge.

"It was no malfunction," Ansel said. "*She* did it on purpose. Didn't you?"

"*Ha ha ha*." Rosalind laughed. "Who's the bumbling new child you've brought with you this time, girl? Have you found yourself a new boyfriend already? Pidgeon'll be sad to hear it. *Ha ha ha!*"

"He's not my boyfriend," Ansel said, stomping a foot. She could see Ashley blushing out of her peripheral vision and tried hard not to look at him.

"I—It was an accident," Ashley stammered.

"It was *not* an accident, boy," Rosalind snapped. "You're girlfriend here is right about that. The Scientist wants to see you and she couldn't wait until you two split up so here you both are. Now come on in. Right this way." She made a gracious wave of her arm then shoved Ansel and Ashley down the hall toward the door at the end of it where Popeye was waving them on.

"I—I don't—" Ashley stammered, gripping tight to Ansel's shirt.

"She's never gonna convince me to stay," Ansel said, trying to shrug him away in vain. "I don't know what she would have to talk to me about."

Rosalind grinned, still pushing them along. "You'll just have to go in and see for yourself, then. Won't you, *girl?*"

Ansel didn't let the word cut her like she knew it was meant to. She didn't respond to it at all. She just gave up fighting and went in through the door, pulling Ashley along in her wake.

The Scientist was sitting in a puffy chair, under the view of the endless mountain that could never again impress Ansel, indicating for them to take their seats across from her. Ashley hesitated but Ansel had been through all this before. She strode right up and took a chair without having to struggle into it, despite its height. Seeing her confidence gave Ashley some of his own, and soon he struggled into the chair between Ansel's and the Scientist's. When he was finally up and seated, he stared in slack jawed awe at the Scientist who smiled—suspiciously Ansel thought—right back at him.

"I— You're— You can't be," Ashley said.

The Scientist nodded, still grinning. "Yes, child. I can be," she said. "And I am."

"Why did you send for me?" Ansel demanded, ignoring Ashley's fanboy reaction. She didn't care who he thought the Scientist was or how impressed he was by her, Ansel just wanted to get out of there as soon as they could.

"Ansel," Ashley said, "she didn't want to see you. She's too important. She probably doesn't even know who you are. She's—"

"*Actually*, I did want to see Ansel," the Scientist said. "I needed to see her, in fact."

"But you're—" Ashley said.

"The Scientist," Ansel cut him off. "I know."

"Well I was going to say Dr. Haley Walker," Ashley said, "but she is pretty much *the* epitome of a scientist. You're right about that."

"Haley Walker?" Ansel said.

"My true name." The Scientist nodded.

Why had she hidden the name for so long if this kid knew it by the sight of her? "Well what do you want?" Ansel demanded.

"I want to know how your trip has gone, dear." The Scientist smiled—Ansel still couldn't think of her as Dr. Walker, she had been the Scientist for too long. "I want to know if you've changed your mind." Then quickly, as if to prevent the answer she knew was coming, the Scientist added, "I want to know what you want now.

I'm sure you have a better idea for yourself after your little adventure in Four, don't you?"

"What do you know about my adventure?" Ansel asked, wondering who was slipping the Scientist information.

"Not much, child." The Scientist laughed. "Which is why I need you to tell me all about it. Starting with the name of your little friend who you've brought along with you."

"I— I'm Ashley Tyson," Ashley said, squirming in his seat. "I'm a topological physicist myself, ma'am. Can I say that I admire you more than any scientist who has ever lived. Like, for real. *You're my hero.*"

The Scientist chuckled. "You can, but you wouldn't be the first." She winked. "And that's about enough said. Let's talk about something interesting for a change. Where did you and my dear Ansel meet?"

Ansel resented being called "her dear" by the Scientist, but she didn't get a chance to respond because Ashley was too eager to speak. "Well I was down in the Labyrinth, ma'am—forgive the colloquialism—but I was monitoring Walker-Haley field function for class credit when she appeared out of nowhere and ran right into me. I thought she was my replacement, you know, but then she said she had come through the seams of Sisyphus's Mountain without the protection of a transport shield or radiation suit, and I wouldn't believe her. I mean, I thought that was impossible. It is impossible, isn't it? She didn't really go through the fields naked. *Did she?*"

The Scientist was chuckling for most of his long rant, shaking her head, and she continued on after he stopped. "I don't know," she said, looking at Ansel for confirmation. "Did you?"

Ansel shrugged. "I found an escape from your mountain wilderness and I took the opportunity, if that's what you're asking."

"By the elevator?" the Scientist asked.

Ansel nodded. Of course the Scientist knew about the seam already. Getting Ansel to tell the story out loud was just some sick power trip.

"It's always tricky keeping the fields contained in such tight spots," the Scientist said, more to herself than either of them. "I'll have to take a closer look at that in the morning."

"So she did go through naked," Ashley said, glancing wide eyed between the Scientist and Ansel. "You weren't lying?"

"Of course I wasn't." Ansel scoffed. "I wouldn't."

"And there are worlds we haven't been told about," Ashley said to the Scientist. "Aren't there?"

"Beyond your imagination." The Scientist nodded.

Ashley seemed to fall into his own mind, lost trying to determine the possibilities created by the new information he had just been given. Ansel wasn't impressed, though. "Is this all you brought me here for?" She scoffed. "To impress some white coated flower from another planet? Can I leave now?"

"Not in the least," the Scientist said, getting serious now. "But the rest, I'm afraid, the reason I really brought you here, that has to be taken care of in private. Ashley, friend, you'll have to wait in the other room with Rosalind. I'm sorry."

"I—but—" Ashley complained as the office door opened and in came Rosalind. "I have so many questions to ask you."

"C'mon, kid," Rosalind said, jerking a thumb toward the door. "You heard the lady. Let's go."

"In due time," the Scientist said, standing to help Rosalind guide him out of the room. "All your questions will be answered in due time."

Ansel heaved a sigh of relief when he was gone. The sooner they were alone, the sooner she could leave, and that was the only thing Ansel wanted. "So," she said expectantly as the Scientist retook her seat.

"So, my dear." The Scientist smiled. "Your trip. How did it go?"

"Ashley already told you most of it."

The Scientist chuckled. "He told me nothing, how you met. I want more. I want to know everything that happened after, everything that happened before. I want to know everything. Did you climb the mountain?"

Ansel nodded.

"And what did you see?"

"Myself," Ansel said without hesitation. She had thought about that view so many times since she had seen it that she could respond by reflex. "My future, my past...*me*." She shrugged.

The Scientist nodded. "Sure," she said. "Sure it was. It was almost like that, at least. You can never get over the mountain, though, so it's only ever your present, really."

"But I did get over it," Ansel said defiantly, puffing out her chest. "Three times."

The Scientist chuckled. "And how many more mountains were there after that?"

Ansel shook her head. "Is this all you brought me here for? To toy with me? I'm pretty sure by now that it's the only reason you let me go out there in that wilderness in the first place."

"No, dear. Settle down, now." The Scientist tried to calm her. "We can move on if that's what you want. I'd still like to know what happened after you met Ashley, though. Did you enjoy your time in Four?"

"What's Four?"

"The world you were in, my dear. You understand how these things work, now, don't you? I'm told you visited a zoo. That had to be illuminating."

"The whole world's like a zoo, isn't it?" Ansel demanded, searching the Scientist's eyes for some deeper meaning beyond her words.

"I think that's always been true," the Scientist said with a smile. "It has been for as long as I can remember, anyway. And that's a long time, mind you."

"No, I mean we're all caged up like those animals I saw. We have no means of escape. Though I did escape, somehow." Because the Scientist had plucked her out of her world, but the Scientist knew that and Ansel wasn't ready to give her the credit. "But everyone else is stuck where they are."

"My previous comment still holds true." The Scientist nodded. "It's been like this pretty much forever. Though I know what you mean. And yes, at one time we were using the Walker-Haley fields to fence things in, but now the entire universe consists of fences and walls, making it all but indistinguishable whether we're in the wilderness or the reserve. There's no separation anymore. You don't even have to say we're *like* the animals kept in the zoo that you visited. In essence, all the worlds of Earth are a part of the same network of habitats making one total zoo."

"And you're the zoo guard," Ansel said, shaking her head. "You make sure everyone stays in their places and the walls stand tall and strong."

"I brought you out of the Streets, didn't I?" the Scientist said.

"I didn't force you to live in Six forever, the lowest of the low."

"My parents got me out of the Streets," Ansel snapped. "That wasn't you. That was our own hard work, and if they hadn't been killed, I could have gotten out of Six—or whatever you want to call it—myself."

The Scientist chuckled. "And how do you think they got their hands on those printers that got them their promotions, huh? *I* got you out of the streets, *I* got you out of Six entirely, and *I* want to give you more than that. I want to give you all the worlds on a platinum platter."

Ansel scoffed. "Yeah, right. To do what with them? Tinker and toy like you do? No thanks."

"*Ba ha ha.*" The Scientist shook her head, waving a finger at Ansel. It reminded her of the same gesture her mom used to make. She didn't know whether to be endeared or angry at the reminder. "Not so fast, Ansel. You'll want to consider this offer and consider it well."

"Well..." Ansel said.

"Well, dear." The Scientist smiled. "Before I give you the offer, you must first answer me one question. What is it that you want most in life?"

Ansel groaned. She had had enough of the Scientist's pseudo-spiritual mumbo jumbo. "What if I don't want to answer that question?" she asked, playing the Scientist at her own games.

"Then you'd be answering my question." The Scientist grinned. "You want not to answer the question. Though I figured you'd want a little more out of life than that. Not answering one question isn't a lot to work with." She chuckled, pleased with herself for some stupid reason.

"What does it matter anyway?" Ansel asked.

"What could it hurt to tell me? You're only wasting time. I know you want to hear my offer. Your curiosity's been piqued. And I won't tell you what the offer is until you answer my one simple question, easy as that. So what do you say? What do you want most in life?"

Ansel sighed. The Scientist was right. The worst that could happen would be that the Scientist didn't offer her what she said she wanted. Who cares if the Scientist learns what that is? "My parents to be alive again," she said.

"Oh, well…" A tear came to the Scientist's eye and she quickly wiped it away with the long white sleeve of her coat, trying to be discreet. "I knew this would be your first request but I didn't think it would hit me so hard. I'm sorry." She wiped her eyes again. "I'm afraid resurrection's not possible, though. Where would we be if it was? Do you have any other desires?"

Ansel shook her head. "You asked for what I wanted most in the world and I told you. Now what's your offer?"

"My offer pales in comparison to your need for a family, Ansel. I've already offered you what family I can and you rejected it. Instead I'm here to offer you independence. You're on your own now—though my offer a family still stands, mind you—but with that in mind, and resurrection off the table, what do you want?"

"Nothing! I don't want anything else. I want everything to go back to the way it was before you killed my family!"

"What next then? What are you going to do when you leave here? Where will you go? Where do you want to go?"

Ansel worked to calm herself down, taking deep, heaving breaths. She wasn't quite sure. She could go back to the Streets, try to hook up with Katie again, relive the life she used to live before everyone started trying to turn her into a garden flower. Or she could try to convince Pidgeon to live out in the endless mountain with her. She could teach him a few things about hunting, and he would be close enough to the elevator that he could get whatever his heart desired to eat from the Scientist's 3D printer. Or she could go do chemistry and stare at bizarre animals with Ashley, maybe even get a white coat of her own some day. She didn't really want to do any of those things, though, and she kind of wanted to do them all at the same time. What could she say? She couldn't decide. "I don't know," she finally did say after too long thinking about it. "I want to do a lot of things."

The Scientist smiled. "Name a few."

"Maybe I want to go back to the Streets to find my old friends. I haven't seen them since I moved to the Belt."

"But you wouldn't want to live there again, would you? Not after everything you've seen out here. Not now that you know how you could be living otherwise."

"Well maybe I want to go back out to the wilderness, then. I bet I could convince Pidgeon to come with me."

"Out there on Sisyphus's Mountain? You think that *wilderness* is big enough for you?"

"No, well... I would like to do chemistry, too. *Ooh*, and free those animals in the zoo. They deserve a bigger wilderness as much as I do."

The Scientist chuckled. "Well, you do want a lot of things. Don't you?"

"Yeah, so?" Ansel crossed her arms, self-conscious and regretting that she had told the Scientist anything.

"So do you think it's possible for you to do all of them at once?" the Scientist asked. "Do you think you can get everything you want? How likely do you think it is that you could even get one of them?"

Ansel shook her head, not saying anything. She had said too much already.

"Well, I'm here to tell you that I can give you all of them, everything you want. You won't have to choose. I'll give you more than that on top of it. In fact, I'll give you everything, period. All of this. All of my power, my knowledge, my walls. I'll teach you chemistry, show you how to control the elevators so you can get to the Streets, or the wilderness, or wherever you want to go whenever you want to be there. I'll give you control over all the walls in existence, even the walls of the zoo where you'll one day be the zookeeper who has the power to expand or detract the habitats as you see fit. I'll give you all of it."

"That's ridiculous." Ansel scoffed. "You would never—"

"I will, dear. *I am*. I've been building up to this all along. You were chosen from the beginning, ever since I gave your parents the printers that helped pluck you out of the streets. This has been the plan all along. Rosalind will tell you."

Ansel looked up and Rosalind was in the room with them, hovering by the doorway. How long had she been there?

"If you're ready to learn, girl." Rosalind smiled.

"And if I'm not?" Ansel demanded. "What if I don't want any of this?"

"But you just told me you did." The Scientist stood from her chair, reminding Ansel of how tall she was. "This is everything you want. Come with me. I'll show you."

She took Ansel's hand and led her out past Rosalind through

the door, but they didn't emerge into the hall. They were somewhere else, in another world entirely. A world in which reality seemed to morph and change around them. There were others there, too. Anna and Rosa, some fat guy like the babies she had seen crying at the dinner party, and a couple of people who she didn't recognize. Ansel didn't know what to do. She tried to turn and run but the Scientist grabbed her by the rucksack, trying to stop her. After a short tug of war and a tussle, Ansel's bag fell to the ground between them and the tent that Rosalind had given her opened up inside, expanding until the rucksack burst, pushing the Scientist deeper into the patchwork nonsense world they had stepped into and Ansel in the opposite direction, back into the office they had come from, where she landed, stunned, at Rosalind's feet.

"What the fuck was that?" Rosalind demanded, rushing to the door which wouldn't open now. "Where'd you go?"

"I— I don't know. There were people" What had she seen? It couldn't have been real. Who was that girl among them?

The door finally opened, but only to the hall. Rosalind burst out through it then back in again. "She's gone," she said. "*The Scientist.* Come on. I need your help."

Rosalind ran out toward the elevator and Ansel was left stammering, "I— I don't— I—" before she forced herself to stand up and follow.

ঽ ✼ ঽ

LXIII. Mr. Walker

"Haley, my dear," Mr. Walker said, standing from his chair, his intent driving his pneumatic legs toward her. "You—*You're alive.*"

"Hello, Lord Walker," Haley said, curtsying.

At the same time, in an all too artificial voice, the robot standing behind him, the one that had been trying to pass herself off as Haley, said, "Of course, Mr. Walker. I'm right here, sir." and curtsied. Lord Walker knew she curtsied without having to look at her. Just as he knew that the curtsy paled in comparison to what the real Haley, the divine image standing before him now, was capable of. "Shut up!" he turned fast, shaking a balled solid fist at the fake Haley who was just out of reach of hitting distance. "Get out of my sight, you imposter!"

She cowered away from him. "But, sir..."

And Mr. Walker ignored her, turning again to the real Haley. "How are you, my dear? What have they done to you?"

Mr. Walker had never seen the face that Haley produced in response. He didn't know she was programmed with the ability to make it. The contempt in her eyes stung hotter than the loss of his Lordship. Haley crossed to the shadow of herself to comfort her doppelganger, and Mr. Walker's heart hardened at her lack of a response. Who was she but another robot? She wasn't much better than her replacement, in fact. He told himself that, but he knew it was a lie.

"Now, now, Walker Man," Lord Douglas said, standing between Mr. Walker and the Haleys, as if his frail little body could hold back Mr. Walker's wrath. "You'll treat your secretary with respect if I have anything to say about it."

"You don't!" Mr. Walker boomed. "That's why they call her *my* secretary. *Both of them are* as a matter of fact. Come on, Haley. We're leaving."

"Enough!" Mr. Walker had never heard Lord Douglas's voice get so loud. "I dare say you know the terms of service for the secretaries, Mr. Walker," Lord Douglas went on in a calmer tone.

"You wrote those terms yourself if I'm not mistaken. So you know firsthand that any improper use of android technology results in ownership of the violated property reverting to Waltronics AI Inc, owner of which just so happens to be yours truly as of five minutes ago. So I'd watch my next move carefully if I were you."

Mr. Walker reared up as if to hit Lord Douglas and end this charade of comradery once and for all. As if Lord Douglas hadn't done enough to end it already. But just before he let his stone fist drop on the Duggy Doug's melon skull he relented, smiling and chuckling to himself. *"Ho ho ho,* Lord Douglas. *Ho ho ho!"*

Haley carried wannabe Haley away and out of the office without a second glance at Mr. Walker who had sustained her life for centuries, ever since she was created. What little gratitude humans were capable of, robots could always do them one worse. Which is why the age of robots was over. Their usefulness had been overplayed, and now they were nothing but burdens. Mr. Walker was more than delighted to get rid of those twin android anchors who were only weighing him down on his new path to success.

"You'll regret this, you will," he said. "You're a stupider man than I thought you were if you think you won't. You'll never keep the crown of Lordship for long making decisions like this one."

Lord Douglas grinned. His white teeth stood out against his dark skin just like Jorah's always did. Mr. Walker took a note of the fact and thought to fire Jorah as soon as possible for the resemblance. Why had Mr. Walker ever gotten into bed with the fool anyway?

"What? What do you have to say for yourself?" Mr. Walker demanded. "Speak up, boy. Now's the time to say what you've always been waiting to say to me."

"I'm not a boy," Lord Douglas said, still giving his white toothed grin. "Nor a man."

"You don't have to tell me that. *Ho ho ho!"*

"I'm something more than you've ever expected, Walkie Talks. I'm your worst nightmare. I'm the Robot Lord at the head of what was once your empire of android soldiers. How easy do you think it is to break those terms and conditions you wrote, *boy*? I mean, you yourself have already broke them and you're the owner who wrote them. How many people other than you do you think have even read them?"

Mr. Walker expected a fight from Lord Douglas, but nothing at this level. He had put the failsafe in the terms and conditions, sure, but he had never actually used it. This, however, this was madness. "A robot Lord, huh?" Mr. Walker chuckled, trying to cover his nerves. "So you're nothing but property, then. Is that about right? Who is it that owns you?"

"No one owns me." The look in Lord Douglas's eyes was too human for him to actually be a robot. He was lying, playing a game, trying to make a legend of himself. This was nothing more than another ploy in his gambit to retain the Lordship. "I am myself," he went on. "I am an independent android. No one can ever own me."

"*Ho ho ho.*" Mr. Walker took out his monocle and twirled it on its chain. "But you just admitted to being a robot. Which makes you property, in effect rendering any orders you've proclaimed as Lord fraud. You're nothing but a construct, Dug. You're zeroes and ones, software, incapable of emotion. How could you ever dream of dethroning me? How could you even dream?"

"Yet I am still Lord." Lord Douglas grinned. "And at our next meeting, as Lord of the Fortune Five, I will move to remove you as the director of the protector force. Things only continue to get worse under your watch, Walker, and I think the board will agree that's it time for a change of management."

"Things will only continue to get worse until I decide to make them better, Lord Douglas," Mr. Walker snapped. "And relish that, because it's the last time I call you my Lord. The next time you see me I'll be at the head of a *human* army, Dugtrio, and they'll be Hell bent on deposing you for your crimes against humanity. I'm sure the Fortune Five will have some thoughts on your so called Lordship as well, once they hear all the things *my* protectors have found that you've been up to. It's really a shame for you to lose the crown like this, but all's fair in money and war, and I'm afraid this is about both now."

Lord Douglas chuckled. "And we'll see how the Fortune Five feels when the price of robot labor gets dearer, Walrus. We'll see whose side they stand on in the end. *Ha ha ha! We'll see.*"

"And maybe we'll see before then," Mr. Walker snapped, "when my soldiers put an end to the strikes and your days of ease. Good day, Duggy. It may be your last." Mr. Walker almost called for Haley before catching himself. He didn't need any robots anymore anyway. He was done with them. He stormed out of the room and into the elevator to yell, "Garage." then, "No, home." not wanting to drive himself without a chauffeur. The elevator fell into motion and when the doors opened up again, Mr. Walker wasn't at home.

Where was he? It couldn't be said to be anywhere, really. More like it was everywhere. It wasn't one place but many, stitched together with ever loosening threads that looked like they might give way at any moment. Here was the border between his elevator and— was that Rosa? what was she doing here?—what looked like a cement wall. Then it was all cement wall. Then it was all elevator. Then half and half again, the borders ever shifting. Mr. Walker feared that he might tumble out of view—maybe out of existence entirely—like the rest of the worlds around him.

"What is this?" Mr. Walker demanded of Rosa who was across the room one second and behind him the next, the cement walls of the room she was in transporting around her with every blink.

"Lord Walker, is that you?" she called back, not sure which way to look herself. At least it suggested that the sights Mr. Walker were seeing might not be hallucinations after all. The world really was pulsating and shifting around him.

Rosa disappeared—no wait, she was only behind him—and in her place were two young girls he thought he recognized. "You there," he called out to them. "Who are you? Where is this? What's going on?"

They both stared at him in surprise. The one with glasses on—who wears glasses in this day and age?—started to say, "It's him. He's Lor—" but she couldn't finish her sentence before she disappeared, too—or rather teleported, moved along with the backdrop around her to another position in the shifting swirling mass of confusion.

The walls shuffled and molded around Mr. Walker. Elevator mirrors, drywall, wallpaper, brick, wood. He was everywhere at once and no one else could be there with him. They could come and leave but never remain. Mr. Walker was getting motion sickness at the thought of it, at the sight of the pulsating, breathing, living walls. He was bending over to wretch but his pneumatic pants held him too tight and wouldn't let go of even his insides. They were as disoriented as he was. He was fighting and fighting against them, trying to do something, anything, and the world stopped.

A face appeared before him. A face from deep inside his subconscious. At first he thought it was Haley, come home to take care of him once and for all. And it was almost, but this Haley had aged, this Haley had once been the Haley who his Haley and her doppelganger were modeled after, who they paled in comparison to, one after another, but no longer. Her skin sagged in certain places, and her eyes, those piercing, inquiring eyes which had haunted him through the longest of nights, made all the pulsating, bulging motion around him disappear for a moment in which he could finally stand steadily on two pneumatic feet.

"Haley," he said, reaching a hand out to grab her hand. "It's been so long since we've spoken face to face. I hope you don't mind that I call you Haley."

Haley smiled, accentuating her crow's feet, and Mr. Walker thought he would kiss even them if she would let him. A tussle of white—how long *had* it been since he'd seen her?—hair fell into her face and she brushed it away with a gloved hand, clad in her scientist uniform as always. "As long as you don't mind if I call you Walker," she said

He grabbed her, wrapping her tight in his safe soothing folds. She tried to hug him back, he could feel, but she only managed to pat his stomach because she couldn't wrap her short little arms around his gargantuan, manly girth. "Of course, sweetheart. Of course." Walker almost cried as he said it. "Call me anything you want to as long as you're talking to me." And he did let out a few tears for two lost Haleys and an old Haley found.

She pushed away too soon, though, and he was left to wipe his own tears. "I—*uh*— Did you see Ansel?" she asked. "The little girl. She might have come through with me."

Walker remembered where he was. His eyes went back to the shifting walls and his motion sickness returned. There were too many breakfasts in his stomach to waste them now—and the pneumatic pants wouldn't let him vomit if he wanted to—so he choked it all back and spit out, "Where are we?"

"Essentially nowhere," Haley said, feeling along the walls even as they mutated and changed form under her hands. "Not yet, at least. This place is in flux. That's why it keeps changing. You better stick close to me or we might lose each other."

Walker scurried closer to her, bumping his bulbous stomach into her back and almost knocking her head into the wall she was searching. "I'm sorry," he said. "I— But— Lost? In flux? What's going on?"

"Whoever brought us here hasn't decided where they want us yet. From the looks of it they're trying to make a new plane for us, for a lot of us."

"Brought us here? Who? Impossible. But you said—*you* control the walls. Who could do this but you?"

Haley chuckled, looking away from her investigation of the ever morphing world for the first time. "You really are clueless, aren't you? Hackers have been getting in for years, Walker. This was inevitable. I've been winning the arms race until now, but—"

"There he is again!" a voice called from behind them. "And he's with *her*. I told you they were working together."

Walker turned to see the girl in the glasses and her friend who he thought he recognized.

"Nikola, Tillie," Haley said, crossing to them. "Stay close now. We'll all be safer if we stick together."

Walker hurried closer to them, taking Haley's advice.

"Where have you taken us?" the girl in the glasses demanded. "What have you done?"

"I haven't done anything," Haley said. "We're all in this together. I think—"

"Enough!" The unknown girl, the one who wasn't wearing any glasses, stomped a foot. "Enough, enough, enough. We can stop this petty arguing at least until we get out of whatever the fuck this is. I can't take it anymore. Hand!" She stormed off and the girl with the glasses chased after her, calling, "Tillie, wait!"

Haley chased them and Walker had no choice but to follow. The room became a hall of shifting walls as they ran, and the hall a labyrinthine maze. Soon Walker was praying to the Hand and every other god of Outland that his pants wouldn't give out when he needed them the most. Just as he thought the pants were done for, ready to putter out, their procession stopped in front of Rosa and her rude partner Anna.

"*You*," Rosa said, staring angrily at Haley. "This is your doing. Isn't it?"

"*See*," the girl with the glasses said, "I told you."

"No, it's not—" Haley started.

"Sure," Rosa cut her off, "It has nothing to do with our war on the robots, right? That's why you have him here, too." She pointed at Walker who raised his hands in defense, shrugging as if he had never met Rosa before. After this was all done and over with, he would have to give her a little lesson on tact, teach her about the concept of classified information.

"What is that supposed to mean?" Haley asked, looking at Walker with those piercing eyes of hers.

"Don't ask me," he said.

"It means," Rosa said, "that he and I are going to destroy your robot army, and you've brought us here to try to prevent us from doing it. Well, I'm afraid to tell you that the Family lives on even without us."

"*You didn't*," Haley said, still staring into Walker's soul. "Tell me you didn't."

"I—I'm a businessman," he stammered. Why was he making excuses to someone who had abandoned him so long ago? "I did with my property what was in my best interests. You can't argue against that."

"What about us?" the girl with the glasses cut in. "We're not with them. We want to help the androids. Why are we here?"

Haley just stared at Walker, shaking her head in disappointment.

"Look," Tillie said—at least Walker thought her name was Tillie, he still wasn't sure who was who in this chaotic mess. "It's obvious that none of us here are responsible for this. Just look around you. The walls are still shifting, the world is still changing around us. I mean—Nikola, you said this was like an elevator tunnel, right?"

The girl with the glasses—Nikola—nodded and Walker filed the name away in his head. Of course, Nikola and Tillie from the uproar in Two. How could he forget? And maybe some evidence as to why they were all there.

"Well the tunnel's still moving," *Tillie* went on. "Someone has to be controlling it, right? And none of us can be doing that from in here, so... Are y'all following me?"

"You know, it may be possible to—" Haley started.

"Are *you* doing it?" Tillie cut her off.

"Well, no, but—"

"Anyone else?" Tillie asked the rest of them, and everyone shook their heads. "Then we can stop asking which one of us did it."

"That's very astute," Haley said with a smile Walker was glad to see.

"And useless." Rosa scoffed. "We still have no way out of this...whatever it is."

"What *is* this anyway?" *Mr.* Walker interjected, feeling the conversation needed an owner's opinion.

"It's a spacetime overlap," Haley said at the same time that Anna said, "It's a big problem."

"Probably, yes," Haley said.

"Too many paths are overlapping at once," Anna went on. "I don't like the look of those walls. Have you seen them?" She and Haley crossed to a wall to inspect its ever morphing characteristics.

"I think we should get out of here," Nikola said, trying to pull Tillie, who didn't budge, along with her.

"You two do know each other, though. Don't you?" Tillie said to Walker.

"*Ho ho ho*, dear. I know many people," he replied. Too many people if you asked him, and none that would do something like this. "What's it matter to you?"

"So how do we get out of this?" Rosa asked, ever ready to get down to business. "That's all I want to know. I don't care what or where it is, I just want to get home."

"That's up to me," a child's voice said from nowhere and everywhere all at the same time. Whichever way Walker looked he saw nothing but shifting walls. "And how y'all react," the voice added.

Suddenly the walls stopped moving and changing form. They coalesced into a small square room with cement walls, binding them all together as one. Apart from them, in the direction everyone was now staring, sat a little girl, cross-legged on the ground, tapping and swiping at a tiny computer pad in her lap.

"*Roo*," Haley said, taking a step closer to the girl. "What are you—"

"Careful," the girl—*Roo*—cut her off. "Don't take another step. I don't know where you'll go if you attempt to approach me, but it'll be far away from here, I can promise you that. It's okay, though. I won't hurt you as long as you stay put right where you are. I just want to talk."

"I demand to know the meaning of this," *Lord* Walker said, stepping to the front of the group of women so he could finally assert control over the situation. How could a little girl be holding all of them hostage right now? He had to put an end to it.

"Your demands are meaningless," the little girl said—was she grinning? It was so hard to tell from that far away. "What makes you think this has any meaning at all?"

"Well you brought us here for something," Nikola said.

"Actually," the girl said. "With the two of you I'm afraid I've quite literally brought you here for nothing. I've never even met you. I'm sorry you're caught up in this, but as long as you cooperate and remain quiet, no harm will come to any of you."

"Wait," Nikola complained, "just let us go then."

"I can't without letting the rest of you go, too," the girl said, shaking her head. "I'm sorry. Sometimes the world just works out that way." She seemed so much older than her appearances let on. "There's nothing else I can do for you until I'm done with them so let's get on with it. Anna," the girl—Roo—said, squirming this way and that in her seat, trying to see around Walker's large frame. "I know you're here somewhere. Now come on out."

Walker stepped aside to let Rosa's little partner step forward.

"What do you think of this, Anna?" the girl asked, smiling. "A pretty beautiful symphony, wouldn't you say?"

"It's dangerous," Anna said, shaking her head. "*Wreckless.*"

"But isn't it beautiful? That's the point. Look, you can even see yourself in it." The girl swiped and tapped and disappeared. In her place there was an exact replica of Mr. Walker and the group he stood among. There were infinite replicas in all directions, as if he were in a room lined with mirrors that somehow reflected them from behind. It was dizzying to see. Just before Mr. Walker tried to vomit again, the sight vanished and the girl returned, laughing, in its place. "Does that frighten you?" she asked, still chuckling. "Make you sick? *Huh ha.* Or do you think it's fun?"

"Who are you?" Nikola, the girl with the glasses, demanded.

"What is this?" Rosa did, too.

"No child can speak to me this way," Walker said, not wanting to be left out.

Only Haley and Anna could get through to her, though. "I've been there before, child," Haley said.

"I feel your pain," Anna said.

"No you haven't," the girl said, standing up and dropping the tablet from her lap. For a second she disappeared and the mutating walls returned, but she was soon back and saying, "No you don't!" She was standing now, closer to them. Walker thought he could reach right out and grab the little tablet out of her hand, but he didn't dare try. There was no telling what would happen to him if he crossed that invisible barrier. "You know nothing!"

"What is this?" Walker demanded. "You, child— Wait, you— You're the director I was interviewing. What are you—"

Roo laughed. "I'm no director. I'm every person you've ever trampled over to get what you want. I'm the end of everything for you. I'm here to show you that you don't control as much of the universe as y'all think you do. None of you!"

"Roo, no," Haley said, and all eyes turned to her natural magnetism. Why had she and Walker ever parted? "You don't understand what you're doing. This isn't good. We can't all be here in one place like this for much longer. All the space you have folding into one tiny spot right here, it's too much. The system can't handle it."

The little girl laughed, pacing the small space she had to walk in. "The system can't handle it, huh? Well maybe I can't handle the system."

"*Right on*," Nikola said, pumping a fist at the little girl. "You tell 'em. We're on your side."

"Shut up!" The little girl stomped her foot. "All of you just shut up until you're spoken to or I'll leave you here forever. There's no way out, okay. I made sure you were far enough away from everything so you'll never be found. Now shut up!"

"This can't be true," Rosa said, imploring Anna. "She couldn't— That little girl did all this?"

"There is a way out, isn't there?" Walker demanded of Haley. "I cannot be stuck here for much longer. I can already feel my stomach grumbling."

"I told you to shut up," Tillie said to Nikola.

"As I told all of you." The girl disappeared, all of the walls, the ceiling, and the floor with her. Walker was free falling into nothingness. They were all falling just the same. They were surrounded by the complete blackness of space that Walker had only ever witnessed on TV, and now he was in it, the stars all around him, his breath escaping him and his head feeling like it was going to explode, but still the beauty got through, and hanging above it all, Haley's aged face, a diamond among the rough and tumble rabble that was free falling through space with them.

Then the walls came back, gravity with them, and the cold hard floor for everyone to fall into a jumble on top of. The velocity of a free fall drop from space ended in a belly flop into a too full room. The fall wasn't as far as it seemed, though, the fear being the worst part, and soon Walker's pneumatic pants had him up and staring at the little girl's smiling face before anyone else in the tiny cell with him could stand.

"What power do you have now?" The girl cackled. "What hope is there for you? *Ha ha ha*!"

"Why are you doing this?" Anna begged, still crawling on hands and knees, trying to get up from the fall. "Why us?"

"Why anyone?" The girl laughed. "There's no logic to it, is there? You thought there was when your life was going as planned, when y'all were on top, putting your boots into our face and keeping us down, but what logic is there now that you're the ones in the mud? Is that about right?"

"None!" Nikola said, seeming to cheer the girl on.

"Your logic," Haley said, still trying to convince her to do the right thing. "This is your logic bringing this upon us, Roo."

"I didn't choose to become this," the girl said. "This is what you made me."

"I didn't make you into anything," Walker said.

"You did! And there's no stopping me now."

"Enough!" Mr. Walker yelled. "I've had enough. Now, child, I don't know who you think are, but enough is enough. Let us go this instant or I'll— I'll… I'll just—"

"*You'll do nothing*. I'm the new Queen of the Walls. I'm the best bender that's ever been born. I'm the future of these worlds and it's time that y'all start to realize that. These are my worlds now, not yours. So get over it."

"Now, I never—" Walker said.

"Child, you better—" Rosa said.

"We did nothing—" Tillie said.

"But the fields," Haley said. "They can't—"

And the little girl disappeared. The walls started moving again. The world was in flux and there was no telling where it would lead. Walker stumbled back on his pneumatic legs. Even the ground seemed to be changing beneath him as he tried to move. Everyone stumbled around him.

"What's going on?" Rosa demanded.

"Where'd she go?" Nikola asked.

"What's the meaning of all this?" Walker huffed, finally regaining his balance.

"There's too much pressure," Anna said.

"The walls are closing in," Haley said.

"What do we do?" Tillie asked.

And the worlds broke apart. How else could Walker's mind comprehend it? It happened in a flash and it took an eternity. Fissures cracked through everything. The walls. The ceiling. The floor. Even the poor girl Nikola's head. There was no telling how long it actually took her to die, though. Each separate half of her body kept reacting as if they were still connected and alive for some time—what amount of time, though? because if it was any time at all it must have been forever so how could it have ever ended?—before the two halves slumped, falling and twitching into—what?—Walker could not tell.

What was it? That thing that lies between the fabric of reality, between here and there when here is right next to there. Whatever was between molecules, and atoms, and nothingness, she fell into that, each piece of her in time—what time, though?—forever, and whole chunks of the universe fell in with her.

Walker's legs were carrying him somewhere. Was there still solid ground to walk on? He felt like he was floating through space again. They weren't just carrying him, they were following somebody. *His Haley.* He heaved a sigh of relief, leaning into the motion to give his pneumatic pants some leverage, and noticed that Haley was following Rosa and the other one—*Anna.* Did names matter with the universe falling apart around them, though?

How many tunnels they went down Walker would never know for sure. The halls, corridors, and tubes were already muddling themselves up together in his mind as he went through them.

Brick wall turn left wall turns into chain link fence looking out onto space keep running not questioning why air is still there only breathing it happily and hoping for more walls and tunnels and oxygen.

At one point, he couldn't tell if he was moving forward or if the walls were flowing by him, creating an illusion of motion. He really was the Red Queen now, and as much as his pants ran, they couldn't catch up to Ann or Rosa or even his Haley.

His pants hissed. His legs stopped moving. He tried lifting his left leg with all his might and felt the air coming out of his pants. Any more movement like that and he might not be able to stand at all. "Haley," he called, keeping his legs as still as possible and feeling them get heavier with every second. "Haley, I'm stuck!"

"Hey, wait," Hayley said, stopping and turning. Rosa and Anna stopped with her. "What's wrong?" She took two steps toward him and a rift started breaking between Rosa and Anna, a rift into that same unknown which the other girl had already fallen to pieces inside of. The world was falling apart and there was nothing Walker could do about it, not even run away, because his stupid pants had failed him at the worst possible time, just like the robot they were.

"I'm not staying for him," Rosa said, the only one on the other side of the rift. "Anna, come on. I think I can see our basement over there." She held her hand across the wrench in reality, and though it didn't cross through the nothingness, it did appear on the other side of the chasm in one piece.

Anna looked at the disembodied hand, then back at Haley. "You know how this is going to end," she said. "We have to get out of her before it does. Leave him." She grabbed Rosa's hand and teleported from one side of the rift to the other then disappeared into the shifting worlds which were getting fewer and further between.

"Haley. *My love*," Walker said as she came closer to him, the fabric of reality disintegrating behind her. "I knew you'd come back to me."

She smiled again, her crow's feet dancing on the brink of happy eyes. "I never left you, Walky. I've been looking out for you all this time."

"Then why'd you have to leave me in the first place?" Walker asked, his legs twitching nervously and his pants deflating that little tiny bit faster with every tiny movement. "I still needed you."

"Why'd you abandon me?" Haley asked, her face changing to something Walker would rather not remember, something he thought he was over when he saw Haley from this new perspective.

"I never did," he said. "I've been running Waltronics and the Walls since they existed. I still run the Walls—your baby—and I only just sold off Waltronics in the hopes of winning it back by force. What more could I do for you?"

"You could have listened to me, dear." Haley smiled, taking on the appearance of her old self again, her younger self, the one Walker missed and loved and had tried to replicate in her android replacements. "That's all I've ever asked," she said, "treat me as your equal."

"Listen to you when?" Walker scoffed, the universe getting tinier around him as the foundations of space and time disintegrated from overpressure. "You never came to talk to me. How should I know what you want? I'm not a mind reader."

"I came to you on Christmas, didn't I?" Haley said, trying to push Walker, trying to move him somehow, but only failing. Without the pants to carry him he was stuck there, and they both knew it.

"Did you?" Walker asked, groaning against her useless straining to budge him. "I was a little distracted with the terrorist attacks."

"Which happened after my speech," Haley said, fidgeting with Walker's pants and reminding him of a time long gone when they weren't pneumatic yet. "Not to mention every Christmas before that."

"*Ugh.*" Walker groaned. How much had he missed Haley, the real Haley? "I know. I never should have—"

She fell away from him. A rift in reality tore them apart. But at the same time Walker's legs kicked into motion. She must have known what she was doing down there. He stood and reached for her, but she had no footing upon which to reach back and grab on, and all Walker could do was call, "Haley, I love you!"

The world ended right then and there. It might as well have. Haley had disappeared into that nothingness and there was no way she was ever coming back out of it. Walker didn't care about anything else in the universe. His pants—reactivated by the only person who could have ever saved him—were carrying him of their own accord now. Or was he falling? It didn't matter to him. There was no ground anymore. There was no space at all. There were no walls or ceiling. There was only Walker, the endless dark expanse of space behind him, and the labyrinthine tunnels of possibility still branching out in front of him. Where would that darkness push him? Where would his pants take him? How would he ever survive? There was only one way to find out.

ᖫ   End of Book Three   ᕉ

Thanks for reading. If you enjoyed that please join us at

www.BryanPerkinsAuthor.com

to keep up to date on future releases in the Infinite Limits series.
And if you're so inclined, don't forget to leave a review on Amazon,
Goodreads, or any other site you might frequent.
Thanks again, until next time.

-Bryan "with a Y" Perkins

Acknowledgements

Again again let's thank Sophie again, and again again let's thank David. They always deserve it.

Thank you also to Megg and Chris Faussett for the chair I sat in the entire time I edited this thing—the same chair I'm sitting in now—and for the giant forest scene that lets me feel like I'm outside even when I have to stay in and work.

Thank you, of course, to Mom, Dad, Tor Tor, and Rob, my Human Family. And thank you to Mr. Kitty, my not so human family.

And thank you, dear readers. Thank you for finally existing when you finally do read this. We've been waiting for you to join the party so thanks for coming along.